FROM THE DEPTHS

Book 2: Of Mountains and Seas

EMILY RENK HAWTHORNE

Published by Hawk Ridge Press
Author Website – www.EmilyRenkHawthorne.com

Cover Illustration by Bookfly – www.bookflydesign.com
Developmental Edit, Line Edit, and Proofread by Goldenhorn Editing – www.goldenhornediting.com
Yuras Map by Ryan Lynch – Instagram and TikTok @outrider-creative

ISBN (paperback) 979-8-9905979-5-2
ISBN (hardcover) 979-8-9905979-7-6
ISBN (ebook) 979-8-9905979-6-9

For a world still learning to choose understanding over division

HOSPITAL
MAIN STREET BOUTIQUE
REDWOOD CAFÉ
LIBRARY
NIVI'S HOUSE
PINE LN.
MAPLE LN.
MAIN ST.
AMBER'S HOUSE
ARAV'S HOUSE
FOREST LANE
REDWOOD ROAD
ABANDONED HOUSE
CLIFF TRAIL
YURAS
PENINSULA

"A strange water emerged, and the killing flowed forth..."

—*The Classic of Mountains and Seas,*
Fourth Century BCE

The Sinkhole

Yuras, California ~ Fall 1990

T HE YOUNG SHIFTER POLICE officer led Senator Ariana Peters through the house. A small group of people stayed huddled in the home's foyer, suspiciously eyeing the strange sinkhole in the corner of the living room. Like the other homes on Redwood Road, this one would have had a cozy cottage feel with its stone fireplace and vaulted wood ceilings, if it wasn't for that fist-sized sinkhole.

"Careful, Senator," the officer said, dropping her voice and putting out a hand to keep Ariana back. "These can be deadly."

"And that is based on what evidence?" This was the first Ariana had heard of such a danger.

"There's been talk around the neighborhood of pets disappearing into these holes."

"That's not really substantiated evidence." Ariana glanced back and forth between her body and the small-sized hole with a pointed look. "I think I'll be okay."

She took a step forward, and the officer again blocked her. "Senator, I must insist."

Ariana's tone hardened. "I've got it from here, *officer*."

This officer was obviously new and overly cautious. Where was Chief Buhl, the head of Shifter police? Why had he left her with this newbie?

The officer pressed her lips together but nodded and retreated to the front door to stand watch.

It's just a sinkhole, Senator Ariana Peters told herself despite the officer's warnings as she stepped closer to investigate.

As she neared the hole, a sense of unease creeped up the back of her neck, as if the hole had a gravitational presence beckoning to its depths. There was no discernible bottom. For all she knew, it was an infinite abyss, sinking straight to the core of the earth. Although that wouldn't be infinite, would it? Infinite would mean it'd go straight through the earth and beyond.

Get it together, Peters, she told herself. *There's no room for error here.*

Around the edges of the sinkhole, translucent and gelatinous tendrils branched out like veins establishing a new blood flow. Tiny cilia lined the tendrils and cast a silver bioluminescent glow that swirled and rippled across their surface. As Ariana took a step forward, a tendril oriented toward her, glowing more brightly. Stretching. Reaching.

It was no ordinary sinkhole. That was certain. This was the fourth home in which one of these had developed. Beginning at the northwest end of Redwood Road, the holes seemed to be following the road southeast and popping up in each home along the way. As far as she could tell, they hadn't spread outside of the area yet. The Shifter police had been right to call her in to evaluate, but did the holes warrant an evacuation?

The management of this area was within her purview now, and she had to plan her actions just right. Not only was this a chance to do good for her people; it was a chance to show she was capable in her new position. Only a week ago, the fire at Chairperson Dawan's house had claimed several lives, and now these sinkholes were spreading down the street from his home. It had to be related, but how? Ariana was still reeling from all the changes—including her recent promotion to senate leader—and was struggling to make sense of it all. Davis, now Chairperson Davis, wanted the matter closed as soon as possible. But how could she close the matter if she didn't know what she was dealing with? The police chief had briefed her on the nature of these sinkholes, but she needed to see for herself what they did.

Ariana turned away and walked to the door.

"I'll be right back, Liz," she said to her assistant who was hovering outside the circle of people.

"I'll come with you, ma'am," Liz responded.

Her youthful energy and desire to please could be helpful but were often too much. In fact, all these new staff members appointed to her were too much. Did she really need a whole entourage to travel?

"No need. I just need a minute."

Subdued, Liz turned back to chat with the other team members by the door, her flushed cheeks betraying her disappointment. Ariana ignored the guilt that popped up in response. This was no time to be waylaid by the easily hurt feelings of an assistant. She stepped outside and glanced around. The forest road was eerily quiet since the Shifter police had cleared the area while they investigated. The residents were being housed at a local hotel while they waited for news on the sinkhole situation. It was up to her to wrap things up before rumors got out.

She picked up a rock, returned inside, and held it over the hole at waist height. *Let's see how these holes make things disappear.*

Out of the corner of her eye, Ariana could see Liz watching expectantly as she let the stone fall. It hit the surface of the sinkhole but didn't sink as expected, instead encountering a slight resistance before the depthless darkness lit up like mercury aglow. The liquid silver bubbled up, enveloping and sucking the rock down like a ravenous pool of mud. She stepped back, but not quickly enough. One of the tendrils whipped out, wrapping around her booted foot and the exposed skin of her ankle. She recoiled, snapping the tendril off. A bit of silver remained on her ankle, a gelatinous blob clinging to her skin, while the rest of the tendril retracted toward the hole. Holding back a surge of revulsion, Ariana leaned down to swipe at the substance, but it disappeared before she could reach it. A patch of cold lingered on her ankle where the silver had touched her. Did it dry up that fast? Or had it sunk into her skin? Ariana shuddered.

A cool feeling spread up her leg. She was probably just imagining it. The stress of the situation was getting to her. But the chill kept creeping through her body, higher and higher, through her leg and torso. As it rose up her neck and into her head, a silver haze swept over her vision. A voice—no, a thought—crossed her mind.

Get rid of them.

"Is it bad, ma'am? What does it mean?"

Ariana's attention snapped back to Liz who stood directly behind her, her eyes wide, her bobbed hair cupping her jaw.

Ariana shook her head, both to answer Liz's question and to clear the strange sensation clouding her mind.

"I don't know yet—"

Another silver tendril crept toward her foot. She stepped back. Was it attracted to her? Or to people in general?

Get rid of them.

A need to clear the area surged through Ariana's subconscious. But that was natural, right? She *should* clear the area due to this unknown and potentially dangerous substance. *Permanently.* Still, how would she convince everyone not to return to their homes?

Liz cleared her throat, and Ariana realized she had drifted off in the middle of their conversation. What was going on with her today? This leadership business was too much for her. She preferred following directions to being the leader. *I am following directions. Chairperson Davis's directions.*

A commotion from the front door interrupted her thoughts as the officer yelled at someone outside. "How did they get past the barricade?"

She pulled a walkie talkie from her belt and spoke into it. "We have a breach!"

Before the officer received a reply, a new voice spoke from outside the house.

"I just want to know what's happening!"

Ariana went to the entrance. A small man with dark hair and gentle eyes stood outside, holding the hand of a boy who couldn't have been more than five years old. Ariana glanced at the wall of photographs in the foyer, recognizing the man as Mr. Garcia, the home's owner, and the boy as his son, Jorge. Upon seeing Ariana, Mr. Garcia pulled Jorge forward and pushed into the house.

"Senator—"

The officer moved to block their advance, but Liz jumped in front of Ariana first, her arms spread out. Ariana appreciated her protective instincts, but Mr. Garcia was harmless.

"That's okay, Liz. I'll talk to him."

Liz lowered her arms but remained vigilant at Ariana's side. The officer stepped back against the wall and watched with her arms crossed.

"Mr. Garcia," Ariana said. "I'm very sorry, but these sinkholes are spreading. You will have to relocate along with the rest of the Shifters in this area until we can contain them and figure out what is going on."

"But this is the home we shared with my wife." Mr. Garcia hugged his son closer. "His mother. It's all we have left of her."

Get rid of them.

A wave of nausea hit Ariana. She needed air.

"I'll... be right back."

Ariana left the concerned-looking father and son with Liz and stumbled out of the cabin, shutting the door behind her. When she reached the edge of the driveway, she interlaced her fingers behind her neck and stretched, taking several deep breaths. The coolness of the forest swept down Redwood Road, rustling the trees and scattering pine needles onto the dirt road. Maybe she wasn't up to this promotion. How could she fill the shoes of the great Meng Zhang? Meng seemed to have stepped into her new role as vice chairperson with ease. Davis had also taken over the chairperson position as if he were born for it. How had they both coped with their new roles in addition to Chairperson Dawan's demise so professionally? Maybe she should resign and go back to being a representative, at least until she had more experience.

The surrounding forest was eerily quiet, no people, no wind, no bird chatter. The lack of people was to be expected, as the barricade started at the beginning of Redwood Road next to Main Street, but why had the birds gone silent?

A soft crunch.

Ariana snapped her head forward, heart racing, searching for the culprit. Reflexively, she raised her arms, lifting off the ground and pulling the air's moisture around herself until a dense fog hid her shrinking form. Feathery brown wings with white stripes replaced her arms. They beat rapidly, allowing her to hover like the bird from which her Shifter form's name was derived—the hummingbird moth. From the safety of her camouflage, she watched, sensing the air with her antennae.

Dappled lighting danced in unreliable streams from above, doing more to obscure than illuminate. Between the pine trees ahead, yellow-green eyes pierced the shadows, followed by a large feline form. Sleek black fur rippled against a muscular body as the jaguar strode to the edge of the road and crossed it in two bounds.

Ariana dispersed the fog from herself and descended to the forest floor, shifting midair in a well-timed feat that allowed her to land softly on human feet. Her body reabsorbed the modified hair scales that covered her moth body, revealing her human skin and light blue pantsuit.

"Chief Buhl," she said with a sigh of relief. What had made her so nervous?

She straightened as the jaguar approached while repeating to herself, *You are capable. You are a professional.*

The jaguar didn't break its stride even as its shoulders and spine cracked. It pulled its front legs up as its posture shifted back onto its haunches. The forearms shrank in length, and the fur disappeared and reformed as a black police uniform. Somehow, Chief Donald Buhl's human form was almost as large and muscular as his jaguar form. Each bicep was as big as his clean-shaven head.

Across the street, two more forms emerged from the forest: another big cat, this one a massive tiger, and a large, gray, prehistoric-looking bird that stood over six feet tall. Officers Nicola Barmann and Eric Okello.

The gray bird had a thick, stork-like build with an enormous shoe-shaped bill that curved upward and ended in a sharp point.

A shoebill, Ariana remembered Eric telling her. A bird common in his ancestral homeland of Uganda.

The tiger leaped, and the shoebill half jumped, half glided across the road. They shifted into their uniform-clad human forms and came up to either side of Donald. Nicola's hair, as bright orange as her tiger fur, was in a long braid down her back. A full tattoo sleeve of tigers covered the pale skin of her left arm in a Japanese style that reflected her ancestry on her mother's side. Besides the tattoo and a slight upward tilt of her amber eyes, she looked mostly Caucasian.

Eric stood stiffly and slightly behind Donald with his arms crossed.

Get rid of them.

Arianna winced.

"Everything all right, Senator Peters?" Donald asked.

"Yes. Did you find any other sinkholes out there?"

"Nope. And nothing out of the ordinary in general."

Ariana glanced at Nicola and Eric, but they only nodded without adding anything. "I see." She paced as she spoke, thinking aloud. "These sinkholes, I believe they might be dangerous."

"That's why we called you in, Senator," Donald said. "We need the clearance to permanently clear this area."

"That will take a long time in the courts. Too long." Permanently removing Shifters from their homes, even if done through the legal system, would cause a lot of discontent with the new administration, and Chairperson Davis wouldn't be happy with that. On the other hand, Shifters who thought they *wanted* to move wouldn't cause any issues. "But I do have authority for oblivion tincture use."

"You want to OT all these Shifters?" Eric said.

Donald cast him a dark look, and Eric shifted in discomfort.

"Only to relocate them. For their own safety. They'll retain most of their memories, just in a different location," Ariana said, feeling the need to justify her methods. "Think about it. There'd be no suffering, just a new reality. We don't want to cause a mass panic about something we don't understand yet, and we could always nullify it and send them home later once everything was settled. In the meantime, the inhabitants of Redwood Road will be safe. And they'll be happy."

And Chairperson Davis would be happy. What better way to showcase herself in her new position? Unlike marks, which stripped Shifters of their powers and left them fully aware of that torture, oblivion tincture simply erased any problematic knowledge, leaving the affected Shifter blissfully unaware.

A sense of calm replaced the anxiety she'd felt since stepping out of the Garcia home. The oppressive and cold brain fog lifted. Yes. The plan would work. The residents of Redwood Road would be safe. Wasn't that what everyone wanted in life? To be safe and happy? She would always do whatever it took to make sure her people had that.

Donald's shoulders relaxed, and he turned to Nicola to give her a small nod. Eric crossed his arms, his mouth in a thin line.

With the head of Shifter police in agreement, Ariana returned to the Garcia home. She knocked and entered without waiting for a response. Mr. Garcia and his son stood up from where they'd been sitting on the living room couch.

"Liz," Ariana said. "Can you gather everyone and wait outside?"

Liz nodded and herded Ariana's team out the door. Despite her overzealousness, she was efficient and good at following orders. Once the staff was outside, Donald, Nicola, and Eric entered the home. Donald indicated for the young officer stationed in the house to follow Ariana's team outside and then closed the door.

Ariana walked up to Mr. Garcia. Putting a hand on his shoulder, she spoke in her most sympathetic and reassuring voice. "It will be all right. I promise."

She nodded over to Donald. He and Nicola approached Mr. Garcia and Jorge, each holding a vial of black liquid. With quick and practiced hands, the officers removed the vial lids, dabbed the black liquid on their index fingers, and touched it to Mr. Garcia's and Jorge's foreheads.

Ariana listened to the officers speak, repeating one of their key phrases to herself in a murmur.

"You will find peace and happiness in your new home."

June 2000

My Dear Nivi,

Destroy this once read.

I've heard Ariana Peters has become the new chairperson. Her strict anti-integration policies will include the liberal use of oblivion tincture. As one who used to administer this tincture, I can tell you that when they come for you, it will be unexpected. Say nothing of your ability to nullify magic. All they know at this time is that you can block physical magic attacks with a shield of fire, and it is imperative they do not find out that the oblivion tincture will not work on you.

I fear this is goodbye for now. Stay strong. It will be lonely being the only one with the truth. Take comfort in knowing I have your grandmother as my companion. Cherish your mother's presence, even if her reality cannot be what you want it to be for now. I have hope that things will change. And when they do, you will reunite us.

Until then,

Meng

FALL 2000

An Unusual Catch

Aleutian Islands, Alaska

Waves crashed against the navy-blue hull of the crab fishing boat, obscuring the red lettering of "The Crabby Lady." Maria Akayux, the boat's captain, ran back from the railing to grip the helm wheel while yelling to the two-person crew.

"Let's go! Let's go! Let's go!"

At forty years old, she was experienced and at the top of her game, physically and mentally. Her muscular, agile frame complemented her eagle-eye vision. Her calloused hands had complete control of the boat. Even as her black hair whipped across her face, the rough conditions didn't phase her. She enjoyed the sting of salt spray in her eyes the way others would enjoy a cup of hot tea and a warm blanket. This was her home. The sea ran in her blood. Her Aleut ancestors had inhabited this area for nine thousand years. Squinting at the rolling waters, she welcomed the challenge. *Bring it on.*

Shawn Murphy, a twenty-three-year-old of Irish descent, yelled back. "Aye, aye, Captain!"

Maria looked back at the stern while he activated the hydraulic pot puller. It sprang into action reeling in the crab trap lines, its droning muffled by the waves.

Alek Ivanov, a large man in his fifties with black hair and a graying bushy beard, waited to guide the trap onto the boat. His yellow waterproof gear added bulk to his already substantial figure.

"Come on, greenhorn! Don't keep me waiting," Alek called. He spoke with a hint of a Russian accent, even though his family had been in Alaska for several generations.

It didn't matter that this was Shawn's second fishing season; he was still a greenhorn to Maria and Alek. And it didn't help that Shawn's own attempt at a beard was patchy and scraggly, made worse by the fact that his blond hair barely registered against his pale skin.

They braced themselves as the boat rocked side to side and the hydraulic pot puller began to lift the trap. The hydraulic arm shook and the boat tilted.

"It's gonna be a big one!" Shawn said.

Alek beckoned to the waves. "Come on, baby!"

The hydraulic arm bucked, and Shawn almost fell. He grabbed the railing just below the gunwale and steadied himself.

"Keep it together, greenhorn!" Maria called.

Something emerged from the surf, wrapped around the seven-by-seven-foot rectangular cage trap. It was large and sinuous, its skin glistening white, blending with the foam atop the turbulent waves.

Shawn leaned forward. "Is that some sort of giant squid?"

The trap swung toward the boat. Shawn and Alek grabbed the metal-ringed sides. Bracing their legs against the floor, they guided it onto the deck, out of the onslaught of water.

Alek poked at the side of the creature. "Whatever it is, it's dead."

Shawn walked around the trap, evaluating the beast. Suddenly, it thumped against the deck. The two men jumped back. Next to Shawn, the coiled body exposed a large, serpentine head.

"What the... ?" Shawn said.

He bent down to inspect the head. Even from where she stood at the helm, Maria saw the serpent's eyes move. Through the mist of sea spray, they glowed bright red.

IRIS

ALEUTIAN ISLANDS, ALASKA

I RIS BAI COULDN'T MOVE. Frozen in her Shifter form, she felt the chill of the ocean water seep into her skin like tar through sand, imprisoning her muscles in its thick and viscous grasp. She was lying on the deck of a boat, struggling to maintain consciousness. The various powers that roiled through her system were too much. They were shutting her down. Even if Davis had succeeded in taking the powers of everyone on the Shifter Council, he wouldn't have survived long after. Davis wouldn't have survived. He didn't...

Memories of her last interaction with Davis surfaced in her semi-conscious state. The San Francisco Shifter City Hall. Walls of underwater glass glinting behind... a man. No—a monster. Bulbous, contorted flesh. Tentacles, fangs, claws. Flashing, crazed eyes glaring... at her.

Voices exclaimed around her, awakening her from her dreams. Her nightmares. She twitched on the boat deck. Waves splashed on her side. But her consciousness didn't last. Her mind faded back into darkness and with it came more memories.

She was responsible for Davis's death. She had tried to save him, tried to bring him to the surface so he could breathe, but the new powers had blackened her vision and clouded her mind. When she'd awoken, he was nowhere to be found.

She was a murderer, a real political gangster, just like her mother. Despite her conflicting feelings about Davis, overwhelming loss struck her. Guilt formed a pit so heavy and deep in her stomach it threatened to pull her down to the ocean floor. The stolen powers rumbled through her body. If the powers killed her, wouldn't she get what she deserved?

But what about all those people who had been stripped of their powers? She couldn't leave things as they were. She needed to return the powers. That would make things right. It would justify what she had done to Davis and gain the trust of the council members. She could still redeem herself and become a leader. It couldn't have been that long since she'd jumped off the dock in San Francisco—maybe it was even the same day. But the excess powers were muddling her brain. She couldn't be sure.

At some point after she had tackled Davis into the water, she had gone back to the transfer stone mine. She had collected as many stones as she could, taking advantage of her new powers to claw through rock and store the stones in a depthless, hidden pocket at her side. Had it been in a state of panic—spurred by a need of self-preservation—that she had mined the stones? Or had it been with forethought, knowing she would return the powers to their original owners?

Pain ripped through her body, her nerves firing indiscriminately. Heat surged through her chest. Too strong. Too hot. She couldn't see. She couldn't feel…

The world came back into focus. Water continued to splash against her side, sliding around the wooden deck that rocked beneath her. A young blond man and an older bearded man wearing yellow plastic outfits cautiously approached her, a fishing net in their hands.

Sensations returned to her. She could feel now, and it felt like she was dying. She *was* dying. If she was going to survive—if she was going to return these powers to their rightful owners—she had to act now.

She tried to focus her finding power to direct her to the San Francisco Shifter City Hall, but the effort made her dizzy. She tried to slither across the deck back into the ocean, but her body twitched uselessly. It was too late. The powers were shutting her down.

The blond man kneeled beside her and began pulling the net over her body. He was close enough to touch. If only she could form a human arm or a tentacle, she could grab a transfer stone and transfer the power to him. That amount of power would kill him, but not right away. It would give her time. Spurred by the panic of being on the precipice of death, she didn't allow herself to think too much about it. She put all her remaining energy into forming an arm.

Her head spun, and her vision blurred. Slowly, muscles cramping and bones aching, an arm split away from her side, and then a hand formed. She blindly groped in the hidden, bottomless pouch where she had stored the stones, her fingers spasming with the effort. A stone slipped through her fingers. And another. She held her breath in an attempt to steady her trembling hand and tried again. She felt for the smooth surface and gingerly closed her fingers. There! She had one! She withdrew her hand and tilted it toward the young, blond man, using the last of her energy. All she could do was wait for him to brush against the stone of his own accord. Belatedly, she realized he had no exposed skin besides his face. He was wearing rubber gloves, boots, and the yellow plastic overwear with a hood that covered his head. The last of her hope petered out, and her hand started to slacken.

The man neared her outstretched arm. "What the... There's someone under the serpent! Alek, help me lift the beast to get 'em out!"

The big, bearded man dropped his end of the net and ran over. The young man knelt and removed a glove to take hold of her hand... and Iris released her powers through the stone.

White light erupted where their hands met the transfer stone. The blond man slackened in her grip, and the bearded man fell back, shielding his eyes. As the power drained from Iris's body, her mind cleared. An internal gate slammed down in her system, stopping the transfer so that only a handful of the powers left her system, enough for her to regain some of her faculties. She looked at the older man, and an idea formed. She could spread out the transfer of her powers between the crew members.

The bearded man crawled forward to check on his crewmate. Dropping the used stone, Iris grabbed another and touched it to his face as soon as he was near enough. Another flash of white light. Another slamming shut of her internal gate to stop the flow of power. She felt better. More stable.

She looked at the two bewildered men sitting on the deck. A human explaining their new situation would be more approachable than a giant snake with one human arm. With her new vitality, she completely transformed into her human form and reformed her black pantsuit. She brushed her long hair from her face and took a step toward the men, trying to look as innocuous as possible. She wobbled, the dizziness returning with full force as she tried to walk on the rocking boat. It wasn't enough. She needed to transfer a little more power to fully stabilize herself.

"What's going on back there?" a voice called from the boat's cabin.

Of course. Someone had to captain the boat.

Leaving the men on the deck behind her, Iris made her way to the cabin on unsteady legs. The men would need a few minutes to recover, which would give her a little time to transfer more power and then figure out what to tell them. And where to put them. She couldn't just unleash new Shifters back into a world of Statics, especially Shifters with multiple powers that weren't theirs and no idea how to use or control them.

She entered the cabin where the captain held on to the wheel with one hand while leaning over the dashboard controls, a yellow rubber coat hanging from the back of her chair. The petite and muscular woman looked at Iris with dark eyes that showed only a hint of surprise. Her long, black hair blew around the brown skin of her exposed shoulders. Iris didn't waste any time. She strode forward and touched a stone to the captain's arm. The stone flashed, and the woman wobbled to the ground.

Again, Iris shut off the transfer after a handful of powers left her system and grabbed the wheel. She knew nothing about piloting a boat but fortunately, she had other means of moving it.

Taking account of her surroundings for the first time, Iris noted several land masses in the distance. Islands. She summoned her power over water and created an ocean current to direct the boat toward the smallest and farthest of the islands. Hopefully, the island would be isolated enough to leave the crew there until she could return the other powers to their rightful owners. After that was done, she'd return and reclaim the crew's powers. She would make a few runs to the mainland first to make sure they were well stocked with food, water, and shelter. Maybe she could get her hands on some oblivion tincture and send the crew back to their normal lives after all this none the wiser.

The captain spoke from the floor, defiant even in her unsteady state. "You better have a damn good story."

"Oh, I do," Iris said with a small smile.

AMBER

UNALASKA, ALASKA

AMBER SAT IN THE Alaskan dockside café, a script for the show *Unsolved Mysteries* in her hands. This was an amazing opportunity, she reminded herself. Not only would she be on national television, but she and Arav were also getting credit for being away from school to work on a special project—a research report about the propagation of local legends and their roles in modern society. It hadn't taken much to convince their parents to come along once Amber and Arav explained the school credit aspect, and they even seemed excited about taking a family trip.

Even though filming was done, Amber couldn't stop reviewing the script, her unease building each time.

UNSOLVED MYSTERIES

SEASON 11, EPISODE 7

MYSTERY: THE CRABBY LADY

PARANORMAL SIGHTINGS: SHAPESHIFTERS

MISSING PERSONS: MARIA AKAYUX, ALEK IVANOV, SHAWN MURPHY

ORIGINAL AIR DATE: FRIDAY, NOVEMBER 10, 2000

HOST ROBERT STACK WALKS IN FRONT OF A SCREEN DEPICTING A SCENE AT NIGHT WITH VAGUE SHAPES AND BLURRED LIGHTS.

ROBERT STACK

Tonight's episode features a trio of mystery, paranormal sightings, and missing persons. Join me in Unalaska, Alaska. *You* may be able to help solve a mystery.

THEME MUSIC PLAYS.
CLIPS OF ALASKAN WILDERNESS, MOUNTAINS, AND BEARS. A BOAT HARBOR AND SHOTS OF FISHERFOLK ON THEIR BOATS. ROBERT STACK'S DEEP VOICE NARRATES THE SCENE.

ROBERT STACK (VOICE-OVER)

On the morning of Sunday, October 8, 2000, the Alaskan king crab vessel *The Crabby Lady* set off to sea from the Carl E. Moses boat harbor in Unalaska, Alaska. Aboard were Captain Maria Akayux and her two-person crew: Alek Ivanov and Shawn Murphy.

PHOTOS OF MARIA, ALEK, AND SHAWN ABOARD *THE CRABBY LADY* APPEAR ON THE SCREEN.

ROBERT STACK (VO)

On Tuesday, October 10, only two days later, *The Crabby Lady* was spotted floating along the northern coast of Unalaska Island. Locals instantly noticed that something was amiss.

A BEARDED MAN IN HIS FORTIES APPEARS ON-SCREEN. A CAPTION ON THE BOTTOM OF THE SCREEN IDENTIFIES HIM AS DALTON HAI, LOCAL FISHERMAN.

DALTON HAI

There was nobody on board. Nobody! No people. No crab. Everyone was just... gone. It was like a ghost ship. Then that night, I was standing on that cliff there looking out to sea, and I saw a white serpent. Enormous. Just gliding through the water. I ran to get my brother Petey so he could see, but when we got back, it was gone.

ROBERT STACK (VO)

Soon, news of the serpent spread, bringing visitors to the area.

A TEENAGE GIRL AND BOY APPEAR ONSCREEN. A CAPTION ON THE BOTTOM OF THE SCREEN IDENTIFIES THEM AS AMBER SU AND ARAV MARKSON, REPRESENTATIVES FROM MONSTER HUNTERS OF YURAS, CALIFORNIA.

AMBER SU

Young people like us are the future, and we need to be involved in situations that may affect our future welfare. This serpent case shows similarities to strange occurrences in our town. We are gathering proof that there are shapeshifting people among us.

ARAV MARKSON

I know from personal experience what it's like to have family members attacked by these *monsters*. We need to spread awareness and band together to keep our communities safe.

ROBERT STACK

So what happened in the two days that *The Crabby Lady* was out at sea? Did monsters attack the boat like these visitors claim? Or was it simply a matter of disastrous weather? Stay tuned to find out more in this episode of *Unsolved Mysteries*.

Amber put aside the script. Tremors shook her hands. She put them under her legs in an attempt to still them, but the nervous energy only transitioned to her feet, which began to tap under the café table. She tried to resume her studies, but her attention kept straying from her books to the dockyard outside and the camera crew gathered there. The late afternoon sun scattered across the water. Splotches of reflected light danced on the boats and darted between the people walking around the dock, wavering their silhouettes like television static. Through the glare of the window, she tried to make out Arav among the camera crew. What was taking him so long?

Even though it was warm in the café, Amber shivered. She averted her eyes from the cold Alaskan sun. When had she become the party pooper? Wasn't this the big thrill she'd always been looking for? But she couldn't shake the feeling that they'd gone too far, following some rumors to Alaska. It was one thing to go to community monster hunter meetings to support Arav when his brother had initially been injured, but Kabir was completely healed now and back to work on the police force.

The café door swung open with a swish of crisp air, and Arav walked in, beaming. The wind had loosened the gel in his short, curly hair, giving him an untamed look, and his brown skin glowed with frenetic energy. He was in his element. Amber's stomach fluttered, not just because of how attractive Arav looked in his fitted fleece jacket that hugged his muscular chest and arms, but also because she was about to dampen his spirits.

Arav scanned the café and smiled when he saw Amber. He walked over, words pouring out before he even sat down.

"I was talking to Dalton, the local fisherman who saw the ghost serpent, and he says he heard of more strange activity off the northern coast of the island. I'm thinking we should check it out. Make sure nothing falls through the cracks. This could be it. What we came here looking for! I can't wait to get home to tell everyone about this, especially Tom."

"Who's Tom?" Somehow, her short reply sounded both exhausted and exasperated. She tried to cover up her feelings by smiling and widening her eyes in feigned interest.

"He's the new kid in Monster Hunters United, remember? The skeptic. But once I tell him everything we've found, he'll be a believer for sure."

Despite her best efforts, the exasperated tone returned. "But... we haven't *found* anything."

"Not yet. That's why we need to go check out the northern side of the island."

The thought of chasing more rumors sent her tapping feet into a frenzy. Arav continued, his voice pitch and speed increasing with an accompaniment of sweeping gestures.

"If we leave now, Dalton said he could give us a ride up there."

Amber's feet tapped. "We'd have to tell our parents first."

"Of course! It won't take long to stop by the hotel."

Tap. Tap. Tap. "What *are* we looking for, exactly?"

"Information. Anything we learn about these monsters will help us protect ourselves and others against them, especially with the new policies coming."

"New policies?"

"Haven't you been paying attention in the meetings?"

She hadn't. There wasn't ever anything new or interesting in those MHU meetings. It was mostly just elderly men who liked to hear themselves drone on and on about the same conspiracy theories. She got the sense it was their only social interaction all week. It made her sad to think of those same elderly people spending most of their days alone at home. *At least they have MHU... I guess.* Playing chess or showing off their stamp collections, or whatever old people did, seemed like a better community activity than always complaining and blaming societal problems on supposed *monsters*.

Why not brainstorm ways to improve their community together? Because that was harder than just complaining. MHU gave them purpose and a sense of control in a messed-up world without the responsibility to fix it. It was why she initially supported Arav joining them after Kabir's accident. He'd seemed so lost, and the meetings gave him a reason to carry on through his day. A place for unhappy people to complain with like-minded individuals was innocent enough, if tiresome and annoying, but at least it was just words, right?

"... and they could always claim it was a hunting accident," Arav was saying.

Is he still talking about the meetings? "Right..."

"Anyway, once we're up there, we can walk through the town and talk to more locals. Or maybe we could get someone here to take us around the coast on their boat, and we could check out some of those little islands—"

Amber pushed away from the table and stood up. "Stop!"

Arav flinched and several café customers turned their way. Heat rushed to her face, and she quickly sat down again. Arav's brow furrowed as she continued in a lower voice.

"I can't go. I need to study."

"You came all the way out here to *study*? What, are you becoming like Nivi now?"

"We *do* have this project to finish, *remember*? And there's nothing wrong with studying *or* Nivi."

Arav scoffed. "That's not what you made it seem like. You were always complaining about how much of a loser she was."

"I never said that."

"'Nivi never goes out.' 'Nivi's always studying.' Nivi this. Nivi that. I thought you'd be happy to finally be rid of her. She was only holding you back."

Arav was right. She had complained about Nivi—a lot—but only because she wanted Nivi to participate more. And just when they had really begun to understand each other, Nivi had changed schools. Just like that. With no regard for Amber's feelings. Part of the reason she'd agreed to go to Alaska was because she missed Nivi so much. She wanted a distraction from the anger and hurt, and she wanted to feel less alone, but Arav's words only brought all those emotions to the surface. Before she could stop herself, she lashed out.

"You know what? Nivi was right about you. You really are a dumb jock."

Arav became very still. His voice trembled with anger and almost a hint of sadness. "You used to be fun."

Amber was instantly sorry. The words were out and she couldn't take them back, but she could try to reason with him. "I'm sorry. I just—it's too much. Even Kabir isn't looking for these *monsters*."

Arav frowned. "He doesn't remember what happened to him. I do. I *saw* it." His voice dropped. "His wounds. They were the same claw marks that were on my mom's body."

Her heart went out to him, but he was making connections that weren't there. "I know what you *thought* you saw, but I was there too, and I only saw Kabir fall. Yes, he fell in a really weird way, but that was it. I know from experience how stress can make you see *things*. When the high school caught fire, I thought I saw Nivi—"

"Are you serious right now?"

Amber flinched at Arav's tone. She wasn't used to his anger being directed at her, or even him being angry at all. But ever since he joined the monster hunting group, the shifts in his mood had increased.

"I thought you believed me," Arav continued. "I thought you knew how much this meant to me. To avenge my mom *and* my brother. To protect others from harm."

"I'm sorry for what happened to them, but we don't know if these monsters exist."

"I *know* they exist."

Amber put up her hands. "I don't want to do this anymore. You go if you want to. I'll see you back at the hotel."

She gathered her books into her bag and got up to go, but Arav followed and grabbed her wrist. "Wait."

Amber tried to pull her arm away. Her emotions were racing, spurred on by the adrenaline rush of their argument. Heat flooded her body, and a pounding pushed inside her skull. It was too hot in the café. She needed to get outside. She needed air. Again, she tried to remove her arm from Arav's grasp, but he held on tighter. The pressure in her head increased. Her heart beat erratically. She felt like her chest was going to explode.

The pressure gave way. A bolt of energy ripped through her core and straight into her wrist.

"Ouch! What the—?" Arav let go of her and stepped back, shaking his hand as if he'd scalded it.

Amber's skin shimmered with a smattering of blue scales where Arav had gripped her. She clutched her arm in surprise, but when she removed her hand, the scales were gone. She was seeing things. Her emotions were making her confused. She just needed to get outside. Out of the heat. She darted out of the café with Arav close behind.

"You're one of *them*!" he cried.

His voice sounded far away, buried beneath the pounding in her head. She didn't want to be here any longer. She just wanted to go home. She closed her eyes and steepled her fingertips along the bridge of her nose. The cool air filled her lungs.

Her headache disappeared, and an intense clarity took over. Even with her eyes closed, she sensed the world come alive around her. Dockworker voices carried on the breeze, crisp and clear. Water lapped against the hulls of moored fishing vessels, complementing the cacophony of seabirds in the ship masts. Her skin prickled in the chill air. Tiny droplets from the humidity beaded along the upright hairs of her arms. She opened her eyes, and there Arav stood before her, brown skin aglow, sparkling in the sunlight that reflected off the sea.

She smiled slightly at the sight of his handsome, glowing face before his grimace reminded her that they were having an argument. "What were you saying?"

He repeated himself, this time in a lowered voice. "You're one of *them*."

"One of whom?"

What were they arguing about again? Her blood rushed through her veins, filling her with energy and life. How could Arav be upset when they were surrounded by so much beauty? The glittering ocean. The sea salt on her lips. The smell of pungent fish and fresh ground coffee beans in the air. They were here. They were now.

In the distance, something caught her eye. On the small road that separated the sea from the corrugated green hills, two people were walking toward the dock. One of them had bright orange hair, and the other had dark hair, but other than that, they were too far away to make out their features. What drew her eye to them was the fact that they seemed to glow as Arav did in front of her now.

Arav's voice brought her back to the present. "What are you looking at?"

What had he been saying? That was right. Arav wanted to continue searching for monsters somewhere up the coast. "You go ahead. I want to enjoy this day. I'll meet you back at the hotel."

She wandered away, caught up in the ecstatic thrill of the day. Her senses continued to fire, her whole-body awareness of the environment dulling the curiosity of her mind. She didn't care. She just wanted to enjoy the day.

Arav's voice called after her. "That's not what I'm talking about."

She waved absentmindedly at him. What *was* he talking about? It didn't matter. All she wanted in that moment was to bask in sensory glory.

The sun hovered above the ocean as a fogbank descended along the coast, tucking the harbor in a blanket of golden mist. As the sun dipped out of sight, a white glow lingered at the horizon before extinguishing in the waves.

Amber glanced at the hotel lobby clock. Ten thirty p.m. No one had come or gone from the hotel in hours. The hotel clerk had long ago stopped giving Amber questioning glances and was now relaxing behind the lobby counter, reading a book. The day's unexplained bliss had faded, replaced by a heavy, sinking anxiety.

Down the hall, the elevator doors opened, and Amber's mother stepped out.

"Amber, dear. Are you still waiting for Arav?"

Amber sighed. "Yeah."

He should've had plenty of time to explore the northern side of the island and be back by now.

"Arav's father doesn't seem concerned. He's already gone to bed."

That wasn't really a ringing endorsement for Arav's safety. Maybe she should look for him back at the dock, but he was probably fine. He probably just got caught up in an exciting, delusional lead. The initial surge of energy she'd experienced during the day had worn off. Her body slumped, and the temptation of sleep weighed down her eyelids. Her mother took her arm and led her into the elevator.

Back in the room, Amber drew the room curtains closed and fell onto the bed without pulling back the covers.

A sunray hit Amber's eyelids. She shielded her face and turned over just as the hotel room door opened. Happy chatter burst into the room, followed by her parents holding blueberry muffins. Amber groaned and covered her face with a pillow.

"*Good morning*, Amber," her dad teased.

"Go away." Amber groaned.

"Looks like it's just us here for the next couple of days."

"What are you talking about?"

"We saw Frank Markson this morning," her mom said.

Amber removed the pillow from her face and sat up. "And?"

"It seems they had some kind of home emergency. Right, dear?"

Her dad nodded and handed Amber a muffin. "Yes. Burst water pipe. What an inconvenience."

"You saw Arav, too?"

"No. But Frank wouldn't have said '*we* have to take the first flight home' if he was going alone."

Amber bit into the muffin to hide her annoyance. Was their argument the previous day so serious that Arav just left without saying goodbye, abandoning her and her supportive parents in this cold and isolated place when the only reason they were here to begin with was his vendetta against some made-up creatures? Worse, what if his delusions now extended to her, and he was going to turn all of Monster Hunters United against her? Rage rushed through her tingling veins and into her fist as she crushed the muffin. She squeezed so hard her nails bit her palm, stinging like an electric zap.

Her mother sniffed. "Is something burning?"

Amber looked down at the crumbs falling from her hand. The buttery edges were singed black.

WINTER 2000

NIVI

SEQUOIA NATIONAL FOREST, CALIFORNIA

NIVI DAWAN SAT AMONG the majestic sequoia forest on the perimeter of the Shifter Academy. In the shade, warm air came only in sporadic ribbons, hints of a reality that would never quite take hold. Snow would be coming soon enough.

After several months at the school, Nivi still felt like an outsider. She missed her simple life in Yuras. She missed her best friend Amber and her grandmother Ling. Everything had been taken away. Erased. Even though Nivi now had her mother Ji, their relationship was a facade because Ji didn't remember the past. Nobody remembered anything. Nobody... except for Nivi.

That day in San Francisco seemed so long ago. The feeling of relief when Iris had taken Davis into the water and when the Shifter police failed to find any indication either of the two had survived. The security of being surrounded by her family and friends. The promise of a return to normalcy. Never to be.

Shortly after that day, Nivi and her mother had been called in to the Shifter headquarters for a debriefing. Several officers stood in the room with them, including Donald Buhl, the head of Shifter police. As soon as their statements had been given, the officers had descended upon them, fingers glistening with black liquid. Thanks to Meng's letter, Nivi expected the oblivion tincture would be used and knew to play along when her mom slipped into a brief unconsciousness, and afterward, to blink blankly when Davis's or Iris's name was mentioned.

And it hadn't stopped with the two of them. Nobody at the Shifter Academy knew who Davis or Iris were. Nobody remembered any of the other council members who had lost their powers to Davis. History had been erased and rewritten.

The school bells tolled the end of break time. Nivi stood up but lingered a moment longer, kicking at the dirt next to one of the wooden posts that bordered the school's property. She wasn't supposed to go past the posts during school hours, especially unaccompanied and without her camouflage pendant. It was the tiny bit of rebellion she allowed herself, lingering at the border of two separate realities—one where she had been May and Nivi, the daughter of Ji and Jackson and the granddaughter of Ling; and one where she was only Nivi, daughter to a single mother whose husband had died in an accident before a healer could arrive. A fallen tree of all things. The fact that her father, the chairperson of the Shifter Council, had been assassinated in a magical fire had to be hidden because it would lead to questions, and the Shifter government wanted Davis and his attempted coup erased from history to avoid potential unrest.

She stared at the invisible border. She could cross over and no one would know, but she wouldn't do it. She couldn't. The safety of her family and friends was at risk.

In the distance, laughter and the crunching of footsteps approached, and soon a group of hikers came into view. Statics. They passed by Nivi, looking through her like she didn't exist, and continued on their way, staying clear of the school boundaries.

It wasn't anything new, and it shouldn't have bothered her. The mottled green camouflage stone on the wooden post prevented the hikers from seeing and approaching her or the school's property. But she was tired of not being seen, whether inside or outside of the Shifter community.

Something kicked up from the dirt as the Statics moved farther away from her. It fluttered in the breeze and blew across the invisible camouflage barrier, catching against a tree trunk. Nivi hurried over to it and picked it up, succumbing to her instincts of wanting to be helpful even though she couldn't actually give it back. It was some sort of flyer, and her heart raced as she read what it said.

WE BELONG HERE

NOT HIDDEN. NOT ERASED. NOT SEPARATE.

INTEGRATION IS NOT EXTINCTION

Could this be what she thought it was—pro-integration propaganda? The bottom of the paper was torn, so she couldn't read what had been written below. It seemed like it could've been a date or the name of a location. She spun around, clutching the paper in her hand, not sure whether she should keep it, hide it, or destroy it.

The bells continued to ring. Nivi shoved the paper into her jacket pocket and jogged into the clearing that surrounded the school. Fading violet lupines sagged into the golden grass-covered meadow, and a flock of quail, disturbed by Nivi's motion, flapped up to the trees. Students gathered at the school entrance—two massive wooden doors in a building made of even more massive, monolithic stones. Everything about the place was impressive and beautiful. The natural way the monoliths leaned against each other, creating a building that blended into the landscape. The sudden cool dampness when she walked inside, and the lush ferns that hung from the second-floor balustrades like streamers or curtains. The light coming into the building between the angles of stone, creating a soft, illuminating glow. It all made Nivi feel small and out of place.

Nivi made her way through the students gathered in the school atrium as they steadily funneled into classrooms, feeling more alone than ever with the secret of her discovery. The more she thought of it, the more unlikely it seemed that the paper was related to pro-integration matters. It could've been about anything, like the lyrics to a song. Even if it was pro-integration propaganda, how would she know who she could safely talk to about it?

In the middle of the atrium, Nivi waited for their teacher, Mr. Cho, to arrive. She didn't bother removing her quilted green coat—part of the school uniform—because they wouldn't remain inside for long.

Mr. Cho strode in from the dining hall, waving Nivi and her classmates over.

"Gather 'round, class. Today's lesson is going to expand on yesterday's. We will work on your secondary powers in both human and Shifter form. When we get outside, you can transform back and forth at will, but wait for me to come to you before you practice your secondary powers. This is important for your safety. Okay, let's go!"

The students walked outside and around the back of the school building, spreading out around a large pool of water. Nivi's skin tingled, her powers ready to break free. She stared down at her hands, clenching and unclenching them. All the students around her were already shifting.

Jorge Garcia, a skinny boy with glasses, pushed past her as he dashed to the pool. He was a few inches shorter than her, so probably about five foot four, with brown skin and black eyes. Nivi wondered about those glasses. Didn't all Shifters have perfect vision? Maybe she was wrong about that.

Jorge jumped, his black, straight, chin-length hair blowing back like a model's in front of a fan, and transformed midair before he hit the water. His Shifter form, an ahuizotl or spiny water dog, was also small, about the size of a raccoon. The mostly black dog entered the water with barely a splash. Waterproof, marbled gray-and-black fur spikes protruded above the water from its back as its monkey-like hands paddled around. Jorge swam up to the pool's edge, reaching for his friend Ai Lu's leg with a claw at the end of his prehensile tail. Ai sidestepped the claw and shifted into a tiangou or celestial dog—a large, long-limbed, muscular beast with a white spot on its forehead in its otherwise glossy black fur. Like its long tail, the fur on its shoulders feathered out like wings into long, flowy strips with a gradient of purple to blue.

In response to Jorge's attempt to grab their leg, Ai opened their canine mouth and swallowed the light in their vicinity, plunging the area directly in front of them and Jorge into darkness. Jorge momentarily disappeared from view, and then Nivi saw him swim out of the range of Ai's eclipse. He remained underwater for the next few minutes, swimming along the pool's floor. Bubbles floated up from where he swam. Nivi had seen on several occasions that his Shifter form had gills on the side of its neck.

"I said no secondary powers without my guidance," Mr. Cho called from across the pool.

Ai closed their mouth, and the darkness in front of them faded.

Jorge climbed out of the pool and shook out his spiky fur before transforming into his human form. Ai followed suit. In their human forms, they couldn't have been more different. Ai dyed their cropped, black hair to match the purple-blue gradient of their canine fur feathering. The white spot in the middle of the celestial dog's forehead translated into a hypopigmentation spot on Ai's tan skin. Jorge, with his green school uniform hanging loose over his slim and compact body, looked almost frail next to Ai's tall, muscular form and broad shoulders. In addition to constantly pushing up his glasses, Jorge had a tendency to hunch and hug himself as if he were always cold, which was funny considering his affinity for pools of cold water. In contrast to Ai's unapologetically direct style of communication, Jorge had trouble making eye contact and tended to speak softly. There must be something about their shared canine experience that drew them together. If two people so different could be good friends, why couldn't Nivi make any friends? She knew why. She had to protect her family until she could get them back, and that meant keeping people at a distance to prevent them from discovering all the truths about her.

"Hey!" Ai said. "You got a staring problem?"

Nivi quickly averted her eyes and tried to hide the warmth in her cheeks by transforming as quickly as possible. Shifter forms had the advantage of masking human emotions. Heat rose in her core and spread to her limbs, igniting flames around her ankles and wrists. Iridescent green scales formed across her skin, replacing her clothes as her hands and feet turned into gold hooves. She let out a deep breath, her muscles unknitting and her joints popping. There was something about being in her qilin form that gave her a simultaneous spark of energy and calm, like she could leap across the massive pool because she'd suddenly been relieved of the burden she carried. She reared onto her hind legs and spun in a circle before reining in her enthusiasm. She glanced around, embarrassed by her outburst. No one was paying her any attention. Of course they weren't. Good. That was what she wanted.

Mr. Cho made his rounds, spending an efficient couple of minutes with each student before he gave his blessing to practice secondary powers. Before long, it was Nivi's turn. She formed her shield, a bubble of thin fire that she kept just large enough to encompass her qilin body. Mr. Cho stood before her and formed a ball of ice in his hand. He tossed it gently at Nivi's shield as if they were playing catch. The ice ball evaporated as soon as it encountered the shield with only the slightest ripple in the fire bubble.

"Very good," Mr. Cho said. "But Nivi, I feel that you're still holding back. There is a lot of potential there, if you would only allow yourself to access it."

There was something about Mr. Cho's bushy black eyebrows and the way his eyes stayed permanently crinkled that reminded her of Amber's dad, and that made his disappointment at her self-limitation all the more palpable. It killed her to be a subpar student, but this was how it had to be for now. No one could know the extent of her powers.

"I've found that meditation can be very helpful for self-discovery," he continued. "Start with just a few minutes a day. Find a quiet place where you can sit undisturbed, close your eyes, and just breathe. You can count your breaths to maintain your focus. Let me know how it works for you in a week or two. For now, try focusing on a distant spot like a tree at the edge of the glade."

Nivi transformed into human form and nodded. "Yes, Mr. Cho."

He moved on to Ai, and the local vicinity darkened as the celestial dog swallowed the light. When they finished, Mr. Cho turned his attention to Jorge. Nivi couldn't see what skill they worked on together, but she assumed Jorge's secondary power had to do with his underwater breathing abilities. Mr. Cho moved on, and Ai and Jorge sat down to chat.

Nivi tried to focus on a tree in the distance like Mr. Cho had suggested to show him she was trying, but it didn't matter because she wasn't going to access any more of her powers either way. Instead, she ended up eavesdropping on Ai and Jorge's conversation without meaning to. She kept her eyes on the tree at the edge of the forest so they wouldn't know she was listening. She'd already embarrassed herself enough with Ai in one day.

Ai opened their mouth and swallowed enough light to put Jorge's head into darkness.

"Hey!" Jorge scooted out from the darkness, waving his hands around. "If you keep disobeying Mr. Cho, you'll be turned over to the..." Jorge lowered his voice but Nivi could still make out his words, "OT police."

Ai closed their mouth and allowed the light back in. They rolled their eyes. "Mr. Cho already gave me the go-ahead to practice my eclipse how I see fit. And don't tell me you believe in that story. That's just something parents tell their kids to make them behave."

Jorge removed his glasses and polished them on his clothes before replacing them on his nose. "All stories are based in truth."

Nivi realized she was staring at them again and quickly refocused on the tree. OT police? "OT" had to stand for "oblivion tincture." How did Jorge and Ai know about that?

A splash of water hit Nivi in the face, and a large, blue fish tail disappeared into the pool. "Fish tail" wasn't exactly accurate. The tail branched into two clawed and webbed appendages. Vera

Browning's head emerged. Barnacles covered her greenish-blue skin, and her green hair bobbed around her shoulders like kelp. Her eyes were completely gold, even the sclera—mirror-like metallic surfaces able to see in the dark. The gold retracted back into small flecks, revealing green irises. As she made her way to the shore, her generous curves glided effortlessly through the water. She seemed so confident and carefree in her skin. In the past few months, Nivi's body had also begun to fill out, but unlike Vera, Nivi covered herself up with baggy clothes.

"Sorry," Vera called, waving a webbed hand. "I meant to hit them." She pointed at Ai and Jorge, flipping her fish tail with another splash.

Jorge transformed and jumped back into the pool as Vera laughed and dove underwater. Together, they swam across the pool. Nivi shook the water from her head, a pang of jealousy and loneliness tightening her chest. This was how it had to be.

After several more half-hearted attempts at her fire shield, the bell rang, and Nivi reentered the school building. She fell in line behind her fellow students for Ms. Collins's history and government class. Unlike the school's entrance, the classroom doors were a more restrained size, as were the classrooms themselves. The external monolithic rocks formed one wall of the room, letting in the same soft lighting as in the atrium through glass-filled spaces between the rocks. The wood ceiling that separated the first floor from the second-floor dormitories above was only about ten feet high. The desks and blackboards were the same as back in Yuras. Even the decorations Ms. Collins had hung around the room—global maps and posters of notable people through history—made Nivi feel like she was back in her Yuras high school.

Nivi removed her coat and hung it on the back of her chair before sitting down. The normalcy she felt from the room's decor was short-lived. Ms. Collins jumped right into the lesson, reviewing the structure of the Shifter Council. Lies, lies, lies. With each word from Ms. Collins's mouth, Nivi shrank farther into her chair as if doing so would distance her from the lies she heard. She couldn't fault Ms. Collins, though. The teacher was a victim of oblivion tincture, just like everyone else.

At least Ms. Collins spoke with a gusto that showed she loved her job, even if what she taught wasn't true. As she turned to the chalkboard, her red-and-black braids caught the light, fiery like her personality.

"Formed in 1789 alongside the Static government, the United States Shifter Council has been a model for Shifter governments around the world, always governing peacefully and democratically."

Except for that one time when Davis stole the powers of half the senators.

"Chairperson Ariana Peters oversees twenty-five senators."

There used to be fifty senators. Why didn't they replace the other half?

"And the senators oversee each state's representatives."

The lies kept coming. So. Many. Lies. Blood pulsed behind Nivi's eyes, causing black spots to dance around her vision. The world began to tilt, and she gripped her pencil hard to maintain her sense of balance. Too hard. The pencil snapped in her hand, startling her so much that she jumped up. Her desk lifted in the process and banged down, and her pencil case dropped to the floor, scattering its contents. Ms. Collins stopped speaking, and the whole class turned to look at Nivi.

"Nivi," Ms. Collins said, a crease between her brows, "are you all right?"

Nivi swayed where she stood, her sheer embarrassment not enough to flush away the feeling of the floor moving beneath her feet. She grabbed the sides of the desk to steady herself and sank back into her chair.

"I'm fine," she mumbled.

Someone gasped to Nivi's right, and when Nivi turned to look, she saw the reason. Blood dripped from her hand where the snapped pencil had punctured her skin. She clutched her left hand over her right to stanch the flow.

"You better go see the healer," Ms. Collins said.

Unable to speak from the dizziness and embarrassment, Nivi only managed to nod. She slowly stood to go, her legs shaky.

"And someone better accompany you."

Nivi cringed. She'd made such a mess of things. Not only had she failed to stay under the radar, now she needed a babysitter to take her to see her own mother for healing.

Ms. Collins looked around the room. Before Nivi could protest, a hand tentatively raised.

"I... could go with her," said a soft voice.

It was Jorge. Why did he want to help her? Ms. Collins nodded at him, and he got up and came to Nivi's side.

"Is it okay if I hold your elbow?" he said.

Just wanting to get out of there, she let him take her elbow to lead her from the room. Even though he was shorter than her, his grip did feel supportive, and it felt nice not to be alone.

They walked in silence through the atrium and into the administration office. There wasn't anything to say. Even if he had questions and she wanted to answer them, she probably wouldn't be able to answer truthfully.

Bernard, the administrative assistant, looked up from his desk when they entered, his fingers stroking his scraggly beard. He saw Nivi's hand and motioned down the hall behind him.

"Go on back, Miss Dawan. Your mother's free right now."

Jorge walked with her down the hall to a frosted glass door with the words "School Healer" at the top. He knocked with his free hand, and a voice came from inside.

"Come in."

Nivi took her arm back from Jorge. "I'm fine... thanks. You should go back to class."

"Are you sure?"

Nivi smiled weakly and nodded.

"Okay. I'll, uh, see you later."

He backed up and bumped into the wall, his face turning red, then turned around and quickly walked away.

Nivi waited until he was gone before opening the door.

"Hi, Mom."

Ji stood up from her desk, somehow looking chic even in scrubs. Her black hair was in a shoulder-length bob, and the gray streak at her forehead was swept to the side. Her shirt had a mock wrap design that tied at the side, making her look like she was going on vacation, not mending students. The white scrubs fit her lithe body in a way that was fashionable yet professional. Nivi had always favored loose clothing, and she embraced it even more now as she filled out with curves that made her look less and less like her mother's daughter every day. Something new hung from her mother's neck—a jade pendant of some kind of animal.

"Nivi? I thought I heard a boy's voice out there."

"Uh, yeah. That was Jorge. A classmate."

"Oh?" She started to give Nivi a half smile with a raise of an eyebrow but quickly backed off when Nivi stiffened.

Ji could always read Nivi well, and Nivi was grateful for not having to explain herself. Even if she wanted to, she didn't really know what to say. She knew her mother was worried about the fact that she didn't really have friends, so maybe Ji had been excited about a potential friend for her daughter, but Nivi suspected it was more than that. In Yuras, it had seemed like everyone around her was dating, and even more so here at the Shifter Academy—something to do with powers emerging in conjunction with the hormones, she guessed. There was too much going on in her life to have any romantic interests, but even before all this, she had never felt that way toward... anyone.

"What happened?" Ji said, looking at Nivi's clasped hands. At least the bleeding had stopped.

"I—I broke a pencil."

Ji furrowed her brow and motioned for Nivi to take a seat. She gently unclasped Nivi's hands and ran her fingertips over the wound. A warm tingling sensation tickled Nivi's palm, and Ji's gray strip of hair shimmered like silver rain. The frayed skin tightened as the wound knit itself back together, expelling several shards of pencil wood in the process.

"Thanks," Nivi said, rubbing her hands together when it was done.

She got up to wash the blood off, and Ji did the same.

"Nivi," Ji said as Nivi turned to leave. "What's going on with you?"

"What do you mean?"

"You haven't been yourself ever since we moved here. Maybe my presence here is too much? This is an important time in your Shifter development, and I don't want to get in the way."

"No—" Nivi started with a bit too much force. The last thing she needed was for her mother to leave her here on her own. Then she would truly be alone. "That's not it."

Ji sat down. "Then please, tell me what it is. Is there anything I can do?"

Nivi sighed and sat down next to Ji, fiddling with the newly healed skin on her palm.

"I'm just... adjusting."

She looked up from her hands but avoided her mother's eyes, instead focusing on the jade pendant that hung from a red string around her neck. It was an oval shape with a rat carved in the center. Its back arched artistically so that its head almost touched its swirling tail.

Ji's eyes followed Nivi's gaze, and she brought a hand up to touch the necklace. "I just found it this morning in a box I hadn't fully unpacked. I'd completely forgotten about it until now."

"I've never seen it before."

Ji's eyes softened. "Po Po sent it to me when you were born—you know, because you were born in the year of the rat. We weren't talking much at the time because... Well, that's not important. What *is* important is that we treasure the time we have together because we never know how long we'll have. I wish I had tried harder with my mother..." She believed Ling was dead, and Nivi had to let her keep believing that. "I'm not sure if you know, but I was born in the year of the ox, and the ox is the secret friend of the rat."

"What does that mean?"

"The ox helps the rat without it knowing. So I want you to know that I'm always here for you, even if it doesn't always seem like it."

Nivi blinked back tears. Thankfully, at that moment, the bell rang, giving Nivi an excuse to turn away and hide her moist eyes.

"I should go."

Ji patted her hand. "I'll be here."

Nivi nodded and stood. She glanced back at Ji before heading out of her office and the administrative wing. Students poured out of the classrooms, and Nivi had to dodge her way back to Ms. Collins's class to gather her things. Ms. Collins handed her a sheet with the class assignments, and Nivi thanked her before she could ask the dreaded *Are you okay?* She made her way outside and dropped her backpack against the wall near the corner of the building. Students rushed past, spreading out into the field, happy to be done with the school day. Where should she go? To the library as usual to study and wait for her mom to get off work? Back to the forest's edge?

Before she could decide, a couple of students began talking, their voices drifting around the corner. Again, Nivi found herself eavesdropping.

"Where are you thinking of going for college?" a voice said. It was Jorge.

"Where do you think? It's not like there are many choices for us." That was Ai.

"Well, there's the college in DC, and London, and Beijing..." Jorge said.

Ai sighed loudly. "You know what I mean. We have maybe one college per continent. Statics have hundreds if not thousands of choices per continent."

"But there are far fewer of us."

"Why should that limit our choices? I'm tired of having to hide in the shadows. My whole life I've had to keep a part of me hidden. I don't want to repress any part of myself anymore."

Jorge lowered his voice. "Careful, this kind of talk could get us the OT. There's always someone watching or listening."

This was the second time she'd heard Jorge mention oblivion tincture. He *knew* they were being monitored. She found herself drifting around the corner of the building, wanting to be part of the conversation. If Jorge knew the truth, she wasn't as alone as she thought she was.

Nivi had thought about using her powers to nullify the tincture's effect on Ji, Ling, and Meng, but she didn't want to risk being caught. Even if they weren't caught, what good would it do if it was still illegal for Shifters and Statics to interact? Better to let her family live in blissful ignorance for the time being. But if other Shifters already knew the truth, maybe change was coming and she was closer to reuniting her family than she thought.

Ai continued. "Or is that what they want us to think? Anyway, it's not like the Statics would know the difference if I went to one of their schools. They can't tell who's a Shifter and who isn't."

"Yeah, I guess. As long as you moved away after a few years before anyone noticed you weren't aging as quickly."

"But even then, why should we care? We're more powerful. What are we afraid of?"

Ai had a point.

"Maybe we were more powerful a century or more ago, but Shifters haven't kept up with technology the way Statics have. Because we increasingly isolated ourselves this past century, we're now at a disadvantage. Statics have missiles and nuclear weapons. How can our increased lifespan, strength, or even Shifter forms and powers compete with that?"

Jorge had a point too.

Both Jorge and Ai suddenly became quiet and turned to see Nivi, their expressions falling. Jorge hunched, and his hands fidgeted. His delicate composition assumed an even more worried appearance than usual. Except for the white hypopigmentation spot on Ai's forehead, their whole face and neck flushed crimson.

"How long have you been eavesdropping?" Ai said.

"I—I'm sorry," Nivi stammered. "I wasn't—not on purpose."

"What did you hear?" Jorge said.

Nivi put out her hands quickly to assuage them. "I agree with everything you said."

Ai crossed their arms. "How do we know your goody-two-shoes ass won't go turning us in?"

Jorge looked chastened. "Come on, Ai. I don't think she meant any harm."

"I didn't," Nivi said. Something in her resolve cracked. Maybe she was tired of being alone for so long and this presented a moment of connection, or maybe she was tired of keeping secrets. "I can prove it."

Ai and Jorge looked expectantly at her, Ai's eyes narrowed and Jorge's widened. Nivi glanced back and forth between them before looking down at a spot on the ground by her feet. Even though it was winter and they were in the shade of the building, she was starting to sweat. This was a mistake. What was she thinking? She couldn't tell them what was really going on and endanger them, herself, and her family. Her loneliness had dragged her into this situation. And she *was* lonely. So, so lonely. Before she could stop herself, she was babbling a bunch of half-truths.

"I'm different. I don't belong here, and I feel so alone. I can't talk to anyone about it because they're watching me, and if they catch me, they could hurt my family."

Ai and Jorge stared at her. Suddenly, Ai burst out laughing. Jorge chuckled, too, although he looked a little uncomfortable about it, like he didn't want to hurt her feelings. Nivi blinked at them, not knowing what to say. And then Ai did something else she didn't expect. They strode forward and put an arm around Nivi's shoulders, pulling her into a side hug.

"Who would've thought we'd find someone even more paranoid than Jorge?" Ai said jovially. "And are you really complaining about being different to *us*?"

Ai looked so strong and cool with their cropped hair and vintage black leather jacket, which they wore instead of their uniform jacket—stronger and cooler than Nivi would ever be. She never thought Ai would feel like an outsider too. Nivi wasn't sure if it was the sudden human contact or the relief at voicing some of her fears aloud, but her lower lip began to quiver.

Jorge stopped smiling and stepped forward, rubbing his arm. "Come on, Ai. You're upsetting her."

Ai looked down at Nivi and hugged her tighter. "Aw, don't be like that. You're not alone anymore. You have us. Welcome to the club that no one wants to belong to." They winked.

That made Nivi smile, and then she was laughing uncomfortably too. Jorge smiled and briefly placed a welcoming hand on Nivi's free shoulder. At five foot seven, Nivi seemed to stand exactly between Jorge's and Ai's heights, like she was meant to be part of their group. It was a silly reason, but for the first time since she'd moved to Sequoia, she felt like she belonged.

Before they could say anything else, a loud commotion came from the edge of the forest. There was a bang and then shouts. Nivi, Ai, and Jorge ran to the front of the building to see what was going on.

Several students rushed across the meadow, carrying someone between them.

"Help!" the group yelled as they ran.

"What happened? Who are they carrying?" Jorge said, his voice filled with dread.

The students entered the school, and Nivi, Ai, and Jorge followed. A crowd formed around someone lying on the ground. Nivi crept closer, straining to see past all the people. Her foot slipped on the wet stone floor, and she looked down. Blood pooled out from the body on the ground, the iron tang thick in the air. Nivi stood frozen even as her brain screamed at her to recoil. Suddenly, she was back in the Shifter headquarters, and all she could see was Meng on the floor, bleeding from Davis's repeated attacks.

Someone yelled. "We need a healer! Hurry!"

"Nivi!" Ai said, grabbing her and knocking her out of her daze. "Where's your mom?"

Of course, her mom. Nivi ran into the administrative wing to the left of the atrium. She ran past Bernard and rapped on the school healer's door.

"Mom! We need help! Someone's hurt!"

Ji ran out of her office and followed Nivi to the school atrium. The crowd parted for Ji, and Nivi gasped. Mr. Cho lay on the ground, pale and bleary-eyed. It was as if his left leg had exploded.

Tatters of his jeans framed exposed sinew and bone. His jeans, soaked in blood, looked black. Nivi wobbled and tried to crouch down to steady herself before she remembered the ground was covered in blood. She backed up and leaned on a wood post, taking slow breaths to hold back her nausea.

Ji kneeled, seemingly unperturbed by the blood, and ran her hands over Mr. Cho's leg. She closed her eyes, her jaw tensing while she moved her hands back and forth. Blood soaked into her white pants and smeared onto her olive skin. The gray strip of hair at her forehead shimmered. Mr. Cho took in a breath and then let it out, the anguish on his face subsiding. Ji opened her eyes and looked back at Nivi.

"Can you get me a towel?"

Nivi forced herself up and ran back into the office, glad to put some distance between herself and all that blood. The short reprieve helped, and she was able to hand over the towel without trembling. Ji wiped the blood off her hands and Mr. Cho's leg. The bleeding had stopped. The hole in his leg was shrinking. Several small pieces of round metal popped out of the hole as it closed. Ji lifted a piece up and looked at it. At that point, Principal Johnson joined the crowd and settled down next to Ji. She always wore coordinated skirt outfits, and today was no different with a white blouse, a black V-neck vest, and a knee-length black skirt that flared out as she crouched next to Ji, unflinching at the blood touching her skirt.

"Buckshot." Principal Johnson said to Ji and then addressed Mr. Cho. "What happened?"

"I—I don't know." His eyes fluttered shut for a moment, and it looked like he had fallen asleep. But then he stirred, his voice soft. "I was patrolling the school boundaries, and I saw several Shifter auras just past the boundary. I saw one of our students, Vera, and figured they were all students playing. I rushed over to reprimand them. I heard a scream, then a bang, and then my leg was on fire."

Shifters past the boundary? Could this have had anything to do with the paper Nivi had found earlier? Guilt gripped her conscience. Maybe she should've reported the paper instead of hiding it.

Jorge stepped beside Nivi, his voice a whisper. "Vera?" He looked around. "Where is she?"

"Did you pass the boundary before you were shot?" Ji said.

Mr. Cho shook his head.

"Did you see who shot you?" Principal Johnson said.

Mr. Cho shook his head again. "I only know they took Vera."

Everyone became silent. Jorge went stiff. Tension filled the room. Nivi knew what the rest of them must be thinking. If Mr. Cho hadn't crossed the boundary, then it wasn't a Static who had shot him and taken Vera. It was another Shifter. One of them.

AMBER

YURAS, CALIFORNIA

AMBER WALKED DOWN MAIN Street as fast as she could, wearing a large sweatshirt with the hood pulled up and keeping her eyes on the ground. For the past few months, she had avoided gatherings in general, grieving and fuming at Arav's dumping-and-disappearing act. Hanging out with their mutual friends would have felt like pouring salt on her gaping wounds, so she went straight to the library after school and then home. On the plus side, all that studying had dramatically improved her grades. If she kept it up, she could have some very good college options in the future.

If these had been ordinary circumstances, Amber would have laughed at how like Nivi she'd become, but people were becoming worried about her world-shunning behavior, specifically her parents. To ease their worries, if only for one night, she volunteered to pick up a pizza for dinner on her way home from the library. That should show them that she still went out in public, and they'd leave her alone for a while. As she neared the Coastal Crust Pizzeria, some sort of flying insect whizzed by her ear and collided with the side of her head. Trapped in the strands of her hair, the bug banged back and forth against her neck, causing Amber to shriek and pull off her hood. For a moment, she forgot all about her incognito appearance as she swatted at her neck and whipped her hair around to dislodge the bug. Only when she was satisfied the insect was gone did she realize that someone was standing in front of her.

He looked familiar, but everyone did in such a small town. She would nod politely and continue on her way, undisturbed. But he advanced toward her as if to make conversation, and her stomach dropped as she realized where the familiarity was from. She'd seen him at a Monster Hunters United meeting. It was only now that Amber realized how scared she'd been of encountering an MHU member. Even though Arav had falsely accused her of being a monster, she still worried that he might have mentioned something to them before he'd left Yuras, something that could make her a target.

"Hey Amber! It's Tom. Tom Ross from MHU. Not sure if you remember me. We only met once before you left for Alaska."

This was the Tom Arav had mentioned. The skeptic. Someone who could be on her side. Amber relaxed a little. Tom seemed to be acting normal enough, and even if Arav had mentioned anything to him, he hopefully wouldn't have believed it, being the skeptic that he was. He seemed like a pretty nice guy, if a little dorky. He was a couple of years older than her, tall, pale, and lanky, with a long neck and a pronounced Adam's apple. Maybe she could get by him with just some quick pleasantries.

"Oh, yes. Of course. Hi, Tom. I'm actually on my way to pick up a piz—"

"I'm so glad you're back," he cut in.

Amber held in a sigh. It seemed she'd have to chat a little longer.

"To be honest…" Tom glanced around as if checking to make sure no one was listening. "I only joined because my parents were getting on my case about making friends. Cryptids fascinate me, in the way that any monster can be fun and fascinating, like Frankenstein's monster or the yeti, but I know they're not actually *real*."

Or maybe he'd do the chatting for the both of them.

"So it was cool to meet you and Arav. You both seem more 'normal.'" He raised his hands to air quote the last word. "Not that the others aren't normal, but they sometimes take things too seriously. For me, this was just supposed to be fun. So I've been looking forward to the two of you coming back from Alaska so the more chill aspect of the club could be restored. Things have been getting a little heated recently, especially with the new policy and all."

"New policy?" Amber managed to get in before Tom resumed talking. Arav had mentioned something about a new policy too.

"Oh yeah, the 'shoot first' policy for all the licensed hunters, me included."

"MHU has licensed hunters now?"

Tom laughed. "No, not licensed monster hunters, just the typical deer and boar hunters in the area. MHU has been pressuring me to start patrols too, but I don't feel right about it. Nothing's happened yet, fortunately."

Hunters patrolling Yuras with a policy to shoot first? A sense of dread began to fill Amber's stomach. It could be nothing. Hunting was a normal pastime for many Yuras residents. Maybe this was just MHU riling itself up over nothing again.

"Sorry, am I talking too much?" Tom asked. "How was Alaska, by the way? We haven't seen you at meetings for a while."

Amber waited a moment for Tom to talk more, but he stood there watching her expectantly, his brown eyes shining under a mop of dark brown hair. He must be done.

"Well, it was all right. We didn't really find anything. And I thought it'd be awkward to go to a meeting since Arav and I broke up."

"You broke up?"

Heat rose up her neck with the raw emotion that saying it aloud brought. But this was another plus. If Arav hadn't told the members they broke up, it most likely meant he hadn't mentioned any of his accusations either.

"Yeah. I haven't heard from him since Alaska."

Tom looked sympathetic. "That's too bad. None of us have really heard from him. His dad has some half-baked story about him visiting relatives, but it doesn't add up."

That was strange. Why would Frank lie about where Arav was? Was it possible something happened to him? She hadn't considered that. Her anger and grief hadn't allowed her to.

"You don't think Mr. Markson did something..."

"No, no. I'm not trying to start any rumors. Frank loves Arav, but something's off. He's the most zealous member in MHU, so you know how he can get with his theories. Come to our meeting tonight. Talk to Frank. You'll see. Something's up."

Was Arav really missing? Despite Tom's reassurances, he sounded unconvinced about Frank's intentions. The heartbreak she'd been fighting welled to the surface but also mixed with... hope. That was silly. Even if Arav wasn't avoiding her of his own accord, he'd called her a monster and basically accused her of having something to do with his mother's death. She should go to the meeting to keep up appearances and prove she had nothing to do with Arav's strange disappearance.

Disappearance... The thought that something bad had happened to Arav... No, she couldn't focus on that. It might not even be true. He could have just gone to visit a relative like Frank said, to avoid seeing her. If she was being honest with herself, she wanted to hear more about Arav, even from the silly MHU members. Any information was better than the complete silence she'd endured so far. And as much as she'd been trying to avoid people, this small bit of interaction with Tom felt nice. Also, it would be good to find out more about this new policy, if it was something she needed to be concerned about.

"Okay, I'll be there. See you tonight."

Floral lotions and scented candles greeted Amber at the front of Main Street Boutique. The familiar fragrances and cheery displays did little to calm her nerves as she made her way through the clothes racks and out back to the enclosed patio. As usual, there was a sign-in sheet, snacks and drinks, and a group of about twenty people chatting and milling about. Potted succulents lined the back-wall ledge. That was new. Frank Markson was there, and Tom. All other regulars, too, except Arav.

It seemed like so long ago that Amber had entered this patio with Arav for the first time. She had wanted to be supportive of Arav at the time in light of what had happened to Kabir, but what had joining this group accomplished, really? There were always purported monster people sightings but no actual proof. It seemed more like a social club for people who loved conspiracies or wanted something to direct their negative energy toward. And it had driven Arav and her to Alaska, which had caused their breakup.

All of a sudden, she no longer wanted to be there. It was a mistake to surround herself with these people—to dredge up her anger and grief—but before she could duck out of the patio, the meeting was brought to order. Everyone sat down as Frank went to the front of the patio to go over the last meeting's minutes. Amber took a seat near the back and tried not to think of Arav, tried not to miss him and hate him and love him. Reports of sightings and their follow-ups droned on, but then the conversation turned to new business.

One of the older group members, Jerry Pei, stood to talk about something he'd seen in the forest. "I was out on my patrol, and

I swear I saw a road I've never seen before. There are all these abandoned houses. How could I live here my whole life and hike every part of that forest and only find that road now?"

"Sounds like we're going on a field trip," Frank said. "If there are no other announcements, I motion for the meeting to be adjourned."

Ayes resounded around the room, and then everyone was getting up and filing out through the boutique and onto Main Street. Amber followed them, swept up in the crowd. The sun had gone down, and it was dark outside. This could be a good chance to slip away and head home.

"This way," Jerry said, leading the group down the street.

"Hey, Amber," Tom said, coming up on her left and preventing her escape. "This is an exciting development, assuming Jerry actually knows what he saw. He's getting along in his years, so I wouldn't be surprised if there *wasn't* a random road of abandoned houses."

"Uh, yeah." Amber chuckled uncomfortably.

"Have you gotten a chance to talk to Frank yet?"

She was trapped. She thought about making an excuse that she needed to get home. The thought of talking to her ex's dad didn't do anything to calm her nerves, but she needed to do it if she wanted to learn anything about Arav's whereabouts, otherwise, she would've just sat through that boring meeting for nothing.

"I'll go find him now."

Amber caught up to Frank and Jerry as they led the pack of monster hunters south on Main Street. She hung back for a moment, listening to Jerry babble about the abandoned road and catching glimpses of the side of Frank's face. He looked different—good even. For as long as she'd known him, he'd always seemed either drunk or hungover, but right now he was cheery and alert in a way she'd never seen before. His complexion looked better. The small blood vessels that had formed a rosy spider web on his cheeks had faded. His eyes were bright, no longer droopy or yellow. Had he stopped drinking?

Jerry crossed Main Street just before they reached Cedar Lane where the library was located. He pointed. Sure enough, there was a dirt road leading to the forest that Amber had never seen before. Behind her, several other MHU members gasped and murmured as they also saw the road. How could this be? Maybe it was recently created by a local's tractor? The dirt didn't look or smell freshly turned, though.

"Come on," Jerry called, turning on a flashlight and waving his hand in a gesture to follow. "The abandoned homes are just ahead."

Frank looked back at the crowd behind them and noticed Amber. "Amber! So nice to see you." He hung back to walk with her while several people passed them to accompany Jerry.

"Hi, Mr. Markson." She didn't know what else to say, so they were both silent for a while. Frank seemed unconcerned. Unlike Tom, he didn't seem surprised to see Amber after so many months. He walked beside her with a strange, peaceful smile on his face. Finally, she ventured to ask a question. "How's... Arav?"

"Great! He's having a blast." He pulled out a flashlight from his belt and turned it on as they entered the woods. Flashlights were a key accessory that many MHU members carried with them since sightings inevitably occurred at night and in the forest.

"Oh... that's great." Amber's face flushed with anger and humiliation. It didn't sound like Arav missed her at all. "What's he been up to?"

"A little bit of this. A little bit of that. School. Sports. You haven't talked to him?"

That was strange. Did he not know that they'd broken up? Even though Frank had his drinking issues, Arav still talked to him. Frank always seemed to know what was going on in Amber's life when she visited.

"Um... no." She didn't know if she should be the one to fill him in on their breakup. "Who's he staying with again?"

"An aunt."

"I didn't know Arav had an aunt. What's her name?"

"Ms. Markson. She's my sister."

She never knew Frank had a sister, either, let alone one Arav would want to live with. And was Frank always so formal when addressing his relatives? He'd always insisted she call him Frank, but her upbringing was too strong for her to be on a first-name basis with her boyfriend's dad. Ex-boyfriend, that was. "Um... Where does Ms. Markson live?"

"Down south. Again, I'm surprised you haven't talked to Arav about it."

Was he being evasive on purpose? Should she push him on the matter? "I must've forgotten. What was the name of the city again?"

"It's far south. Just outside LA."

Again. Evasive. It was like Tom had said. Something was up.

Anxiety tensed her muscles. Her pulse increased in speed. Heat flared in her chest, and a tingling spread to her fingertips. The air around her felt charged, electric.

Up ahead, Jerry stopped and swung his flashlight from side to side. Amber and Frank caught up, and Frank shined his own flashlight on the ground. Sure enough, a road of abandoned homes stretched ahead. Amber was so surprised, she forgot about her anxiety regarding Arav's whereabouts.

Jerry was mumbling to himself, his free hand in his hair or what was left of it. "I swear... The road kept going through here. And there were houses."

He couldn't see the houses? But they were right *there*.

Frank put a hand on Jerry's shoulder, but Jerry walked forward.

"It must be a little farther," Jerry said.

"That's all right, Jer," Frank said. "Let's come back in the morning when there's more light."

Frank continued to try to reason with Jerry, but the other members turned back toward town with hushed disappointment and exasperated whispers. Amber felt bad for Jerry. Should she say something to support him? But what did it mean that no one else could see the road? She was afraid to find out, so she kept her mouth shut.

Even after the crowd had gone, Jerry refused to leave.

"Just a little farther…"

Jerry stopped at the edge of the flat piece of land. It was a *very* flat piece. In fact, it almost looked like a pool of water. A silver glow emanated from the edge closest to Jerry, probably from his flashlight.

"Jer…" Frank said. "That looks like water. I don't want you trudging through that in the dark. Could be a sinkhole."

Jerry took a step forward, and he stumbled as if his foot were stuck. His flashlight lit up the area around his foot. No… his flashlight was pointed ahead. The water was glowing on its own!

The glowing substance rose up around Jerry's foot and crept up his ankle, encasing his leg in a gelatinous sheath. Tiny silver lights flickered across its surface, similar to the fiber optic lamp in Amber's science classroom. Jerry yelped and tried to pull his foot away, but instead, off balance, he fell forward into the pool. He managed to right himself but was stuck to the spot.

And then he started to rapidly sink.

Amber's heart raced and the heat in her chest returned. Beyond Jerry and the silvery pool, the road of abandoned homes flickered in and out of view.

"Jer!" Frank yelled.

He ran forward, keeping his feet on solid ground, but by the time he grabbed Jerry's hands, Jerry had sunk to his waist in the gelatinous substance. The silver reached up Jerry's sides and sucked him down to his chest… shoulders… neck… chin.

"Help me, Frank!"

Frank pulled and pulled, but he was no match for the glowing ooze. Amber watched in horror as Jerry's mouth, nose, and eyes sank beneath the semi-fluid substance. When only Jerry's hands remained above the surface, she realized Frank was still holding on. Terror froze her limbs and tears stung her eyes, but she forced herself to yell out.

"Let go, Mr. Markson! Let go before it gets you too!"

Despite her cries, Frank held on. She would have to watch two people get eaten alive by that carnivorous goo. Not only had she lost Arav, but she was going to lose his dad too. And still, she couldn't move. Inside her frozen body, her heart raced so fast she thought it would burst. Hot blood pumped through her veins—so, so hot that her fingertips burned. So much pressure in her chest. It was too much. The panic. The heat. It had to go somewhere. It had to break free.

Heat jolted from her chest, through her muscles, and released her arms. They instinctively reached for Frank in a futile attempt to help. A metallic taste filled her mouth, and pressure rang through her ears. An electric shock hit her hands, causing them to spasm. Blue sparks erupted from her fingertips, arched through the air, and zapped Frank in the hand that held on to Jerry. He yelped and let go, falling back just as the tips of Jerry's fingers sank beneath the surface. The gel lapped over the spot where Jerry had been, glowing brightly, and then it faded, and the only light remaining was from Frank's flashlight where it lay on the ground.

Amber stumbled forward on trembling legs, all the heat and energy dissipating, and sank down beside Frank. What *was* that?

That... *power*. It must've been related to the crazy glowing gel. That was the only explanation. And was Mr. Pei really... *dead*?

She picked up Frank's flashlight and held it tightly, if only to have something to steady her hands. The silver pool was tranquil, with no glow or sign of movement. When she looked up at Frank, the placid smile on his face had disappeared. His eyes were wide and unblinking, and he spoke quietly at first as if in a trance and to no one in particular.

"They have him. They have him." He turned to Amber and grabbed her by the shoulders, the volume of his voice rising. His eyes gleamed silver in the flashlight. "*They* have him! The *monsters*! They have him!"

The crazy, ranting Frank she'd been familiar with was back, except this time, Amber believed him.

ARAV

UNKNOWN LOCATION

A RAV STOOD ALONE AT the edge of the Yuras cliffs, peering toward the horizon over the ocean. High above, a golden eagle soared on the breeze, swooping and circling. Something looked off about the bird, not from the front but from the side. It was too large. Much too large.

The sun momentarily blinded Arav as he tried to discern the peculiarities of the eagle. He shielded his eyes. When he lowered his arm, the eagle was swooping toward him, its massive claws inches from his face, its sharp beak open, screeching.

He startled awake to the sound of a commotion down the hall. The soft bedding stuck to his sweat-soaked skin. The sun shone brightly through the skylights. *Another* strange eagle dream. They started once he arrived at this prison, and they were getting more frequent. How long had he been here now? Two, three, four months? He would've been carving notches in the wall like they did in the movies, if he had something to carve with.

He sat up on the small bed and pushed himself to his feet. The cold stone floor brought welcome relief to his overly warm body, still radiating from the adrenaline of his racing heart. The prison cell was maybe ten-by-ten feet, not including the bathroom, with very tall ceilings that made it feel more spacious than it was. A floor-to-ceiling glass wall faced the hall and connected perpendicularly on either side to a two-foot-wide panel of glass that transitioned to a smooth gray wall. That panel of glass allowed for some contact with the prisoners in the adjacent cells if one wanted it, except there were currently no other prisoners around him. He was alone.

He walked over to the enclosed bathroom and splashed water on his face. The amount of privacy he had was surprising for a prison, even if he was being held without due process. Although the authorities, whoever they were, made it clear they would know if he was trying to do anything suspicious. As if what they were doing wasn't suspicious. They even called themselves "shady" or "shifty" or something like that.

The commotion that had awoken him continued. Two guards were arguing out of view. Usually, when the guards came and went, sometimes bringing another prisoner, sometimes taking one away, they never seemed to care if he could hear what they said. Strange and concerning. Was that because he would never leave this place? Or at least not alive? He pushed away the thought and walked to the front of the cell. He picked absently at the lunch tray by the door as he stared out the glass wall and tried to listen to what the guards were saying.

In the months he'd been in this place, no one had been in a cell close enough for him to talk to, if they could be called cells—they were more like modern, capsule hotel rooms with all that glass, gray stone, and dark wood fixtures—so he found himself excited to hear a conversation, even if it wasn't directed at him.

"I said to *hold* your fire," one of the guards said. The tension in her voice made Arav think she was speaking through clenched teeth.

"He came at me so fast," the other guard replied, sounding shaken. "Did you see his Shifter form?"

That was the word they were always using to refer to themselves. *Shifter*. It probably meant the same thing as "shifty."

"No," the female guard replied.

"Exactly. It was a crow, except with three legs, so fast that all I could see was a streak of black."

A three-legged crow? Were they hunting for natural oddities or something?

The anger left the female guard's tone. "Still, that was too messy. The chairperson will be upset."

The male guard groaned. "So will Buhl. This will *not* help my case. He's had it out for me since the beginning."

"What do you mean?"

"It's because I'm not a big cat like you two."

Big cat? That must be some police lingo. Arav was having such a hard time following their conversation.

"That's not true—"

"It is. You know it is." A sigh. "Let's just get this one situated before she wakes up."

Footsteps approached. The guards came into view—the ones who'd kidnapped him from Alaska. Nicola and Eric. They were both taller than him, maybe just over six feet, and more muscular, dressed in their typical black tactical gear with a patch over their left shoulders that looked like a white chevron with some sort of half-human, half-animal design. Nicola was pale and had fiery orange hair and a tattoo down one arm. Eric had dark brown skin and wore his coily hair cropped. Between them, they carried an unconscious girl who must've been close to Arav's age. She had skin as brown as his own but with more of a sun-kissed golden tone, and her shoulder-length, wavy hair was a green-tinged, white-blond that looked as if she had spent too much time in a pool. As the guards carried her, her full curves bounced in a way that was hard to ignore, especially in the skin-tight, white crop top and low-cut jeans that exposed the soft roundness of her belly.

Arav averted his eyes. What was he doing? He wasn't some lascivious animal lusting after girls like they were pieces of meat, even if this one happened to be attractive. He was a respectful and civilized guy who judged each person on their character. At least he tried to. Plus, he had a girlfriend. *Had.* That was the key word. Amber was one of *them*, one of those *uncivilized* monsters that had killed his mother. She had been lying to him this whole time. Still, he missed her. He longed to talk to her to make things right. Maybe it was all a misunderstanding. Maybe he hadn't been doing a good job recently of judging people by their character. Maybe he just longed for company, any company.

Arav pulled his shoulders back and stared at the guards as they walked in front of his window, ready to pound on the glass with his questions and demands and fully expecting them to pass by without acknowledging him as usual, but he also didn't want to startle the sleeping girl. The guards stopped and opened the cell door across from his own. His heartbeat quickened. A person to talk to. Maybe she would know what was going on.

Nicola and Eric put the girl on the bed and left, but they soon returned with a small tub they proceeded to fill with water in the center of the room. Strange. Was the shower broken in her cell? His face warmed as he realized that if she did use the tub, she would be in full view of him.

Once the tub was full, the guards locked the door and did something else that was surprising. They walked directly up to where Arav was standing and spoke, their bodies seeming to glow. Must be something about the way their uniforms reflected the light.

"Are you ready to tell us the truth?" Nicola said, staring at him with intense amber eyes.

"I don't know what you want from me," Arav said. "Why won't you let me go?"

Eric stepped forward. "Why were you out with Statics without a camouflage stone?"

"I don't know what that means."

Nicola shook her head. "He's not going to talk. Leave him. He'll reconsider eventually."

"Wait!" Arav said. "Please, I'm telling you the truth."

She seemed to consider his words before speaking again. "Tell me, who was that Static with you in Alaska when we took you in?"

"I don't know what a Static is, but I was with my dad."

The guards exchanged a glance, and by the looks on their faces, Arav knew he had said the wrong thing. They turned to go.

Arav spoke again, hating the desperation in his voice, but he couldn't stay here any longer. His brother and dad must be worried sick. Amber too. He just wanted to go home.

"It's the truth! Why won't you believe me?"

Eric scoffed. "We know you are lying because a Shifter cannot have a Static as a parent."

They walked away, mocking his response as they went.

Arav stood silently, dumbfounded. He didn't know how to respond to words he didn't understand, but there was that word that they called themselves, again. *Shifter*. And apparently, they considered him a Shifter too. As the guards disappeared from view, his heart sank. He was going to rot away here. His family would never know what happened to him, and he didn't even know why.

He sat down on his bed and put his head in his hands, mulling over what else he could say to get them to let him go. He lifted his head and looked over at the girl on the bed across from his cell. Green-and-gold eyes looked back, turbulent like whirlpools glinting in the sun. Like with the guards, there was a surreal glow about her. It had to be the lighting. He probably looked like he was glowing too.

Hope and excitement surged through him. She was someone new, someone who could have information that could help him, and she was awake.

6

LING

YURAS, CALIFORNIA

THEY SAT SIDE BY side on the porch bench, sipping tea, Ling with a book from the library, Meng with a newspaper. A typical weekend in Yuras. Despite the cool day, the direct sun created a warm microclimate on their porch, so neither of them wore jackets. In fact, Ling noticed with a feeling that lingered between amusement and embarrassment, their outfits almost matched. Ling wore a long-sleeve yellow dress with white tights, her salt-and-pepper hair loose and running down her back, and Meng wore a yellow shirt paired with light jeans, her shoulder-length hair curled and dyed jet black. It was true what they said about couples starting to look like each other over time.

"Gwendolyn Brooks died," Meng said from behind her newspaper.

"That's too bad," Ling said. "She was such a trailblazer. I liked her poetry."

"She was eighty-three."

Ling took a sip of tea. "Mm. Do you think we'll live that long?"

Meng put down her newspaper and arched an eyebrow. "Do you *want* to live that long?"

"Only if you'll still have me when I'm that wrinkly and saggy." Ling squeezed Meng's hand, and Meng scoffed playfully.

Meng folded up her newspaper. "I'm going to go inside."

"I'll join you in a bit."

Ling nestled back into the bench with her book, feeling the sun against her face. She enjoyed being outdoors, reading, working in the garden, whereas Meng couldn't tolerate as much heat and liked to keep her complexion pale. Must be due to her years living in England.

Just as Ling was getting immersed in her reading, movement caught the corner of her eye. She looked up from her book and jumped. A woman stood on the porch by the front door. Where had she come from? Ling hadn't seen or heard anyone approaching.

The woman was Asian with sharp, angular features and an expression as if she had eaten something unpleasant. She wore a black pantsuit, which was strangely formal, and she was tall, especially compared to Ling and Meng who were barely above five feet.

Ling put her book down on the bench and attempted pleasantries even though her heart was pounding thanks to the woman's sudden appearance. "May I help you?"

The woman looked confused. Maybe she hadn't heard her. Maybe Ling hadn't spoken loudly enough.

"Hello," Ling said, raising her voice. "How can I help you?"

The woman seemed to evaluate Ling, then a tone of amazement entered her voice. "You don't know who I am."

"Should I?" Ling knew she was getting older, but her memory wasn't deteriorating yet.

Meng's voice came from inside the screen door. "Did you say something, darling?" A moment later she came out. "Oh, hello. I didn't realize we had company."

The woman tensed at seeing Meng but immediately relaxed. "You don't know who I am either."

"Did we meet here in Yuras?" Ling said. "I thought we met all our neighbors, but we only moved here a few months ago, so I'm sorry if you're slipping my mind right now."

Meng stepped forward with an outstretched hand, always willing to take control of an awkward situation. "Let's reintroduce ourselves. I'm Meng, and this is my partner Ling."

The woman gave an uncertain laugh as she shook Meng's hand, then suddenly appeared worried. She looked around the street, as if she thought she was being watched. "Is it all right if we go inside?"

"Certainly," Meng said. She led the way in.

Ling followed behind. "I didn't catch your name. Or the reason for your visit." Meng would chastise her for being rude, but she had a right to know who was entering their home.

The woman turned and looked at Ling with a strange expression, as if there was so much more behind what she was saying.

"I'm Iris, and I'm here to return something to you."

NIVI

SEQUOIA NATIONAL FOREST, CALIFORNIA

SEVERAL HOURS AFTER THE attack on Mr. Cho and Vera's abduction, the school bells chimed, signaling for all to meet in the dining hall. The atrium remained crowded, abuzz with murmurs, since classes had been canceled for the rest of the day. The students slowly emptied out of the atrium through the doors to the dining hall. Nivi stared at the remaining streaks of dried blood while Ji picked up the blood-soaked towels.

"I'll take it from here, Ji," Michael, the janitor, said while bringing over an empty bucket and a mop.

Ji nodded and stood, handing over the red towels. "Thank you, Michael."

Michael set down the bucket and mop and placed the towels in the bucket. He waved his hands over the floor. Water streamed out of his fingertips in a fine, pressurized mist. Once the floor was sufficiently damp, he mopped up the blood and wrung the mop into the bucket.

Nivi and Ji stepped away to give Michael room.

"Will Mr. Cho be okay?" Nivi asked Ji.

"Yes. He needs some time to recover from the blood loss, but he'll be all right."

"What about Vera?" Jorge said from beside Nivi.

Nivi jumped, having forgotten he was there.

"The council is sending a search team out. Don't worry. They'll find her." Ji gave a sympathetic smile. "I'm going to get cleaned up. You better all head to the dining hall." She left the atrium through a hallway that led to the faculty residences.

How could her mother be so calm? All that blood. And Vera was missing.

It was because she didn't remember. She didn't remember they'd been through this before. Through violence and pain. Why was it happening again?

Nivi's gaze returned to the ground where the mop swept through the remnants of blood, a macabre watercolor of crimson on stone.

A hand touched her lightly on the shoulder. "Come on," Ai said, the usual edge in their voice softened.

Nivi nodded, but before walking away, she remembered she'd stepped in the blood. She asked Michael for a rag to wipe off her shoes.

The atrium had cleared. Of the students, only she, Ai, and Jorge remained. Ai's full lips were pressed into a thin line. An expression that looked like a mix of anger and concern furrowed their brows. Despite their softened voice, they looked like they wanted to beat someone up. Jorge looked as queasy as Nivi felt. His dark complexion had taken on a gray tone. Sweat beaded on his nose, fogging up his glasses. He wiped his hands on his jeans, then wrapped his thin arms around himself, all the while muttering about Vera and blood.

The three of them walked to the dining hall. Even with ceilings as tall as those in the atrium, the room buzzed with the frenzied commotion of all five hundred Shifter Academy inhabitants in one place. Tables, chairs, and benches made from wood stumps and carved boulders were divided into five seating areas. The teachers, faculty, and staff sat at the front, followed by side-by-side tables for the seniors and juniors. Nivi took a seat at the freshman table at the back of the room beside the sophomore table, and Jorge and Ai sat on either side of her after hanging their winter coats on pegs on the rock wall behind them. At the front of the room, a single monolith on its side formed the stage. A small waterfall trickled over the moss-covered stone wall behind the stage.

Ji entered the room with Principal Johnson—both in fresh clothes—and they quickly made their way to the head table. Soon after, two people entered the hall, and a hush went through the room.

"It's the chairperson," Ai whispered. "And vice chairperson."

Nivi glanced at Ai, whose eyes tracked the politicians. On Nivi's other side, Jorge's legs shook, and he squeezed his hands together, blanching the skin over his knuckles.

"This can't be good," he muttered.

Chairperson Ariana Peters walked down the aisle to the stage, followed by Vice Chairperson Anthony Cruz. The shoulder pads in her light blue suit gave a stately appearance to her tall, thin frame. She had a deceivingly unhurried gait, traversing the dining hall in a matter of seconds while her shorter colleague scurried to keep up.

Anthony had the compact form of a featherweight wrestler. His dark brown hair, swept back high over his head, looked light and fluffy, probably styled with lots of mousse. Positioning himself to Ariana's left on the podium, he smiled as if the awkwardly quiet room were applauding his arrival. The overhead lights gleamed off his diamond ear studs and overly white teeth.

Ariana spoke, her strong voice filling the room as if she were giving a campaign speech, her eyes glinting silver under the dining hall lights. "Thank you all for gathering on short notice."

A smile touched her thin lips, repeatedly pulling down the tip of her aquiline nose in a manner that seemed to crack her calm facade. It gave Nivi the creeps. What kind of false front were these politicians trying to put on? Mr. Cho almost died, and Vera was missing. Why were they smiling?

Ariana ran a hand over her light brown hair. "It seems you all had quite the scare today, but I'm here to tell you everything is all right."

A wave of murmurs flowed through the hall, whispers about Vera and Mr. Cho. Anthony nodded enthusiastically, never losing his movie-star smile.

"Mr. Cho will make a full recovery, and your classmate, Vera, has been found," Ariana continued.

The crowd erupted into gasps of relief, including Jorge at Nivi's side.

"And we have taken care of the perpetrators," she continued. "It seems Vera wandered past the camouflage stone barrier and into a group of troublemaking Statics. Mr. Cho tried to help her and got caught in the fray. Fortunately, there is no lasting harm, but I must reiterate the importance of staying within the school borders and wearing your camouflage pendant while outside. Instances like this are why we must maintain the strict boundaries between Shifters and Statics—to protect ourselves and each other."

Anthony began a slow clap, speeding up when several hesitant claps joined in. Eventually, the majority of the room followed suit. Nivi didn't clap, feeling ill at ease. It didn't make sense. Had Mr. Cho lied about staying within the boundaries of the camouflage stones so he wouldn't get in trouble? Or had he just been mistaken?

Ariana cleared her throat. "We'll be meeting with groups of you to get all the details of the incident. While you wait your turn, enjoy lunch provided by the council today."

She descended from the stage and walked down the center aisle to exit the dining hall, nodding at students with the same calm smile. Anthony followed closely behind, waving and shaking a couple of students' hands.

As soon as they left the hall, several uniformed officers entered carrying boxes of pizza and cupcakes. Happy exclamations and chatter commenced with the arrival of the food, and soon students were eating and laughing as if they were celebrating a birthday. Jorge scarfed down a slice of pizza and then another.

"Anxiety makes me hungry," he explained. "I'm so relieved Vera is okay."

Nivi took a bite of the pizza in front of her, forcing herself to blend in with the crowd despite her apprehension. Was she the only one who thought something wasn't adding up? Why would Ariana need to meet with groups of students if she already knew what happened? After the first bite, hunger flared in her stomach, and she finished off the slice without a word. Ai didn't touch their food.

"Are you serious right now?" Ai said.

"What?" Jorge said, mouth full of food.

"You believe that bullshit? I thought *you* were the paranoid one."

Nivi appreciated Ai so much at that moment, not only for welcoming her into their group but for validating her suspicions.

A tremor returned to Jorge's hand, and he dropped what remained of his pizza on his plate. "What do you mean? Vera..."

Ai glanced at the door that led back to the atrium.

"What do you see out there?"

More officers in black uniforms walked by the doorway. Jorge's face paled.

One of the officers walked toward their table. Nivi's heart raced. It was getting hot in the room. Too hot.

Ai reached behind Nivi to nudge Jorge, speaking in a hushed tone. "Do it. Now!"

Jorge nodded right as the officer arrived. Nivi looked at Jorge. He just sat there. What did Ai want him to do?

The officer passed their table and went to the sophomores first. "Please follow me," he said to a few students at the end of the table.

Three students rose and followed the officer out of the room. When they were out of sight, Nivi whispered to Jorge.

"What are you doing?"

"I'll tell you later," he said, looking around nervously. "If Ai's right about what's going to happen."

"What's going to happen?" Nivi said.

Ai leaned forward, the three of them forming a conspiratorial group. "I hate to be an enabler of Jorge's paranoia, but I'm really good at reading people. Get ready for your new reality." They mouthed the words *oblivion tincture*.

Ai was completely right. All the officers. The chairperson's sudden arrival. They were erasing what happened today. But why? What were they trying to hide? And it was so hot in the room. Didn't anyone else feel how hot it was?

Jorge sat back and put his arms to the side as if to steady himself. One of his hands touched Nivi's wrist, and he quickly pulled it back. A strange look came over his face, and his eyes widened. He sat unmoving for several seconds, various emotions flashing across his face. Eventually, he leaned over to Nivi and whispered. "What—How—Did you *do* something?"

Nivi looked at Jorge, confused. She glanced at her arm where Jorge had touched her. Glowing red veins bulged from her skin. Oh, no. The heat. It wasn't the room. She'd let the stress of the day activate her powers, and when Jorge had touched her, she had nullified the oblivion tincture that must've been used on him in the past. What was he remembering? Panicking, she shook her head furtively at him, her eyes pleading for him to stop talking before Ai or someone else overheard. Thankfully, he didn't say anything more, but he looked very distressed.

Another guard walked by, and Nivi winced. Jorge shook his head as if trying to clear it. She could only imagine the chaos going through his mind.

"They're going to erase them again," he muttered, though she wasn't sure if he was speaking to her or himself. His dark eyes focused on her in an intense stare. "They're going to erase what happened to Mr. Cho and Vera."

Nivi nodded. "You won't remember anything."

Ever the observant one, Ai narrowed their eyes at Nivi. "Don't you mean *we* aren't going to remember?"

Nivi realized her mistake. Too late. She was really screwing up today. All this secrecy was too much to contain. This was bound to happen eventually. That was why she should've stayed away from others instead of trying to make friends. What could she say to get out of this one? Did she want to get out of it? Today had been the most connected she'd been to others in so long, and it felt so nice.

Jorge leaned into their conspiratorial circle, pushing up his glasses. "It's okay. You can trust them." He nodded toward Ai.

Jorge and Ai had such a close connection, and they had accepted her into their group. Maybe she could reveal a little bit more without telling the whole truth.

"I'm... kind of immune."

Ai raised an eyebrow. "Immune?"

"To the OT."

Jorge sucked in a breath. She'd said too much. Now he knew she was immune *and* able to break the tincture's spell on others. She should've just said she could nullify oblivion tincture, and then she wouldn't have revealed more about herself. Still, it felt good to have someone know almost the full truth about her.

Ai's mouth fell open, but they looked intrigued.

Nivi continued quickly. "They wiped my mom's memory, and they tried to wipe mine, but it didn't work. So I know, more than anyone, what it's like to be watched. And controlled."

"Why did they want to wipe your memories?" Jorge asked.

Nivi hesitated. How much more should she say? She was in too deep now. "We were involved in a—uh—heated political situation. I think Chairperson Peters was afraid if we remembered the events, there would be chaos in the community."

Ai scooted closer, their accusatory tone replaced by glistening eyes. "What kind of political situation?"

"It's complicated," Nivi said. "Let's just say there used to be many more senators in the council."

Jorge waved an arm up and down. "See? Didn't I tell you? Weird things keep happening. Like in that *Unsolved Mysteries* episode in Alaska where someone saw a giant white serpent or snake after a fishing boat crew disappeared. A Shifter, and *more* missing people."

"What did you say?" Nivi said. A giant white snake? Could that have been Iris?

Ai jumped in before Jorge could respond. "Didn't *I* tell *you*? If we don't start standing up for ourselves, we'll never have control of our lives."

Jorge shushed Ai and looked around. "It won't matter if they just keep wiping our memories again and again. We have to stay under the radar for now. And this time, I'll know for sure if they do it."

Nivi wanted to ask Jorge how he'd know, but another officer entered the dining room. The three of them fell silent, watching the officer gather three more students from the sophomore table before leaving the room.

Nivi thought back to the flier she'd found on the outskirts of school. It was conceivable that not every Shifter had been OT'd, or that not every Shifter had been OT'd properly. She wasn't sure if she was summoning false hope, but it gave her some strength. Maybe word had gotten out, and Ai and Jorge were in on it.

Jorge broke their silence. "My mother was right." Nivi and Ai turned to look at him, and Jorge explained. "She thought the Shifter Council was going to become more anti-integration over time. There was a pro-integration movement for a while, but she said there was always a rebound effect, like a pendulum."

"I wonder what she'd think of this?" Nivi said, casting a glance at the officers out in the hall.

"She died when I was young, but I remember her talking to my dad about it, and I recently spoke more in depth with him about it when I started to suspect something was going on."

"My dad died when I was young too." Feeling like she needed to prevent any pity, Nivi quickly added, "But I barely remember it now."

Jorge and Nivi's eyes met, and Nivi looked away. If he only knew the circumstances of her dad's death.

"Even though it might seem like you barely remember," Jorge said, "it'll always affect you."

Nivi looked up at Jorge again and returned his small smile. Maybe he did understand a bit.

"I always thought you were so stuck up," Ai interjected.

Nivi was taken aback when she realized the comment was directed at her.

"Ai!" Jorge said. "Way to ruin a sensitive moment."

Ai held up a hand. "Hold on. I didn't finish. I always thought you were so stuck up, *but* it turns out you just have a bunch of baggage, like us."

This made Nivi crack a smile, and they all started giggling.

"I'm adopted," Ai said after a moment. "I'm only sharing this so you know my history too. Like you, I don't want any pity." Ai's perceptiveness was so uncanny. "My birth parents died when I was a baby and my adoptive parents are amazing. I have no complaints. Life is what it is." Ai seemed to decide something and suddenly changed the subject. "Say, what are you doing next weekend?"

"Nothing." Since moving to Sequoia, Nivi never had anything to do on the weekends. She mostly just hung out in her room in the two-bedroom staff housing she shared with her mom while the other kids played in the yard or went home to visit their families if they were locals.

"Why don't you come to SF with us? There's a group of us like-minded people meeting there. And by 'like-minded' I mean people with Jorge's type of OT paranoia and pro-integration beliefs like mine."

Nivi hesitated. "SF?"

"Yeah," Ai said. "San Francisco. Have you heard of it?"

Nivi began to protest but then realized Ai was teasing her.

"You should come," Jorge said. "It'll help keep us from feeling so powerless in this *situation*." He glanced over at more sophomores following an officer out.

"I don't know. I doubt my mom would let me."

Ai put an arm around Nivi. "Let me take care of it. I have a way with parents. Plus, it'll be supervised. Just remind me about it if I don't remember this conversation tomorrow." For a moment Nivi didn't understand what they meant, and then Ai continued in a whisper. "Since you're *immune* and all."

Oh yeah. Depending on how much the officers erased today, there was a chance Ai and Jorge wouldn't remember what she had said. Wouldn't that be better? For her to keep her secret and her family safe? She couldn't help but feel a little sad at that prospect.

The last of the sophomores cleared their table, and soon an officer with orange hair and a tattoo sleeve down her left arm entered the room and approached their table. Even though Nivi knew what to expect, her stomach still dropped when the officer stopped in front of them.

"You three," she said, pointing at Nivi, Ai, and Jorge. "Come with me. Bring your things."

Nivi pushed back from the stone table and stood up, glancing around at the room full of chatting and laughing students oblivious to what was happening. They grabbed their coats from the wall pegs. Ai and Jorge walked silently ahead of her, and Nivi tried to look as casual as possible as she followed them out of the dining room and into the atrium.

The officer waved her hand. "This way. We'll be heading upstairs."

Ai and Jorge glanced back at Nivi before following the officer up the stairs to where the student dorms were located. It made sense, Nivi realized, because oblivion tincture caused the affected person to pass out for a while before waking up with new memories, so they needed to put the students somewhere to recover. Although from what she remembered, the effect was relatively quick.

The officer stopped just before the dorms and indicated a small room that Nivi hadn't known existed. Two other officers waited for them on one side of the room in front of a slit of glass between two monoliths that looked out to the field beyond. The younger one with brown hair and skin was as tall and muscular as the orange-haired woman who'd brought them in, but the third officer dwarfed them both. Nivi almost stumbled when she recognized the large, Caucasian man with a clean-shaven head that gleamed in the overhead lights and muscles that bulged through his uniform. Chief Donald Buhl. The head of Shifter police. He'd been present when they'd used oblivion tincture on her and her mother. She quickly returned her gaze to Ai and Jorge's backs to avoid attracting suspicion. There was no reason she should recognize him unless the oblivion tincture hadn't worked on her.

"Have a seat," the officer with brown hair said, taking a step forward to indicate a set of chairs against the opposite wall.

Donald put up a hand to stop the first officer's advance.

"I've got this, Eric—" he cleared his throat. "I mean, Officer Okello."

Officer Eric Okello tensed, then stepped back and crossed his arms while leaning against the wall. The sides of his jaw flexed repeatedly.

"Have a seat," Donald repeated in a deep, resonant voice.

The three of them sat quickly and obediently. Both Jorge and Ai looked as nervous as Nivi felt, which gave her some hope that she didn't stick out. She'd expected Ai to have some of the sass they usually exuded, but there wasn't a trace of defiance in their face.

Donald paced with slow, deliberate steps in front of them. "I'm Chief—"

"Buhl," Ai said with a huff. "We know."

So Ai still had sass. Nivi flinched, waiting for the officer's rebuke, but Donald looked briefly amused before resuming his stoic pacing.

"Can you tell me where you were at the time of the incident?"

Ai spoke for all of them, which Nivi appreciated, and Jorge didn't seem to mind either since he was balling into himself. His arms were tight around the coat in his lap, and his chin dug into his chest.

"We were outside together against the east wall of the school. I know because we were in the shade."

Nivi marveled at Ai's quick recollection and ease of speaking in this tense circumstance.

"So you didn't see anything?" Donald asked.

"No, we only heard the commotion when a group of students brought Mr. Cho across the field and into the school."

"What did you do then? Did you talk to Mr. Cho?"

Ai was sitting at the edge of their chair, back straight. "Not directly. We followed the students into the atrium and saw Mr. Cho's leg had been blasted apart. He said some people took Vera, and when he tried to help, they shot him."

"Who shot him?"

"He didn't say. All he said was that he hadn't passed the camouflage stone barrier."

Donald stopped pacing and stood facing them. "Do the two of you have anything to add?"

Jorge shook his head without looking up. Donald then looked at Nivi, meeting her gaze. Was that a look of recognition? Did he suspect she remembered him? Nivi quickly looked at her knees and shook her head as well. She could feel his gaze still on her, and she tried to steady her breathing. Donald finally shifted and moved away.

"As you heard Chairperson Peters say earlier," he said, "Mr. Cho did unfortunately pass the camouflage border where he was attacked by the dangerous Statics. It's easy to lose track of your surroundings during stressful events, as you may imagine. That's all for now. Officer Barmann will show you out, unless there's something else you wanted to add?"

Nivi and Jorge shook their heads, mumbling their thanks as they rose from their seats and shuffled out of the room.

"It was our *pleasure*," Ai said, not disguising the sarcasm in their voice.

The officer with the orange hair and tattooed arm walked Nivi and Jorge out of the room. Ai trailed behind. Nivi glanced at the officer's badge and saw her full name was Nicola Barmann.

"Follow me," Nicola said, leading them downstairs.

Eric ran up from behind and joined Nicola as they walked. They spoke in lowered voices but didn't seem to care if the three of them overheard their conversation.

"You know, he only treats me like that because I'm not a big cat like the two of you," Eric said.

"Not this again," Nicola said. "We've been over this. It's because you're new. He treats all newbies the same."

"I doubt that," Eric grumbled.

"Just fall in line and do what you're told. You're trying too hard to prove yourself by taking command. That's Buhl's job. Our job is to follow orders."

"I thought our job was to protect our people."

Nicola scoffed. "Is that what you were doing earlier? Protecting?"

"I *told* you, *that* was an accident." Eric lowered his voice to a whisper.

Nicola put up a hand to stop Eric from saying more as they approached the school entrance where another officer guarded the door. She turned to address Nivi, Ai, and Jorge.

"Please remain outside until we finish questioning all the students. The school bell will ring when it's time for you to come back in."

With that, Nicola and Eric walked back into the building, still discussing Eric's grievances. Nivi, Ai, and Jorge continued outside, and the remaining officer closed the door behind them.

"That was weird," Ai said as they walked to a cluster of rocks halfway between the school and forest border. "But hey, no OT. Looks like your paranoia is overblown."

"*You* were the one who thought they were going to OT us," Jorge pointed out while sitting on a rock.

Ai sat on a rock next to him. "Only because you've been getting these ideas into my head."

"Why *didn't* they OT us?" Nivi said. "You were both there. You heard what Mr. Cho said versus what Chairperson Peters said."

"Maybe Mr. Cho was confused," Ai said with a shrug. "They don't need to OT us if they're telling the truth."

"Or if they think we already believe their lies," Jorge said. "Have you ever known Mr. Cho to be confused?"

"I've never known him to be shot in the leg either." Ai patted their leg in emphasis. "That kind of trauma can definitely confuse a person."

"We could just ask him."

"*Really*, Jorge? *You're* going to question Mr. Cho's memory?"

Despite his ability to stand up to Ai, Jorge shrunk into himself when faced with the possibility of interrogating a teacher, and it was obvious to Nivi that he wouldn't do it. It was funny—before today, Ai was much scarier to Nivi than any of the teachers, but her perceptions had changed. Maybe Ai was right. Nivi had baggage like the rest of them, and that baggage made them all paranoid. But there wouldn't be any harm in asking.

"I'll do it," Nivi said.

Both Ai and Jorge looked at her, and even though Nivi wanted to shrink away like Jorge had, she held their gazes with what she thought was a steady, calm facade.

Ai's expression became thoughtful. "Cool. Well, there he is."

Nivi followed Ai's gaze to the school entrance where Mr. Cho was walking out. They wanted her to do it now? Great. Well, she'd gotten herself into this. She couldn't back down after saying she'd do it. She set her jaw and walked to Mr. Cho. Ai and Jorge watched her, looking impressed.

"Mr. Cho," Nivi said hesitantly when she reached him. "Are you okay?"

"Ah, Nivi," Mr. Cho said. "I am now. Thank you so much for your concern."

He started walking toward a group of other teachers who were standing together in the field. Nivi followed.

"Mr. Cho, um, I have a question."

For some reason, the simple act of speaking to Mr. Cho was causing her to heat up again. No, she wouldn't let the stress activate her powers. She would stay in control this time.

Mr. Cho stopped and faced Nivi, his face pleasant and patient. "Yes?"

Nivi glanced around to make sure no officers or other people were within earshot.

"I guess it's more of a statement I want to verify. Earlier, when you were injured, you said you hadn't passed the school boundary, and that someone past the boundary shot you."

Mr. Cho furrowed his bushy eyebrows. "Is that what I said? I must've been confused. I was careless and stepped past the boundary, exposing myself to those Static troublemakers. Very foolish of me."

Could he be speaking the truth? Or was it oblivion tincture? Why OT the whole school when just one person would do?

Nivi's fingertips twitched. She reached for Mr. Cho's hand. Power flowed down her arms and pulsed hotly in the veins of her wrists. It would be easy to verify his claims. All she had to do was touch him. But what if it *was* oblivion tincture? She'd be exposing her full secondary powers to Mr. Cho as well as all the Shifter police who were still roaming the school. She let her arm drop.

"Was there something else you wanted to ask?" Mr. Cho said.

Nivi shook her head. "I'm just glad you're okay."

Mr. Cho smiled and walked away to join the other teachers. Nivi returned to Ai and Jorge who waited with expectant expressions. She sat on a rock across from them.

"What did he say?" Jorge asked.

Nivi looked at Ai and shrugged. "You were right. He was confused."

Ai jumped up and clapped their hands. "Ha! See!" They pointed at Jorge. "I told you."

Jorge rolled his eyes and hunched over, grumbling something under his breath. Nivi found herself chuckling at their interaction despite her lingering unease.

They spent the next hour chatting in the glade, the direct sun warming them enough through the winter air that they unzipped their coats. More students gathered in the clearing as each group was questioned and released from the school. Eventually, it seemed like all the students were outside, a grove of forest green uniforms, and the only people remaining inside were some faculty, staff, and the Shifter police.

It wasn't long before more faculty trickled outside, including Ji. She scanned the field and lit up when she saw Nivi with Ai and Jorge. It was the first time Ji saw her with friends at the Shifter Academy. Friends. Is that what Ai and Jorge were? Maybe not quite yet, but they were on their way, especially if she ended up going to San Francisco with them. That was *if* her mom let her go.

"What's wrong?" Jorge said.

Nivi startled. It seemed Jorge was always noticing how she felt. "Oh, I'm just thinking about how my mom won't let me go to SF."

"Allow me." Ai laced their fingers and stretched, cracking their neck from side to side. "Ready to witness the magic?"

"It's just..." Nivi said, starting to panic a little. "She's very... *supportive* of the current institution." She didn't want her new friends to judge her or her mom. It wasn't Ji's fault she currently thought that way, but the fact that Ai and Jorge knew that was almost as bad as if they believed Ji was an anti-integrationist of her own accord. It meant Nivi's secrets were out in the open, and Ai and Jorge had power over Nivi and her family, if they chose to use it.

"Don't worry," Ai said with a smile. They playfully patted Nivi on the shoulder and stood up. "It doesn't matter. I can convince her either way. Be right back."

They waved and walked up to Ji. Nivi cowered, straining to hear, but they were too far away.

Jorge gave her a reassuring smile. "Ai really is very good with parents. I don't know how they do it."

Nivi ventured a glance at her mom and saw she was smiling and nodding. She relaxed a little.

"Nivi," Jorge said, "while Ai's busy, can we talk about what happened earlier?"

"Oh..." Nivi's stomach dropped, any relaxation gone. "Yeah. Sure." She paused, not knowing how to start. "You can't say anything. If any of this gets out, it could put me and my family in danger."

"I would never do or say anything to put you or your family in danger," Jorge said solemnly.

"Okay." Nivi took a deep breath, not quite ready to share everything. She needed to know how much Jorge remembered first. "I'm assuming you remember something that had been erased from your memory?"

Jorge removed his glasses and rubbed his face. He was silent for a moment, staring at the glasses in his lap.

"My home…" he finally said. He lifted his head and looked at Nivi. "The one my dad and I shared with my mom before she passed away. They made us leave it and move here. I'm originally from a small coastal town called Yuras."

Nivi's mouth fell open in surprise. "Yuras? I'm from there!"

Jorge's brows lifted. "You are? Wow. What a coincidence."

She wondered if they'd ever crossed paths. It was unlikely since she'd been raised as a Static, and Jorge had most likely been hidden from her by camouflage stones before her powers developed, but still, being in the presence of someone else from her hometown made her so nostalgic for the life she used to have that she wanted to cry.

"I don't understand," she said. "Why would they erase that?"

"There was something in our home, some kind of sinkhole. I was young so I'm not sure of the details, but it wasn't safe."

"But why would they erase your memory? If it wasn't safe, wouldn't you have moved voluntarily?"

Jorge shook his head. "I don't know."

He looked at her, having shared his piece, and now it was her turn. She could do this. It would be okay. Jorge was technically in the same position as her now, remembering something he shouldn't.

"When I said I was immune to the OT," she began, trying not to let her voice tremble, "that was only part of the truth. Basically, magic doesn't affect me. I can negate magic in addition to shielding against it."

Jorge's eyes widened slightly, but he didn't say anything as he patiently waited for her to continue.

"I'm the only one in my family who remembers what happened. I haven't told anyone until now because I need to keep them safe, but I feel so helpless. There's nothing I can do to help them, and I'm so tired. Tired of pretending to be the best version of myself. Sometimes I wish I had an excuse to be the worst version."

"I get it."

"Please, don't tell anyone what I told you."

"I won't," Jorge said. "But when you feel ready, you can trust Ai. You'll see when we go to SF. We're all in this together."

Nivi smiled, and Jorge returned the smile.

"Can I ask you something random?" Nivi said.

"Sure."

"Why do you wear glasses? I thought all Shifters had perfect vision."

Jorge laughed nervously. "It's kind of silly, but these are plain glass lenses. No prescription. I used to wear glasses before my powers emerged, so this feels like me, like I'm preserving a part of myself from before. That probably sounds weird."

"Not at all."

"Bernard wears glasses too, but his are actually for vision correction. It's rare, but some Shifters don't have perfect vision."

That was right, now that she thought about it. How had she missed that Bernard wore glasses when she passed by his desk every time she went to her mom's office?

An outburst of laughter brought Nivi's attention back to her mom and Ai. Ji was laughing. And then she *hugged* Ai! What was going on? She released Ai and looked over at Nivi, giving her a thumbs-up before turning to speak to other faculty members.

Ai walked back to them with a look of triumph.

"What did you say?" Nivi said, unable to hide the awe in her voice.

Ai shrugged and smirked. "Oh, you know." They continued in a dramatic announcer's voice. "Pack your bags for San Francisco!"

AMBER

YURAS, CALIFORNIA

AMBER CLUNG TO FRANK'S arm as they walked back to Main Street, half supporting him and half supporting herself. With each step, her brain struggled to comprehend what she'd seem. Or what she *thought* she'd seen. It was just like when she thought she saw Nivi setting the school on fire. It seemed so real but at the same time so absurd it couldn't actually be real.

Frank hadn't said anything since they left the silver pool, but his face had taken on a determined look. His jaw muscles were taut, and his narrowed eyes stared straight ahead at some unseen villain. Amber realized the tremors she felt in his arm weren't due to instability, they were due to anger.

"Mr. Markson," Amber ventured. "What..."

She didn't know how to continue. There were too many questions. *What happened? What was that? What do we do? What do we say?*

Frank seemed to understand her unspoken questions, or maybe he already had a plan of action. Either way, he stopped on the red brick sidewalk of Main Street and turned to her.

"Listen to me. Don't tell anyone what happened. They'll just think you're crazy."

"But..." Amber blinked and then gestured to the MHU members that were still milling about on the sidewalk ahead. "Don't we have a whole group of people who would support us? We need to find Mr. Pei. And Arav. You said *they* have him."

Frank chuckled without any mirth. "That's the thing, isn't it? People can be so ardent about their beliefs, but they don't actually want to face the truth, even if it agrees with them." Amber started to protest, but he continued while leading her to the MHU group. "Watch and you'll see. There'll come a time when I can mobilize the group against those monsters, but until then, remember, you saw nothing strange."

Tom stood at the front of the group chatting with a couple of members—a skinny middle-aged man and a tall young woman whose names Amber couldn't remember.

"Back already?" Tom said when Amber and Frank joined the group. "Where's Jerry?"

"He probably wandered off," someone said from the crowd. "You know how Jerry gets."

Frank kept his tone flat. "Actually, he was eaten by a giant pool of silver slime."

There was a moment of silence, then the tall woman and skinny man burst out laughing.

"Who said sober Frank wouldn't be as fun?" the skinny man said, slapping Frank on the shoulder.

The tall woman turned to talk to members behind her who also started laughing. Pretty soon, the whole group was murmuring and snickering.

Amber couldn't bring herself to laugh along. Tightening her grip on Frank's arm, she fought desperately to keep tears away. Tom smiled politely at those around him, but he didn't laugh. A slight crease was present between his brows, and he watched Amber and Frank with an intensity that could only be labeled as scrutiny. Did he suspect them of wrongdoing?

"Come on," Frank said gruffly. "I'll walk you home. It's not safe out here."

His last words brought on another round of chuckles.

Amber waited until they were out of earshot and crossing the street onto Maple Lane before she spoke again. The tears had stopped threatening to form, but her voice still cracked.

"What happened back there?"

Frank didn't speak right away. He walked her to her doorstep, and she released his arm.

"When I was trying to help Jerry," he said, his voice softening at the mention of the elderly man, "I touched a little of that silver stuff. I felt it remove *something* from me. It's hard to explain, but after that something was gone, I could remember." His voice began to shake. "They took Arav. In Alaska."

Now the tears came, a couple falling down Amber's cheek. "Who took him?"

Frank shook his head. "I don't know who they were. Just that they were dressed in some kind of black uniform. They touched my forehead and told me to sober up and that Arav would be moving in with an aunt—my sister. I don't have a sister! But once they said it, it was like it was true."

Amber felt weak with a combination of relief and newfound fear. Relief that Arav hadn't intentionally left her. Fear for his safety. "Why would they take him? What do we do? We have to find him! Are you sure MHU can't help us?"

Frank shook his head. "I've been a joke to them for so long. Before, all I cared about was the bottle—anything to shut it all out. They never took me seriously, and they aren't going to start now. Not until there's danger right in front of 'em."

Amber wanted to scream. But she also understood. No one had believed her, either, when she'd told them what she'd seen during the high school fire.

"Get some sleep," Frank said. "I'll let you know when it's time to act."

"But what about Mr. Pei? What about that glowing pool?" Surely, if the MHU members saw the pool, they'd believe them.

Frank fixed a stare on Amber, and the porch light glow reflected silver in his eyes. She felt an urge to back away from that cold, metallic gaze.

"Remember, you didn't see anything strange."

Was that a warning? Feeling suddenly devoid of emotion, Amber wiped her eyes and nodded. Retreating quickly into her house, she watched Frank walk down the street before she fully closed the door. Her hand lingered over the doorknob before she reached for the dead bolt and locked the door.

"How was your club meeting?" her dad said from the couch where he and her mom were watching TV.

Amber jumped. She hadn't realized they were sitting there, even though the TV was clearly audible. Frank had spooked her, but why? He was only looking out for her, wasn't he? She slowly turned around. Her dad must've seen the expression on her face because he grabbed the remote and turned off the TV. Her mom rushed over and wrapped Amber in her arms.

"What happened, sweetie?"

Amber could only shake her head. Even if Frank hadn't scared her into keeping what she'd seen to herself, her parents would never believe her. They hadn't believed what she'd seen during the Coastal High fire, and they wouldn't believe her now.

Her dad joined them and placed a hand on her back. They stood silently while Amber tried to swallow the lump in her throat.

"We've been thinking," her dad said gently. "You've been working so hard at school. Maybe it's time for a break? We could go out of town. Take a real vacation. We could go to San Francisco?"

Amber shrugged off her parents' hands. How could they think of traveling so soon after Alaska? Didn't they realize how awful that trip had been? She pushed past them, ran to her room, and slammed the door behind her.

Early next morning, after a night of fitful sleep, Amber walked down Main Street, a hood pulled over her head. Bare maple trees lined the brick sidewalks, their skeletal fingers scratching at the cloudy, gray sky. She kept glancing around as if Frank would appear any second to question where she was going, but the sidewalks remained empty. She knew she should stay away, but she had to know if what she thought she'd seen was real. If the pool was still there, that would be enough to prove to MHU that they were telling the truth. Anxiety grew in her stomach as she got closer. What would she find in the morning light? Jerry's remains stripped of flesh by that carnivorous goo?

Soon enough, she reached the previously unknown dirt road branching off Main Street. She walked to where the pool had been, gingerly taking each step, afraid she'd step into it like Jerry had. The road kept going deeper into the forest. It was definitely fully formed, and it wasn't new. Pine needles and new growth covered the firmly packed dirt. And just like she'd seen the night before, there were houses up ahead. All in disrepair. Abandoned. Jerry had been right all along.

Amber backtracked to where she thought the silver pool had been, but it was nowhere to be found. Had she imagined it? But then Frank would've imagined the same thing. She refocused her eyes and checked again. The road here was smoother and wider than in other places, and there were no signs of new growth or pine needle accumulation. Something *had* been here.

She shuffled her feet along the edges of the smooth ground, tracing a line in the dirt. It matched the outline of the silver pool as she remembered it. It had *definitely* been here. But where had it gone? Soaked back into the ground? Maybe Jerry was all right, then. She had to let someone know.

She turned to run into town and tripped over something solid on the ground. Shaking off the sting in her big toe, she rolled the object over with the tip of her shoe. It was a wooden post, about three or four feet long. An old one. Whatever. It was probably some old trail marker for the road. She started to walk away, but something about its appearance brought her back to take a closer look.

One end of the post looked almost like it had melted. What could've caused a mark like that? The same thing that had sucked down Jerry? If Frank had succeeded in pulling Jerry out, would Jerry's leg be melted off at the end?

Glancing down the road into the forest, Amber looked for signs of other wooden posts. Maybe if she found another, she could compare them to see if she was imagining things. She didn't want to send people blindly after Jerry without more information to help them. The last thing she needed was to witness the whole town get sucked down by that carnivorous pool.

As she walked along the overgrowth at the edge of the road, she felt something warm emanating from the shrubs just ahead. She bent over, examining the ground through the vegetation, and the warmth increased, like it was in her own chest. There, just ahead, was another wooden post, obscured by the overgrown brush. A tingling sensation went through her fingertips as she touched the wood. Hopefully, it wasn't due to a toxic mold or an allergic reaction. The post wobbled under her touch, no longer firmly in the ground. She shook it back and forth until it came loose and picked it up. It wasn't very heavy at all. That was a surprise. She carried it back to the edge of the forest and laid it next to the first post. At first glance, they looked the same—rounded pieces of wood darkened by age—except the first one was slightly shorter. She hadn't imagined it. The first post had definitely melted off at one end.

There was something at the upper end of the second post. A mottled green stone embedded in the wood. She reached forward to touch the stone, and both the warmth in her chest and the tingling in her fingers increased. Had the first post had a stone like this, too, before the silver goo melted it off? Confused, she stood up and took a step back.

"Whoa! Where did you come from?"

Amber whirled around at the voice. Tom stood at the start of the dirt road, his eyes wide.

"What do you mean?" she said.

Why did he look so shocked? Was he spying for Frank?

"It was like you appeared out of thin air."

What was he talking about? Some of her previous sass entered her voice. "I was crouching down, and then I stood up. What are *you* doing here, *Tom*?"

Tom narrowed his eyes but then seemed to let the matter go. "Jerry didn't come home last night. His wife called me this morning. She's been calling all the MHU members asking if they've seen him, so I came back to retrace his steps. It's really awful that Jerry is missing. We used to joke together about my cryptid obsession. I don't really see the difference between cryptids and the monsters MHU is hunting, but Jerry had a whole criteria list that differentiated them. Anyway, here I am to help find Jerry. Oh gosh, I'm talking too much again, aren't I?"

So Tom wasn't Frank's spy. He was a concerned citizen. The previous night's horror barreled into Amber at full force. Her heart raced, her throat constricted. Could she bring herself to recount what had happened? Frank already had, and everyone laughed. Everyone except Tom. Something in Tom's eyes seemed like he was willing to listen to what she had to say, that he was willing to believe, and she really needed someone to believe her. Where was the Amber she used to be? The feisty, carefree Amber who could tell it to people like it was and not worry about their reaction? If she looked really hard, that Amber was still in there, hidden beneath protective layers which now included an oversized sweatshirt. She could do this. She could be who she was. It was the right thing to do.

"That's why I'm here too." Her voice came out so timidly. She cleared her throat and tried again. "What Mr. Markson said last night was true. It sounds crazy, but there was a pool here last night, and Mr. Pei got too close, and it sucked him in." Tears sprang into her eyes, and her voice grew strained. "There wasn't anything we could do."

Tom's voice was analytical and matter-of-fact. "So it was an accident. He drowned."

"It wasn't an accident. That pool, or whatever it was, was *alive*. It *glowed*. It *pulled* Mr. Pei in."

Tom stared at Amber for several seconds and then sighed. "Why didn't you say anything last night?"

"I was scared, and everyone laughed at Frank. What else could I do?"

"You should've said something. Don't be afraid to speak your truth."

"You're one to talk," Amber shot back, "trying to fit in with this group who makes fun of the things you like."

"That's different."

"Uh-huh," she said skeptically.

Tom pouted and crossed his arms. "Anyway, there will be more members here soon to help look for Jerry. I'm not going to say anything to them, and I suggest you keep what you said to yourself, too, for the time being."

He was just like Frank, wanting her to keep this horrible secret to herself.

"You just told me to speak my truth. So you don't believe me?" Amber said, her tone defiant. She was so sick of not being believed.

"I don't *not* believe you," Tom said. "But, as you know, I'm not like the other members. I don't want you putting a target on your back. Also, I don't see any pool of water or anything else right now."

"I know! It just *disappeared*! But that means there's hope for Jerry. He might've gone down this road."

Tom's demeanor brightened. "Really? Which road?"

"This one, heading into the forest."

"Uh, which one?"

Amber waved toward the road. "This one." *Obviously.*

When Tom still looked confused, Amber took a few steps down the road and spun around with her arms out wide to make a point. Tom's reaction was not what Amber expected. His head lurched back, his eyes so wide the whites made his dark brown irises look like points. He looked back and forth so quickly, Amber was afraid he'd strain his neck. No matter where he looked, his gaze never focused on her, instead bypassing her like she wasn't there. It was a disconcerting thing to feel as if she didn't exist.

"Tom? What's wrong? I'm right here."

Tom showed no indication that he heard her. Amber walked toward him, and he jumped back with a yell.

"Ahh!"

Amber jumped as well and spun around, looking for the source of his fear and ready to run if she needed to, but he pointed at her, his long finger trembling.

"You—you disappeared. And then reappeared. *Again.*"

"I don't know what you're talking about!"

Was Tom seeing things? He seemed like such a nice, normal guy at first, but appearances could be deceiving. This was like when Arav accused her of being a monster. Could it be that both Arav and Tom were in the wrong? Or was there actually something wrong with her?

"Well, *something* is making you disappear." Tom took a step forward.

"It wasn't me!"

Indignation heated her face, and a crushing pressure built in her chest. She took a step back, and her heel caught on one of the posts by her feet. She fell back and landed with a jolt on her butt, the shock of the fall sending an electric charge through her. The hairs on her body stood on end. Convulsions shook her arms as the pressure in her chest released. Bright blue electric bolts shot out from her fingertips, arcing and sizzling through the air. One of them hit Tom in his shoulder, knocking him to the side as he yelped and grabbed his arm.

This couldn't be happening.

Her ears rang with the hum of a thousand mosquitoes. A metallic taste coated her tongue. She pulled back her hands and rubbed at the fingertips, which still cracked and sparked with residual electricity. The sparks faded, and fatigue cramped her muscles. She wanted to call out to Tom, to reassure him it wasn't her, that she hadn't meant to do it, but her voice wouldn't emerge. She hadn't been breathing and it hit her now as she hunched over, coughing and gasping.

"Amber? Amber?" Tom called out, looking back and forth while still holding his shoulder. "Where are you?"

"I'm here," Amber croaked.

The fabric of Tom's jacket was singed. Was his shoulder injured as well? Amber hadn't done that. She couldn't have. But she had seen the electricity emerge from her hands, felt the power rush through her body. Had Arav been right? Was she actually a monster?

Tom didn't seem to hear or see her. He kept calling out and looking past her. Amber scooted forward, and her fingers encountered something warm and tingly. She lifted her hand. It was the green stone embedded in the crumbling wood of the post. There was something about that stone that gave her pause, but Tom's calls drew her back to the present. She put the post down, pushed herself to her feet, and walked toward Tom, still coughing. Tom startled when he saw her, then rushed over.

"Are you okay?"

Amber nodded. "Yeah."

"I don't know what's going on, but I definitely believe you about Jerry now. We need to warn the others!"

"No," Amber said with sudden dread. She couldn't have the MHU members suspecting her of any wrongdoing. "I mean, I don't want to scare them away. We need them here to search for Mr. Pei and Arav."

"Arav?"

"I think whatever took Mr. Pei also took Arav. And I think you were right about—"

The sound of voices came from down the street. Amber flinched and took a few steps back. There was no reason to panic. No one suspected her of anything yet, except maybe Frank. He told her to keep things to herself, and she hadn't, and she had been about to tell Tom that Frank was acting suspiciously. If that was Frank coming down the street, she needed to get out of there. Pressure and heat built in her chest. Oh, no. Not again.

Tom took a few deep breaths, looking more pale than usual, then set his jaw with a firm nod of his head. "That's probably some of the members. When they get here, we'll form a search party."

The voices grew louder, and MHU members showed up on the sidewalk next to the dirt road. Tom turned to greet them.

Amber's arms tingled. The sizzling pressure grew. She had to leave, now.

Too late. Electricity crackled from her hands and zapped into the ground by her feet. At least her hands had been pointing down, but some of the MHU members saw, including Frank. Gasps arose from the group. Tom turned around, confusion on his face. Amber backed up and tripped again on that stupid post she'd left on the ground. This time she caught herself before falling. More gasps arose from the group.

"She disappeared!"

"She's one of *them*!"

"A monster!"

Tom put out his arms in a futile attempt to placate the crowd. Amber turned and ran down the dirt road into the forest. A debilitating fatigue swept through her body, but she pushed herself to continue. What was she going to do? They were going to attack her and possibly her family.

After a few minutes, she realized no one was following her. Gasping, she slowed to a walk and cut through the trees toward her home. She took the back way to Maple Lane, emerging from the forest and cutting through the neighbor's yard at the end of the cul-de-sac. When she was sure no one was on the street, she ran down the sidewalk. Something pinned to a tree wavered in the corner of her vision, and she paused to look at it. It was a missing person flier with Jerry's photo, fluttering feebly in the wind like a moth specimen pinned to a collector's board. She shivered and ran faster.

She burst through the front door to her home and slammed it shut behind her.

"Mom! Dad!" She found them in the kitchen. "I want to go to San Francisco. Today!"

She regretted her previous reaction to their suggestion. All she could think about now was getting away from the surreal nightmare she was living.

Her parents' eyes widened, and they exchanged a silent conversation of raised eyebrows, shoulder shrugs, and nods before they turned back to her.

"Of course," her mom said and smiled. "I think this trip will be good for all of us."

Relief coursed through Amber's body. "Thanks, Mom. I'm going to start packing."

Even though she was exhausted, she went to her room and flung clothes into a bag, desperate for anything that would distract her mind from plunging into despair.

9

Arav

Arav stood slowly from his bed as if he were afraid of startling a timid animal, but the girl watched him cooly, flecks of gold glinting in her green eyes.

"Hello," Arav said, walking up to the window.

The girl rubbed her eyes and sat up in bed, her brows furrowing as she put a hand to her head.

"I had a bad headache at first too," he said, feeling strangely happy to have this mutual experience with someone, even if it wasn't a pleasant one. "It's from whatever they drugged us with. Water helps, though." He indicated the bathroom.

The girl followed Arav's gaze, then stood—she was almost as tall as he was—and walked across her room while muttering to herself. She dipped her fingers into the tub the guards had left, and Arav could've sworn her fingers turned blue beneath the surface of the water, but when she withdrew them, they were back to normal. The lighting in this place really was strange.

Before he could say anything else, the girl entered her bathroom, and Arav found he was disappointed to have lost communication already, but a moment later she emerged with a glass of water. She pulled a chair from the small table by the bed over to her glass wall and sat facing Arav while sipping her water.

"So," she said between sips, her thick blond lashes grazing her round freckled cheeks. "You're claiming to have a Static for a parent?"

A bead of water stuck to her full upper lip. Arav watched it move slowly down until her tongue flicked out to catch it. He quickly averted his gaze but in the wrong direction, landing on the curves of her chest as she took a deep breath. To hide the flush creeping up his neck, he retreated from the glass wall to get his own chair, taking his time to position it across from her until he was more composed.

I am a respectful person. I do not objectify women, he repeated several times in his head.

What was wrong with him? He was never this affected by a girl, not even Amber. It had to be because he was starved for human interaction, or maybe it was because he was from a small town and had limited experience with girls he hadn't known since grade school. Still, there was something about her. Something different. From the contrast of her white-blond hair and her brown, freckled skin to the way she sat poised, confident, and fearless despite the situation they were in. And then there was the glow and the warmth he felt when he looked at her. It was the same he'd started feeling with Amber, and he had assumed it was because he was falling in love with her. But that was *before*. Before Amber had revealed her true colors. And he didn't know this girl. He couldn't be falling for her at first sight, could he?

Arav realized he was staring again, and he hadn't answered her question. She watched him patiently, the corner of her lip slightly quirked. Did she know the effect she had on him?

He cleared his throat, coming off gruffer than he meant to. "Static? Will you please tell me what that means? And why don't you seem upset to be here?"

"Oh, I am. I'm pissed. But I already know why *I'm* here. Once they've cleaned up the mess they made, they'll let me go with new memories. I'm more curious who you are and why *you're* here."

Arav tried to absorb what the girl was saying. "How do you know that?"

"It's amazing how much people say when they think you're still knocked out."

This girl was sneaky. Could she be trusted? He could at least try to get some information from her before he shared any details about himself. "I'll make you a deal. I'll answer one of your questions for every one of mine you answer."

The gold in her green eyes sparkled. "Deal. I'm not the one with anything to hide."

"I don't have anything to h—" Arav stopped himself, flustered. How was she getting under his skin already? He was probably just out of social practice, thanks to being locked up in here. He needed to keep his cool. She could be working with the guards. Why else would she be so calm and collected about this whole situation? He needed to be smart and establish a rapport to feel her out. He took a breath and started again. "What's your name?"

"Vera." She raised an eyebrow. "And yours?"

"Arav."

The corner of her mouth lifted again. "Nice to meet you."

Arav snapped his attention back to her eyes. "Yeah. You too." She continued to look at him with an amused expression, and he realized he was supposed to ask another question. Maybe that was enough rapport-building. "So what's a Static?"

"Someone without powers."

What did that even mean? He was about to ask another question, but Vera spoke first.

"Who are the members of your immediate family?"

Arav hesitated. Why did she want to know about that? He didn't want to give away information that could be used against him or his family. Vera seemed to sense his hesitation and spoke again.

"I promise I'm not working for our captors."

Arav still didn't speak.

Vera sighed and leaned back in her chair. "Here, I'll even tell you what I overheard from the guards. It seems that our current chairperson is trying to stoke anti-integration sentiment by kidnapping Shifters and putting the blame on Statics. It's all about power and control. That way she can continue her strict oblivion tincture policies." She suddenly looked defeated. "I don't know what to do—how to beat the OT. But, if it's my new reality, and I don't know any better, will it even matter?"

Arav shook his head. "I don't understand anything you just said."

Vera regarded him for a few moments and seemed to come to a decision. "I believe you. The guards and the chairperson think you're involved in some secret resistance organization. That's why they haven't let you go yet. They want to learn what you know. But you don't know anything, do you?"

"No. I don't know anything." Relief rushed through Arav. Someone finally believed him.

Vera seemed to be talking to herself. "A Shifter who doesn't know he's a Shifter. I've never known a Shifter with a Static parent, but I guess it could happen, if the other parent is a Shifter." She focused back on him. "Can you tell me about your parents and maybe we can figure this out together?" Arav stared at her with what must've been a blank look. "Oh, yes. I'm sorry. Let me explain. Like I said before, a Static is someone without powers, while a Shifter can shapeshift into another creature and also has a secondary power that may or may not be related to their shapeshifting."

A chill ran through him. Shifters were *monster people*. Did she just say one of his parents must be one? Maybe he misheard. Maybe this had something to do with his mom's death. Maybe he could find out who killed her. Could he trust Vera with this information? His mom was already dead. What would it matter if he told Vera about her? She couldn't be used against him. He took a deep breath.

"My mom died a couple of years ago. She was killed."

Vera inhaled sharply, her demeanor changing to one of surprise and sorrow. "I'm so sorry."

"My dad always thought she was killed by a monst—a *Shifter*, as you call them. I thought he'd gone crazy with grief until I saw one of them attack my brother. He left the same kind of claw marks on my brother that were on my mom." A lump in his throat cut off his speech. He'd thought he would be able to talk about his mom without emotion, but it still affected him.

Vera's expression was hard to read. She seemed to be deciding what to say. Finally, she leaned forward, her elbows on her knees.

"Again, I'm so sorry. Is your brother okay?"

"Physically, yes. I've tried to talk to him about it, but he says he fell on a branch. The only person who believes me is my dad." Arav chuckled wryly. "Maybe I'm as crazy as him."

Vera shook her head. "They probably got to him. The OT police." At his confused expression, she explained. "'OT' is short for 'oblivion tincture.' It wipes a person's memories, and then new memories can be placed. In the past, it was only used on Statics who saw too much of the Shifter world, but the current administration has a strong police force that has been using oblivion tincture more liberally. It's gone too far. It's being used on Shifters and Statics alike, on anyone who does anything the chairperson deems *inappropriate*. She's saying it's for our safety, but it's all about power. Control. It's likely that the same Shifter attacked both your mother and your brother, and they're trying to cover it up for some reason."

The *same* Shifter. Arav hadn't considered this possibility. His heart raced. All Shifters were evil, bloodthirsty monsters, constantly on the hunt for their next human meal. Didn't they all have large claws capable of inflicting damage like the kind done to his mother and brother?

"How could you tell if it's the same Shifter? Aren't they all the same?"

Vera tilted her head. "You mean, do all Shifters have the same form? No. They vary widely. That's why, if the claw marks you mentioned looked identical, it's likely they came from the same Shifter, or maybe two Shifters with similar Shifter forms."

Wait a minute... He looked at Vera, suddenly filled with suspicion again. "Just how do you know so much about Shifters?"

She stood up and stretched, the movement creating another distracting display. "I guess now's as good a time as any."

She walked over to the tub in her room and hoisted herself onto the edge, letting a leg dangle into the water. *Was she going to bathe right now?* Arav averted his eyes, the flush back, but stronger than before. Then he realized she was getting into the bath fully clothed.

"What are you doing?"

Vera lowered herself into the bath and submerged her head. This girl was not right. He couldn't believe he had shared so much with her. He watched the tub, mouth agape, waiting for her to reemerge. When she didn't right away, he started to worry. A minute went by, then two. He jumped up and banged on the window.

"Hey! Are you okay? Hey!" He continued to bang on the window, then called out to the guards for help when there was no response.

Finally, Vera's head popped up from the water, and Arav almost collapsed into his chair from relief. But then he registered her changed appearance.

Her hair had turned green, and her skin was... *blue*. And were those *barnacles*? And her eyes! Shining pools of liquid gold with no trace of her pupils or the whites of her eyes. She lounged back against the tub, letting her arms—which were also blue and barnacle-covered—hang over the sides. She flipped a tail—or some kind of fin-and-scale covered leg fusion—over the tub edge where it dripped water from webbed claws onto the floor.

Arav's stomach turned. She had *claws*. Claws like the ones used on his mom and Kabir. On her hands *and* tail. He was going to be sick.

Vera wagged a webbed, clawed finger at him. The gold in her eyes shrunk and fractured into flecks, and her pupils and green irises reappeared.

"Don't look at me like that. These claws are way too small to do more than a little surface damage."

She smiled, and sharp, pointy teeth shone from between her lips. Arav put his head in his hands, shaking it in disbelief. Not only was he imprisoned in this place for the foreseeable future, but he was also here with one of *them*. A monster person. Or Shifter. Or whatever they were called.

He was sweating now, heat coursing through his body. Dark spots dotted his vision. He looked up and tried to stand to get some water or at least get farther away from *her*.

Vera sat up in the tub, revealing the bare skin of her torso that was mercifully covered in barnacles. Where had her clothes gone? She waved at him. "Get on the floor!"

What? Why should he get on the...

The black spots in his vision grew, and he barely registered the thud of his body against the cold ground before all went dark.

IRIS

YURAS, CALIFORNIA

I RIS SAT ON A couch across from Meng and Ling in their humble living room. She squirmed uneasily, not just from the discomfort of the worn-in fabric and padding, but at the discordant sight of these very ordinary women who had once been so powerful. In the past, Iris would have had some satisfaction at seeing these politically powerful Shifters become simple, Static nobodies, but something had changed within her. Maybe it was the breaking of Davis's mesmerism spell. She could now judge the world for herself, but even so, what were her motivations? They had aligned with Davis's for so long that even with the mesmerism spell gone, she couldn't be sure if her thoughts were truly her own. No. They were her own. They had to be. Her near-death experience and her failure to save Davis had changed her views and put everything into perspective.

At the thought of Davis, his eyes wide as he drowned, tears came to her eyes. She held them back before they could trickle down her cheeks. The two women regarded her with patience and curiosity, waiting for her to speak. How much should she tell them? How much would they believe? Would they think she had wanted to help Davis? To save him?

All that power, exhilarating and terrifying. Euphoric and painful. She could see why Davis was drawn to it. Even through her resolve to return the powers to their original owners, something inside her urged her to keep them for herself. The magic was already corrupting her mind, just like it had Davis's. She needed to get rid of the powers as soon as possible. No wonder Davis had completely lost it. This much power would make anyone crazy, not to mention a Static who was not built for the power to begin with.

Iris...

A wordless call beckoned her outside. Water. Whooshing. Crashing. Even seated in the little beige house, Iris could sense exactly where the call came from. From off the Yuras cliffs.

Maria. Iris responded with her own thought and turned to glance out the window behind her. Somehow, she knew the captain of the fishing crew was summoning her.

No. The fishing crew should still be safe on the island. It was all the powers in her system, making her hear things that weren't there, starting to drive her mad.

Ling cleared her throat, bringing Iris's attention back to the little aging woman on the padded seat. Meng elbowed Ling as if to chastise her for her rudeness. Ling swatted Meng's elbow away. All the while, they both kept their patient smiles.

"How 'bout I get us some tea?" Ling said.

Iris nodded, and Ling got up and left the room. Meng and Iris looked at each other awkwardly for several moments before Meng stood up as well.

"I'll... go help her."

Iris didn't mind. It would give her time to collect her thoughts and figure out her strategy. By the time they returned with a pot of tea and three cups, Iris had decided to go with a simple and direct approach.

Meng placed the cups on the coffee table, and Ling poured the tea. Iris accepted a cup, a fragrant mix of herbs and flowers, and took a sip. When they were all settled in their seats, Iris took a breath and spoke.

"There's no easy way to say this, so I'll just be direct. You two have had your memories erased. You are actually magical humans called Shifters with the ability to shapeshift into a particular creature, among other things." Iris waited for their reactions before proceeding.

Ling and Meng were in the middle of sipping their tea. They paused, set their cups down, and exchanged a glance. There was no meaningful change in their expressions. Good. Maybe they would be reasonable. Iris would have more of a chance to explain before providing proof.

Then Meng's serious expression cracked. Just a quiver at the corner of her mouth was enough to trigger a titter from Ling, and before long, both of them were doubled over with laughter.

"Wait, wait," Meng said, wiping her eyes. "Tell me what I can transform into. No, don't tell me. I want to guess. A platypus? Oh, please let me be a platypus. Such bizarre little creatures."

"A dragon," Iris said, an irritated tone marring her words. "And not just any dragon. You were the vice chairperson of the Shifter Council." Patience. She must be patient. These two were basically hearing this information for the first time.

"Vice chairperson!" Ling said with mock deference. She turned to Meng and flourished a hand in the air before bowing her head.

"Oh, stop," Meng said and pushed Ling away playfully.

Iris sighed. "This is serious."

Ling and Meng sat up straight. Quivering lips punctuated their attempt at solemn expressions. It took a few tries, but they were finally able to maintain some semblance of seriousness.

"Please," Ling said, a slight waver in her voice. "Tell me what I can transform into."

Iris opened her mouth, hopeful for another chance to explain, but Meng turned to Ling first, mouthing the syllables pla-ty-pus. Their decorum dissolved again into a mess of giggles.

Children. Iris was dealing with children. Whoever had administered the oblivion tincture probably thought they were getting a laugh by reducing these two distinguished Shifters to this puerile state, but it was clear that Meng and Ling were actually getting the last laugh.

Iris reached into her hidden pocket and took out a transfer stone. She rolled it between her fingers, searching through her powers. Even through the tumult of magic, each power was distinct. She could feel the heat of Ling's vermilion bird and its associated fire power. It bubbled at the surface of her awareness and tingled through her veins, as if it knew its original owner was near. If she was careful, if she really focused, she could transfer back just Ling's power.

"I'm going to have to show you," Iris said, leaning forward. She touched Ling's hand while focusing on extracting her specific powers.

A flash of white illuminated the living room. Power flowed out of Iris and into Ling in translucent white strings. A tiny bit of heaviness lifted. Her headache diminished. The knives in her muscles stopped twisting as much. It worked! Only some twenty-five more powers to return.

Ling yelped before slumping in her chair, causing Meng to scream in response and jump to Ling's side.

"Darling! Darling!" Meng shook Ling's shoulder, but Ling's eyes remained closed. "What did you do to her?" Meng looked at Iris with wild eyes, then ran to the fireplace and grabbed an iron poker. She brandished the weapon at Iris.

So some of Meng's fiery nature did remain.

Iris held up her hands. "Hold on a moment. She's okay. Let me explain."

Ling lifted her head from the chair. "Meng? Are you there?"

Meng dropped the poker and ran to Ling's side, taking her hands. "Yes, darling. I'm here. Are you all right?"

"Yes. I feel… great."

"Thank goodness."

A glow began to emanate from Ling's core. There she was.

"I've given you back your powers," Iris said. "Look at me, do I look *different* to you?"

Ling turned from Meng to look at Iris. "You're... glowing."

"As are you. This is how you know if someone is a Shifter. Only Shifters can see each other's auras."

Ling looked down at her hands. "My skin tingles." She rubbed at the backs of her hands, then began to scratch them.

That was strange. She shouldn't have the urge to transform so quickly. "Try to relax. I need to explain some things to you."

Ling continued to scratch, progressing from her hands to her arms and shoulders.

Meng rubbed Ling's arms. "Are you sure you feel well, darling?"

"Yes. Great." Ling beamed even as her scratching became more intense.

"You're scratching too hard," Meng said. "You're turning red."

Ling's skin shimmered. Goose bumps dotted her arms.

"Just take a deep breath," Iris said. "Don't give into the pull yet."

Thin, red stalks erupted from each bump. Fluffy down followed, elongated, and quickly matured into smooth, iridescent feathers, red from one angle, orange and gold from another. Ling raised her arms with a squawk. Her joints popped, and her bones cracked.

Meng pulled back, her hands over her mouth. "Oh, my!"

Ling jumped up from the chair, her legs bending, her feet curling into claws. The feathers replaced her clothes and skin like a red superbloom of flowers across a plain, cascading from the crest on her head to her fiery waterfall of a tail. A dagger of a beak gleamed on her face, and gold eyes darted side to side.

Her great wings pumped chaotically, their twelve-foot span unable to complete a full flap without hitting the ceiling and floor. Her body bobbed and crashed down onto the coffee table. Teacups scattered. Chairs fell over.

"Do something!" Meng shouted.

"We just need to calm her down," Iris said.

Ling attempted to take off again and crashed into a wall. She tumbled back, screeched, and righted herself before immediately crashing into the wall a second time. Meng ran around the clumsy giant bird, hands waving.

"Just take a deep breath, darling!"

Iris rubbed her face. This was going to take some time. At least she hadn't given Meng her powers back first.

NIVI

SAN FRANCISCO, CALIFORNIA

A I AND JORGE WALKED straight through a packed San Francisco street without hesitation. The crowd parted before them like water around a ship, never aware of their presence. Nivi lagged behind, flinching and dodging pedestrians, unaccustomed to the camouflage stone dynamics. It was a wonder she was even here, that her mom had agreed to go to San Francisco and then stayed back at the hotel to let them explore on their own. Ai's persuasive abilities were more magical than the camouflage stones.

"What did you say to my mom this morning?" Nivi said.

Ai smiled and shrugged. "Nothing. I had my parents talk to her. They probably mentioned the many reasons why she should give her teenager some independence—substantiated in research, of course—and then convinced her to join them and Jorge's dad on a tour."

Nivi laughed. "Did you use that same argument when convincing her to let me come to SF?"

"Oh, no. *That* was my typical boasting disguised as small talk. I already have the highest GPA in our class, *and* I'm the youngest National Scholar Award recipient. Plus, I told her we were attending a meeting for gifted and talented youth. Most parents are happy to let their kids be around me, thinking my talents will rub off on them." They chuckled half-heartedly. "It's not the parents I have trouble with. It's the kids."

Nivi pushed aside a slight twinge of academic competitiveness. "Well, I'm glad I'm around you."

"Not me," Jorge said with a smirk. "My dad's forcing me to join you two in hopes my grades will improve."

Ai hip-bumped him. "You're a lost cause."

They all laughed and turned the corner, but soon Jorge's jovial mood faded. He stared at the ground, dragging his feet.

"It doesn't feel right. We shouldn't be here having fun while Vera is still recovering from her ordeal. She always came with us on these trips."

"She'd want us to have fun for her," Ai said.

"Keep telling yourself that," Jorge mumbled.

"And we aren't having fun; we're meeting up with the *others* to continue planning."

Dread began to take form in Nivi's gut. How had she agreed to meet with people she knew nothing about? What were they planning exactly?

"Who are these *others* again?" Nivi said.

Ai looked around as if they were afraid someone was listening before they got closer to Nivi and spoke in a low voice. "It's a pro-integration group. We've been meeting to plan a campaign to win the next election."

"And also to stop OT use," Jorge chimed in in a whisper. "There's something seriously wrong if a government has to wipe their citizens' minds to keep control."

"But how does this group know about OT use if they've had their memories wiped?" Nivi said.

"They haven't been able to get everyone," Jorge said. "And they've started a compilation of evidence in a secret location that not even the OT police know about. So even when the government wipes someone's memories, they haven't wiped the knowledge of that evidence."

That was great news. It gave Nivi hope. The thought of political conflict increased her anxiety, but she knew better than anyone how it felt not to be in control of her memories, or at least her family's memories. And if this pro-integration campaign worked and the OT police were disbanded, her family could be reunited.

"I'm in!" Nivi said, shaking a fist.

Ai stopped and looked at Nivi like she was the dumbest person in the world. "Yeah. We know. That's why you're here, isn't it?"

Nivi retracted her fist under an arm, heat rising to her cheeks. Jorge and Ai exchanged a glance. They were probably wishing they hadn't invited her. She shouldn't have come. They were looking at her like something was wrong with her. Then, straight ahead, standing outside a coffee shop, she saw her salvation. A distraction.

"Shifter!" Nivi said in an excited whisper as she pointed.

Sure enough, a Shifter glow emanated from a girl leaning against the wall next to the coffee shop entrance.

"She looks our age," Jorge said. "But I don't recognize her from our class."

"Or our school," Ai said. "Interesting."

Nivi tried to see who the Shifter teenager was, but Ai and Jorge moved in front of her, so she only caught glimpses of the girl. She wore an oversized gray sweatshirt with the hood pulled up. Her face wasn't really visible, just her long, black hair that hung out from the hood.

It wasn't until they were right in front of the café that Nivi got a clear view. She froze. It couldn't be. How... Nivi tried to turn around. Too late.

The girl looked up. "Nivi?"

"You know her?" Ai said.

Jorge turned his head toward them and lowered his voice. "She's not wearing her camouflage stone."

The wearing of a camouflage stone created a telltale shimmer around the Shifter's aura, almost like specks of gold glitter. Sure enough, Amber's aura lacked that sign.

Nivi tried to sound normal and happy, unsuccessfully. Her voice wavered nervously. "Amber!" She gave Amber an awkward hug.

How had Amber recognized her? Wouldn't the OT police have erased Amber's memory too? And more importantly, how did she have a Shifter aura?

Amber embraced Nivi and didn't let go. "I'm so glad to see you. You have no idea."

Nivi had missed Amber, too, had missed having a close friend and confidant.

Amber finally let go of her and stepped back. "You look different."

It was true. Nivi had grown in the months they'd been apart. At five feet seven inches—the same height as her mother—Nivi had several inches over Amber now, and her curves had filled in. Amber was still almost waiflike in comparison.

"Um, are you here with Arav?" Nivi blurted. It was a dumb question because of course she was. They were always together outside of school.

Amber's face fell. "No, uh... It's complicated."

Nivi was stunned. Had they broken up? Despite Nivi's dislike of Arav, she had to admit they were crazy about each other.

"Oh. I'm sorry."

Amber shrugged, obviously not wanting to talk about it. It hurt to know Nivi hadn't been there for Amber when she needed it, and that she wouldn't be able to be there for her in the future either because they lived in different worlds. Except, did they? Neither of them had addressed their auras yet, the glowing elephant in the room.

Amber shifted her attention to Ai and Jorge. "Are these your new boarding school friends?"

Nivi glanced at Ai and Jorge. Would they object if she said yes? Luckily, she didn't have to answer because Ai jumped in first.

"I just want to say, you are so badass. Can't believe you're just out here like this in the open. Way to make a point! Are you here for the meeting too? What school do you go to?"

Amber wrinkled her forehead. "Uh, thanks? Coastal High. You probably haven't heard of it."

"Isn't that where you went, Nivi?" Jorge said.

How did Jorge know that? But then she realized that since he was from Yuras, he'd know of the only Static high school there.

"Yeah, Amber's my best friend."

"Who she hasn't spoken to all year." The resentment in Amber's voice was clear.

Nivi tried to shrink in on herself. This wasn't supposed to happen. She tried to change the subject.

"What are you doing in SF?"

"My parents thought it'd be nice to do a quick trip. Just some local travel for now since we were just in Alaska."

"You were in Alaska?" That might explain how the OT police had overlooked her, but not the Shifter aura part.

"So how is it, mingling with everyone like you're a Static?" Ai said.

Again, Amber looked confused. "What's a—?"

It dawned on Nivi that Amber didn't know about her powers. Could it be that they were hidden like Nivi's had been? For her protection? If so, she needed to keep Amber's secret until she had a chance to talk to her alone. She cut off Amber before she could finish and grabbed her arm, pulling her off to the side.

"I need to talk to you. Where are you staying?"

Could it be that Amber had been a Shifter this whole time? That would be amazing. Amber could come to the Shifter school, and Nivi wouldn't be alone anymore.

"I'm staying at the Hyatt. Just there." Amber pointed to the street corner. "We're supposed to head back to Yuras tomorrow..." She tensed and trailed off. Was she afraid of something? But then she pulled her arm out of Nivi's grip and returned to her usual flippant self. "It's really nice to see you. Just being here with you, I'm feeling all warm and fuzzy inside."

Nivi let out a weak laugh. Would Amber still feel happy to see her once she knew the true source of that warm, fuzzy feeling? It didn't matter; she needed to tell Amber. It wasn't safe for her to be walking around like this. She opened her mouth but didn't know where to start.

Through the café window, Nivi could see Amber's mom walking toward the door and... She didn't have an aura! Mr. Su stood at the counter, also without an aura. How was this possible?

"Random question," Nivi said. "Do your parents have round, red scars on their left shoulders?"

"Uh, no..." Amber gave her a quizzical look as she dragged the last word.

Mrs. Su reached the doorway and called out to Amber. "Did you want anything, dear? Your father's about to order."

"Mom! Look who's here!" Amber gestured to Nivi.

Mrs. Su looked right through Nivi with a perplexed expression. "Who, dear?"

"We need to go," Jorge whispered, appearing next to Nivi.

"Now," Ai agreed from behind Jorge. They raised their voice to Amber as they linked their arms through Nivi's. "Sorry, something came up. So good to meet you."

Ai and Jorge quickly pulled Nivi down the street as she protested.

"Your friend's badass, I'll give you that," Ai said. "But it's one thing to make a point with well-planned action and another to sit so openly for so long at a café without a plan. So you can stay if you want, but we're out of here."

Ai was right. Nivi couldn't risk this exposure either.

She yelled back at Amber. "I'll find you later at your hotel!"

AMBER

SAN FRANCISCO, CALIFORNIA

AMBER WATCHED NIVI LEAVE with her new friends. She looked so cozy with them, their arms linked through hers. How quickly Nivi had adjusted. Shy and reserved Nivi who hated being around people. Apparently that wasn't the case anymore. She had moved on, just like Arav had.

No, Arav had been taken, she reminded herself. It was getting harder to hang on to that belief, harder to hang on to the memories of all her recent experiences. Had Jerry really been consumed by a glowing pool? Quicksand could look like a pool, and the moon could've been reflecting off its surface.

She wanted so badly to tell Nivi everything that had happened, but Nivi wouldn't believe her. The last time she'd tried to talk to Nivi about what she'd seen during the Coastal High fire, it'd led to a big fight.

Maybe she was losing it.

But Frank had seen the same thing.

Maybe Frank was losing it.

Maybe Arav really was with an aunt or a family friend he called an aunt? Maybe Arav had been sent away because Frank couldn't take care of himself, let alone Arav.

Even if it hadn't been an unfortunate quicksand incident and Jerry had actually been consumed by a glowing pool, did that prove there were shapeshifting monsters out there? Or that Arav had been taken? The existence of supernatural glowing sludge didn't prove the existence of monsters, just... supernatural sludge. The more she thought about it, the more the surreal aspects of that night faded away. Logic took their place. Frank was losing his mind. Arav had been sent to live with a responsible adult. Jerry perished in quicksand or a sinkhole. Her eyes had been playing tricks on her in the dark, that was all.

"Amber?"

Her mother's voice brought her out of her daze. "Yeah?"

"Who were you talking to?"

Amber glanced down the sidewalk at the shrinking shapes of Nivi and her friends. She imagined all the questions her parents would have if they knew she'd seen Nivi, and she felt exhausted thinking about it.

"Oh, no one."

Amber followed her mom into the café and joined her dad at the counter where she ordered a croissant. The barista handed it to her, and she headed to a corner seat by the window while her parents waited for their drink orders at the counter. She picked at the croissant and stared outside, feeling the sun warm her through the windowpane.

The leather seat cushions across from her groaned as two people sat down. Amber turned away from the window, expecting to see her parents, but it wasn't them. The unfamiliar man and woman seated across from her looked like some kind of police officers, tall and built, wearing black uniforms with a white patch on the shoulder. The man reminded her a little of Kabir—they had similarly wide-set eyes—and that made her think of her embarrassing interrogation after the Coastal High fire, which made her think of Arav, which made her angry and sad and irritated all at the same time.

"Can I help you, *officers*?" she said, putting aside her croissant. Her irritation tinted her words even though she tried to hide it.

The man leaned forward. His name tag read "Eric Okello."

"You better have a good excuse for being out and about without your camouflage stone."

Since when was having or not having a stone illegal?

"I don't know what that is," Amber said. "I'm just waiting for my parents over there."

She pointed to the counter, hoping her parents' presence would make the officers go away, being that she was a minor and all. The officers looked over and then back.

"Your... *parents*?" Eric said.

"Yes. They're right there!"

The other officer, whose name tag read "Nicola Barmann," turned to her partner.

"*Right...*" She brushed her orangish-red hair back with her tattooed arm.

"Tell us why you're really here, and we'll let you on your way," Eric said.

Unease trickled through Amber. What were these officers accusing her of? "I just did. I'm just visiting with my parents."

Eric shook his head and spoke to Nicola. "Looks like we got another one."

"Another what?" Amber said.

"If you insist on lying, we're going to have to take you in," Nicola said.

Amber's voice quaked. "I'm—I'm not lying. I'm telling the truth."

Eric reached into a pouch on his utility belt and brought out a greenish stone on a chain. He handed it to Amber. "You can put this on, or I can put it on for you."

Amber took the necklace, her hands shaking, and slipped it over her head without arguing. If this weirdo cop wanted her to wear a necklace, she'd do it just to keep him happy for the time being. She kept glancing over at her parents, hoping they would rescue her from this strange situation at any moment. Why were they taking so long?

Eric nodded at Nicola, and she got up from the table, taking a small vial of black liquid out of her utility belt. She dabbed a couple drops on her fingers and approached Amber's parents.

"What are you going to do?" Amber called after her, but she didn't respond.

Amber turned back to Eric who had also taken a vial out of his utility belt. His fingertip glistened with some kind of milky liquid. He stood up and then dabbed the liquid to her forehead before she could pull away. She would've cried out in disgust if a strong desire to sleep hadn't instantly come over her. It was all she could do to brace herself as her head fell toward the table.

IRIS

YURAS, CALIFORNIA

THEY SAT AT THE dining room table while Iris explained. Ling was flushed, her hair disheveled, and Meng was visibly on edge. In the living room, broken teacups littered the brown carpet next to an overturned coffee table and several holes in the drywall. Luckily, the teapot hadn't broken and was now safely on the kitchen counter in the process of a new brew. Iris explained how transfer stones worked, how the person in possession of a stone could give or take powers, and how the stone was inert after that transfer was completed. Then she went over her relationship with Davis and their political struggles, as well as Ling and Meng's history.

When Iris finished her story, Meng spoke first. "Let me see if I got this right. Ling and I used to have magical powers. Someone named Davis took them, using these transfer stones. Then you took them from Davis. And now you want to give them back to us because you have *too much* power?"

Iris nodded.

"And where is this Davis now?"

Iris swallowed her guilt and kept her voice as even as possible. "He drowned."

"Huh. Seems like he could've used some of these powers."

Iris winced. If only she could've saved him... No, she wouldn't go there right now. She had to focus on the task at hand.

"Okay," Ling said. "If we are these shape-changing people—"

"Shifters," Iris said.

"Shifters," Ling repeated. "Why don't we remember anything?"

Iris leaned forward, happy to be getting somewhere. "Oblivion tincture."

"But what about our neighbors?" Ling said. "If I've been living here for as long as you say I have, then wouldn't the neighbors know?"

"They've probably had their memories wiped as well."

"Seems a bit convenient," Meng mumbled, crossing her arms.

Ling went to pour new cups of tea for everyone and brought them back to the table.

Meng took a sip from her cup. "What if I don't want your powers?"

"But it's *your* power," Iris said, a bit of panic rising in her voice. She could always force the powers back on each person, but that wasn't how it was supposed to work. She was supposed to help them feel whole again. They were supposed to be grateful. "It's part of you. You aren't you without it. Tell her, Ling."

Ling closed her eyes and took a deep breath. She opened her eyes to look at Iris and then shook her head. Iris's hopes fell. If she couldn't do this, couldn't redeem herself, then she might as well have died at the bottom of the ocean with Davis. But then Ling chuckled.

"I wouldn't have believed it if you hadn't shown me. It's true. I feel amazing. I feel myself again. Like you said. I feel *whole*."

"You can't be serious," Meng said.

"I love you, honey," Ling said, patting Meng's leg, "but this is probably the best I've ever felt."

Meng crossed her arms again, her fingers tapping, then she uncrossed her arms and stuck out a hand. "Okay, then. Hand them over."

It took Iris a moment to realize Meng had agreed to get her powers back. She jumped up, reaching for a stone from her pocket, but then had a thought.

"We should probably go outside for this."

Meng raised an eyebrow. "Outside?"

"You're a dragon, remember? Your Shifter form is a bit larger than Ling's."

Iris looked through the sliding glass door into the backyard. "Is there somewhere outside that is shielded from the view of others?"

"We could go into the forest," Ling said.

"That works, but we have to be careful and fast. Anyone could be watching at any time."

They collected their things and set out for the forest. To avoid detection, Ling took them through the backyard fence to the undeveloped land beyond their neighborhood street. Only a few trees dotted the immediate vicinity. Mostly there were shrubs and grasses, all rustling in the ocean breeze. They walked west along the peninsula toward the forest, the sun shining down from a clear, blue sky. The nearby waves twinkled and enveloped them in briny mist. Soon enough, they were in the pine forest, safely ensconced from prying eyes, or so Iris hoped.

Ling paused and looked back at Iris. "How far do you want to go?"

Iris glanced behind. She couldn't see the neighborhood through the trees, but it still felt too close. "A little farther."

They continued walking, Ling leading the way, turning slightly left to follow the curve of the peninsula. They stepped into what Iris at first thought was a small clearing. The trees were thinner here, but they grew in a winding pattern that stretched away in each direction. It was a road.

"What is this place?" Meng asked.

Ling shook her head. "I don't know."

That didn't mean much since oblivion tincture had wiped both their memories, but something felt off about the area. For one, the road looked like it hadn't been used for a long time, not by hikers and definitely not by cars. Pine needles covered the uneven dirt, and small bushes and trees grew all around.

They continued walking down the unused road. Up ahead on the left, a home came into view from behind the trees. Any apprehension Iris may have had that they would be seen by the inhabitants faded as they neared the structure. Squirrels scattered at their approach, one between the remaining glass shards of a splintered window frame, another through a gaping hole in the wall. Birds flew in and out of the second story, the roof long since collapsed in. The front door hung at an angle, creaking faintly, and peeling paint fluttered in the breeze. Here and there, the entire home uttered a collective groan, a warning of more collapsing to come.

Meng and Ling didn't seem to sense the strangeness of this place. They passed the dilapidated house with only a cursory glance, continuing down the road.

Why did this place feel so familiar? The farther they went, the more Iris was sure she had been here before. Well, of course she had. Her parents had lived close by, and she and Davis had mined transfer stones by the cliffs for years. And Chairperson Dawan had lived in this area too. It wasn't inconceivable that she'd come across this road during that time, but why didn't she remember it? Up ahead, she could see another abandoned house and then another. She was sure she'd remember a road full of abandoned homes.

The ocean breeze continued to stream through the trees, but it no longer felt refreshing. Instead, it sent a chill down Iris's spine. Goose bumps spread across her arms, and with them, a realization began to take hold. What if the reason she didn't remember this place was because of oblivion tincture?

Meng paused, stretched her arms out to the sides, and turned around. "Is this enough room?"

"Hmm?" Iris said, jolted from her thoughts.

"For my *transformation*."

"Oh. Sure."

Iris removed a stone from her bag and walked to Meng, who stiffened at her approach.

"Don't worry," Ling said, placing a hand on Meng's back. "It doesn't hurt. Well, not really."

"Comforting."

"It's hard to explain, but it's worth it."

Meng nodded and squared her shoulders as Iris touched her with the stone. A bright white flash. The release of power, and with it, a slight lifting of the weight Iris carried. Meng gasped as the light filtered through her body, then went limp. Ling caught her before she fell and lowered her to a sitting position on the ground. Meng instantly tried to stand up.

"Better to rest first," Iris said. "Your body probably has muscle memory to shift like Ling's did, but it's still been a while."

Ling sat down next to Meng. "She's right. Let's rest here for a little bit."

While Ling and Meng chatted quietly on the ground, Iris roamed the edges of the dirt road. Between a couple of trees, a wooden post leaned at an angle. It looked like one of those used to border Shifter territory. She approached the post and gripped the top to push it straight. There should have been a camouflage stone embedded there, but it was missing. A gouge remained in the wood where the stone should've been. It was enough to confirm her suspicions. This road had been Shifter territory.

Iris let go of the post. Instead of falling, it wobbled in place before slowly leaning back to its side, as if it had been plunged into a bowl of jelly. She straightened the post again and let go. Again, it wobbled, this time sinking a bit deeper before settling to the side. Crouching, Iris pushed aside some shrub branches to examine the ground at the post's base. There was some kind of muddy hole about twice the diameter of the post. She pushed the post straight and wiggled it around, and the mud suddenly emitted a silver glow while moving up the base of the post, sucking it deeper into the hole.

Hello, Iris.

Iris lurched back, landing in the shrubs. She had the urge to brush off her hands as if something foul had gotten on her skin. Inside her mind, the silver substance seemed to beckon to her again, a sickly ooze trickling into her brain. It was not unlike the call she'd thought she'd heard earlier from Maria, but something about this one felt terrifying. It reminded her of a documentary she'd seen on African social spiders and how the spiderlings greeted their mother, thanking her for birthing them before draining her of her bodily fluids.

Several tendrils branched out from the hole, pretty silvery lights scintillating across their surface. Touching them probably wasn't a good idea, but their beauty was entrancing, and before she knew it, she was inching toward a tentacle. As her foot neared, the tentacle shrank back and disappeared into the hole. She moved her foot toward another tentacle, and it also retreated into the hole. Behind her, a deep groan erupted from the abandoned house closest to her. The noise was frighteningly loud, and it broke her fixation on the silver substance. Dusting herself off, she made her way back to the dirt road, making a note of where the hole was so she could come back to investigate more.

The groaning grew louder. The walls of the house shuddered and then fell inward with a great crash, sending dust and leaves into the air. Birds chirped their complaints and fluttered off while Meng and Ling scooted away from the destruction. When the dust cleared, only a few wood beams remained of the house, slowly sinking into a silver gelatinous pool that hadn't been visible before. The pool glowed around the beams as it sucked them down.

Iris's skin prickled. She could feel that silver stuff *everywhere* under the forest.

"What's going on?" Meng yelled. Blue light pulsed from her body.

Iris shook off the eerie sensation and ran back to Meng and Ling. She could only deal with one thing at a time. First Meng, then the silver.

"Take a deep breath, Meng, or you're going to transform."

"Well, it's going to bloody happen sooner or later. Isn't that why you wanted me to do this outside?"

Sure enough, blue scales clanged into place across Meng's skin while her clothes faded and her body elongated. Long and sinuous, it whipped side to side, nearly knocking over Iris and Ling while they scrambled out of the way. Sharp claws gouged the dirt, and a toothy jaw snapped in a terrifying yet seemingly joyous manner. Her tail cracked against a pine tree to the right and then another to the left, leaving fresh, fragrant wounds. The dragon ran down the road and, before long, began to lift off the ground, feet alternating between clawing at the ground and grasping at the air.

"Meng! Try to take some deep breaths!" Iris yelled. A blue dragon flying above the trees would be much harder to conceal than one hidden by the forest. She nudged Ling. "Can you get her to calm down? We need to get you both back home."

Ling nodded and ran after Meng with preternatural speed, soon catching up and keeping pace. She jumped into the air and transformed into her vermilion bird form with ease, her shifting muscle memory apparently revived. Red feathers streaked alongside undulating gem-blue scales like a dance of fire and water. Then Ling flew past Meng's head and transformed into her human form, impressively sticking her landing. A plume of dust rose by her feet as she held out a hand and spoke in a strong, commanding voice.

"Stop!"

Meng skidded along the ground, the back half of her body folding and crashing into the front half before she completely toppled to her side. Ling didn't flinch even as the dragon slid to a stop at her feet. A cloud of dust momentarily obscured Ling from view. When the air cleared, Ling leaned over and touched Meng's scaly, horned head.

"Sorry for that, honey. Now, just try to breathe and relax."

Even from where she stood some distance away, Iris could see an inhalation rattle through the dragon's sinuses and puff out of its mouth. The snake-like body went slack and then began to shrink, claws retracting, scales fading, and clothes reforming until Meng's human form sat on the ground before Ling, looking exuberant.

"I know what you mean now," Meng said, taking Ling's out-stretched hand and getting to her feet.

"You're glowing," Ling said with a smile.

"You too."

Iris walked up to the couple, surprised by her nostalgia at their "first" experience with transforming. It hadn't been so long ago that she had stepped forward to protect Anna Sun from her father, unaware of the powerful creature she would become in that moment. What happened to that courageous little girl? The one who didn't hesitate to defend against the abuse of power? Instead, in an ironic twist of fate, she'd become an accomplice to the power-hungry son of the man she had originally defended against.

Meng looked back at the collapsed house. "What was that silver stuff back there?"

Iris looked back as well. The silver pool had become still and almost hidden, its metallic surface reflecting the forest around it. Its pull toward her had also subsided.

"I don't know." Iris started to say something more about the silver but stopped herself. Even if Meng and Ling had known what was going on in the past, they wouldn't know anything in their current state, thanks to oblivion tincture. Better to wait until she could find out more information or figure out how to nullify the OT. "We should get back to the house for now, to keep you both out of sight and safe until we can get some answers."

Ling and Meng nodded. Hand in hand, they strolled back the way they had come, chatting in soft, excited tones about their experiences. Iris followed a step behind. A breeze wafted between the trees, carrying with it strong ocean scents and a sting of salt. Iris blinked at the prick of tears the salt brought to her eyes, or was it the memories? Another breeze floated by, this one markedly colder, tickling her ears and lifting the hairs on the back of her neck.

Iris.

Iris turned around. Behind her, the remnants of the abandoned house had completely disappeared. Through rustling pine trees, sunlight oscillated on the now dull and motionless pool. It would have blended in with the forest floor if Iris hadn't known where to look. No. It wasn't the pool calling her. It was something else. Someone else.

As she followed Ling and Meng out of the forest, the ocean breeze engulfed Iris in a barrage of sensory assaults.

Iris. Iris. Iris.

Her ears tingled, and her mind filled with the repetition of her name. *Come, come,* it seemed to convey. The salt sting spread from her eyes to her nose and skin, burning with a need to be by the sea. The breeze itself changed course, dragging and pushing her toward the northern coast. When she allowed herself to look in that direction, she saw a rising swell in the ocean approaching the cliffs, unusual because the rest of the water was flat.

"You go ahead," she said to Meng and Ling without understanding what compelled her. "I... need to check on something."

Meng and Ling paused only briefly to look at her and nod, too trusting in their small-town life. They continued toward their home without arguing, still caught up in the excitement of their recent transformations.

Iris made her way to the coast, her feet moving of their own accord, her mind allowing it as if in a daze. Without the cover of the trees in this area, the wind pulled her hair loose from its bun and whipped it wildly about, but strangely the surrounding tufted grasses remained still. As she neared the cliff, a figure appeared at the edge, dressed in a fleece jacket and utility pants, gazing out at the ocean. Had they been here the whole time?

She studied the figure as she approached. That lean and muscular form... That brown skin and black, waist-length hair... There was something familiar about it all.

In her heart, she knew who it was, but she couldn't believe it.

"Maria..." she said, a chill going through her body at the confirmation.

Maria Akayux. Captain of *The Crabby Lady*, whom Iris had left stranded with her crew on an Aleutian Island. How did she get here?

A tear glistened on Maria's cheek, and she spoke without looking at Iris. "The ocean has always been a part of me. Since I was a child, I felt it call to me. I could understand its language. But now..." She shook her head and turned to Iris, a faint smile curling her lips. "This is so much more."

Iris. Iris. Iris. The words swirled through her mind, murky and tumultuous like a stormy sea.

The swell in the ocean suddenly rose up in front of the cliff and over Iris's head. She barely had time to exclaim before the tidal wave encompassed her and knocked her to the ground. Her mind flashed back to her underwater struggle with Davis. Davis's wide eyes and shocked expression. Gasping for air. His hand reaching for her.

The water was gone as quickly as it had arrived, flowing back over the edge of the cliff. In its place stood a stocky, middle-aged, bearded man and a young, pale, blond man. Alek Ivanov and Shawn Murphy. Maria's crew.

Somehow their combined powers must have allowed them to transform together into one joint form. Shifter magic had been combined in the past for varying effects. That was how camouflage and transfer stones and oblivion tincture were created. But she'd never seen Shifter powers combine like this.

Iris jumped to her feet, her body tense and her blood rushing, ready to transform.

Alek stepped forward. Water dripped from his black-and-gray beard. "You left us on that island—"

Shawn cut in. "She told us her plan when she left us there."

"Shut it, Greenhorn," Maria said.

"Yeah, let the *men* handle this," Alek said. When he saw Maria's glare, he lost all his bravado. "I mean—the women—wo-*man*. I mean captain—"

"If you don't stop talking, Ivanov, I'll make Iris turn back into a snake and bite off your head."

"Yes, Captain."

Iris's muscles relaxed, the guilt of what she'd done sapping away her energy. "I—I was going to come back for you. All of you. I just needed a little more time."

Maria put up a hand, smiling. "I believe you. I bet you're surprised to see us."

The two men smirked.

Iris nodded, able to utter only one word. "How?"

"My crew and I have always worked well together. Once we were in tune, we could feel you."

And Iris could feel them. The transfer of magic must be connecting them all more than she'd realized. Now that she knew what the sensation was, she realized she had felt them all along. If she wanted to, she could summon them the way they had summoned her. Her mind shifted to Ling and Meng. Strange. The same sensation and connection were present there as well, even though the magic had gone back to the rightful owners.

Maria continued. "It took us a while to figure out how to use these powers, but once we did, we were able to track you. And we could feel this *place*. Something bad is going on here."

The silver. Could that be what she meant? Iris considered showing them the pool, but Shawn's head snapped up.

"Someone's coming."

Iris followed Shawn's gaze in the direction Ling and Meng had gone. Two figures approached through the shrubby grass, both with Shifter auras. They were too far away to make out their features, but she immediately assumed they were Ling and Meng. Why were they coming back? Iris had told them to wait for her at home. Too many Shifters in one location were sure to attract the wrong kind of attention. She turned back to the crew.

"It's not safe for you here. Is there somewhere you can go until I can get more information on how to make this all right? I'll try to get in touch with you as soon as I can. I promise."

Maria looked out at the sea and nodded, that dreamlike expression returning to her eyes. With a lift of her hand, a wave crashed over the cliff, and the three of them dissolved into the retreating water. It was amazing to see their transformation, and Iris wished she could tell the Shifter Council about the crew's ability. Imagine the new discoveries they could make about their powers! They would hold her in such high esteem for this discovery. They'd teach about her at the Shifter schools, eventually, after she made everything right.

Iris glanced back along the grassy cliffside. The figures were gone. Maybe Meng and Ling had decided to go home. Her mind replayed the image of the two Shifters in the distance. Something wasn't right. Meng and Ling were petite, and those approaching Shifters had seemed much taller—

A hand grabbed her wrist from behind, and something constricted into her skin, almost to the point of pain. She looked down and saw the restraint at the same moment she recognized the magical tingle of power in it. Before she could react, another band snapped into place on her other wrist, pulling her arms behind her. She twisted and turned, rifling through her multitude of magical abilities to no avail. She wasn't able to transform. She wasn't able to use her secondary powers. The restraints prevented the use of magic. Panicking, she lifted her head to meet the gazes of the two Shifters who each gripped one of her arms. Black uniforms. White shoulder patch. Shifter police.

NIVI

SAN FRANCISCO, CALIFORNIA

THE EVENING AIR REMAINED surprisingly warm as Nivi and Ji headed to the meeting location, not like the thirty-degree drop when the sun went down in Sequoia National Park.

"What exactly is this meeting about again?" Ji asked as they walked arm in arm past a quiet stretch of stores that had closed for the night.

Nivi tensed. What could she tell her mom that wouldn't cause her to turn them around and go back to Sequoia that instant? She wished she could've left Ji at the hotel, but her mother had insisted on coming along. Ai's magical persuasion had only gone so far, or maybe it had made the meeting seem a little too enticing.

"Um, it's for gifted and talented youth to—uh—get more involved in politics." That was partially true. Maybe she could distract her mom once they were there. Ai hadn't seemed overly concerned about Ji coming. They thought it could be good for her to be exposed to pro-integration ideas. Maybe her mind could be changed.

Nivi stopped in front of a building with a tall hedge bordered by a decorative, wrought iron fence with a leaf and floral motif. An iron gate led through an arch cut into the hedge where a wooden sign reading "KW's Bookstore" hung overhead. She checked the building addresses. They had arrived.

"This is cute," Ji said. "But why's it so dark?"

"Maybe they don't want to disturb the neighbors," Nivi lied, knowing full well that the exterior lights were off to prevent unwanted attention. "There's enough light from the streetlamps, anyway."

On the other side of the gate, a large tree sat in the middle of a cobblestone courtyard, clinging to the last of its red and yellow leaves. They passed under the tree and approached the bookstore, a stone and wood building that seemed plucked out of a fairytale. A soft glow emanated from the stained glass windows, indicating activity inside.

Nivi reached for the blue, arched door. "I wonder if Ai and Jorge are already inside?"

They'd left for the meeting earlier to help set up. Their parents had let them go alone.

Before she could touch the handle, the door swung open, and a young Shifter Nivi didn't recognize ushered them inside. A stained glass lantern hung overhead, dimly lighting the entryway in a kaleidoscope of colors. The young Shifter, whose name tag read "Thy," held out a hand.

"Camouflage stones, please."

Nivi glanced nervously at her mom who looked shocked, a hand protectively over her necklace.

Thy's cherubic features remained expressionless. "This is an in-clusive space."

"What does *that* m—" Ji began.

"Mom, please." Nivi whispered through gritted teeth. She felt guilty uttering the next words, but she knew they would work. Especially since her mother was so concerned about Nivi making friends. "Don't embarrass me."

Ji went rigid for a moment, then her shoulders slumped. She removed her camouflage stone and handed it to Thy, who affixed a tag to it, hung it in a box with hooks, and handed back a ticket number. Nivi followed suit, and they continued into the book-store.

The entryway opened to a two-story circular space with a wood-en, spiral staircase in the center. Driftwood fanned out on the ceiling like the branches of a tree. More stained glass lanterns hung from the ceiling, speckling the rows of bookshelves throughout the store and along all the walls. To the right, a small crowd was gathered on couches and cushions in what looked like a reading space. Those without seating stood in the back. A full-figured woman with dark blond hair stood on a platform at the front of the crowd.

"Hi, everyone," she said. "Thanks for coming tonight. For those who don't know me, I'm Rowena, one of the local organizers, and I'll be your host tonight." Her bright blue eyes shone in the overhead lights. "Without further ado, let me introduce our first guest!"

The audience began to clap, but Nivi couldn't see who was being introduced without getting closer. She stopped paying attention to what Rowena was saying as she surveyed the room. Even at a glance, it was obvious that the crowd was a mix of Shifters and Statics, and Nivi knew her mom instantly noticed.

Ji gently grabbed Nivi's arm and pulled her to her side. "*Nivi,*" she said, her voice strained. "What's going on here?"

Nivi opened and closed her mouth. She'd been fixated on getting to this meeting, and now that they were here, she didn't know what to say next. Maybe whoever was speaking could inspire some dissent in Ji. Even as she thought it, she didn't believe it. This was a bad idea. What had she been thinking? The oblivion tincture used on her mom was too strong. Whatever lies she had been told had formed roots too deep. Ji was more likely to turn them all in than change her mind about the system. Nivi should've turned down the invite from Ai and Jorge rather than come here and risk everything.

A man about Ji's height broke away from the back of the crowd and approached them. He wore a fitted black tee and chinos, the clothing emphasizing his lean and muscular build. The stained glass lights danced off his dark skin and short Afro as he walked, and even though he was a Static, it was like he was surrounded in magical fairy light.

"Ji?" he said. His handsome face looked confused and even pained.

Shocked, Nivi glanced back and forth between Ji and this man.

Ji went pale. Her hand fell away from Nivi's arm, and she took a step back, her voice a startled whisper. "Kellan."

A strange feeling grew in Nivi's stomach. Who was this man, *Kellan*? How did her mom know a Static? And why were they looking at each other like they'd seen a ghost?

Arms suddenly surrounded Nivi from behind, and she stifled a yelp.

"You finally got here!" a voice said.

A small form stepped before her. "Glad you could make it."

It took Nivi a moment to register Jorge and Ai, distracted as she was. They pulled her to the crowd, speaking quickly and quietly about what she'd missed.

"You gotta hear this guy. His story is so inspiring," Ai said.

"He'll make you a believer," Jorge said. "Maybe even your mom."

Nivi only half paid attention, struggling instead to look back and hear what Ji and Kellan were saying to each other.

"You left," Ji was saying.

Kellan stepped closer to Ji, his hands spread open. "I'm so sorry. All I know is one day I was in Yuras, and the next I had moved back to San Francisco, and I didn't know why. But now, after being involved in this group, I'm pretty sure I know what happened to me. They erased some of my memories."

Ji shook her head and turned away. Kellan touched Ji's shoulder, and that sinking feeling hit Nivi's stomach again. Who was this guy? His touch was too *intimate*.

Then Nivi was in the crowd, and she could no longer see Ji and Kellan or hear their conversation. Ai and Jorge led her down to some cushions on the floor. Nivi was still trying to look at Ji through the people standing at the back of the crowd when she heard a familiar voice.

"I was a child separated from my family, my own *Shifter* family. Who gave the Shifter Council the right to separate families? If it happened to me, it could happen to any of you."

A chill went down Nivi's spine as a loud murmur of assent washed over the crowd. That voice. She slowly turned to see the speaker, hoping her ears were playing tricks on her. It had to be the din of the crowd or the distortion of the microphone because it wasn't possible. It couldn't be. But her ears were not mistaken.

There he stood in his usual tailored suit, tall, lean, with black hair that was longer than she remembered, and still as handsome and charismatic as ever. Davis Sun. How was he alive? Nivi had seen him disappear into the depths of the ocean. The Shifter military had found no signs of him or Iris. Had he retained the ability to transform into a sea creature or breathe underwater? That would explain how he'd stayed submerged and survived. But... but! Were her eyes deceiving her? Because here was Davis, alive, leading a joint Shifter and Static revolution, and he had *no* aura. He was... a Static.

This must be a trick. They were all in serious danger. Davis had some plan to fool them all so he could steal their powers and reclaim control of the Shifter Council. Seemingly far away, Davis continued to speak, his words dissolving into the haze of Nivi's mind as she stood up and backed away. She saw him gesturing grandly with his arms. Heard the crowd grow louder and louder, clapping and voicing their frustrations, their anger, their agreement. Felt the temperature rising with the bodies in the room, thick, sticky, suffocating.

"The time for integration is now," Davis said, and the crowd chanted along.

"The time for integration is now! The time for integration is now!"

Ai and Jorge turned to look at Nivi, their expressions of jubilation fading to concern as they reached for her, their mouths moving. Blood whooshed through her ears, her heart, her legs. She had to get away.

She tripped over someone seated on a cushion behind her, vaguely aware of a gruff reprimand.

"Sorry," she mumbled.

She pushed past the rows of standing people at the back of the crowd, looking for Ji. Where had they gone? She found them next to the bookshelves, a few rows back. They were still talking, still too close.

Ji saw her approach. "Nivi, what's wrong?"

Nivi swayed. The room blurred. She couldn't stop the panic flooding her system, couldn't make herself speak to warn them.

Arms caught her on either side, steadying her. Ai and Jorge. They had followed her.

"What's going on?" Ai said.

Nivi opened her mouth. Willed the words to emerge. But what could she say? None of them would know who Davis was. She was the only one, apart from maybe Chairperson Peters, who had retained the memories of what he'd done.

Suddenly, the front door burst open. Bright flashlights swept across the room, followed by shouts from a stampede of uniformed Shifters.

"Stay where you are! Hands out where we can see them!"

The stream of officers closed in on the crowd, not seeing Nivi where she stood with Ji, Kellan, Ai, and Jorge. Ai and Jorge jumped into action, dragging Nivi, Ji, and Kellan in the opposite direction and behind a bookshelf.

"What's happening?" Kellan said.

Ai shushed him and spoke in a whisper. "Shifter police."

Kellan looked through the stack of books. "I don't see anyone."

"That's because they have camouflage stones on."

Ji pushed past them, trying to get past the bookshelf. "It's okay. They're on our side."

Ai pulled Ji back. "No, they're not."

Ji tried to shake Ai off. "I'm sorry, Nivi. I wanted to be supportive, but I found that paper in your jacket pocket this afternoon, so I alerted some of my superiors."

Paper? Oh, no. Nivi's heart sank as she realized it must've been the pro-integration propaganda she'd found by the school border. She'd forgotten about it. No wonder her mom had insisted on coming tonight.

Ai dropped Ji's arm and glared at Nivi. "We've worked so hard for this. How could you betray us?"

Nivi's intestines twisted into a tight ball of dread. "I swear. I didn't tell her anything."

Despite everyone's efforts to keep the meeting's agenda secret, Ji had betrayed them. But how could Nivi blame her? Ji had been an ardent supporter of the current administration ever since they had used oblivion tincture on her.

Nivi peeked out from behind the shelf. Shifter police were handcuffing Statics and Shifters alike and marching them out the front door. The Statics were understandably confused as they were hauled away by invisible forces, while some Shifters tried to quickly explain the situation before being detained themselves. At the front of the crowd, Rowena jumped into action, delivering a karate chop to one officer who reached for her with cuffs before spinning and side-kicking another. Several more officers approached Rowena warily, and she launched into the air, transforming mid-leap into a pale-winged bat.

While Rowena kept those policemen busy, another officer handcuffed Davis and pushed him toward the door. Nivi might have found a small satisfaction in that if she weren't so terrified. From outside came the sound of car doors slamming; no doubt Shifter police cars waiting to take everyone away. As the crowd slowly cleared, a couple of officers began to search the rest of the bookstore.

"Follow me," Kellan whispered. "There's another exit this way."

Ji still resisted. Ai clapped a hand over Ji's mouth to prevent her from calling out.

Jorge attempted to help restrain her. "Please, please, please. You don't know what you're doing."

Nivi was torn. What should she do? If the OT police got them, she would still retain her memories, but everyone else, all these people resisting the regime, would essentially be nullified. Nivi would be more alone than she had thought she was before. She didn't want to endanger her family, but hadn't she been waiting for the right time to do something? If she didn't act now, they wouldn't escape. When would she get another chance to change things for the better and reunite her family?

She had stayed silent for so long; kept this secret burden all to herself. If the walls between Shifters and Statics were breaking down, did she need to keep her secret any longer? If the size of the crowd tonight and the mysterious relationship between Ji and Kellan were any indication, things had been moving in the right direction for a while. Maybe Ji had been part of these meetings before her memory was wiped, and that's how she knew Kellan. The thought of her mom working to upend the system gave Nivi strength.

She clenched and unclenched her hands. Blood pulsed to her fists. Her veins rose to the surface, hot and red like molten lava. She turned to Ji, who was still struggling against Ai and Jorge, and placed a hand on her mother's shoulder. Ji's eyes met her own, questioning despite her obvious agitation.

Tears blurred Nivi's vision. "Mom. Remember." She closed her eyes and willed the heat from her chest to spread until she knew her whole body was glowing.

"Nivi, what are you…" Jorge said, hesitation and awe in his tone.

The rush of blood in Nivi's hands slowed and her body cooled. She opened her eyes and watched Ji's brows furrow then relax.

"It's okay," Nivi said to Ai and Jorge. "She understands now. You can let her go."

With confused looks, Ai and Jorge let go, and Ji embraced Nivi.

"Can someone tell us what's going on?" Ai said.

Nivi wiped a tear from her cheek. "There's no time right now."

"As much as I'd like to know as well," Kellan said, "I agree. We need to go. Now."

He tiptoed between shelves, hunching over, and they followed him one by one until they were behind the spiral staircase. Kellan reached down and pulled a metal handle on the floor—a trap door. Fortunately, the noise from the officers and their detainees was loud enough to mask the squeaking of the hinges. Kellan motioned for them to descend the wooden steps to the dark space below. Ji went first, followed by Nivi, Ai, and Jorge. Kellan came last, closing the door behind him. Nivi felt around blindly, grabbing a hand she hoped was Ji's. A dim light bulb came on. They were in a basement storage space full of boxes and books, and Nivi was holding Jorge's hand. He gave her a small smile, and she quickly released his hand without returning the smile. It was just a harmless mistake. Anyone would've done the same thing if they were in this scary situation. No need to make anything of it.

"There's an exit up those stairs," Kellan said, pointing to the opposite wall from where they had come down. "You all head up first, and I'll turn off this light and follow."

They did as he said, exiting into a small garden that must've been at the back of the bookstore. The light in the basement went off, and Kellan came up the stairs a few moments later, closing and locking the door after him.

"How did you know about this exit?" Ai said.

"I'm KW. Kellan Williams. This is my bookstore," he explained, his expression turning sad. "Or at least it was. Not sure what'll become of it after tonight."

"You don't have to come with us," Ai said. "You could turn yourself in. They'll just wipe your memories, and you can go back to your life as you knew it before."

"No way," Kellan said. "Not again." He glanced at Ji, and again Nivi had that strange sensation. What exactly *was* their relationship?

"Where can we go?" Jorge said. "Since Ji alerted her superiors, the police will probably be waiting at the school to detain us."

Everyone was silent while the sounds of shouts and slamming car doors continued on the other side of the bookstore.

"I know where we can go," Nivi said. "The Shifter police already swept through the town earlier this year, so they won't be thinking of looking there again so soon. At least I hope not."

"Wait," Ai said, turning to Jorge. "Can we trust her or her mom after she just ratted us out?"

"We can," Jorge said.

Ai huffed. "Seems like everyone knows something except for me."

"I promise I'll explain everything once we're away from here," Nivi said.

Ai crossed their arms. "So where are we going?"

Nivi took a deep breath. "It's a small town called Yuras."

When no one spoke, Kellan stepped forward. "Yuras it is. Let's go. My car's over here."

"No, I'll drive," Ji said. "They'll be looking for your car since this is your bookstore."

"Won't they be looking for you too?" Ai said. "Since you informed them and all?"

"I left an anonymous message."

Ai looked skeptical but didn't argue. They didn't have any other choice. They couldn't transform without attracting unwanted attention, and even if they could, none of them had a form that could travel the distance to Yuras faster than a car anyway.

The five of them piled into Ji's tan Toyota Camry with Jorge offering to sit in the middle back seat since he was the smallest of them all. Nivi scooted in next to him, emotion choking her throat as she buckled her seat belt.

She was going home.

Arav

Unknown Location

THE COOL STONE FLOOR throbbed against Arav's face. Or was his face throbbing against the floor? He pushed himself onto his hands and knees, every muscle aching and every joint creaking as if he had just run a marathon and then rolled down a rocky hill. Even his eyelids hurt.

He sat back on his heels and attempted to stand. Wrong move. The floor rushed at his face again, and it was all he could do to brace himself with his limp hands and cushion the impact. He gritted his teeth against the searing pain through his palms.

"You'll want to take it easy," came a voice through the fog in his mind. He shook his head, not understanding. The person spoke again. "It's the first time, right?"

Slowly, very slowly this time, Arav pushed himself up into a sitting position and held his knees in front of him as nausea roiled through his intestines and his vision clouded. Vera sat on the floor behind her glass wall, a look of sympathy in her eyes. For a moment, fear, disgust, and panic rushed through him as he remembered the monster in the tub, but she was perfectly human now. Had he imagined it?

"First time?" he managed to grunt in response to her question.

Vera ran her hands through her damp hair. So she *had* been in the tub. She didn't have any blue scales or barnacles though. His gaze briefly ran over her form-hugging shirt before he caught himself and quickly returned it to her face. Maybe he had just freaked out because a girl had bathed in front of him?

"This isn't going to be easy for you to hear," she said.

Arav rested his head on his knees. Thank goodness the nausea was passing, and so were the body aches. He raised his head, and his vision was clear. "What?"

Vera looked at him, unblinking. "You're a Shifter."

Half a laugh escaped Arav's mouth, the words not finding purchase.

"And from what I've gathered, so was your mom," she continued.

Another disbelieving laugh caught in his throat. He wanted to say *You can't be serious* or *I'm not a monster*, but Vera spoke again, pointing at his body.

"Look at your hands."

His hands? Arav looked. Hard, pebbled scutes lined his hands in a brown hue not too different from his usual skin tone but with a slight golden sheen. He blinked several times. Surely, it was just his blurred vision. But when he glanced back at Vera, she was in perfect focus. He extended his fingers one at a time. One, two, three... four.

Where were his fifth fingers? His pinky fingers were gone! And his *nails* were long, black, and sharp. Capable of inflicting the kind of damage he'd seen on Kabir and his mom.

He jumped back as if doing so would separate him from what he saw. The pebbled skin smoothed in front of his eyes, the black talons retracted, resuming the normal shape and color of his nails, and a pinky finger reappeared on each hand. Nausea cramped his stomach again as he struggled to make sense of his situation. His breaths came in short gasps, and the edges of his vision again became fuzzy.

"Take a deep breath," Vera said. "Or you'll make yourself transform again. And I don't think you can handle it again so soon, mentally or physically."

Arav shook his head, forcing himself to take several deep breaths. "This is some kind of trick."

"I'm afraid not. I don't have that kind of secondary power."

Secondary power? What did that even mean? "My confinement here is messing with my brain. I just need some fresh air. To see the sky." The sky. Like in his dreams, when he was soaring, the wind supporting his wings. He covered his face with his hands and mumbled to himself. "This isn't real. This isn't real."

Vera's firm voice came through the turmoil of his thoughts. "Arav. Arav, look at me."

Arav lowered his hands and looked at Vera. His vision had always been really good, but now, as he gazed through his glass prison wall at Vera, marvelous and minute details flooded his vision. The gold in Vera's eyes twinkled, flecks of suspended gold dust rotating and migrating around her irises. Warm light emitted from her chest as if the golden glow of her eyes extended through her whole being. Somehow, through the haze of his panic and disbelief, that warm glow brought him some comfort.

Vera spoke with a serious and yet somehow still sympathetic voice. "This is real, Arav. You're a Shifter. You might've noticed before this transformation that I have a glow. And the guards do too."

Arav shook his head, but he *had* noticed. It wasn't just the lighting.

"That's the Shifter aura. It's how we recognize each other. If what the guards said about your father being a Static is true, you most likely inherited your powers from your mother." Vera paused for a moment and continued when Arav didn't respond. "Let me guess, you've been having dreams about large, winged creatures with sharp talons?"

Arav stopped shaking and looked up, immediately suspicious. "How did you know that?"

"It's common to have dreams about your Shifter form before your first transformation. My Shifter form is a mermaid, so I used to dream about swimming around in the ocean and seeing large fish-like creatures. Yours is a griffin, so that's how I guessed what your dreams were about."

A griffin. The recurrent dreams of giant, four-legged eagles—well the front half was an eagle, and the back half was a... lion? Now they made sense.

Vera looked chagrined. "Oh, I'm sorry. I ruined the surprise for you. It's customary for first-time Shifters to see their form themselves without being told what they are, but since there are no mirrors in here, I guess you wouldn't have had the chance anyway."

He scoffed. Like it would have mattered if he had seen his form or not. An unexpected surge of elation filled his chest. Power, strength, joy. He almost smiled, but he fought it back along with an urge to jump into the air. Vera must've seen, though, because she smirked.

"It's hitting you, isn't it? Doesn't it feel great?"

He cleared his throat, but his voice still came out gruff. "Earlier you mentioned a secondary power?"

She nodded. "All Shifters have secondary powers. Mine is seeing in the dark. My eyes turn fully gold in the process." She closed her eyes for a moment, and when she opened them, they were a solid, reflective gold. After a few blinks, the gold shrank and fractured back into flecks. She winced. "It hurts to do that when it's light out."

It was getting harder to hide his emotions now. He was downright giddy. This wasn't right. It was unnatural. He was a monster. *She* was a monster. And yet he felt even more drawn to her. If he had this much trouble controlling his feelings and transformations, wouldn't his mother have struggled with it too?

"My mother wasn't a monst—a Shifter. We would've seen her change at some point." Doubt crept into his voice. "Wouldn't we?"

Vera glanced up while tilting her head. "Not necessarily. She probably would've gone somewhere private, and, depending on the size of her Shifter form, she could've even been doing it at home. Usually, we can go days or even weeks without needing to transform, and some of us can go longer, although it gets uncomfortable and less predictable."

At home? During the school year, his mother had been home alone for most of the day unless he or Kabir were home sick, so there was no telling what she'd been up to. But during the summer... His mother had her weekly relaxation bath days when she wasn't to be disturbed, and she always emerged looking so refreshed and happy. Not just happy. Vivacious. He cringed. Had she been soaking in the tub in some kind of monstrous form like Vera? Or was she fluttering around like a butterfly? He'd never know. A wave of sadness overtook him, not just for the loss of his mother, but for all that she had kept hidden from them. All that she must've given up.

"She must've felt so alone," he said.

"She wasn't the only one, you know. There are other Shifters who have Static partners. Because of the laws, they either have to give up their powers to openly be with them or keep their relationships secret. It's one of the things we're trying to change." She smiled as an earnest tone entered her voice. "She must've loved you and your father very much."

Arav's stomach flipped. It was such a pretty smile that rounded her cheeks. Try as he might to remain steadfast in his beliefs, his anti-monster convictions were fading. After all, he was one now.

And wasn't it possible that, just like in the rest of humanity, not all Shifters were bad? His mother for one. And himself. And maybe Vera?

He realized they had been staring at each other for a moment too long, long enough to make things awkward. Before he could think of something to say, the sound of doors slamming broke the silence. Footsteps and voices followed. Arav and Vera got to their feet and pressed against their respective glass walls to try to see who was coming. The same guards who had brought in Vera appeared, gripping the upper arms of an Asian man wearing a suit. Unlike Vera, the man was awake.

As they neared, Arav noticed the man's hands were restrained behind his back, but he didn't glow like Vera or the guards. Did this mean he wasn't a Shifter? What had Vera called those without magic? Statics?

Vera's eyes were wide and glossy, and her cheeks were slightly flushed as she watched the man approach. Did she know him? Did she *like* him? Arav supposed the man was handsome for an old guy. What was he? Thirty? He was a little taller than Arav, but not as muscular. Was it the suit? The chiseled jaw? The way he looked so suave even while handcuffed? Arav didn't trust him.

The guards led the man past them and into the cell directly next to Vera. Great.

"The chairperson will be here shortly," Eric said while the restraints dissolved from the man's wrists.

Nicola locked the cell, and they walked back down the hall the way they had come, slamming the door again on their way out.

Vera rushed to the two-foot-wide strip of shared glass that separated her cell from the newcomer's.

"Davis," Vera said. "What happened?"

So she did know him. Arav crept a little closer to the front corner of his cell to hear their conversation better.

The suave man, Davis, rubbed his wrists, straightened his suit jacket, and smoothed his hair before approaching the glass between him and Vera. What a douche.

"We were ambushed at a meeting," he said. "Someone must've informed the Shifter police."

Vera inhaled sharply. One hand wrapped around her waist as the other went to her mouth. "How many did they get?"

"As far as I know, everyone who was in attendance. They've already OT'd the rest. I assume the chairperson wants to speak to me personally since I'm the lead Static organizer."

"How will we recover from this?"

Something twanged in Arav's chest at the despair in Vera's voice. He cleared his throat. "What's going on?"

Davis seemed to notice Arav for the first time. He inclined his head in greeting, and Arav nodded stiffly.

Vera turned to face Arav, her voice wavering. "There's a group of us, Shifters and Statics, working to make things better. We want integration between Shifters and Statics so no one would have to hide their relationship or who they are. We're trying to fight the gross abuse of power by these Shifter police officers who take us and erase our memories to keep the chairperson in her absolute power." She sank to the floor and put her head in her hands. "But it's over now. It's all over."

Arav didn't know what to say. In an instant, Vera's spunk and spirit were gone, and he couldn't help but associate Davis's appearance with this change, especially because he now lay cavalierly in the bed in his own cell like he didn't have a care in the world.

"What's your deal, Davis?" Arav called. "Why don't you seem worried?"

Davis sat up in his bed with a somewhat amused look on his face. "And you are..."

"Arav Markson."

Davis seemed to scrutinize Arav's face. "You look familiar. Have we met before?"

That question startled Arav. "Not that I know of." Was it possible they had?

Davis narrowed his eyes, and Arav stared back. What was this guy's deal? Suddenly, Davis's eyes widened and a small gasp escaped his mouth.

At that moment, Arav's pulse picked up, and his surroundings blurred. His awareness propelled forward, and he was suddenly on the Yuras cliffs, staring out through Davis's eyes.

Kabir lay on the ground in front of him, clutching a gash in his side. Blood seeped through his fingers...

Arav's awareness shot back to his cell. He grabbed his head to steady his vision. What had just happened? He'd felt something similar when he was arguing with Amber in Alaska. But why had he seen his mom? Was it a memory? Was Davis playing some trick on him? But Davis didn't have any powers.

"Did you say something?" Davis said.

Arav shook his head.

Davis shrugged and lay back down. "Well, *Arav*. There's nothing to be done right now, so why waste time worrying?"

It took Arav a moment to remember that he had asked Davis a question. This man was infuriating. How could he be the leader of any movement? Who would respect him? Arav looked back at Vera, who was still on the ground, her head pressed into the arms that clutched her bent knees. He squatted across from her and spoke in a soft voice.

"Hey, we'll figure something out."

Vera lifted her head just long enough for Arav to see that her eyes were shining with tears. "It was nice to meet you, Arav. Soon I'll have no memory of you, and things will continue on as if we'd never met." She lowered her head again.

Arav's heart constricted at her words. Why did he care? He had thought she was a monster, and now he was disappointed their acquaintance would soon be erased.

"Maybe not," he said, trying to make her feel better. "I've been here a long time."

She raised her head, half laughing, half scoffing. "And that's a good thing?"

"Maybe it means they're running out of tincture and keeping it for more important situations. Why else would they keep me—a nobody—around? Just because one of my parents is a Static?"

Vera tilted her head in that cute thoughtful way of hers. "Maybe. They have been OT'ing a lot of people recently. Or maybe they're afraid. Most people think mixing Static and Shifter blood leads to no magic. They must be trying to verify if that's not the case, because that would be a big hit against the anti-integration movement." She looked hopeful for an instant before her eyes became downcast once again. "But none of this will matter if we don't remember it."

Not knowing what else to say, Arav went to his bed to lie down and wait.

A day and a night passed without much talking. Davis seemed content to lie around all day, staring at the ceiling as if he were watching a movie. Vera spent most of her time submerged in her tub, and Arav paced and did jumping jacks and push-ups, unable to rid himself of his nervous energy.

Finally, the sound of doors opening and people approaching broke the silence. Arav jumped up from where he was doing push-ups and pressed himself against the glass wall, fogging it up with his body heat and breath. A woman he hadn't seen before came into view followed by the same two familiar guards. She was tall and thin, with light brown hair tied back at her neck, and she wore a tailored black suit. Something about her calm demeanor almost reminded him of Davis. It was the small smile she wore—so fake.

She strode right by his and Vera's cells and stopped in front of Davis's glass wall. Davis continued to lie in his bed, arms behind his head, one leg bent and the other crossed over.

"Hello, Davis," she said in a cool tone.

Davis turned his head without sitting up from the bed.

The woman smirked. "Imagine my surprise to hear you'd come back from the dead, and as a Static, no less."

At these last words, Vera popped up from her tub with a startled expression, an inner pair of clear eyelids pulling back from her gold eyes as they reverted to green. Apparently, she could hear underwater.

Davis looked back at the ceiling. "Ariana," he said in a bored tone. "Always so desperate for respect. And even now that you've taken over my position, you struggle to maintain control without wiping everyone's memories. Are you afraid they will see you for the pathetic leader you are?"

Vera's mouth dropped open. She climbed out of her tub and walked over to the glass strip between her cell and Davis's.

Ariana scoffed, but she visibly stiffened at Davis's words. This guy was so good at being a douche that Arav would've felt annoyed on Ariana's behalf if he hadn't been trying to digest all the information their conversation had just revealed.

"I have the ability to shape your life in any way I choose," Ariana continued, a slight edge creeping into her voice. "So I caution you to know your place when you address me."

Davis almost seemed like he was going to yawn. "As I said, so desperate for respect. Why don't we skip these niceties, and you ask whatever it is you came all the way here to ask?"

The guards stepped forward, but Ariana waved them back. She clenched and unclenched her fists, then regained her cool composure with a laugh.

"I don't have any questions."

This seemed to pique Davis's interest as he turned his head to look at Ariana, although he still appeared bored.

"I just wanted the pleasure of telling you to your face that I've verified the rumors." Her voice sounded gleeful.

Davis narrowed his eyes. "What rumors?"

Ariana began to pace in front of Davis's cell like she was lecturing to an audience.

"You may not know this, but my mother was a servant for a wealthy family in Los Angeles." She waved her hand as if to dismiss a concern. "We came from humble beginnings, and I'm not at all ashamed of it. She had servant friends in other households, and they swapped gossip about their employers. One of her friends, I believe her name was Margaret, was a servant in the Sun household. Here's where it gets *really* interesting. It seems they had a son who happened to be a Static. A Shifter family with a Static son. Uncommon, I know. It must've been a disappointment to them, to have such a stain on their family name."

Davis was sitting up now, his jaw tight and his mouth in a thin line.

"Shall I continue the story?" Ariana said. "Somehow that son discovered special stones—stones that allowed him to steal powers. With those stolen powers, he rose in the ranks of Shifter politics, culminating in an attempted coup." She stopped pacing and faced

Davis, her voice turning icy. "How dare you steal *our* powers and try to pose as one of us. If not for Representative Bai—rest her soul—you might have caused more damage than you already have. Thankfully, I've restored calm and integrity to our community and discovered your secret society before it was too late. Now I can rest assured that the greatest threats to Shifter society have been taken care of."

Vera's face fell. She backed up from her glass wall, shaking her head in disbelief, and disappeared into her bathwater.

Arav didn't fully understand everything that had been said, but there was something sinister in Ariana's voice that made him call out.

"What are you going to do to us? Are you going to kill us?"

Ariana looked at Arav as if noticing him for the first time. A note of mirth tinged her response. "I'm not a *monster*."

A chill ran down Arav's spine. Did she know about his involvement with the monster hunters?

"Enjoy your memories of Shifter society for now," Ariana said to Davis. "You will remain here as long as it takes for you to tell me *everything* about your underground movement. When I am satisfied there are no more loose ends, I will personally see to the administration of your oblivion tincture."

She straightened her suit jacket, turned, and walked away, the guards close at her heels. All was quiet except for the slamming of the doors at the end of the hall.

DAVIS

UNKNOWN LOCATION

DAVIS WATCHED ARIANA LEAVE, his practiced cool and relaxed smile fading as the doors closed behind her. He turned and walked straight to the little bed against the wall, barely pausing to throw off his suit jacket and kick off his shoes before he lay down. Everything drained from him. His energy, his ambition, his hope. The universe had been against him since his birth. All that waited now was the oblivion tincture, and in a way, he welcomed its arrival. The erasure of his memories, and the ability to start anew.

Especially the freedom from his memories. They haunted him.

Even now, in the quiet of the cell, people flashed through his mind. His mother as she touched him with a transfer stone and the light left her eyes. His sister with her nonstop adoration of him and crumpled face as he betrayed her trust. Jackson Dawan, full of disgust and engulfed in flames. The random Shifter woman on the cliffs of Yuras who just happened to see him coming from the transfer stone mine, and her fear and panic as she ran from him and fell to her death. The scores of Shifters he had stolen powers from. Worst of all, his father, with his twisted mouth hidden beneath his mustache and his daily scorn that Davis still couldn't escape.

After stealing his family's powers, Davis had visited his childhood home in secret. Hidden behind a tree or bush, he watched as his father and sister aged. As Statics, they lived a reclusive life, subsisting on their fortune and servants. Over time, Randall became wheelchair bound, and Anna became his caretaker. Even in that feeble state, Randall still held power over Davis. Everything Davis had done, he'd done to prove himself to his father, but nothing seemed good enough to warrant approaching him after all those years. He'd been determined to do it... one day. Every day he'd been making progress, advancing in Shifter politics, becoming more powerful.

And then he was elected vice chairperson. Elated, he rushed to his childhood home after the swearing-in ceremony was over, but as he approached the tree-lined property and the gleam of the white stone mansion, he balked.

He has to accept you now. He has to forgive you. You've proven yourself worthy. You're strong. You're powerful.

But part of him told him he'd never earn his father's approval, no matter what he did.

As he stood behind a tree, looking for movement in the upstairs arched windows, a black car rolled up the road. Davis stepped behind the tree to keep from being seen. Was John still the family driver? Probably not since he was a Shifter.

As the car turned onto the round driveway of the house, something about it looked different. It was too long and boxy to be the family car. The car stopped in front of the house and a couple of people got out to open the trunk, both dressed in black. The front door of the house opened, and Anna stepped out, also dressed in black. She was middle-aged now. Strange that his younger sister looked older than him.

Her face grim, Anna fully opened the mansion's double doors and stepped aside as the people from the car walked inside. A moment later, another black car drove up to the house. That one *was* the family car. The driver, who wasn't John, got out with three other people Davis didn't recognize. They greeted Anna and went into the house. Davis watched intently, looking for his father. What was he planning?

Then the people emerged, and Davis's stomach dropped.

The six strangers squeezed through the double doors, their steps slow and strained due to the casket they carried between them.

It wasn't his father. It couldn't be, but he knew in his heart it was. As the pallbearers loaded the casket into the hearse, Davis leaned against the tree he'd been hiding behind for support. Anxiety shook his legs, a sense of a purpose unfinished, lost. His father couldn't be dead. He couldn't. How dare he die and ruin all of Davis's plans? Who was Davis now that his father was gone? Nothing and nobody, just as he'd always been.

Anna watched the hearse drive away, followed by the family car. She turned and went into the house without a second look, and Davis left, never to return to his family home.

During the first weeks in his position as vice chairperson, he wallowed in his emotional void. Things might have continued on that way until his powers ran out and he was forced from his position but for a chance encounter. On one of those nondescript mornings, after Davis had wandered morosely through the underwater Shifter Council building, staring listlessly at passing fish, Marcus the administrative assistant called his office.

Davis answered the phone. "Yes?"

"Vice Chairperson Davis, you have a visitor," came Marcus's voice.

He sighed loudly. "Who is it?"

"She says her name's Iris."

Iris? Was it the same young girl he'd coached through her time at the Shifter Academy in hopes she'd one day use her finder skill to find him more transfer stones? If it was her, did he even want to pursue that course anymore? He just wanted to let all his powers fade, let himself fade away from Shifter life and politics and truly embrace being a nobody. But something about hearing Iris's name at that moment sparked what was left of his ambition.

"Let her in."

Iris entered the office. She was taller than he remembered, but still just as pretty. Her youthful, heart-shaped face had elongated into an eye-catching sophistication that broke into a charming, nervous smile when she saw him.

"Mr. Davis," she said. "I mean, I guess it's Vice Chairperson Davis now. I happened to be in the council building—I'm doing an internship—so I just wanted to say hi and congratulations."

This was a sign that maybe he wasn't done with Shifter life after all. There was more power to be had, more changes to be made in the system. He would show his father, alive or dead, what he could accomplish.

He returned Iris's smile. "Thank you. I guess that means we'll be seeing more of each other."

Davis smiled wryly to himself as he lay in the prison cell. He would've never guessed where his time with Iris would lead him. All that time, he'd thought he'd been controlling Iris, when in the end, she had changed his fate more drastically than he could've imagined. Iris. Why did everything keep coming back to her?

Just months ago, he'd awoken on a beach north of San Francisco, choking on seawater, barely alive. He'd clutched at the sand, an intense relief calming the panic of his near-death experience. He was *alive*. What had he been doing with his life?

All the powers were gone. All his hard work for nothing. He was weak, a failure, worse than a nobody. He was a pariah. His father had been right about him. He'd always been right.

It was strange being himself for the first time since he'd been a teenager. He had cloaked himself in the comfort of power for so long. Without it, he was small and alone. The euphoria of being alive faded into depressive self-loathing. For what felt like hours, he lay there on the beach, wishing he had died. What was there for him now?

Iris was somewhere out there with *all* of *his* powers. He tried to get angry, but the feeling didn't come. Emptiness. He had dropped as low as he could go, and somehow his gratitude at being alive began to percolate back in. He had survived for a reason. Maybe he'd been going about things the wrong way. Instead of stealing powers and forcing Shifters to accept him, maybe he should get back to the root of the problem—integration policies—but this time as a Static. There must be other people like him. He'd find them and gather them together. He'd start a revolution.

He knew where to go and what to do. He'd done it before, when his father had first kicked him out of the house. So he'd stood up, rubbed the salt from his eyes, spit the sand from his mouth, and made his way into town. He had washed up in Marin County, not far from Sausalito. After some inquiries and more than one strange look, he located the nearest homeless shelter, the Marin County House of Hope.

At that point, fate seemed to take a turn again. It took a little bit of clever questioning to find out that someone at the Marin County House of Hope had dealings with Shifters. Everyone thought that person was crazy, of course, because he'd talk about shapeshifters as if they really existed, but through him, Davis met more Statics who knew about Shifters.

It turned out that Davis wasn't the first Static who'd wanted to organize a revolution. There was a pro-integration group, a mix of Statics and Shifters, that was growing but poorly organized. They'd been waiting for someone with the ability to lead, someone like Davis.

One of the members, Kellan Williams, was a local bookstore owner. Davis suggested holding meetings there, and then he began to speak at meetings. It didn't take long for him to grow his own following. He would do things differently this time. He'd do things right.

The doors opened down the hall and footsteps approached. Davis snapped out of his reverie and smoothed his hair. Even in his gloom, he could still look and act dignified. He wouldn't let Ariana get the pleasure of thinking she'd won or knowing his spirit had been crushed, even if it had. So he took deep breaths and waited for the guards to appear.

ARAV

UNKNOWN LOCATION

AFTER THE SHOCK OF Ariana's visit, Vera had sunk back into her tub. Davis lay in his bed, all his obnoxious energy gone. Not knowing what else to do or say, Arav went back to doing push-ups in his cell. Down and up. Down and up. It felt good to obliterate his thoughts with muscle pain, yet his nervous energy lingered even as his arms and chest gave out. As soon as he collapsed to the ground, all the soul-crushing thoughts rushed back. The impending doom of oblivion tincture. It was hopeless.

It shouldn't bother Arav so much. His memories would be erased, and he'd go back to living his life without knowing any better. But would he? Now that he knew he was a Shifter, what kind of backstory memories would they create? It was a personal attack to have his memories wiped and replaced. He'd forget about key aspects that made him who he was. It wasn't right. He hated to admit it, but that Ariana person was even worse than Davis. But what could he do? What could any of them do? Davis had said everyone else involved had already had their memories erased. They were trapped here with no way out, awaiting the oblivion tincture like inmates on death row.

At some point, Arav must've fallen asleep on the cool stone floor. The sound of doors opening and footsteps approaching startled him awake. Heart racing, he rose to a sitting position, stretching his back and neck that ached from the hard floor. Was Ariana back already? Was this it—oblivion?

The guards strode in with a prisoner. They half carried, half dragged a girl between them. She was slight of frame, and her head hung forward, her long, black hair obscuring her face.

That looks like Amber. Heart racing, Arav quickly got rid of the notion. There was no way Amber would end up down here, but the initial thought still sent shock waves through his mind, and he realized how much he missed her. What would she think if she found out he was one of the monsters he'd accused her of being? Was she actually one too? Or had he caused that reaction on her wrist with his own powers? Would she forgive him? It didn't matter now. He'd probably never see her again.

The guards brought the girl into the empty cell next to Vera's, which was across the hall to Arav's right. They laid her on the bed, closed and locked the door, and left again without a word.

From the cell on Vera's other side, Davis stood at his window looking down the hall. "It's a party now," he quipped.

No one responded, and Davis seemed to lose interest, going back to his bed to lie down.

Arav couldn't stop staring at the new girl sleeping in her cell. Part of him hoped it was Amber, just so he could see her face and tell her he was sorry, but he knew it was just wishful thinking.

Soon the girl began to stir. She moaned, rolled to the side of her bed, and sat up. She brushed the hair back from her face and... It *was* Amber.

"Amber!" Arav called out before he could stop himself. He couldn't believe it. Why would Amber be here?

She rubbed her face and looked over at Arav. Slowly standing up, she made her way to her glass window and pressed her hands against it.

"Arav?"

"What are you doing here?"

Arav wanted to cry and hug her, but he was also devastated that she was here in this prison. Then he saw it—she was glowing. The *Shifter* aura. She *had* been a Shifter this whole time, just like him. He glanced over at Vera, who had gotten up from her bed. For some reason, Amber's aura was much fainter than Vera's.

Amber shook her head. "I don't know. One minute I was with my parents, and now I'm here. What is this place?"

"This is a prison for Shifters," Arav said. "People like us."

Amber shook her head again. "For what? I don't understand." She sounded a little panicked, and Arav's heart went out to her.

"Another Shifter who doesn't know she's a Shifter?" Vera said. "Interesting. How do you know each other?"

"She's my girlfriend—" Arav began protectively and then hesitated, feeling heat creep up his face. Why was he embarrassed saying this to Vera?

"*Was*," Amber said.

The comment was like a punch to his stomach, but she was right. They had fought, and he'd accused her of being a monster. He hadn't wanted anything more to do with her at the time, but it still hurt to hear her confirm the breakup. But things were different now. He knew his true identity, and they were one and the same. Would that change things between them?

"Sounds like you two have some talking to do," Vera said.

"It really is a party now," Davis said from his bed, somehow sounding excited and bored at the same time.

"Ignore him," Arav said to Amber.

"Why are you all so calm?" Amber said, her voice rising. "We're prisoners here and you're making *jokes*?"

Arav sighed. "We've been here... a while."

Amber put her head in her hands and sank to the floor. Her shoulders shook a little and then stopped. When she looked up, her eyes were red. "How long have you been here?"

"Ever since Alaska. I was taken from in front of the café, right after our... fight."

Amber nodded, chewing her lip. Her voice dropped to a whisper. "I thought you'd left me."

"No," Arav said. He put a hand up on the glass, his heart breaking.

"So we're stuck here? Forever?"

"Not forever." He wanted to make her feel better, but he didn't know how. "Just until they wipe our memories. Then they'll send us home."

"Oh. Great." Amber threw her hands in the air. "They're going to *wipe our memories*? How is that even possible?" She brushed a tear from her cheek before assuming a look of determination. "Okay. Tell me everything I need to know."

Amber was strong. She was able to bounce back from adversity. That was one of the things Arav loved about her. But where should he start?

"Look... the way I left things... I'm so sorry. I know the truth now—"

"Which is what?" Amber snapped.

"I—I'm..." Why was he having such a hard time?

Vera got into her tub and transformed into her mermaid form. "I'm going to help you out because this awkwardness is killing me. He's a Shifter. You're a Shifter. You both have powers, and you're able to transform into other creatures. Our current government doesn't like Shifters who don't follow the rules, so they gather us up and keep us here to question us. And then they wipe our memories and send us home none the wiser."

Amber stood up from the floor and gawked. Vera, in all her blue-scaled, green-haired, clawed-fin glory, waved back from her tub. Amber gasped and then covered her mouth like she was embarrassed for her rudeness.

"Um, who are you? *What* are you?" she said, lowering her hands.

"I'm Vera. This is my Shifter form." Vera gestured to the cell next to hers. "And that's Davis."

Amber paced in front of her glass wall, covering her mouth with both hands. "This isn't real. This can't be real."

"Sorry, hon, but it is," Vera said with a touch of sympathy. She paused as if something had caught her eye and turned to examine Amber through the panel of glass between their cells. "That's weird. Why's your aura so faint?"

Amber looked down at herself. "My what?"

Arav explained the Shifter aura to Amber while she watched him incredulously.

"Does that mean that I—that I can—" She looked at her hands like she expected them to grow claws like Vera's. After a moment her shoulders slumped. "I didn't even know I had one, so I have no idea why it'd be faint."

All of a sudden Davis was in the corner of his cell, trying to look over at Amber. "I have an idea why."

Everyone looked over at Davis, and he took his time, clearly enjoying the bit of power he was holding over them.

"Spit it out, Davis," Vera said.

"So impatient." Davis tsked. "It's not like we have somewhere to be."

How could this guy have been a leader when he was *so* infuriating? Arav felt heat rise within his chest and the muscles constrict over his ribs. He locked eyes with Davis, and again the world blurred around him as if he were rushing forward.

He was on the Yuras cliffs, and his mom was running just ahead. She was running away from something. She was scared.

And then she tripped... and fell over the edge!

He jumped forward and grabbed at her with lion's paws, claws extending. They dug into her back and chest, but she slipped through them and continued to fall.

Arav reached forward, and his hand banged into the glass wall in front of him. He pulled it back with a stifled yelp and glanced around, orienting himself. He wasn't in Yuras. He was in a prison for Shifters. Why did that keep happening? Was he starting to remember something? Was *he* responsible for his mom's death? No, he couldn't be. He had been home with his dad when it happened. He took a deep breath, shuddering, not wanting to black out again and wake up with talons or claws for hands.

Davis watched him, narrowing his eyes, but then seemed to move on. "Did you by chance encounter a special kind of stone?" he said to Amber.

Arav thought of the mine he and Amber had found, and Amber seemed to think of the same thing at the same time as she met his gaze, her eyes wide.

"You did, didn't you?" Davis said. "Interesting. But you don't know what it does?"

"Cut the suspense and just tell us," Vera said.

"Looks like someone took something that didn't belong to her," Davis said with a slight singsong to his words.

Vera pushed herself up with a huff. "This is getting us nowhere."

She swung her tail out of the tub and shook the water from it. Arav averted his eyes as Vera got out of the tub and transformed into her human form, her wet hair dripping down her crop top and snug jeans, but his eyes drifted back to watch her walk into the bathroom. He looked back at Amber who was giving him a strange look.

"Oh, you're no fun," Davis called after Vera. "Okay, fine. I'll tell you. The stone you found can transfer powers, or steal them, from Shifters. Did you ever touch it to someone, see a bright light, and feel a sudden surge of energy?"

"No. Never." Amber paused and her eyes met Arav's. "But there was a stone at Nivi's house that looked like it had electricity in it. Do you remember? I brought it to show you, but by then it was dull and dark. That electricity I saw was gone. And I do remember feeling some sort of shock when I touched it."

Arav nodded. "I remember you being excited about a stone, but there was nothing special about it."

"Interesting," Davis said. "A darkened stone means it was used. I didn't realize the stones could hold power as well."

"What?" Vera snapped, emerging from the bathroom. "Already planning another takeover?" Davis didn't respond, and Vera turned to Amber. "So your aura is faint because you touched a stone that . . . What, held someone else's powers?" She glanced back at Davis, but when he stayed silent, she scoffed and faced Amber again. "So I guess that makes you part Shifter? Interesting. I always thought that either you're a Shifter or you're not, but judging by this group we've got right here, it seems to be more of a spectrum."

"It definitely seems more complicated than that," Amber said.

"You could say that again," Arav mumbled.

NIVI

YURAS, CALIFORNIA

As soon as the car was on the freeway and they were sure they weren't being followed, Ai and Jorge peppered Nivi with questions while Kellan listened intently from the front passenger seat. The cathartic effect was immediate as Nivi explained what Davis had done, the OT police, and her additional secondary power. She hadn't realized how much she needed to share her story.

"The Davis we know doesn't seem anything like the one you knew," Ai said after Nivi recounted the attack on the Shifter Council.

"Ai!" Jorge exclaimed. "That's so inconsiderate of Nivi's experiences."

Ai put up their hands in a placating manner. "I completely believe you and support what you went through, Nivi. I'm just wondering... Could he have changed?"

The question reverberated through Nivi's body, tensing every muscle in its wake. *Could Davis have changed?* He had *killed* her father. He had stolen the powers from *half* of the Shifter Council. Because of his actions, anti-integration sentiment had increased, and Chairperson Peters had resorted to oblivion tincture overuse, causing Nivi to again be separated from her family. So what if he had changed? Did that excuse everything he'd done in the past?

"Hey," Ji said softly from the driver's seat, breaking Nivi's spiral of anger. "He's in custody now. After what he did, there's no way they'll let him out."

Kellan shook his head. "It sucks being deceived like that."

"We thought he was our salvation," Ai said, "but it turns out we don't need him. We only need you!"

"What?" Nivi asked, feeling self-conscious.

"Don't you see what this means?" Ai said. They reached across Jorge to grab Nivi's hands. "This is how we win!"

Nivi shook her head, confused.

"With you! *You* are our secret weapon! You can nullify the OT on everyone. Everyone! Once everyone remembers what's happened, there's no way they'll let Chairperson Peters continue what she's been doing."

"I—don't know."

"What's not to know?"

Jorge pushed Ai's hands from Nivi's. "It's not like she can do it all at once."

"Nullifying that many people at once would drain her," Ji added. "It'll take time."

Ai's enthusiasm wasn't deterred. "So we start small until we have the numbers we need. And we start now!" They grabbed Nivi's hands again.

Nivi looked at Ai, still not comprehending. The night's events had overwhelmed her, and sharing all her secrets had wiped her out. All she wanted to do now was sleep.

"With me, silly." Ai shook their hands. "Nullify the OT on me!"

"On you?" Nivi freed her hands.

"So *now* you're a willing believer of the OT?" Jorge said. "You never believed me when *I* told you."

"Of course," Ai said. "Nivi being immune trumps your secondary power."

Nivi was confused. "What does breathing underwater have to do with knowing about the OT?"

"My ahuizotl form can breathe underwater," Jorge said. "But that's not my secondary power."

"In a way," Ai said, "it's like he has two secondary powers too."

That was indeed surprising. Nivi watched Jorge expectantly, waiting for him to elaborate.

Jorge startled when he realized the attention was on him. "Oh, right. Well…" He pushed his glasses up his nose and placed his hands in his lap, fidgeting. "I guess it's better to show you." He reached up and turned on the overhead light then pushed up the sleeves of his black long-sleeved shirt to expose his forearms.

Words formed on Jorge's inner forearms as if an invisible hand were tattooing him in elaborate script. It was beautiful, the swirls of black against his brown skin, and it gave Jorge an unexpected edge to his outwardly meek self.

Kellan turned around to look. "That's dope, man."

Jorge beamed.

Nivi read the words as they appeared on Jorge's left arm first. "Shifter police, black liquid, touched forehead." The phrasing seemed rushed and unfinished. She read his other arm. "Shifter police, black liquid, again?"

"I can write or draw anything on my skin in any color," Jorge explained. "If I want to keep something hidden, I write it in transparent script, and I can always darken it later like this. It's why I have to wear long sleeves on test days, so I don't cheat." He grinned sheepishly. "I also do it whenever there's something interesting that I want to remember. Every so often, I run out of space, so I check what I've written on myself before I erase it. One day this note appeared." He pointed to his left arm. "I had no memory of putting it there and no idea what it meant until it happened again. By then, there were whispers of what the OT police were doing, and these notes confirmed it for me."

Ai reached for Nivi. "Will you please nullify it now?"

Nivi took a deep breath and clasped Ai's hand with one of her own. The heat in Nivi's chest soared and rushed down her arms until it met Ai's hands. From there, it radiated outward, prying away the oblivion tincture's grip until it drifted away as harmless as water vapor.

Ai gripped the sides of their face, wide-eyed. "Oh my god. It's all back!"

Jorge grabbed Nivi's hand from Ai, startling Nivi. "Me too," Jorge announced with a glance at Nivi, as if to say, *We don't have to say when I got my memories back.*

"What did they erase?" Nivi said.

"The structure of the Shifter Council, for one," Ai said. "And Davis as chairperson! Wow, that's trippy. The second time was for gossiping about what the OT police were doing. I'm surprised the meeting tonight was organized as well as it was with how often the OT police were crawling around. What about you, Jorge?"

"Same," Jorge said. "And some earlier stuff from when I was maybe five years old. The memories are coming back, but slowly. They made me leave my old home, in Yuras, because there was something strange in my house. At first I thought it was a sinkhole, but there was also some kind of goo in the corner that my dad told me not to touch."

"Goo?" Ai said.

Jorge shrugged and continued. "Something silvery, not quite liquid, not quite solid. Then some people from the Shifter Council came to check it out. She told us it was dangerous."

"She?" Ai said.

"It was Chairperson Peters. But she was a senator back then."

Ai started to sound excited again. How did they have so much energy? "Great! We have a plan. Once we get to Yuras, we need to go to your old home, Jorge, and check out what this goo is. See why Chairperson Peters wanted to erase your memory over it and move you away."

Ji cut in from the driver's seat. "That's a good idea, but why don't you all rest right now? We have a long drive ahead."

Nivi hadn't realized her eyelids had drifted shut and, and, she was grateful for the quiet following her mom's words. She leaned against the window, exhausted but full of hope inspired by Ai's enthusiasm. As she drifted off to sleep, she held on to the thought that maybe she could nullify the OT on enough people to bring about the pro-integration revolution Shifters were craving.

About halfway into the seven-and-a-half-hour trip from San Francisco to Yuras, they stopped for gasoline and bathroom breaks, and for Ji and Kellan to swap places. Nivi tried to listen to the whispered words from the front seats, but they were few and incoherent, so she ended up dozing for most of the drive. Somehow, her head kept bumping into Jorge's head as she slept.

"Sorry," Nivi said for probably the tenth time when her head hit Jorge again.

"It's okay."

Jorge was looking down at his forearms. Passing streetlamps illuminated shifting inky designs on his skin.

"What are you doing?" Nivi whispered so as not to wake Ai and Kellan.

Jorge glanced at Nivi before returning his attention to his arms.

"I'm trying to remember what she did. My mom. She had the same secondary power as me, and she used to make these designs on her body."

"Does it mean something?"

"Our Aztec ancestors used body paint for different purposes like protection or to signify a specific deity. My memories are still splotchy, but there was a specific deity she used to invoke. It was like a party trick. My dad would smile when he talked about it."

"A party trick? So it had some kind of effect?"

"I'm not sure."

Nivi left Jorge alone to concentrate and fell back asleep. It was almost five in the morning when they arrived in Yuras. The dark of night obscured most of the scenery outside Nivi's window, but as they exited the freeway, she immediately recognized the row of lamps glowing softly in front of the hotels on Ocean Lane. They passed the apartment building she had stayed in with Ji for a few days after they'd been reunited and before they'd been OT'd. A twinge of sorrow marred that otherwise brief, happy memory.

Her heart beat faster and faster when they turned onto Main Street and then finally Pine Lane. There was the home she had shared with Ling just up ahead on the right.

Kellan parked the car along the curb in front of the house. Through the thick mist that had settled over the neighborhood, the streetlamps glowed like hazy orange bubbles. Nivi stepped out of the car and stretched. The cold pricked her face, and she ran her hands over her curls, which were definitely starting to frizz in this weather.

"It's still pretty early," Kellan said. "Should we wait a little before we knock?"

"No," Nivi said, already walking up to the door. "It's too risky. We should get inside as soon as possible. Plus, Po Po usually gets up early. She'd be getting up in the next hour anyway."

Ji got out and walked with Nivi to the door while Kellan, Ai, and Jorge stayed in the car. Nivi took a deep breath and rang the doorbell. She waited and listened, then rang the bell again.

Footsteps shuffled within, the quick pace matching that of Nivi's heart. A moment later, Ling answered the door wearing a robe and looking very sleepy. She also looked smaller than Nivi remembered, but maybe that was because Nivi had gotten taller. And she was *glowing*. She had a Shifter aura! She had her powers back, which meant the OT must have been removed too. When did this happen? It didn't matter. Nivi gasped with joy and ran forward, grabbing her grandmother in a tight embrace.

Ling stiffened and yelped. "Meng! Help! A strange girl is attacking me!"

Nivi pulled back. It appeared the OT was still in effect, but then how did Ling have her powers? First, she needed to stop her grandmother's cries from waking the neighbors. Fortunately, the nap in the car had helped restore some of her energy, so she was able to immediately draw on her powers. Before Ling could tear herself away, Nivi nullified the OT. Ling stopped fighting and returned Nivi's hug.

"I've missed you so much, Po Po."

"I've missed you too."

Ling released Nivi and looked up at Ji.

Ji stepped forward and embraced Ling. "Hi, Ma Ma."

Suddenly, Meng ran up behind Ling, a broom held like a base-ball bat in her hands, her eyes flashing blue in the dark. She also had a Shifter aura and intact oblivion tincture effects, apparently. "Let her go!"

Ling whirled around. "It's okay. They're family." Meng lowered the broom, a suspicious look still on her face. Ling nodded at Nivi. "Go ahead."

Nivi stuck out a hand as if to shake Meng's, but as soon as Meng took it, she expanded her power and nullified the OT. Meng's expression became serious, and she ushered them into the house with a quick pat on each of their backs.

"Wait," Ji said. "We have a few others with us." She stepped outside to wave at the car.

Kellan, Ai, and Jorge came into the house, and Meng shut the door behind them. Nivi introduced Ai and Jorge. Ji introduced Kellan, and Ling paused with a strange expression before shaking his hand. Meng stared at Kellan's face then glanced sidelong at Ling, who didn't return her gaze. There was definitely something going on here, Nivi was sure of it.

"You must all be tired," Ling said. "You're welcome to rest in our room or our guest room. Actually, it used to be Nivi's room."

"You can use it," Nivi said. "I slept a good amount in the car, but Mom and Kellan probably need to rest."

"We slept enough too," Ai said, indicating themself and Jorge.

"Would you like some tea and breakfast then?" Ling asked.

They nodded enthusiastically. Meng led Ji to Nivi's old room and set up Kellan in her and Ling's room while Ling made tea and warmed some steamed buns filled with meat and veggies.

While they ate, Nivi kept thinking about how Ling and Meng had reacted to meeting Kellan. Had they actually recognized him, or had it been in her head? And then another thought struck her; she had nullified the OT on all of them except one person. Kellan. She was pretty sure the OT had been used on him as well, based on what he had said earlier when Ai asked if he wanted to stay with his bookstore and have his memory wiped. *Not again.* If she nullified the OT on him, would he be able to explain all the strange looks her family had been giving him?

Maybe she should wait to ask her mother first, give Ji the chance to tell her what was going on. Maybe there was a good reason they were reacting the way they were. She should give her grandmother and Meng the same opportunity to be open with her. Based on Ling's history of secrecy, she doubted that route would lead to much, but still, Nivi would give her the chance. She wanted to repair their relationship and work on having open communication with them all. And then, if all that failed, she'd nullify the OT on Kellan.

Lost in these thoughts, Nivi barely heard Ai and Jorge's conversation with Meng and Ling. Twenty minutes passed, then a figure appeared from the hall in the kitchen doorway, startling Nivi in her seat.

"Are you all right?" Jorge asked, instantly turning away from the conversation.

The kitchen light caught the gray streak in Ji's hair as she stepped forward. Of course, it was just her mother. Who else would it be? *Kellan. And all the answers hidden by the OT.* Nivi's heart raced. What was she afraid of? She'd been through worse—losing her parents and her memories at age four, and then losing her family again soon after finding them. The mystery of why Ji, Ling, and Meng seemed to know Kellan shouldn't be too much to bear. But something in her gut constricted further, a deep seed of dread telling her to let things be, to refrain from digging for answers.

Jorge followed Nivi's gaze to the kitchen doorway. "Did you sleep enough, Mrs. Dawan?"

She smiled. "Yes. My healing powers help restore my energy faster. I'm sure Kellan will be a while longer."

"Then this will be a good time to catch up on some Shifter matters," Meng said. She indicated an empty chair for Ji to sit. When Ji was settled, Meng continued, leaning forward conspiratorially. "Iris was here."

"Who's—" Ai began before Jorge nudged them with an elbow. His expression seemed to say, *We can ask our questions later.*

Nivi's mouth dropped open, and across the table so had Ji's. Before she could voice the jumble of questions going through her mind—*what, how, why*—Meng explained.

"She said the amount of power she had absorbed from Davis was killing her, so she was trying to give the powers back to the people Davis took them from. She seemed to be on a mission to redeem herself."

"Did you believe her?" Ji said.

Ling and Meng exchanged a glance, seemingly unsure how to answer.

"Where is she now?" Nivi blurted.

She winced at the desperation and fear in her voice. It made her seem so weak, but the thought of Iris here dredged up all her old anxieties. And Davis! They didn't know yet that she had seen him. She had to tell them. She caught Ai and Jorge watching her, *judging* her. Just as she was starting to make friends, she was going to ruin it with her displays of emotional weakness. She forced herself to calm her facial muscles and still her fidgeting hands while her heart rattled on.

Ling's response didn't help her anxiety. "We don't know. We last saw her on the cliffside as we were walking back to the house."

"And there's something else," Meng cut in. "Something in the forest."

"Is it the goo?" Ai said, ignoring another elbow jab from Jorge.

Ling and Meng both looked surprised by Ai's question, and Ai made Jorge explain his memories.

"I think they must be one and the same," Meng said. She stood up. "But it has definitely grown. We should go now before it gets light outside. Nivi, you come with Ling and me. Your powers may be able to help. Ji, you stay here with Ai and Jorge. Answer any questions they have." She turned to Ai and Jorge. "I apologize for my brusqueness, but we may be short on time."

Ai seemed about to protest, but Jorge jumped in. "We understand."

Ling stood up. "Let's go."

"Wait," Nivi said. "I saw Davis. He's alive and he was speaking for pro-integration at Kellan's bookstore. And he's a *Static*."

Meng's eyebrows rose but quickly relaxed as she seemed to determine something.

"If he's a Static, he must've survived after Iris used the transfer stone. She didn't seem to think he had. Where is he now?"

"He was detained by Shifter police," Ai said.

"If that's the case," Ling said, "we can worry about him later. Right now, we have to go."

Nivi didn't have time to protest as Ling and Meng put on their shoes and grabbed their cardigans from a rack by the door before heading out. Were those matching gray knit sweaters? A quick survey of the living room revealed a basket of yarn and knitting needles with the same color of yarn on top. Which one of them had started knitting? Bemused, she gave a brief wave to Ji, Ai, and Jorge, pulled on her sweatshirt and shoes, and followed Ling and Meng out into the still dark and foggy morning. Just as they started down the sidewalk, the front door opened again and a figure ran out. It was Kellan.

"Wait up," he said, jogging over. "I'm coming with you."

Nivi's stomach jumped. She was hoping she'd get a moment to talk to Ling and Meng alone, but she couldn't ask them how they knew Kellan right in front of him. That'd be so awkward.

"That's not a good idea," Meng said.

"I'm the only one without an aura," Kellan said. "And I'm a sprinter. If you get caught, I can run away and warn the others."

Meng pursed her lips but didn't push the matter, and they continued on in silence.

The fog provided a comforting, if wet, blanket of obscurity as they walked through town. Empty streets stretched into the haze, and Nivi didn't sense any other Shifters around, but who knew if Static eyes might be lurking behind drawn curtains. If Statics and Shifters had teamed up for pro-integration at Kellan's bookstore, couldn't the same be true, even if counterintuitive, for the anti-integration activists?

Even with the cover of fog, Nivi felt safer when they entered the forest. So funny, looking back, how scared she'd been to go into the forest that night with Amber last year. That felt like so long ago. She'd been a different person living a different life then.

Meng produced a flashlight from what must've been a deep pocket in her cardigan and led the way to an abandoned road, the location of Nivi's childhood home. The home where Davis had killed her father. The home that had burned down before Meng and Ling had wiped her memories. Fury kindled in her chest, but she smothered it, soothing herself with the knowledge that Davis had been detained. As for Meng and Ling, they had been trying to keep her safe. Even though it didn't feel good, it had been for the best.

This must've been where Jorge had lived as well. They had been neighbors, and they might've been friends earlier too. A sense of disappointment crept into her mind for these missed opportunities, but she reminded herself that if she had continued to live on Redwood Road, she wouldn't have met Amber, although she and

Amber had also been separated in the end. She stopped that train of thought.

Meng waved Nivi over and pointed her flashlight to the left of the dirt road.

"What is it?" Nivi whispered.

The flashlight illuminated a smooth piece of land that looked like a plot for a house. Too smooth. Not a shrub or piece of grass on the ground. And the flashlight was reflecting off the dirt like a mirror. Then it *moved*. Ever so slightly, a sluggish rippling of water. Meng clicked off the flashlight, but a silver glow remained where the surface rippled. At the edges of the smooth ground, glowing silver tendrils retreated from Meng's feet, illuminating her face in a soft light. Meng took a step forward and the tendrils retracted farther.

The goo, Jorge had called it. "What does it do?" Nivi said.

"We're not sure," Meng said. "But I can feel it. It feels like—"

"Our powers," Nivi finished. She could feel that thrum of energy below the surface. "But why is it here? Where did it come from?"

"That's what we need to figure out," Ling said. "That might give us the answer to how to stop its spread."

Nivi stared at the gelatinous silver pool as if she could see through it. That silvery swirling glow. Her mind drifted to the night Amber had taken her to the transfer stone cave. That's what the silvery swirl reminded her of.

"The transfer stones," she said.

Meng and Ling looked at her.

"This pool, it reminds me of what the transfer stones look like inside."

"The transfer stones," Ling repeated thoughtfully.

"Could their use have created a disturbance in the magic balance?" Meng said. "We're probably somewhere above the transfer stone mine right now."

Nivi mentally followed the path she and Amber had taken into the cliffside tunnel all those months ago. They had gone a good distance underground, so it was plausible they had ended up under Redwood Road.

"What does it mean?" Kellan said.

Ling approached the edge next to Meng and the tendrils retracted even more. "It means whatever this is will continue to spread until the balance is restored."

As if on cue, a creaking groan sounded from a tree at the edge of the pool nearest them. Luminous silver slopped around the base of the trunk. The tree shuddered, scattering pine needles like raindrops over the gelatinous surface, bobbed, and slowly sank. Before long, the entire tree had disappeared into the depths of the pool. A faint tree-shaped glow lingered on the surface before fading out altogether, leaving a darkness that Nivi could feel. It pulled at her like the vertigo of standing on the edge of a cliff. It wanted her. It wanted to consume.

"Nivi," Meng said, pointing at a silvery tendril at the pool's edge. Nivi tore her gaze away from where the tree had been. "Can you see if you can nullify this?" Meng must've seen the horror on Nivi's face because she quickly added, "You don't have to touch it. Just try from where you are."

That was a relief. The thought of touching those ravenous, crawling tendrils with her bare hands made her shudder. She tried to clear her mind of being engulfed alive and suffocated in jelly. Focusing on the tendrils at the pool's edge, she extended the warmth from her chest into her hands and feet. Hot blood pulsed in her veins, igniting small sparks above her skin that burst into flames. The sparks floated into the air and surrounded her body in a bubble-thin sphere of fire. She increased the size of the sphere until the edge touched one of the silver tendrils. The tendril retracted. It was working! She focused her energy into her fire sphere, increasing the pressure of her powers against the magic of the tendrils. She could feel the silver resisting, but it was weakening, losing its hold on the ground before her.

Nivi stepped forward, her confidence building in stride with the retreat of the silver. The front edge of her fire sphere, an iridescent bubble of red and orange, wavered where it touched the pool's edge. She took another step forward, and the resistance increased. Sweat pricked her brow as she put her hands out before her and pushed more of her power through her body and into the sphere. The surface of the sphere rippled violently, the waves increasing in size and frequency. It was becoming unstable.

A silver tendril poked into Nivi's protective bubble. That wasn't supposed to happen. Her powers prevented attacks by all magical forces, unless... Her memory flashed back to her fight against Davis when one of his tentacles had whipped through her defenses and knocked her to the ground. His magic had been too strong.

Summoning the rest of her power, she doubled down on her efforts against the silver. The effort turned her glowing red veins white hot. At first, the invading tendril shrunk back, but then it began to advance again. Panic built in her chest as the tendril shot toward her foot and wrapped around her ankle, cool and surprisingly firm. And then it began to feed, not on her flesh but on her mind. A cold sensation ran across her scalp like icy claws dragging across her skin. At the same time, her foot began to sink into a puddle of silver that had formed beneath it. She stifled a scream and struggled to pull her foot out of the horrific puddle.

The suction was too great. It seemed the more she struggled, the faster her foot sank. She stopped struggling, but the silver continued to engulf her. The icy claws moved from her head to the back of her neck and across her throat. She fell to her knees, and Kellan and Ling lunged forward to catch her.

No! Stay back! Nivi tried to shout, but the cold had reached her neck, imprisoning her vocal cords. Kellan and Ling were too close. The silver was going to get them too.

Drained, Nivi fell toward the ground, her fall broken by Kellan's and Ling's arms. Suddenly, a white light erupted from Ling, diaphanous strings that flowed into the silver puddle at Nivi's feet. The tendril released Nivi's ankle, and the puddle retreated into the main pool of silver. Ling collapsed alongside Nivi.

The edge of the pool glowed brightly, releasing the strings into the air where they floated up into the sky and dissipated like spider silk on a breeze. Nivi tried one last time to manifest her powers against the silver. A tepid warmth trickled down her arms, and a brief surge of heat emitted from where Kellan held her. Her nullification efforts faded there, failing to advance past her hands. The glow of her veins and the silver vanished, plunging Nivi's vision into darkness as her eyes readjusted. Her heart thudded in her ears from her exertion, and a cold sweat covered her entire body.

Meng ran over, sweeping her flashlight over the ground. No glowing. No movement. Nivi's powers had worked. Thank goodness, they had worked. Still, the feeling of those icy claws lingered on her skin—and deeper. A chill was settling into her veins, coursing through her body.

She looked at Ling and realized something was wrong.

"It—it took my powers," Ling said weakly.

Ling's aura... was *gone*. She was a Static, again.

Meng dropped to Ling's side and helped her sit up.

Nivi turned her head from where she lay on the ground. It was all she could manage to do. Meng shone her flashlight on the silver. The tendrils were gone, and the edge of the pool had pulled back by a noticeable amount.

"Did Nivi nullify the silver?" Meng said.

"Or was it the taking of my powers?" Ling said.

Nullify. Silver. Powers. Meng and Ling's words sounded so far away.

Kellan was still kneeling on the ground, shaking his head. Overhead, the sky began to lighten into rosy shades of dawn.

He finally stood, pointing at Ling with a surprisingly hostile tone. "*You*. You kept *her* from me."

Ling went rigid, her eyes briefly rounded as if some realization had dawned on her before her gaze landed on Nivi and softened into... fear? Regret?

Kellan rubbed a hand over his mouth and chin, his long fingers surprisingly like Nivi's own. Morning light streamed in through the tree branches, catching Kellan's light brown eyes in its glow. How light his eyes were. Her own eyes were of a similarly light brown shade, much lighter than her mother's and father's. She had always wondered how that happened to be. A distant ancestor with lighter eyes, perhaps? Genetics were funny that way.

Kellan moved toward Nivi, a devastated expression creasing his glistening eyes. He opened his mouth and closed it. His full lips pressed together and came apart, full lips with a sharp Cupid's bow that mirrored her own. All of a sudden, Nivi couldn't breathe, as if the air had thickened into a gel around her.

Kellan neared her, his mouth moving with no sound, but Nivi heard what he said nevertheless. *My... daughter.*

Cold plunged into Nivi's heart, and her vision darkened. Her last nullification efforts. She had nullified something on Kellan. She had nullified... the OT.

Somewhere in the distance, voices called out, footsteps followed, vague sounds reaching out in the haze of her mind, but she was too far away.

IRIS

UNKNOWN LOCATION

IRIS REGAINED CONSCIOUSNESS IN a bright hallway. Two guards held her by the upper arms, carrying her to a set of double doors. Squinting, she looked around as the fog of sleepiness lifted. She was in a prison, passing empty cells on both sides. She lifted her head and planted her dragging feet flat on the ground.

"I can walk," she said.

The guards loosened their grip on her arms but continued to guide her through the double doors into another corridor of cells. The first few cells were empty, but just up ahead she saw movement. Prisoners approached their glass walls to watch her approach. There were two girls on the right and a boy on the left who all appeared to be teenagers.

Before they reached the first inhabited cell, the doors behind them opened and footsteps approached. The guards stopped and turned Iris around to greet the newcomer. It was Ariana Peters. She must've taken charge after Davis's attempted coup. This was

Iris's chance to redeem herself, to emerge as the savior of the Shifter Council.

"The police found this one wandering in Yuras without a camouflage stone as they were doing a final sweep through," the female guard said.

A look of amazement crossed Ariana's face. "Iris Bai? *Also* back from the dead?"

Also? Who else had Ariana seen? Iris cleared her throat, trying to seem calm. "Hello, Ariana. It's so good to see you. Is it Senator Peters now?"

"Chairperson, actually."

"I see." Iris's response came out a little flat, but she didn't know how she should respond. Was she supposed to congratulate Ariana on a position she hadn't won? A position she'd ascended to by a stroke of luck—or misfortune, depending on who one asked?

Ariana must have expected a different response because a frown flickered across her lips, but she quickly reverted to a pleasant demeanor.

"It's so wonderful to see you alive. We all owe you many thanks for stopping Davis when you did."

"Of course. I was happy to do what I could." Iris looked back at her restraints. "But it seems there's been a misunderstanding."

"I'm sorry about that. After everything that's happened, we have to take extra precautions. I must ask, where have you been all this time?"

"I'm... not sure. After Davis... drowned, I was confused and in and out of consciousness." It wasn't a total lie. Due to the overwhelming powers, she had suffered several blackout spells that she gauged lasted from days to weeks at a time. "I only recently washed ashore in Yuras where the Shifter police found me."

Ariana arched an eyebrow. "And you said Davis *drowned*?"

"I did," Iris murmured with downcast eyes. She hoped Ariana wasn't going to prod deeper into that sore memory or demand proof.

Ariana approached her, and Iris readied her wrists to be released, but Ariana didn't stop. She passed Iris and continued down the hall, past the three teenagers, and stopped in front of a cell just past the second girl.

"I see," she said in a mimic of Iris's previous response.

The guards grabbed Iris's arms and followed Ariana. Something was wrong. Why weren't they freeing her? She almost blurted out that she had a bag of hidden transfer stones ready to return the powers, but the words caught in her throat as they halted in front of the next cell. Someone sat on a bed by the cell's left wall. She gasped.

It was Davis. He was *alive*!

Davis shot to his feet when he saw Iris. Ariana motioned to the guards, and they took Iris into the cell across from Davis. So much emotion and confusion muddled her mind and twisted her stomach that she didn't resist. Once the guards had locked the door, her restraints dissipated.

Ariana stepped up to Iris's glass wall. "What happened to Davis's power?"

Should she tell Ariana her plans for redemption? About the transfer stones? It didn't feel right. She couldn't gauge Ariana's intentions.

"I don't know," she finally said.

Ariana was silent for a moment before she seemed to make up her mind about something. "There's a lot that's not making sense." She waved her hand back and forth between Davis's and Iris's cells. "With so many unanswered questions, I have to play things safe. I'll have to investigate your claims, of course. Again, I'm very appreciative of your *attempt* to stop Davis when you did, but I've worked hard to create a safe system for our community since then, and I can't have you stirring things up, can I?"

Iris didn't respond. She stared at Ariana, torn about whether she was losing her chance to prove herself to the current chairperson, or if she was doing the smart thing by not aligning herself with Ariana. What if she told Ariana about the stones and she confiscated them for herself?

Ariana didn't seem bothered by Iris's stare. She addressed the guards.

"Leave her here until I figure out what to do with her."

With that, she left with the guards.

As soon as Ariana and her guards were out of sight, Iris's legs wobbled. Had she just lost her chance to redeem herself? No, she wouldn't give up. She just needed to find a way out of here.

Her gaze met Davis's. He was *alive*. Alive! That meant she *had* been successful in saving him. She wasn't a murderer after all.

She turned away. New questions and emotions flooded her mind. Why had she cared so much when she'd thought Davis had died? Now that he was alive, she wanted to hate him. *He* was the one who had murdered Chairperson Dawan and made her think she had done it. *He* was the one who had used her to find the transfer stones and then discarded her when he thought he didn't need her anymore. And yet, after everything they'd been through, she still couldn't fully hate him.

Before the transfer stones, she'd respected the work he'd done to promote integration. When she'd wanted to give up politics, he'd been the one to encourage her to continue. Yes, he may have had ulterior motives, but they'd had the same end goal—a world where Shifters and Statics could live openly together. Someone who wanted that couldn't be completely bad.

She paced around her cell, steepling her fingers over the bridge of her nose, trying to hold back tears. They weren't tears of relief. No, they were angry tears. Confused tears. Exasperated tears.

"What's wrong with you?" came that all-too-smug voice from a man who'd always had an effect on others and knew it.

Iris stopped her pacing and looked across the hall. Davis watched her with a quirk to his mouth.

"Damn you, Davis," Iris said in a harsh whisper. "You can't just show up here alive and be all normal."

"Couldn't I say the same about you?"

"Do I *look* like I'm acting normal?"

A slow smile curled Davis's lips as his eyes quickly darted up and down Iris's body.

"You look... like crap."

Iris turned away with a huff. She knew the magic was taking a toll on her body, but did he need to spell it out? That insolent bastard. She was a fool to think he could change even after a near-death experience. But *she* could, and she would make good on her promise to herself to restore all the stolen magic to their legitimate owners.

The curvy teenager to the right of Davis's cell chuckled. "Another couple with an awkward history, it seems."

Heat rose into Iris's cheeks. She quickly resumed her pacing to hide her face.

The girl spoke again. "You're Iris? How do you know Davis?"

So the girl hadn't heard of her, or she didn't remember. She wouldn't put it past Ariana to have used oblivion tincture on as much of the Shifter population as she could.

Iris walked to the far-right corner of her cell, avoiding Davis, to speak directly to the teenager. "And you are?"

"Oh, I'm Vera. Happy to make introductions." She pointed to each person in turn." You already know Davis. That boy next to you is Arav. And Amber is on the other side of me. Welcome to our strange little family. So... Is it true what they said about Davis?"

Iris glanced at the other teenagers. Arav nodded stiffly in greeting. She couldn't really see Amber—the girl would need to press up against the corner of her cell to be visible from where Iris stood. "What did they say?"

"That he used to be chairperson. That he stole Shifter powers." When Iris didn't answer right away, Vera continued, "Not that it matters, since we'll all have no memories of this soon enough, but for the time being, I'd like to piece together my shattered world as much as possible."

A deep sigh came from Davis's cell.

"You don't get to say anything!" Vera snapped. "You lied to us all."

Davis gestured from the corner of Iris's vision, speaking in that suave yet conceited way of his that she hated. Yet, part of him seemed tired and... sad.

"You don't know what you're talking about, little girl. This has been going on for much longer than your, what, fourteen or sixteen years of life?"

Apparently, he'd guessed correctly because Vera scoffed and rolled her eyes.

Iris ignored Davis and focused on Vera. "How do you know *him*?" She waved a dismissive hand toward Davis without looking at him.

Vera sat down facing Iris, her white-blond hair bobbing around her shoulders.

"I guess it doesn't matter if I talk openly about it now," she said with a sigh. "We were part of an underground organization fighting for pro-integration and against the overuse of oblivion tincture. Davis was the head of the Static resistance."

"Oh?" Iris ventured a glance at Davis.

He smirked at her. "Like I've always said, we're fighting for the same thing."

"Everything you heard about Davis is true," Iris shot back to fight the complex emotions that kept trying to rise to the surface. "We were *colleagues* in the Shifter Council."

Vera's throat bobbed, but she seemed to take the information in stride. "Maybe it was a good thing we were caught, then. If anything, it stopped Davis from stealing all our powers."

Davis straightened his white button-up shirt. His suit jacket was draped over the chair at the back of his room. "I wasn't going to steal your powers."

It was Iris's turn to smirk. "Did you forget the way to the mine?"

A hint of red tinged Davis's cheeks. "No," he said, dragging out the word. "I wouldn't have needed the powers if we had been able to implement integration because then we'd all be equal." He stared into her eyes in the sensuous way he'd used to when he'd been exerting his stolen powers over her. His voice dropped in tone and volume, as if he were sharing a moment just with her. "Imagine what we could've accomplished working together."

Iris looked away, unsettled. He had no powers now, so why was her heart fluttering? Even after all this time, was she so easily affected by a pretty face? No, it must just be because she was still so surprised to see him alive.

"You can stop your campaign speeches, Davis," Iris spat, hoping he couldn't see through the unimpressed facade she presented.

She had thought his persuasive words were a result of the allure power he'd stolen from his sister Anna, but it seemed he had a natural ability to charm. It was no wonder he'd become the leader of the Static pro-integration movement in such a short time. But why was he using his tactics now? It must be some kind of ploy.

He simply shrugged and sat back down on his bed, shoulders slumped. His tone sounded surprisingly defeated. "It doesn't matter now."

Iris tried to tune him out, but doubt crept in. Could he be telling the truth? The way he looked and sounded reminded her of their last moments on the San Francisco dock outside the Shifter Council building. At the time, she had been so furious at his betrayal—his insults and refusal to acknowledge how much she'd helped him—that she hadn't considered the deeper implications of their conversation. Due to his father's deception, Davis had thought he'd killed his mother, who had been chairperson at the time. His *pro-integration* mother. How different would things have been if she had survived long enough to enact that change?

She shook away her train of thought. None of that excused Davis's behavior since his youth. *He murdered Chairperson Dawan,* she reminded herself. And just like his father had made him think he was a murderer, Davis had made Iris think she was one too. She began to fume again at the memories. Perseverating on those was a waste of time. She needed to focus. She needed to find a way out of this prison.

The boy in the cell next to her, Arav, started to talk, presumably to Vera or Amber, but Iris wasn't really paying attention while she evaluated her surroundings. Aware of the possibility of hidden cameras, Iris cycled through her variety of less visible secondary powers to see if she could find a weakness in the door or walls. She conjured a sliver of metal that she tried to pass through the edge of the door frame, thinking that if she could get it through, she could make it curve to work the exterior door handle. No matter how thin she made the metal, it stopped at the junction of the door and frame. She tried to dig a hole through the wall of the bathroom. Eventually she stopped caring if there were cameras. She transformed into an ant to walk into the drain and encountered an invisible barrier. Time passed, and she grew weary, the powers sapping her energy. It seemed she was able to transform and conjure magic freely, but none of it had any effect on the cell. It was magically sealed.

"These cells are immune to all Shifter powers. There's no way out," came Davis's voice.

Iris was at the back of her cell, running her fingertips along the grout between stone tiles. She looked back to see Davis watching her. There was no getting around it. If they were going to be stuck here together for a long time, she'd have to talk to him at some point.

She took a deep breath and walked to the glass wall opposite his. "How did you survive?"

"You sound disappointed," he said.

"I'm serious."

He raised an eyebrow. "You... don't remember?" She shook her head. A pink tinge returned to his cheeks. "You put your mouth on mine. You breathed air into me."

Her face heated, mirroring his. She didn't remember that, but it restored faith in herself that she hadn't let him drown, that she had helped him in his time of need.

The snark returned to Davis's voice. "Are you enjoying what you took from me?"

"I don't know what you're talking about."

As if on cue, a tingle of power pricked Iris's skin, the warmth infiltrating her veins and coalescing thickly in her chest like hot tar. Sweat beaded her brow as she fought a sudden urge to gasp for air. This shouldn't be happening. She had returned enough of the excess powers to feel in control for the time being.

Before anyone could notice her change in demeanor, she rushed into the bathroom and closed the door. Turning on the faucet, she tried to steady her breathing. Something poked through the skin on the back of her hands, brightening the vicinity with a flickering red glow. Vermilion bird feathers. Ling. This wasn't good. Why had Ling's power returned to her? What if more powers started returning while she was trapped in this place? Then oblivion tincture would be the least of her worries.

Iris splashed water over her face, the cool liquid calming the excess power enough to stop her from completely transforming. As water dripped down her face, the taste of sea salt entered her mouth, leftover from when Captain Maria and her crew had splashed her with a wave. No, they had *become* the ocean.

Water continued to run from the faucet as an idea began to form. Vera had said this place was immune to all Shifter magic, but no Shifter had been able to *become* an element before. Could this be her way out? Maria had said they had a connection to her, that they could feel her calling to them. She touched the running water and felt for that connection, calling out through the water. *I'm here. I'm here. I'm here.*

The effort combined with the excess magic in her system exhausted her. She needed to lie down. She turned off the water and went to bed. Her eyes drifted close, and her mind wandered off to the Yuras forest. Silver gelatinous pools surrounded her, sucking down trees and houses in their wake. Tendrils of silver reached for her feet, beckoning her to enter their depths. One of the tendrils touched her foot, cold and wet like water.

Iris started awake, damp with sweat. She sat up and used the edge of her sleeve to wipe her face.

"Bad dreams?"

Davis lay on the floor at the front of his cell, one leg bent and the other crossed over his knee, his hands behind his head as if he were watching clouds in the sky.

Iris sat up straight and changed the subject, hoping her tone was as judgmental as possible. "Why are you on the floor?"

He answered in that nonchalant way of his. "I got bored on my bed. I needed a change of scenery."

"Right..."

Again Iris's chest tightened, ruining her attempt to act naturally. She curled over her lap with her arms crossed over her stomach, alternating between shallow and deep breaths until the feeling passed. When she was able to raise her head again, Davis was still lying on the ground, but he had turned his head to look at her.

"It's getting to you, isn't it?"

"I don't—know what you mean," Iris said, struggling through her sentence.

"You know, I used to get nightmares too. A forest with glistening silver pools."

How did he know?

He must've read the shock on her face. "Ahh, so it wasn't just me. It's all that…" Davis sat up and lowered his voice. He made a circular motion over his chest with one hand. *"Power."*

Iris stood slowly and walked up to her cell's glass wall and sat down opposite Davis. She glanced over at Vera, Arav, and Amber's cells, but she didn't hear anything or see any movement. Would it matter if they heard them? Still, it was best to be cautious.

"Tell me what you know," Iris said.

Davis propped his elbows on his knees and his chin on his hands in a way that made him look like an innocent child. *Innocent, hah!*

"I don't know anything." Even his voice exuded innocence.

His posture, his expressions, his voice. He really had a way of manipulating people. Iris turned her face, annoyed. They sat silently for a few moments until Davis let out a somewhat dramatic sigh before he spoke again.

"Look, I want to thank you. And… apologize."

He sounded earnest. Was he? No, it had to be more manipulation. Iris kept her head turned away.

"You don't believe me."

Iris turned to glare at Davis. "Why should I?"

Davis seemed unbothered. "I don't blame you. I wouldn't trust me if I were you either. I was never a good kid. I could blame my father, but..." He shrugged. "At some point, I have to take responsibility for my own actions."

Was he *opening up* to her? No. This was just like when he first told her about his dying mother and the transfer stones. She wouldn't be fooled by him again.

Davis continued as if he were happy to talk whether Iris listened or not. "I won't lie. When my mother first gave me her powers, it was a rush. I'd never felt anything like it before, and I wanted more. But with each power I took, there was something else beneath it all, something dark and festering. That's when the dreams started. That glowing silver pool... It's going to ask you to do things, not with words, but you'll just know. You'll feel it like it's your own will. You'll think it's your own thoughts."

Iris shook her head. "I don't feel or think anything except wanting to be rid of all the power and make amends. And thanks to you, there's a lot of amending to do."

Davis leaned back, propping himself up on his hands, and chuckled softly. "I wasn't as strong as you. I couldn't fight it. I didn't want to fight it. I was so angry about so many things. It's thanks to you that the spell was broken. When you took all that power from me, I could finally think clearly for the first time. I discovered I had a natural ability to lead. I didn't need powers for that. My father is long dead, and it's time I stopped trying to get his approval. I can do better, and that means continuing what my mother started." Again he looked defeated. "But it's over now. So I thank you for giving me this chance, for as long as it lasted. Even if they wipe my memories, I still had the chance to be a better person because of you."

Iris didn't know what to say. Davis didn't seem to have an agenda. He was just... talking, like he was getting something off his chest. But all that hurt and betrayal didn't just go away. All his past evil deeds didn't just go away. The pit of anger still sat solidly in her stomach just waiting for a moment to gush forth. Was this the dark, festering feeling Davis had mentioned? Or just a way for Davis to clear himself of blame?

A realization hit her, one she tried to push away and prevent from taking hold, but it clung to her mind like wet dog fur: *She* was the one at fault. She'd been blaming Davis for everything, for her own actions and her own feelings, but it was more complicated than that. Davis had been influenced by the overwhelming amount of magic in his system after using the transfer stones, and she knew what he'd felt because she felt its influence now. But he hadn't been completely under its control, just like she hadn't been completely under Davis's control. She had still been able to live her own life and make her own decisions. She had wanted to let him influence her, so she could have an excuse to do things she wouldn't have been brave enough to do herself. Having someone to blame took away responsibility so she wouldn't be at fault.

That was the old her. She was reborn, ready to take control of her life and accept responsibility, to have agency in her actions and her future. She had attempted one path, had climbed to the peak of the mountain only to fall to the literal bottom of the ocean, but she was ready to rise from the depths. If she could change, did that mean Davis could as well? And was it really changing or just shifting more toward a side of themselves that had been there all along? The good things about Davis were true as well as the bad. They weren't mutually exclusive. Could he have achieved what he had without all the stealing? Like her, he had probably needed something to give him the confidence and permission to push for what he wanted. For him it had been the stones and powers. For her, it had been Davis.

Davis watched Iris mulling through her thoughts, and she felt an urge to reply to his soliloquy.

She forced the words out. "I'm glad you're a *better* person now."

Davis laughed. "I didn't say I'm a better person, just that I had the chance to be one."

That took Iris aback. Maybe he had changed, or at least was really trying to.

From her tub of water, Vera clapped loudly and slowly. "Bravo. What a moving speech." Her tone was disingenuous. "If you're both finished, some of us are trying to get some rest before our brains are turned to mush."

Davis smirked and turned to Iris with a wink. Iris kept her expression as neutral as possible and got up to return to her bed. She didn't want to feel a connection to Davis. She didn't need his company or for him to commiserate with her. She just wanted to lie down before the powers started to kindle inside her again. But before she could return to bed, she needed to try to contact Maria and her crew again.

In the bathroom, she turned on the faucet and touched the water, sending her thoughts through the cool stream. *Where are you? I need your help. Please find me.* The effort made her dizzy, and she clutched the sides of the bathroom sink before turning off the water. On second thought, maybe they would need a point of entry. She turned the faucet back on just enough so that it dripped and went to bed.

As soon as her eyes closed, the silver pool in the forest returned. It drew her closer and closer, the pine trees at its border shuddering at its pull. A glowing tendril reached for her foot and wrapped itself around her exposed skin. Its touch was so cold, the chill running straight to that pit of anger she kept hidden deep inside. It pried at the stone walls, trying to let loose the fury. *Davis is the enemy. He must be destroyed.* No. She didn't want to kill anyone. She wouldn't. Maybe her past actions made her as bad as Davis, but like he'd said, they had the chance to be better people. When the silver tendrils made no progress on releasing her anger, they continued on, crawling up her body, submerging her flesh and thoughts, and when they reached her head, they spoke.

Iris. We're here.

Iris's eyes fluttered open. How long had it been? She sat up in bed and glanced at the other cells. Everything was quiet. The overhead lights had dimmed.

That dream. The silver called to her in the same way that Maria and her crew had. Were they all connected through the transfer stones? Could the silver have something to do with Ling's power returning to her?

Then she remembered the faucet. She got up quickly and went to the bathroom. The water still dripped in the sink, but the bathroom was otherwise empty. She sighed and went back to sit on the bed. It was too much to hope for. Her only option for escape would have to be some kind of surprise attack. If Ariana didn't suspect her extra powers, maybe Iris could unleash them when the chairperson came to use the oblivion tincture. But there were probably protections in place that would keep Iris from using her powers, otherwise others would have escaped before. Maybe she could strike some kind of deal with Ariana? She could bargain with the transfer stones.

The drip drip drip of water continued in the bathroom. How long should she leave the water on? It sounded louder. More like gushing—and splashing.

Water pooled out from the bathroom floor into the cell. A moment of panic flashed through Iris. The pipes must have burst. Before she could think of what to do next, the water rose up from the ground in spiraling columns and formed three aqueous figures. Their features solidified, and then there they were: Captain Maria Akayux and her crewmates Shawn Murphy and Alek Ivanov.

"You came," Iris breathed.

"It was a little tricky navigating those pipes," Maria said, "but once we allowed ourselves to just follow your signal, the water found the path of least resistance." She looked around. "What is this place?"

"A prison," Iris said. "I'll explain later. We need to leave before they come back and arrest you too."

"Let them try," Alek scoffed. Iris followed his gaze and noted the drain on the ground in the middle of the room. Would escape really be that easy?

A commotion erupted from the other cells as Davis, Vera, Arav, and Amber rushed to their respective windows to watch.

"Uh... What? How?" Vera said.

Davis crossed his arms, the slight upward curve of his lips again eliciting an annoying fluttering in her chest. "Impressive."

Arav just blinked, mouth ajar.

"Let's go," Maria said.

"How do you... do I..." *Become water.* She had seen them do it, so she knew it was possible, but it still seemed impossible for her to do it too.

"It's easy," Shawn said, his blue eyes shimmering like the ocean on a sunny day. "You already contacted us. You feel our connection."

Iris shook her head, not understanding. How did the connection she felt with them translate into turning herself into water?

"We already *are* water," Maria said, her long, black hair beginning to sway like the ocean waves. "It is our life force. Our essence. All you have to do is accept that is what you are."

"I think I need step-by-step instructions," Iris said.

Alek laughed, his bushy beard rippling like Maria's hair. "You feel that tug? That connection?"

Iris nodded.

"Focus on that. Do you feel it moving?"

Iris focused on the connection that had called them to her. Deep in her chest, the warmth, the pull. Sure enough, it moved. It was fluid, waves and currents, ready to assume any form or flow freely.

"Good," Alek said. "Follow the movement. Captain will lead us."

Iris swayed with the connection, not just her body, but her awareness. Maria, Alek, and Shawn's skin became translucent, a thinning membrane under which water rippled. Iris's hair moved back and forth against her back, and the skin on her hands also became translucent. It was working!

"Wait!" a voice shouted behind her. Iris turned and saw Arav banging against the glass panel between their cells. "Don't leave us! Take us with you!"

Was it possible to take others with them? No, they didn't have the same connection. It must have something to do with the transfer stones and the mix of powers they all had in their bodies. Iris turned back to the group, her feet puddling, letting Maria lead her to the drain.

Arav continued to bang on the panel. "Please!"

The desperation in his voice caused a pang in her heart. If she wanted to prove to herself that she wasn't a monster, shouldn't she do her best to help others as well? Once she figured out what happened with Ling's powers, she'd come back for all of them, even Davis.

Before she could respond to Arav, her body disintegrated into a pool of water. Maria and her crew splashed to the floor around her, and together they flowed through the drain in the floor.

Cool darkness enveloped her, chalky minerals, the sharp tang of metals, rushing and trickling. They surrounded her and became her as she flowed through the drainage pipes as one with Maria and her crew.

In that liquid form, she was the budding youth of spring and the eternal nurturer of life. She rushed forward, longing to break free from the rigidity of the pipe. Time moved around her, and she moved through time, aware but unconcerned with its constraints.

A pinpoint of light appeared ahead. It grew and grew and soon they burst out of the pipe, through the air, and into the ocean. Brine and bubbles embraced her, and they were one, gliding through the waves.

A pressure pulled her from the ocean. She didn't want to leave this oneness, but she flew up through the air, crashing over a cliff and onto land. The freedom of form faded away, and she was again a person, on her hands and knees on the ground. Water dripped from her body and then simultaneously absorbed into her and evaporated away. She felt the urge to cough and sputter even though no water choked her lungs. Her body shook, overwhelmed by the exhilaration and perspective change. Maria, Alek, and Shawn stood in a semicircle around her, calm and collected.

"I've never felt anything like that. How did you do it?" Iris asked Maria. "How did you tear us away from that freedom?"

Maria looked out at the sea. Waves reflected in her dark irises, which undulated as if they were still liquid.

"Water... It's a great and beautiful power. We would cease to exist without it. But when your people have been enslaved and had their identity stripped away, not even water can coax you to remain in its confines, no matter how fluid and vast they may seem." Without waiting for Iris to respond, she turned and walked toward the forest. Shawn and Alek followed her. "Come. There's something you have to see."

Iris got to her feet and rushed after the trio. They entered the forest, and she soon realized they were on the same dirt road she had visited previously with Ling and Meng. All around them were the signs of Meng's sloppy transformation—skid marks in the dirt and slashes oozing sap in the bark of several trees. Up ahead, there was a clearing so smooth and devoid of plants and trees that it looked like ice, but as they neared, it began to ripple and glow. It was the silver gel-like substance that had swallowed an entire abandoned home. The silver pool of her dreams.

They stopped a few feet from the edge of the pool, and Maria turned to Iris, the look in her eyes the same far-off look she had when gazing out to sea.

"This thing speaks to us. You feel it too. It wants to expand, to consume. It doesn't want us here. It fears us." She sighed, and her eyes focused on Iris. "You may see magic as a gift. I can see how it can be addicting, the thrill and the power, but it has also derailed our lives in the past months and taken us from our jobs and community." She walked up to the pool's edge and kneeled. "The closer I get, the more resistance I feel. The pool is trying to push me away. I wonder what'll happen if I touch it."

A sudden irrational fear filled Iris. She needed to get Maria away from the pool or something terrible would happen. She lunged forward to grab Maria's arm, but she was too late. Maria knelt and touched a finger to the edge of the pool.

The silver didn't rise to engulf Maria like it had the abandoned house. Instead, it shrank back, but not fast enough to avoid her touch. A white glow emanated from her hand, a plume of hazy white, wafting into the air. The white threads floated toward Iris and then slammed into her. She gasped and leaned over, dizziness causing the world to spin. Blinking rapidly to clear her vision, she saw Maria shaking her head, clearly dazed. Alek bent over to help Maria, getting too close to the pool.

"Stop!" Iris yelled, holding up a hand.

Alek paused his descent and looked up with a questioning gaze.

"It's this silver," Maria said. "It's channeling its fear to her. As long as we maintain this power, it grows stronger. It doesn't want us touching it; that's why it doesn't want us here."

Through her scrambled thoughts, Iris tried to make sense of what had just happened. Maria had touched the pool and then Iris had felt powers return to her. Maria no longer had an aura. Why would the silver return the powers to Iris? The one thing that was clear was that she now had too much power again. Keeling over with nausea, she stumbled forward to the edge of the pool, unable to control her body even as the silver in her mind tried to push her away. Her head spun, and she dropped to her hands and knees. The tips of her fingers dipped into the cool, viscous substance.

A silver glow pulsed around her fingers. The powers pulled through her body, like threads through her tissues, and coalesced above her hand in a faint white plume, just like they had with

Maria. Iris could feel her head clearing, her chest expanding, her body stabilizing. The powers were leaving her. They were *leaving* her! She jerked her hand away from the pool before she lost all of them.

"It's shrinking back," Alek said, still bent over by the pool but fortunately not touching it.

The edge of the pool retreated by a few inches—not a lot but still a noticeable amount. Iris sat back on her heels. Now that her mind was clearer, she could think. Maria had said the silver was speaking to her, telling her to stay away. When Maria had touched the silver, her powers had gone back to Iris. When Iris had touched it, where had her powers gone?

"We're restoring the balance," Maria said. "These powers never belonged to us."

The balance. Of course. This pool must have formed as a result of transferring magic. Which meant—her stomach sank—that her powers had gone back to Davis.

"My powers went back to the person who started all of this," she explained. "He was in the prison cell across from me. I doubt he'll return the powers voluntarily. Instead, he'll go on to wreak havoc on both our worlds. We'll have to bring him here by force to make sure he touches the pool. We'll have to go back to the prison."

Davis had claimed he was trying to change, but how could she trust him? As soon as the powers returned to him, he'd be under the same influence he claimed had made him unable to think for himself before.

"We can't go back the way we came," Alek said. "Without the captain's powers, we can't become water anymore."

"You can do more than you think," Maria said. "Maybe it won't be exactly the same, but each of you has multiple powers you can try to combine into your own formations."

Iris looked at Maria with awe. "How do you know this?"

"I could feel how the powers interacted within me. I'm assuming it's the same for all of you."

In the past months, Iris had been so focused on surviving the excess of powers in her system that she hadn't stopped to consider how the powers could be used together. But Maria's words made sense. Shifters had been combining powers to create all sorts of things, such as camouflage stones, oblivion tincture, and even transfer stones. If Davis had figured this out earlier, he would've been unstoppable. Would he be able to figure it out now?

"We have to go back to the prison right away," Iris said. "We don't have time to experiment, so I'll have to give you some powers back first so you can lead us."

Maria took a deep breath. "All right."

Iris reached into her hidden pocket and brought out a transfer stone. It illuminated in her hand as she brought it toward Maria, ready to transfer her powers, and her veins tingled like she was plunging her hands into hot water. But she hesitated. It felt wrong to use a transfer stone if it had been the transfer of magic that had created the imbalance and thus the silver pool. But how else would she be able to give Maria some powers? She didn't have another choice if they were to get to the prison as soon as possible.

She looked down at the stone. Its gray color had changed to a swirling blue. It looked like... water. The water power Iris had been preparing to transfer—she couldn't feel it in her body anymore. Had it gone into the stone? How had she been unaware that the stones could store powers as well as transfer them?

A faint tremor shook the ground below them.

"Did you feel that?" Alek said.

"You guys..." Shawn said, pointing at the pool.

At the center of the pool, bubbles emerged, small at first like those in a glass of champagne, but larger ones soon followed. They popped at the surface with a sickening wet belch, sending ripples to the shore. The swells grew, glowing with internal silver light that shone brighter and brighter, and a fracture line shot out from the edge of the pool. Shawn jumped back from the fissure.

Again, the ground rumbled. Nearby trees rustled, and pine needles scattered over their heads.

"I think we need to leave," Iris said.

"Good idea," Maria said.

They all backed away from the turbulent pool, down the dirt road in the direction they had come. The shaking increased.

A loud crack!

The fissure split apart and raced toward them, zigzagging through the groaning earth. From within the crevice, silver oozed forth, slurping and suctioning its way onto the road. Some puddled around the base of a large pine tree, which shook at its touch. It creaked and groaned, tipping onto its side in a slow descent before succumbing to the silver.

"It's coming too fast," Maria said.

Iris thought quickly. If a magical imbalance gave the silver strength, it must've been her use of the transfer stone that had caused this earthquake. She threw the activated stone into the crack where it sank into the silver. The water powers rushed back to Iris in diaphanous white ribbons of light, the head rush disorienting. The rumbling slowed but the ground still shook.

"We need to return more power," Maria said, pointing at Alek who was the next closest to the encroaching crevice. He immediately responded to her unspoken command and dropped to touch the substance.

More white haze rushed into Iris, knocking the air out of her. Once more, it put her at a dangerous level of power, and before she could crumble under the weight of it, she ran to a silver tentacle that was working its way out of the crack and touched it, sending more power back to Davis. She shuddered as her power levels returned to a more manageable level and quickly withdrew her hand before more could leave her. Sitting on the ground, she scooted away from the silver, but it didn't follow her. Instead, the tentacle retracted into the crevice and out of sight. The ground stopped trembling, and the fissure in the ground stopped advancing.

"It worked," Alek breathed.

Shawn stepped toward the shrinking pool of silver, his hands outstretched.

"Stop," Iris said, catching her breath. "Keep your powers for now. I'll need your help."

Who knew what Davis would be up to now that he had multiple powers back? Would she and Shawn be enough to force him back here?

Maria walked over to Iris and helped her to her feet.

"Do you have any more of those stones?" Maria asked.

"We can't use them," Iris said, the realization hitting her as she spoke. "You saw what just happened. Transfer stone use increases the magical imbalance, which seems to make the silver stronger."

"I don't want to use them." Maria held out a hand. "I want to check something." Iris put a hand protectively over her hidden pocket where she kept her stash of stones. Maria huffed impatiently. "You think I gave my powers away just to steal them back? Especially after what just happened? I don't want the earth to swallow us whole."

Reluctantly, Iris took a stone from her pocket and passed it to Maria. "Be careful. Don't activate it. If you touch it to a Shifter, you'll feel a pull... just don't allow yourself to open that door."

Maria examined it, taking her time to turn it over and hold it up to the light. Then she chucked it hard at the pool.

"No!" Iris yelled. "What are you doing?"

She needed that stone. Every single one was precious.

The transfer stone hit the surface of the pool, which wavered with the impact. Silver gel rose up over the stone and glugged it down. For a moment, Iris worried that the pool would rise in another tidal wave of tentacles and ground-splitting tremors, but instead, the silver shrank back even more.

Maria turned to Iris, holding out her hand once more.

"It's part of restoring the balance. We need to give them all back."

Iris retreated a step, shaking her head. Panic built in her chest. A cold, silvery haze clouded her mind, telling her that losing the stones would be like losing herself.

"Not yet," Shawn said. Maria shot him a glare, and he immediately lost his assertiveness, averting his gaze. "Uh, that is, Captain, I believe that should be the last step. We might need them in case this Davis person doesn't come back here willingly."

Yes, of course. That was why Iris needed them, why her body had reacted with such alarm. She was just afraid of Davis and needed the stones for protection.

Maria's jaw muscles worked and then loosened, and she nodded. Shawn seemed to relax, and even Iris breathed more freely. The transfer stones would be safe with her... for now. She needed to get herself together, to regain control of the situation, and that meant preparing to confront Davis.

Iris walked away and motioned for them to follow.

"We're going to need backup."

NIVI

YURAS, CALIFORNIA

WHAT A STRANGE FEELING. Nivi was used to fire and roaring heat in her veins, but now a dense cold descended upon her, freezing her blood into an icy sludge and chilling her to the core. And yet it was not unpleasant. After all the tragedy and stress that fire had brought into her life, the cold was a welcome change, numbing out the pain and betrayal. She didn't have to think. She could just be.

Voices drifted in and out of her awareness. Meng's melodious British accent. Ling's matter-of-fact and succinct phrases. Kellan's resonant baritone, so very similar to her father's...

Icy walls slammed down, squashing the flare in her pulse before the thought could take root. She sank down, down, far away from the voices and the world, as if the glowing silver had actually sucked her into the earth. Spots of light flashed in her periphery as hands lifted her from the ground and carried her through the forest. The spots grew in number until her whole mind was a mass of sparkling silver dots in an otherwise dark pit, like gleaming transfer stones in the mine walls.

She was one of them, a stone embedded in the earth, awakened decades before, hidden away from the world, until... A slight breeze disturbed the stagnant, humid air, stirring up aromas of damp earth and bringing with it the brine of the sea. Then, there he was. *Davis*. She knew it in her bones before she could see him. His finger scraped through the imprisoning earth. A tremor went through her body, reaching toward the surface, wanting to break free.

Davis wasn't alone, *Iris* was there with him, the glow of fire in her hand lighting his way. One of the transfer stones fell from the wall into Davis's hand. He took it from the tunnel, and a thrill of power rumbled through the ground. And even though Nivi couldn't see when he used the stone, she felt it, like a pickaxe striking the wall that kept the stones and their powers imprisoned, breaking them free. From the depths, they oozed forth, drop by silver drop. With each subsequent transfer stone use, they grew and grew, their appetite to consume increasing with their size. Davis had set the silver free, but he was also the one who could confine it again.

Ice-cold rage flowed through Nivi's veins. Davis was the one who had started all this, who had killed the father she knew, caused her to be separated from her family, and put the Shifter Council on a militant path with their oblivion tincture use. It didn't matter that he was now a Static. Rage and fear flushed out any rational thoughts, egged on by the sharp cold in her mind. She would find him and destroy him.

And then she was back in her body, lying on a soft surface. She opened her eyes and turned her head. She was on the couch in Ling's living room. Meng and Ling stood just inside the doorway to the dining room and kitchen in the midst of a hushed but heated discussion.

"Shall I continue, *darling*?" Meng said, addressing Ling with a reproachful tone.

"Please do," came a deep voice from someone out of view. Kellan. Emotion frayed the edges of his otherwise controlled voice. "Tell me what's going on. What happened all those years ago?"

"Well?" Meng said, seemingly waiting for an answer.

Ling remained silent, her eyes downcast in a surprisingly resigned expression for someone who was always so strong and reserved.

Meng continued speaking. "I guess I shall be the one to tell you. Ling, here, told me that you, Mr. Williams, had seen her Shifter form and were hanging out around town trying to catch more glimpses of Shifters, stirring up trouble from the local anti-Shifter group and the like. So I used oblivion tincture on you and sent you back where you came from." Kellan made a sound of protestation, but Meng continued. "It was completely in my right to use oblivion tincture for this purpose. Knowledge of Shifters is kept secret from Statics for everyone's protection. But I am so very sorry that I used it on you based on a lie." She cast a narrow-eyed glance at Ling.

Kellan paced into view, balling his fists. His entire body tensed, and when he finally spoke, his voice trembled. "If you used oblivion tincture on me, how did I remember Ji? Even though I knew who she was and what she meant to me, it was like there was some kind of block in my mind because I couldn't contact her or even think about contacting her."

"Because I told you to forget about the vermilion bird, Ling's Shifter form," Meng said, "and to stay away from Shifters in Yuras. I didn't know anything about your relationship with Ji, so all your memories of her would've stayed intact."

I see, Nivi wanted to say in response to Meng's explanation. But she didn't see. It wasn't just the fact that she suspected she still didn't know the whole story. It was the fact that oblivion tincture had torn apart her life more than once, and hearing it mentioned again stirred something from the bottom of her subconscious. Something unpleasant. Something she had been trying to keep at bay. All the secrets, all the loneliness, all the unfairness—it all fueled a fire that was trying to break free.

A new figure appeared in the hallway and broke Nivi out of her thoughts.

"You did *what*?"

Everyone turned to see Ji standing there. Although she sounded tired, the shaky vehemence in her voice sent a chill down Nivi's spine.

Ling broke her silence, desperation in her voice. "It was to protect you."

"It was to protect yourself!" Ji spat back. "You betrayed me! You kept us from being a family!"

A *family*? What was her mother talking about? They had a family—before Davis took it away. The pieces were there in her mind, waiting to be put together, but she couldn't bear to let them touch. It was too much. It was all too much.

Ji turned and rushed back down the hall. The sound of a door slamming followed soon after. Ling started to follow Ji, but Kellan stopped her.

"Let me talk to her," he said, gritting his teeth as he continued. "As hard as it is for me to say this right now, I know you probably had your reasons for doing what you did. But it'll take time for her, and me, to trust you again."

He squeezed around Ling through the dining room doorway, glancing for a moment at where Nivi lay on the couch in the dark, before heading down the hall. He hadn't seen that she was awake, not with the lights off around her. But she had seen him and all those features that were so similar to her own.

No. No. No!

Her whole life was a lie. Again, a cold wall blocked those thoughts from taking root. Rage, so pure and raw and focused, scratched at its confinement, walls that grew ever more brittle. Coldness shot through her veins, giving her a clarity she'd never experienced before.

She must leave. Yes! She must leave *now*, before anyone can stop her, stop her from her mission, to keep them all safe, she has to kill, kill, kill. Kill Davis. Find and destroy him.

The silver pool called to her. It would help her accomplish her goal and lead her to Davis. She rose from the couch, letting the blanket that was covering her fall to the floor. In the other room, Meng and Ling sat at the dining table, whispering. Nivi glided over the carpet to the front door, the soft fibers muffling her steps. The room took on a soft silver glow, and for some reason it didn't alarm her. She slipped on her shoes, gripped the doorknob, and slowly turned, making sure to make no noise.

"Nivi?" came a voice behind her.

Nivi froze and then turned to see Jorge in the hallway.

"Where are you—Your eyes..." He gasped and took a step back.

She didn't wait for him to finish; she already knew what he was going to say. Opening the door, she stepped outside and took off down the street before anyone could follow. A curtain of shimmering silver fell before her, the world rippling as if it was a mirage. She knew her eyes, like the pool in the forest, were glowing silver.

AMBER

SAN FRANCISCO, CALIFORNIA

AMBER SAT INSIDE HER cell bathroom, which was surprisingly bright and modern. It was the only place she could have some privacy while she processed the variety of emotions that rattled her psyche. She was a prisoner because she'd inadvertently stolen magic. Whose magic had she stolen? Would she ever get out of this place? Yes, if she answered their questions, but then they'd erase her memories. Maybe it wouldn't be so bad to go back to life as she'd known it, but did that mean Arav would be erased from her memories? Would it even matter if she didn't remember anything?

And Arav! He hadn't intentionally disappeared on her, and he'd still thought they were together. She should feel relieved. She *was* relieved! Then why wasn't that fact sitting well with her? These last few months were the first time she'd been on her own for as long as she could remember. Sure, she had her parents and other friends, but that was different. She'd been with Arav for a year before his disappearance, but even before that she'd always had Nivi. Without either of them, she didn't know who she was, but she had started to find out. Was that what was bothering her? As alone as she'd been, she'd felt like she was on the precipice of self-discovery. Could she figure herself out with Arav in her life? She didn't know. None of it would matter if her memories were erased.

And what was with the looks Arav kept giving that girl next door? Vera, or whatever her name was? It must be because he'd been trapped here for so long. Months! As bad as she'd had it, he'd had it worse. He needed a friend. Even if it had to be that voluptuous mermaid-creature-thing...

The sound of voices interrupted Amber's thoughts. It was good timing—her thought process hadn't been productive anyway.

She stuck her head from the bathroom to see who was speaking but couldn't see anything from her vantage point. Like the bathroom, the rest of the cell had a light and airy feel. If she *had* to be locked up for a while, this place wasn't *that* bad. At least these Shifters treated their inmates better than Static society did, even if they did erase their memories. She wondered if it would be worse to have a transient stay in an awful prison but keep her memories.

She crept out of the bathroom and moved to the right side of the glass wall where she could see into Arav's and Vera's cells more directly. Through the adjoining glass panel between her and Vera's cells, she saw a blue tailfin peeking over the top of a tub, the translucent webbing catching the overhead lights in iridescent hues of blue, purple, and pink. It was actually really beautiful...

for a fish, she supposed. The fin curled down around the tub rim as if it were grasping it. It *was* grasping it. The webbing stretched between bony projections that ended in claws. Creepy.

The cell directly across from hers was empty. To the right of that cell, Arav was lying in his bed, staring up at the ceiling. The voices were coming from the cells on the other side of Vera's and Arav's. If she pressed herself against the glass, she could just make out the figures of Davis and Iris murmuring across the hall to each other. Her movement must've caught Arav's eye because he sat up, then got up and walked to the corner of his room across from where she stood. He glanced over at Vera's cell a couple of times.

"Looking for someone?" Amber asked in a harsh whisper. "She's underwater."

"She has abnormally good hearing underwater," Arav said.

"So there is something you don't want her to hear?"

"No. Not really. It's just—"

"What?" Amber crossed her arms, heat rising to her cheeks.

She couldn't help it. She *was* jealous.

Arav sighed. A defeated look fell over his face, and Amber was instantly sorry. This situation wasn't his fault. It wasn't Vera's either.

"I've missed you so much. You have no idea."

Amber sniffed. "I've missed you too."

"Hey," Arav said softly, putting a hand on the glass in front of him. "We'll get out of here soon, and we'll go home, and everything will be okay."

"I don't know."

The pain returned to Arav's eyes. "What do you mean?"

She wanted to be comforted by his words, to believe them, but she knew things would be different.

"Even if we get out of here—" she began.

"When," Arav cut in. "*When* we get out of here."

"*When* we get out of here," Amber repeated, "we won't be able to go back to how it was. I'm not like you. You heard Davis. My powers are stolen. I don't know for sure what that means, but I probably won't be able to stay in your world."

Her vision blurred as tears gathered in her eyes.

"Why does it have to be your or my world?" Arav said. "If there is a difference, we need to change things. People who care about each other shouldn't be separated like that."

"I don't know if it's up to us. You're right about one thing though."

"About what?"

"We'll be okay. You'll make new friends..." Amber glanced at Vera's tub before she could stop herself. "And so will I."

"Amber..."

Multiple voices erupted down the hall. Too many voices. Arav's gaze lingered on Amber before he turned and ran to look through the strip of glass between his and Iris's cells. Amber pressed her face up to her own window, and Vera's head emerged from the tub. Blond hair tinged with green cascaded in wet strands down her back and chest. Every inch of her skin was covered in barnacles and iridescent blue scales, including her face. A clear, second lid pulled back from her gold eyes, and the gold fragmented, shrank, and dispersed into a suspension of glittering green.

"What's going on?" Vera said, revealing a mouth full of sharp, pointy teeth.

She pushed herself out of the tub, displaying a brief glimpse of spiny dorsal fins that ran down her back before they retracted into her skin along with her scales. Her white crop top and jeans reappeared at the same time. She really was a beautiful and eerie creature. Amber could see why Arav was drawn to her.

The commotion in Iris's cell grew louder.

Vera rushed to her window. "Uh... What? How?"

Arav pounded on the glass between his and Iris's cells. "Wait! Don't leave us! Take us with you!"

Amber's hopes flared. Were they being rescued?

Arav banged on the glass again, his tone turning desperate. "Please!"

And then... quiet. What had happened? Was Iris gone? Did she escape?

"Well, that was exciting," Davis said.

Arav looked at Davis, his fists clenched and his face red. "Just shut up! Don't you care that we're trapped here? Show some respect and stop making stupid comments."

Before Davis could respond, the door opened at the end of the hall. Footsteps approached. Was this the police coming to question them and then erase their memories? Or were they responding to Iris's escape? Her heart raced as the footsteps came closer.

A familiar figure came into view, walking with determination and intent. Black, curly hair, brown skin, and a curvy figure that was halfway between Amber's and Vera's. Silver eyes gleamed with an internal light of their own.

Amber gasped. She knew the girl, but something kept her from calling out. Instead, her voice emerged as a hesitant whisper.

"Nivi?"

Nivi paused at her name and turned to Amber with those silver, otherworldly eyes, looking at her without seeing her. And then she moved on, past Arav's and Vera's cells, and straight to Davis.

IRIS

YURAS, CALIFORNIA

THE CREW MADE THEIR way out of the forest with Iris in the lead. She squinted at the harsh morning light, not realizing how bright it had gotten while they were in the shade of the trees. They walked through the fields to avoid the streets and prying eyes, wind whipping their hair and clothes, and ended up at the backyard door of Meng and Ling's house. Iris reached over the fence and unlatched the gate.

They filed into the backyard, a microclimate of windless sun, noticeably warmer as soon as Iris closed the gate. It was too early for flowers, but the garden was lush and green from the winter rains. Vines crawled up the fence, plants covered the ground and filled the planters, and birds chattered away in the yard's single tree. A stone paver path led around a patio dining set to a sliding glass door. Iris knocked and peered through the glass.

"Hello? Ling? Meng?"

No answer. She tried the door, and it slid open.

"We're not breaking and entering, are we?" Shawn said.

"Breaking, no," Iris said. "Entering, yes. But I know them."

Iris stepped into the area between the dining room and kitchen and waited for them to follow. Alek and Shawn looked at Maria who nodded to the door, and they all entered. They stood around the dining table while Iris walked through the house, knocking on doors and calling out. She returned to the dining room.

"No one's here."

They stood unspeaking around the dining table for a few moments while Iris tried to think of what to do next.

Shawn tilted his head to the side. "Do you hear something?"

Faint voices drifted in from outside. Iris walked to the front door and opened it. From down the street came the sounds of a commotion. She stepped outside and looked toward where the neighborhood street connected to Main Street. Half a dozen people stood there. Among the group were Ling, Meng, and Ji—what was Ji doing here?—as well as two teenage Shifters and a Static man she didn't recognize. Why were they out in public like that? They were so conspicuous, standing there on the sidewalk in the bright morning sun, and they were putting themselves in danger of being spotted. It didn't seem like many people were awake yet, but they would be soon. Then her gaze swept back to Ling. Her aura was gone, which confirmed what Iris had felt back at the prison. Ling's powers had transferred back to her.

The group was pointing down Main Street, obviously arguing about something.

"Is that our backup?" Alek said.

"Yes..." At least Iris hoped they would be. Of course they would want to stop Davis, but would they trust her?

They left the house, Shawn closing the door after them, and walked toward the group. As they neared, snippets of the argument became clear.

"Jorge, tell us exactly what you saw," Meng said.

Everyone turned to look at one of the teenagers, a small, skinny boy with glasses. His voice and mannerisms were those of someone who'd rather not be the center of attention, but he made a valiant effort, straightening his hunched posture and maintaining eye contact with Meng as he spoke.

"I saw her open the door, and when she looked at me, her eyes were glowing silver. She had this look on her face that just didn't seem like her. It was eerie. And then when I followed her outside, she just... disappeared."

"How did she disappear? Like just poof?" the other teenager said.

Jorge looked up at the teenager whose cropped purple-and-blue curls added to their height difference. "No, she melted into a silver substance, the same color as her eyes, and then it absorbed into the ground."

The Static man took a step toward Ling and pointed his finger at her.

"Don't you see? It's that stuff from the forest. You made her go up against it, and look what it's done! It's taken her!"

Meng stepped between Ling and the Static man, one hand raised toward his chest. "Hold on a moment. We don't know exactly what happened yet."

Ji touched the Static man's arm, her voice wavering. "Kellan... I..." She shook her head. "I'm just so scared."

The Static man, Kellan, turned to Ji, his face softening.

"Nivi's strong," Meng said. "We'll find her, and she'll be okay."

"But..." Jorge began, seeming to summon up more public-speaking courage. "It wasn't Nivi. That's what I've been trying to say. It was her body, but it wasn't *her*."

The group didn't notice Iris and the crew as they approached. Iris tried to process everything she'd heard. Nivi had been here, but she had disappeared by becoming that silver substance from the forest. Kellan said Ling had made Nivi go up against it, which meant Nivi must've tried to nullify it with her powers. It obviously hadn't worked.

Sudden anger swept over Iris. All the transferred powers in her system swirled and raged, pushing her to exact revenge, guiding her to her target—Davis. She swayed, and Maria grabbed her elbow, steadying her.

"Are you all right?" Maria said.

Iris nodded, blinking back her emotions, trying to quell the storm inside her. This wasn't her. Was this what Davis had been talking about? The power of the silver pool flowing through her with all the transferred powers, forcing her to do things? She wouldn't let it. She was stronger than it. She could fight it. And now she knew where Nivi was going.

"Excuse me," Iris said from the edge of the group.

Everyone jumped and turned to look at her, their heads moving side to side as they evaluated her and the rest of the crew.

"So... You came back," Ling said, her expression as icy as Meng's eyes.

Iris was taken aback for a moment. What would've brought on Ling's hostility? Then she remembered Nivi had been here, which meant Ling and Meng and everyone else had their memories back. Good. That would make this easier.

"I know where Nivi's headed."

"Where?" Kellan said, gripping Ji's hand.

Ji looked at Iris pleadingly.

"To a prison," Iris said.

"What prison?" Ji said. "How do you know that?"

"First," Iris said, "I have to explain a few things. The silver was created by the use of transfer stones. It grows larger and stronger whenever a transfer stone is used—whenever the magical imbalance increases. To fight it, we need to return the powers to their rightful owners, but they have to go back through each person who has had them." She addressed Ling. "For instance, Ling must've recently touched the silver because her powers came back to me."

Ling nodded. "I did."

"So in order to reduce the silver's strength and size, I would need to touch it to send Ling's powers back to Davis, and finally Davis would need to touch it to send them back to Ling. Before I found you all, I was in the forest with Maria, Shawn, and Alek." She motioned to the fishing crew. "I touched the silver and felt some of the powers I took from Davis leave me. I'm assuming they went back to Davis. It seems that if anyone with transferred powers touches the pool, the powers will go back to the person who had them just before."

"If you touched the silver," Meng said, "how is it not affecting your mind or eyes like it did Nivi's?"

Iris shook her head. "The silver isn't in me like that. The transferred powers seem to protect me from the silver physically entering me, because the act of me touching the pool sends the transferred powers back to the person who had them before me, thus reducing the silver's strength."

"Let me see if I got this straight," Kellan said. "Transferring powers created the silver. The more powers that are transferred using transfer stones, the bigger and stronger the silver gets. If you don't have transferred powers and you touch the silver, it can enter you and control your mind. If you do have transferred powers and you touch it, the powers go back to the person you took them from, and the silver gets smaller and weaker."

Iris nodded. "You got it. If you don't have transferred powers, don't touch it. The silver wants what every living thing wants... to survive. It can't do that if all the powers are returned to their rightful owners, and there's one way to guarantee the powers are never fully returned."

"It's sending Nivi to kill Davis," Meng said, astute as ever. "If she succeeds, the powers he has will fade with him. It won't be possible to return them. And the powers Iris has will have nowhere to go."

"Why bother with anyone else," Iris said, "if you can focus on just one person."

"The person who started it all," Ling said with a heaviness that spoke volumes.

They had all been through so much at Davis's hands.

"I know where he is," Iris said. "If we hurry, we might be able to get there before Nivi does and force Davis to return the powers."

"How do you know what the silver wants?" Ji said.

Iris ran a hand over her head. "Because I can feel it. I have a connection with it. I believe it's because I used the transfer stones, and I have all these transferred powers in me. It's trying to turn me against Davis, so it must be influencing Nivi the same way."

Ji crossed her arms. "How do we know you're telling the truth, that you won't just help Davis again?"

Iris sighed inwardly. How would they know? "If I just wanted to help him, I wouldn't be getting you all involved."

"Maybe you just want us to stop Nivi so you can help Davis," Ji said.

Iris hadn't thought of that angle. She hesitated, not sure what to say.

Meng saved her the trouble, although she seemed reluctant to admit it. "She *did* come back voluntarily to give Ling and me back our powers, before any of us knew anything about the silver."

Ji didn't seem convinced. Ling turned to her. "It's the fastest way to get to Nivi. We'll have to take our chances."

"Um, can someone explain exactly what's going on and who all these people are?" the teenager with blue-and-purple hair said.

"Let's go back to Ling and Meng's house, and I'll explain there," Iris said, "before we get caught out here by prying eyes."

Jorge nudged the taller teenager and whispered, "We all lost our camouflage stones during the bookstore raid. Remember, Ai?"

"Yeah, yeah," Ai said.

Ling began walking. "Let's get going."

They went back to Ling and Meng's house and gathered in the living room. The mess from Ling's earlier transformation had been cleaned up, although there were holes in the drywall.

Iris introduced them to Maria, Alek, and Shawn and briefly explained how she knew Ling, Meng, and Ji. Ji introduced Kellan as someone who was helping with the pro-integration cause, fidgeting as she spoke. Both Meng and Ling avoided eye contact with him, but Iris didn't ask any questions about why there seemed to be tension. Iris recounted how the OT police had taken her to the prison where she'd seen Davis, how the crew had helped her escape, and how they ended up transferring some of her powers back to Davis through the silver.

"Fascinating," Meng said in response to the crew's combined use of powers.

"But they can't become water anymore," Iris said. "So we'll have to be a bit more visible with our transportation." She looked at Meng, who raised an eyebrow. "You did it for us before. I was thinking you could transform at the edge of the forest and immediately dive down by the water to avoid detection as much as possible. I can use my finder power to guide us."

"There's no way someone won't see her," Ai said.

"If we don't get there in time and Davis escapes, or worse, if Nivi kills him, the silver will expand and this whole area won't exist anymore."

Meng nodded. "It'll be the fastest way." She addressed Iris. "Can you tell us everything about when you were taken by the OT police?"

"I was standing on the Yuras cliffs, and they appeared behind me," Iris said.

"You didn't sense a Shifter aura before?"

Iris thought hard. She had been distracted by the fishing crew's watery appearance at the time.

"I did, but I only noticed them from a distance. I thought they were you and Ling." She scrunched her forehead, trying to remember the details. "My memory is foggy. They must've used some kind of sleep tincture to knock me out. When I came to, I was in the prison. There were some sort of handcuffs around my wrists, like glowing rope restraints that prevented me from using my powers. Once they put me in the cell, the restraints dissolved, and I could use my powers at will, but there was some kind of barrier around the cell that was immune to the powers."

Meng continued her questioning. "Do you know where the prison is located? Is it somewhere isolated or populated?"

"Judging by the path Maria took us after she and her crew rescued me, it's in the coastal region north of San Francisco, which is not populated, but it is a hiking area."

"You won't need us all going," Ling said. "Especially those of us without powers." She took Meng's hand and squeezed it, offering a small smile. "I'll hold down the fort for you." Letting go of Meng's hand, she motioned to Kellan, Maria, and Alek. "You three will stay with me." Then she pointed at Jorge and Ai. "As well as you two. We don't need any other kids getting harmed."

"No way," Ai said, crossing their arms. "I'm helping Nivi."

Jorge pushed up his glasses. "Nivi needs us."

Ling sighed. "All right, but listen to Meng."

"I'm going with them too." Kellan locked eyes with Ling in an apparent showdown of wills, and then he said through gritted teeth, "She's *my* daughter."

That was news. A Static was Nivi's father? What about Chairperson Dawan? Iris glanced back and forth between Ji and Kellan. Kellan did somewhat resemble the late chairperson. Oh-ho, what had Ji been getting up to? Iris instantly sobered up, thinking of her role in the chairperson's demise. She couldn't go down that train of thought, not right now.

Arguments broke out between who would stay and who would go.

Iris stood in the middle of the room and waved her arms to quiet everyone down. "Why don't we all go to the forest together, and we can figure out the logistics on the way? We'll be a large group, but since we're planning to ride on a dragon soon, I'm not so worried about being inconspicuous anymore. Let's just start moving."

Everyone looked around, but no one disagreed. Iris led the way through the dining room and out the glass sliding door. They continued through the backyard and out the gate to the shrubby cliffside beyond. No one spoke as they made their way to the forest.

Iris didn't see anyone as they walked, but she still felt a little safer once they were surrounded by trees. She continued to the dirt road where Meng had transformed earlier. Now that Meng had her memories back, her transformation should be much smoother.

They walked on the road past an abandoned house, and Iris paused before they reached the area of the silver pool. She had heard something. She raised a hand to stop everyone and put a finger to her lips. Tilting her head, she listened.

Footsteps crunched behind them, and they turned to see a couple of Statics approaching through the trees.

At the front was a large man with unkempt brown hair and a shadow of a beard. He wore a red flannel shirt and appeared to be in his forties. "This way, Tom!" he said to the young man behind him.

Tom was also tall, but he was lanky with a mop of dark brown hair and a pronounced Adam's apple. His long face had the smooth appearance of a teenager, although his eyes were unusually steely for his age.

"Hold on, Frank," Tom said. "Why are we heading this way? Who's over here?"

"The camouflage stones on the path are gone," Iris said to the group as if that knowledge would shield them from the incoming Statics.

"Uh-oh," Meng murmured, stepping behind Iris to hide herself, but not quickly enough.

The large man saw her. He had been heading straight toward them as if he'd known they were there.

"It's her," Frank breathed, stopping in his tracks.

"Who is it?" Tom said. He turned his steely gaze on the group, his eyes narrowing.

"We need to go," Meng said in a hushed yell. "Now!"

Ling glanced over at Maria before addressing the rest of the group. "You all go. We'll distract them."

"We're staying with our captain," Shawn said, and Alek nodded beside him.

Meng's expression betrayed a flicker of hesitation before she turned and waved at the rest of the group. "Follow me."

Meng took off at a run, and Iris followed, glancing behind to see Ling, Maria, and her crew standing their ground in front of the two men. It made sense for the Statics to have some Shifter backup, but would Shawn alone be able to protect them? He did have several powers, she reminded herself. She continued running with the others, following the dirt road around a bend before stopping.

"I think there's room here," Meng said. "But you all better stand back. Once I've transformed, climb on. Don't waste any time. Other Statics might be getting wind of us soon. Iris, you'll guide me where to go. Sit up on my head and put pressure on my horns in the direction I need to go." Meng faced the end of the dirt road, then turned back toward them. "Oh, and make sure to hang on."

Blue scales erupted over her skin and clothes, shimmering in the scattered light that filtered through the trees. Her body elongated into a giant serpentine dragon, and her tail whipped out, causing them all to take several steps back. Her four clawed feet dug into the road, producing a small cloud of dust, and electricity crackled across her sides. She lowered her head to the ground. Two branched horns poked through an icy blue mane that matched her eyes. The mane floated weightlessly around her head, fading down her back into spikes and plates. A low rumble emerged through her toothy, whiskered snout followed by hot puffs of breaths that Iris interpreted as *Let's go*.

Ai was the first to mount Meng's head, running forward with gusto and using Meng's horns and spikes to pull themself up to walk along the dragon's spine. They moved halfway down Meng's back and sat between a couple of armored plates, leaving plenty of room for everyone else. Jorge hung back, shrinking in on himself, until Ai motioned and called to him impatiently. He climbed with more calculated caution and took a seat in front of Ai.

Kellan followed with an expression of such awe that Iris wondered if he'd ever seen a Shifter transform before. Ji went next, and Iris last, taking her place at the front of the group on Meng's head. She sat down, hair standing up on the back of her neck and arms with the electric energy surrounding Meng, and took the base of a branched horn in each hand. She was the captain of this magnificent beast.

Meng picked up speed, galloping through the trees, out into the sunlight, and to the cliff edge. She dove over the side of the cliff, down toward the water, and Iris's stomach leaped while several people yelped behind her. Salty wind whipped her hair about her shoulders and chilled her hands as she gripped Meng's horns. Meng straightened out just above the ocean's surface, and her body began a smooth, undulating glide through the air, her scales blending with the glittering ocean.

Iris looked back at the others, briefly worried that one of them had fallen off, but they were all there. Jorge was pale and looked like he was going to be sick. Kellan didn't look much better. Ai smiled broadly and even yelled out, "Woo-hoo!" Only Ji, like Iris, seemed unfazed, although she looked like she was enjoying herself.

Meng headed farther out to sea until the cliffs were a brown line in the distance, and then she continued parallel to the shore. While they rode, Iris tapped into her finder powers. She envisioned the prison, the glass walls, the white stone floors, the dark brown of the bed frames and wall fixtures. Warmth filled her chest and a directional pull tugged at her mind. There wasn't much steering to do yet. They would be heading south along the coast for a while, but Iris pressed her hands against Meng's horns to affirm they were going in the right direction. She didn't know how hard she'd need to push for Meng to feel her, but even with her gentle pressure, Meng seemed to understand and nodded her head before picking up speed.

Iris inhaled deeply as she gazed out to sea. She flashed back to the last time she'd been on Meng's back headed to the Shifter Council building. This time would be different. This time she was going to make things right.

Iris

San Francisco, California

THE WATER RACED BY, the sparkling waves blurring into a vague blue haze. Ocean spray pricked Iris's face and stung her eyes, and she blinked rapidly to clear her vision. Eventually, she gave up and closed her eyes, marveling at how smooth the travel was even at that speed. How could Meng see through the salt sting, ocean glare, and the drying wind that only increased the faster they went? Unlike Iris's snake form that had no eyelids whatsoever, Meng must have a second pair of eyelids. Those creepy, clear ones she'd noticed on lizards and other reptiles would be very useful in this situation.

At some point, Iris felt the destination was near and pulled back on Meng's horns to slow her down. As they gently decelerated, Iris ventured to open her eyes and found it was much easier to keep them open at this slower speed. She pressed on Meng's horns, directing her toward the cliff-lined shore. They followed the curve of the coast, and the gray sky and characteristic rust-red bridge in the distance told her where they were—just north of San Francisco. It made sense that the prison would be close to the Shifter Council headquarters, given how easily Chairperson Peters had made her appearance, but this wasn't good news for them. In such a high-density area, they were sure to be spotted by multiple Static onlookers. They had no choice. They had to get Davis back to Yuras to restore the power balance. Hopefully they weren't too late.

Veering to the left, they neared the cliffs north of the Golden Gate Bridge and landed on a rocky beach tucked into a cove. Meng lowered her head, and they descended one by one before Meng transformed back into her human form.

"That was amazing!" Ai exclaimed.

Even Jorge, who looked slightly green, nodded enthusiastically.

Kellan ran his hands over his face and hair. "That was the wildest experience I've ever had."

He looked at Ji and smiled, and Ji returned the smile while placing a hand on his shoulder. Iris still didn't know the nature of their relationship, but this wasn't the time to find out. She glanced up at the surrounding cliffs, relaxing a bit when she didn't see any hikers. She walked over to the nearest cliff, feeling the tug of her finder abilities leading straight into the wall.

"The prison's here. I just don't know where the entrance is."

"Most likely it's a camouflaged entrance requiring specific camouflage stone clearances to enter," Meng said.

Iris examined the cliff wall. "We escaped by becoming elemental water, but I don't know if there's a way in or out for a Shifter without clearance."

Meng looked up thoughtfully and then set her gaze on the teenagers. "We're going to have to set some bait."

Ai and Jorge looked at each other, and then, surprisingly, the small boy stepped forward.

"I'll do it."

Ai grabbed his shoulder. "Not without me."

Jorge looked about to protest, but Meng interjected first. "Ai's right. We need to do this together. What are your secondary powers?"

Jorge held out an arm on which dark swirls appeared. He was drawing on his skin. Ai opened their mouth and darkness spewed forth, swallowing themself, Jorge, and Kellan who stood nearby. From within that lightless, expanding cloud, someone yelped in surprise, probably Kellan.

"That's enough," Meng said. "Impressive and useful. Thank you for the demonstration."

As fast as the darkness had come out, it flowed back the way it had come, as if Ai were sucking in an unusually large bubble of chewing gum. Kellan spun around as the darkness lifted.

"You're welcome," Ai said when the darkness was gone, seeming very pleased with the compliment. Jorge nodded and stood a little taller.

Meng assumed a position in front of everyone on the beach, looking every bit the leader she was. "Okay, this is what we're going to do. Jorge and Ai will be the bait."

"But they're just kids," Kellan said. "Let me be the bait instead."

"Unfortunately," Meng said, "we need Shifters to attract the attention of the OT police. Hear me out. Jorge and Ai will walk through the forest on these cliffs, pretending to be hikers. It's important for Ai to walk in front and Jorge behind—that way, if the officers surprise you from behind, they will have to take Jorge first. Jorge, you'll need to make sure you yell or say something to make it clear to Ai what's happening. That should give Ai a few seconds to sink the local area into darkness, which will be our cue. The rest of you will—"

A deep rumble erupted from the earth. Small stones scattered down the cliffside. Meng, who was closest to the cliffs, ran back toward the ocean's edge, followed by Ai and Jorge. Kellan and Ji took several steps back, almost bumping into Iris as she prepared to transform and flee, but as quickly as the sound had started, it stopped.

"What was that?" Ji said.

They all stood in a row on the water's edge, the waves lapping at their feet. Before any of them could respond, the cliffs rumbled again, but this time it sounded fainter, like it was coming from within the earth instead of the surface.

"Davis..." Iris breathed, hoping her words weren't true.

"Or Nivi," Meng said. "Change of plans. Iris, guide us to the top of the prison. Let's go!"

She leaped into the air, her body elongating mid-jump. Blue-green scales covered her from snout to tail as she twirled her sinuous body back on herself, as effortless as a ribbon on a breeze. Dipping back toward the sand, she swept over the kids, grabbing Jorge by the shoulders with her left front claws and Ai with her right ones. With the teenagers dangling and screaming in her grasp, she passed over Ji and Kellan, grabbing each of them the same way with her back claws before lifting them to the top of the cliffs.

Everything happened so quickly, Iris barely had time to blink before realizing she needed to follow. Could it be that Nivi alone was causing the cliffs to shake? Nivi didn't have those kinds of powers, so it seemed more probable that Davis would be the one making a ruckus with his newly returned powers. Unless… Did the silver have something to do with this? There was something familiar in the movement of the earth, a supernatural call to join forces and be rid of Davis.

In the turmoil, Iris reverted to the form she knew best, a giant white snake. Lengthening her body, she climbed the cliff, gripping the stony protuberances with her underbelly, slithering and winding quickly to the top. The cliffs here were more sloped than the ones in Yuras, with shrubs growing up the sandy slopes and cypress trees at the top.

Ji, Kellan, Ai, and Jorge stood at the top of the cliff while Meng hovered in the air. Iris slithered through the shrubs, following the guiding pull of her finder abilities to the prison. Not far ahead, she saw the silhouette of a doorway in a crop of large rocks. Nivi must've nullified the camouflage magic surrounding it for it to be so visible. Iris slithered up to the doorway and transformed into her human form. She waved at Meng, who landed gracefully on the ground in her human form.

Kellan rushed to the doorway. "Is this where Nivi is?"

Ji grabbed Kellan's arm and held him back. "Wait, we don't know what's down there."

"I do," Iris said. "There were only a couple of guards, and they didn't stay around very long. I don't think we'll find much resistance from them. It's Davis I'm worried about." *And Nivi.*

That strange feeling was intensifying the closer Iris got to the prison, a twisting of her insides, an increase in tension.

Help Nivi. Kill Davis.

Iris paused at the doorway. White stone walls lined a wooden staircase that descended into the earth. Cool lights illuminated the way from overhead. There was no door.

Faint yelling erupted from somewhere deep down the stairway, followed by more rumbling of the ground.

Ji lurched forward. "It's Nivi!"

She rushed down the stairs and out of sight before anyone could stop her. Without any hesitation, Kellan followed her. The teenagers looked at Iris and Meng, clearly nervous.

"Let's go," Iris said. "If there are guards down there, we'll have to immobilize them before they can use oblivion tincture or handcuff us."

Meng motioned to the teenagers. "Stay behind me and listen for instructions."

They nodded and, with Iris in the lead, descended the stairs.

"What if someone comes across this entrance?" Jorge said from the back.

"I think we have bigger things to worry about right now," Ai said.

"They're right," Meng said. "We'll have to worry about that later."

Iris's finder ability led her toward the cell she'd been locked in. This was the way the guards had first brought her in, but she'd been disoriented at the time, so she didn't want to rely on memory alone. The stairs led to a straight hallway. Up ahead, there was a set of double doors, and at first Iris worried they'd be locked, but as they neared, she could see they were slightly ajar. It must be Nivi's work again, nullifying any magical obstacles along the way. They pushed through the doors and into another hallway. Rows of cells stretched down the hall on both sides. Ji and Kellan were nowhere to be seen.

"This is a prison?" Jorge murmured. "It's fancy."

"You want to be locked up in here?" Ai said.

"I'm just saying."

"There's no one here," Meng said.

"This isn't where we were kept," Iris said. "It's still farther ahead."

Fortunately, there was only this one hallway, so they didn't have to worry that Ji or Kellan had gotten lost. They passed dozens of empty cells with their large glass walls. How many Shifters had been kept here at one time? How much had she missed while she was recovering in Alaska with Maria and her crew? And why did there seem to be only the two guards stationed here at any one time? The more Iris thought about it, the more the reasons became clear.

Ariana Peters became chairperson after Davis had stolen powers from the US Shifter Council, effectively reducing their numbers by half. Why she decided to wipe all Shifters' memories of Davis and those events, Iris didn't know, but this prison must have been used to house Shifters in the interim. At that time, there had probably been many guards, but now that most of the Shifters already had their memories wiped, the OT police were sent on patrol instead of guarding the prison. It was gross, all of it. Wiping memories and imprisoning Shifters who weren't criminals. There would be a reckoning one way or another. Once the powers were put back in balance, the senate would be back to its full strength, and Ariana would have to answer for cutting the affected senators out of Shifter society instead of helping them in their time of need.

But what could she have done at the time? They had thought Davis was dead and all their powers would have disappeared with him. What else could Ariana have done with so many Shifter senators now permanently Statics? Move toward integration, that was what. It was time to finally move forward and stop this antiquated separatist thinking.

They came to the end of the cells, and the hallway made two sharp lefts into another set of slightly ajar double doors. From behind those doors, the yells could be heard more clearly. That, and the hot tug of Iris's finder power in her chest let her know they were here.

Iris pushed one of the doors open enough to peer in, and a jumble of voices and yells flooded out. Nivi stood in the center of the hallway, not moving, just standing and staring at Davis's cell. Ji and Kellan were on either side of Nivi, both of them trying to talk to her and coax her away, but they didn't touch her.

One of the teenage prisoners, Amber, banged against her glass wall. "Nivi! Mrs. Dawan! Can you let us out? Please!"

Arav and Vera also banged against their glass walls, calling out with no response.

Iris couldn't see Davis, but she suspected he was standing opposite Nivi, potentially staring back with a curious and unperturbed expression. She wondered if he was scared.

And then simultaneous urges to help Nivi and hurt Davis rolled over her mind, like a storm clouding her thoughts. At that moment, Nivi turned her head slowly toward Iris, her eyes two silver hollows, empty and beckoning. A silver substance trickled from her eyes like slimy tears, inching down her cheeks and trickling down her neck, shoulders, and arms. The silver dripped from her fingertips onto the floor where it combined into rivulets, eating into the ground. Cracks appeared on the floor and a low rumble followed. No wonder Ji and Kellan weren't touching her. They both took a step back, still calling to and pleading with Nivi to no avail.

No, Iris thought. *It's the silver. I can't let it control me.*

"What are you waiting for?" Ai said in a hushed voice.

"What do you see?" Meng said beside her.

Their voices snapped Iris out of her daze, and she jerked back her head and pulled the door shut. A cold sweat swept over her face, and she closed her eyes, trying to flush out the silver's compulsions.

"What's going on?" Jorge said. "Is Nivi okay?"

Iris opened her eyes and shook her head. "I—I don't know."

"Then we have to help her!" Jorge tried to push past Iris.

"Wait." Iris put out a hand to stop him. "That thing that has control of her... It's trying to control me too. I can't go in there."

"We can't just leave her there," Jorge said. "We have to try."

"We could let the other prisoners out to help," Ai suggested.

"If these cells are Shifter proof," Meng said, "we won't be able to let the prisoners out without the specific stones or keys, or without Nivi's help."

"Then help Nivi," Iris said. The silver swirled in her thoughts, but she pushed it back to the periphery. Maybe Nivi would be able to do the same. "She's still in there, you just have to get through to her. Help her fight against that thing before she kills Davis. But don't touch the silver. It'll try to control you if you do."

Iris pushed the door open while Meng, Jorge, and Ai rushed past. She slumped onto the floor, her back against the open door, willing herself to stay put instead of giving in to the silver. Her hand slipped into the hidden pocket at her side, and one by one she took out the transfer stones and put them into her suit pockets. When she was done, her pockets bulged with their contents.

Just in case, she thought.

She took off her jacket and lay it on the floor beside her while she watched the situation in front of her unfold. Jorge and Ai stopped in front of Vera's cell, throwing their hands up as if to hug her through the glass. Apparently they knew each other.

Meng ran up to Ji and Kellan.

"Don't touch Nivi," Ji said, sounding pained. "That stuff is all over her."

The cracks in the floor lengthened toward Davis's cell, stopping before they touched the glass.

"The powers keeping Shifters in must be keeping the silver out," Meng said. "Nivi, don't give in! Don't nullify the barriers!"

Nivi's body went stiff and then began to tremble. At the same time, a new wave of thoughts flooded Iris's mind.

Come and end it. End Davis.

Iris grabbed her head, trying to keep the thoughts out, but they expanded, a silver haze over her mind, clouding out her resistance. Slowly, she put her hands down and stood up, swaying a little as the last of her will gave way.

I will let you in, and together we will finish him.

The shouts ahead and the pounding on the cell windows drowned out her approach. She just had to get close and wait until the right moment.

Nivi's body stopped trembling, and more silver oozed off her and pooled around her feet. The pool swirled and widened, climbing up the walls and crawling across the ceiling, forcing everyone to the far side of the hallway, everyone except Iris. The floor cracked. A chasm formed in the hall, separating Nivi and Iris from everyone else. From the ceiling, thin slimy tendrils descended, a glowing silver curtain that connected to the chasm. No one would be able to get to Nivi and Iris without touching it.

Iris moved closer to Nivi. As she approached, Nivi turned and smiled, her eyes depthless glowing pools of silver. She raised a hand and pointed at Davis's cell. Iris turned to look. Davis stood in his cell watching them. Surprise flickered across his face when he saw Iris. Although his arms were relaxed by his sides, his body was unusually stiff, and the sides of his jaw tensed on and off.

A red glow emanated from Nivi's outstretched hand, expanding into a translucent bubble of fire. The edge of the bubble touched the door handle of Davis's cell. There was a click, and then the bubble resorbed into Nivi's hand. She lowered her arm and looked at Iris, and Iris knew she was meant to open the door and finish the job. She took a step forward, and the silver on the floor quickly retreated to make room for her to pass. She took another step and another until she reached Davis's cell. Her hand gripped the handle and opened the door.

She stood in the doorway and stared at Davis. His fingers twitched, and a stream of water swirled around his fingertips. Fish scales glimmered across the back of his hands. He was preparing to fight back, but would his newfound powers be enough to stop her and Nivi?

Nivi stayed where she was in the hallway. Except for what was on the ground and hanging in a curtain to block the others from helping, the remaining silver retreated into Nivi. She had done what she came to do. The rest was on Iris.

Scales appeared on Davis's face and then disappeared. Water flowed out onto the floor, creating small waves. Davis must be testing his new powers. Another wave formed, this one up to Davis's waist, and rolled out toward Iris. It wasn't enough to hurt her, let alone stop her. The bones in her legs cracked and lengthened, and she whipped out the white snake tail, knocking Davis to the ground. He smacked onto his back and the water flowed back into his hands. Pushing himself up, he scooted backward on the ground, fear now clear on his face. But he wasn't going down without a fight. His face hardened, and water pooled around his feet. A wave rose and surged toward Iris.

Iris reformed her legs and waited for the water to hit. She could have easily sidestepped it, but there was no need. It wouldn't harm her. The incoming wave paled by comparison to what the silver could do, especially if she used another transfer stone to increase its powers.

Yells came from across the silver curtain and from behind the other cell windows, but Iris barely heard them. She knew what she had to do.

"You won't survive all these powers," Iris said to Davis. His face fell and his shoulders slumped, all the water flowing back into his body. She focused on his white button-up shirt, memorizing the details before she spoke the next words. "Unless you meet me back in Yuras."

Davis's eyebrows rose in surprise.

"Now, go!"

In one smooth movement, Iris jumped and turned, her body lengthening and coiling around Nivi. White scales encountered glowing silver ooze, and as they touched, a force of powers raced through Iris's system. Heat flooded from her chest to her extremities and launched from her skin in white smoky tendrils. They drifted through the air and into Davis's cell.

"No!" Nivi screamed.

The powers ripped through Iris's system, but still she held on to Nivi's squirming body. She thrashed her snake head into the silver curtain and pools on the floor, and more powers left her system. Nivi's eyes stopped oozing and returned to their light brown color. The slime on her skin disappeared, as did the curtain and the pools on the floor. Eventually, Nivi stopped fighting and went limp in Iris's coils. Only then did Iris release her grip, gently lay Nivi on the floor, and transform to her human self. She collapsed onto the ground next to Nivi, breathing rapidly, and looking for Davis.

He was gone.

Beside her on the floor, Nivi began to weep. It was quiet and weak, and Iris knew just how she felt.

"He killed my father. This was my chance to make things right, and you stole that from me."

Iris squeezed her eyes shut to hold back tears. The memories of that burning house haunted her. She opened her eyes and sat up, reaching a hand tentatively toward Nivi, but there was nothing she could say to help. Nivi lay on the ground, covering her face with her hands while she cried.

Then Ji and Kellan were there, Ji cradling Nivi's head in her lap and Kellan kneeling beside her.

"I'm so sorry, my baby," Ji said. "I should've told you the truth about your father."

"Davis killed him," Nivi repeated.

"I know," Ji said. "Nothing can ever fix that. But you still have a father."

Nivi's eyes landed on Kellan. She didn't look shocked or even surprised.

"I know I'll never replace your dad," Kellan said, his voice thick with emotion. "But I'm here for you and your mom. If you give us a chance to be a family, I promise I'll never give you a reason to regret it."

Nivi sat up and wiped her face.

Ji moved around to kneel before Nivi. "It's a lot to take in. We'll take it slow. Nothing has to change right away."

Meng walked up and offered a hand to Iris, who took it. Once she was back on her feet, she leaned against one of the cell walls. All her powers were gone now, except for her own: her snake form and her finder and fire powers. She smiled to herself, glad that she had prepared for this moment by moving the transfer stones out of the magical pocket. They might need them if Davis wouldn't go willingly to the silver. Despite the lingering weakness and dizziness, she felt better. She hoped Davis would listen to her warning and meet her in Yuras. She didn't want to be an accessory to any more deaths.

Meng crouched by Nivi. "I'm sorry to interrupt, and I know you've been through so much already, Nivi, but we're going to need your help to open the other cells."

Nivi looked up and around, seeming to become aware of the other cells and their inhabitants for the first time. Vera, Amber, and Arav had all gone quiet and were standing at their walls, watching. Slowly, Nivi got up, ignoring Ji's outstretched hand, and went to each cell door, touching the handle briefly. A red glow emanated from her hand before the locks clicked open. Vera came out first and wrapped Nivi in a tight hug.

"Thank you."

Nivi stiffened and responded with an emotionless nod when Vera let go. Jorge and Ai ran up to Nivi, hugging her and exclaiming their relief, and then turned to do the same with Vera. Nivi turned away from the three friends reuniting as if it pained her to watch. She moved on to release Arav from his cell. The two of them stood in front of each other awkwardly until Arav put a hand on Nivi's shoulder, thanked her, and walked over to Vera. He seemed equally if not more awkward in front of Vera, almost as if he were shy or embarrassed. Vera hugged Arav with the same warmth with which she had hugged Nivi and then introduced him to Ai and Jorge. Amber watched Arav with a strange expression from her cell while Nivi let her out.

"Oh, Nivi!" Amber cried, throwing her arms around her. "I'm so sorry. About everything!"

Nivi responded with the same emotionless nod and continued walking down the hallway and out the double doors at the end.

Amber looked bewildered, but Arav walked over and gave her a hug. Both of them tensed as they began to chat.

"Wait!" Ji said, running after Nivi.

"Leave me alone!" came Nivi's reply.

A moment later Ji returned through the doors.

"She needs some time to process," Kellan said, giving Ji a hug.

"I'm going after her," Jorge said to Ai and Vera.

He walked down the hall and through the double doors. Ai and Vera started to follow, but Meng stopped them.

"I know you've all been through a lot, but unfortunately we're not done." She looked from side to side as she addressed everyone in the hallway. "We need to go after Davis. And some of us need to head back to Yuras to help Ling and Captain Maria and her crew."

"Who?" Amber said, her eyebrows pinching together.

"The crew of *The Crabby Lady*," Arav said. "Remember the ghost ship from Alaska? They're the ones who rescued Iris, though I have no idea how."

Amber's eyes darted around the room. "There's so much I don't understand, but I'm not even going to try right now."

"What happened to them?" Arav said to Meng.

"Some Statics ambushed us in the forest, and Ling and the others stayed back to distract them."

"Do you think it's MHU?" Amber said to Arav.

"Unfortunately, yes," he replied.

"And who is she?" Amber whispered to Arav while pointing at Meng.

Arav shrugged even as he turned to Meng. "We're coming with you."

"This would be a great opportunity to bridge the gap between Statics and Shifters," Kellan said, "but I want to stay here for Nivi."

"I'll stay here and wait for Jorge and Nivi too," Ai said.

"I'll head with you toward Yuras," Iris said. "I can sense Davis has gone north. Hopefully he's heading to the silver of his own accord. Otherwise, I'll make sure he goes to the pool to give back the powers." She hurried down the hall and picked up her jacket from behind the double doors, patting the stuffed pockets to make sure they were secure.

"Okay," Meng said as she followed Iris. "We'll go back to Yuras the way we came."

"And what way is that?" Amber said.

A small smile touched Meng's lips. "By dragon."

NIVI

SAN FRANCISCO, CALIFORNIA

NIVI STORMED THROUGH THE hall, passing empty cell after empty cell, the glare of glass blinking in her periphery. How could they have let Davis get away? Tears threatened to form again, and she reached for that deep, dark place that wanted revenge, that wanted to hurt Davis as much as he had hurt her, but it was gone. All she found there was an empty and lonely sadness.

She ran up the stairs and into the open air of the oceanside cliff, sucking in the crisp air in deep, choking gasps. She wasn't going to cry again. She wasn't. A dense fog had moved in, obscuring the edge of the cliffs and the ocean below. Ghostly figures of trees swayed in the breeze. The even grayness of the sky made it hard to tell what time it was, and disoriented in time and space, Nivi felt lost. She didn't know where she belonged. Keeling over, she coughed until her breathing slowed and she no longer felt like gagging or crying. But with the calming of her body came a rush of thoughts and emotions. She stood up and took off running through the shrubs and up the sandy mountainside, through a line of tall cypress trees with their leaning trunks and flat canopies.

Up and up she went until the ocean and trees faded into the fog below and the ground beneath her feet turned rocky. Her body grew hot and each breath burned as she raced away from her troubles. Her lungs wanted to explode, so she let them.

She screamed, heat bursting forth from her chest and threading down her arms and legs. Her veins became molten lava, sparks leaping off the back of her hands as they pumped through the mist. Leaping into the air, her body transformed as her scream became a roar. Her glowing fists hardened into gleaming gold hooves. Green scales spread up her arms and across her body, the feeling like dozens of bubbles popping against her skin. Fire flickered up her legs, protective flames that were harmless both to her as well as the surroundings. Her hooves hit the ground, and she continued galloping up the mountain, knocking brambles out of the way with her horned head. Spots of rainbow dotted the ground, firelight reflecting off her luminescent body.

She arrived at the top of the mountain, a geologic formation of large boulders. Her breath puffed in great clouds. Mist swirled around like ethereal ribbons. Rearing onto her hind legs, she roared and whipped her scaled tail back and forth. She didn't care if anyone heard or saw her. None of it mattered anymore, and in a way, despite her rage and despair, it was freeing.

Footsteps crunched behind her, and Nivi whirled about, immediately transforming back to human form out of reflex. When she saw the creature standing there, fire once again licked up her wrists as she prepared to shield herself. A small black dog approached her—except it wasn't a regular dog. Its gray-and-black fur formed spikes along its spine, and instead of paws it had monkey-like hands. A claw at the end of its tail waved back and forth as the dog walked. Was it waving at her? And then the dog was gone and Jorge stood in its place. Of course, it was Jorge's ahuizotl form.

The fire left her, snuffing out around her hands. Her fury wilted, and she sank onto a boulder, sapped of energy.

"I'm sorry I startled you," Jorge said, taking a hesitant step forward.

Nivi turned away from Jorge and stared off through the fog at the ocean. In the distance, it was impossible to see the horizon or differentiate the sky from the sea. Jorge climbed up the boulders and sat beside Nivi, pulling his knees to his chest and hugging them with his skinny arms. He sat silently and stared out to sea alongside Nivi. The remnants of anger stirred in her chest, and part of her wanted to lash out at Jorge. He was an easy target, with his shy and quiet ways. He was always so nice to her. He'd probably let her take out her anger on him without a fight, and that knowledge just made her sad all over again.

"Why are you here?" she finally said.

"Your mom wanted to come after you first," Jorge said.

At the mention of Ji, fury threatened to rekindle in Nivi, but her soul was spent.

"But she figured you'd want some space," Jorge continued.

At least she got that part right.

"And I didn't want you to be alone—"

"What if I want to be alone?" Nivi cut in.

"--even if it feels like that's what you want right now."

"How would you know what I want or need?" she snapped.

Jorge took a deep breath before responding. His tone was gentle and kind even if the point he made stung. "I also lost a parent and had my past erased."

It wasn't the same though. Jorge couldn't understand how angry she was, how betrayed she felt. "Well, I didn't actually lose a parent, did I? Kellan's right there." She waved her hand toward the base of the mountain like she was backhanding a fly.

"You still lost a parent. The only father you knew until now. Nothing replaces that."

Tears formed in her eyes, and she swiped at them angrily with the sleeves of her sweatshirt. "How are you so calm about all this?"

"I'm not." He rubbed his elbow. "At least not on the inside. I'm just not good at showing how I feel." Nivi didn't respond, and after a moment, Jorge continued. "Your family needs you, and so do your friends. Me, for instance... and Ai, of course."

Nivi looked at Jorge in surprise, meeting his eyes for the first time. Their eye contact went on a moment too long, and Jorge looked away, his cheeks turning red. Nivi didn't know what to say. She'd seen Arav and Amber look at each other that way. Did Jorge *like* her? Should she feel something in response? But she felt nothing. Well, not exactly *nothing*. The attention caused her heart to flutter, but there was no attraction to Jorge. And why shouldn't she be attracted to him? He wasn't a bad-looking guy. He had smooth skin, a strong jaw, a prominent nose, and dark eyes with thick lashes. Model qualities, really, except for his shorter stature, of course. And he was loyal, smart, and even-tempered. She *should* find him attractive.

The more she thought about it, the more she realized she had never been attracted to *anyone*. But should that matter? Did she need to feel attraction to have a relationship? Did she even want a relationship? She was so confused.

Jorge got up, saving her the trouble of responding. "I'll give you some space, but I just want you to know you're not alone." He dusted off his pants and got down from the rocks.

He began to walk down the mountain, glancing back at her once with a shy smile. Nivi didn't move. Her anger toward her family had been diffused by the surprise of Jorge's affection, and if she was honest with herself, she didn't want him to go.

A moment of clarity cut through her cooling emotions. Despite her feelings of betrayal, she owed her family the chance to explain. And it was okay to be angry at Davis—he was the one who had started everything—but the anger was gone. In its place was the horror of what she'd almost done. She'd wanted to kill Davis, and in that moment of intense rage, she would've done it if she'd had the chance. The realization terrified her, and she vowed to never let anger control her again. No matter what monstrous things had been done to her and the people in her life, she wasn't a monster. She had family and friends who cared about her.

Jorge had been right. His presence had helped. But now a new fear kept her from following right away—the fear that if she didn't reciprocate Jorge's feelings, she'd lose a friend. An idea flashed through her subconscious, almost a longing for the days when it was just her and Amber and Po Po. Things had been simpler then, but she quickly suppressed the thought. Of course she didn't want to return to those days. She wanted her mother in her life. Maybe even Kellan. She wanted a whole family.

Dappled sunlight broke through the grayness, raining drops of warmth against her face for a moment before disappearing again behind the clouds. Jorge's form shrank as he descended the mountain, appearing even more diminutive as he approached a line of pines and cypresses. Nivi stood and stretched her head back, closing her eyes against the cloudy sky. Ocean whooshes and seagull squawks rose soothingly up the mountain. When she straightened and opened her eyes, Jorge had disappeared into the trees.

Yells erupted in the distance. Soon after, Jorge reappeared in front of the trees, waving his arms wildly and calling to her. Nivi jumped and skidded down the side of the boulders, a panicked energy renewing her muscles.

"What happened?" she said breathlessly when she reached Jorge.

"I don't know, but it sounded like it came from the prison entrance."

"Let's go!"

Fear gripped Nivi, fear that her family and friends would once again be taken out of her life. They jogged down the mountainside, the wind bending the trees toward the ocean as if an unseen force were pulling them in. Emerging from the trees, they continued through the shrubs and sandy ground until they reached the edge of the cliff near the prison entrance.

No one was there. Nivi turned back and forth, listening for the yells, but only the wind and waves howled in her ears.

"Where are they?"

"They were still in the prison when I came after you," Jorge said. "Maybe they're still there? Or maybe they went to wait on the beach?"

They leaned over the cliff edge and looked down at the small cove. There was no one there either. This was all her fault. If she hadn't run off, they would've all left together before trouble arrived, but now she was going to lose her family again. A new determination fired up in her chest, pumping heat through her veins and down her arms. Her veins swelled and tiny glowing sparks shimmered above her skin. She grabbed Jorge's hand.

"Stay in contact with me, just in case."

At her touch, his cheeks flushed, but he nodded solemnly. They walked hand in hand to the prison entrance. As she suspected, only the rock outcropping was visible, no trace of the doorway in the large boulder in front. Nivi placed her free hand on the rock, and sparks leaped from her skin onto its surface. Under her touch, the rock glowed a warm orange and began to vibrate. There was a crack as if the rock was splitting, and then the outline of a door appeared before fading and revealing the entrance.

"What's the chance whoever's down there didn't hear the door open?" Nivi whispered.

"If they're in the last block, probably pretty good," Jorge said with an encouraging lift of his eyebrows.

Nivi adjusted her grip on Jorge's hand and led the way down the stairs. They got to the bottom and made their way to the first set of double doors. Nivi peered through the windows on the doors. No one there. She took a breath and pushed on the handle. Locked. As before, the stream of fire in her veins quickened its flow, glowing beneath her palm, and the lock clicked open. She pushed the door open slowly and went through, pulling Jorge behind her. Then, she closed it just as slowly to prevent it from clanging.

The rows of cells lay ahead, white walls and floors gleaming under the lights. It was so quiet. Too quiet. The hum of the overhead lights was like the roar of the ocean. They took a few steps, and the rubber soles of their shoes echoed down the empty hall. They froze, glancing left and right as if someone might jump out of a cell. After a moment, they continued more slowly. All the beds were untouched as before. There was no sign that anyone else had been through here.

Halfway to the end of the block, Nivi stopped and cocked her head. Other than their footsteps and the humming of the lights, there were still no noises. No talking and definitely no yelling. Could they have been wrong about the yelling they heard earlier? Maybe it was just a passing group of hikers. But then, where would everyone else have gone? They wouldn't have just left without telling her or Jorge, would they? An unreasonable fear flickered through her mind. No. Someone had replaced the camouflage on the prison door, and it hadn't been her friends or family. She began moving down the hall again.

The rock entrance had been so perfectly camouflaged. Camouflage. The word echoed in her mind. Neither she nor Jorge had been able to see it, so it must have been camouflaged against Shifters. What if the OT police were camouflaged too? Camouflaged against Shifters and Statics alike? Panic and heat surged through her system. Her veins swelled and pumped out more sparks, coalescing into a bubble-thin sphere which expanded to encompass her and Jorge in a fraction of a second. As if out of thin air, two people in black uniforms appeared as her fire shield touched them. Jorge yelped in surprise. It was the two guards who had been in the room when Chief Donald Buhl had questioned them at the Shifter Academy. Nicola Barmann and Eric Okello. The guards lunged forward with glowing white restraints aimed at their wrists.

"No!" Nivi yelled.

The force of her exclamation shot through her body and filled her shield with more sparks and pressure. The shield burst forth with a blast of blinding white light that filled the hall. Unlike the last time when her shield had burst in the transfer stone mine, Nivi remained conscious and standing as the light faded, still clutching Jorge's hand in her own. She wobbled but remained upright with his support. Nicola and Eric were on the ground in front of them, expressions dazed and hands empty. The glowing white restraints had disappeared. Behind them, Ji, Kellan, and Ai sat back-to-back on the ground as if they had been tied together. Her nullifying power had removed the camouflage used on them and the magical restraints. They stood up, rubbing their wrists while sidestepping the guards.

"I'm so sorry," Ji said, embracing Nivi.

"Me too," Kellan said from behind Ji.

Ai embraced Jorge and then Nivi.

Relief flowed across Nivi's skin like a cool stream, dampening the heat in her veins. They were all right. Everyone was going to be all right. She realized she was still holding Jorge's hand and let go.

"Where's everyone else?" Nivi said.

"Meng took them back to Yuras to help Po Po and the others," Ji said.

And just like that the panic was back. "What happened to Po Po?"

"We had a little run-in with some Statics on the way here."

A spiteful and exhausted part of her wanted to run away and never look back. All of this trouble... Her family had brought it upon themselves. But she knew that wasn't true. Despite what small role Ling, Ji, and Meng may have had in the series of events that led to this point, it was greater than all of that. This was a social wave of change that they could ride on or let crash into them, but they couldn't avoid it forever.

Nivi stepped toward the exit. "Then we need to go help too."

To her side, Jorge let out an exclamation and vanished.

"What the..." Ai jerked their arm strangely and then also vanished.

Ji's, then Kellan's eyes widened in brief looks of shock that seared into Nivi's mind and lingered in the air when they, too, blinked out of existence. Nivi whirled around, heart pounding, blood pulsing, sparks jumping from her palms. What was happening? She was alone—completely alone—in the hallway. Even the guards were gone.

Something gripped her wrists, tingling and twisting into the tissue and pulling them behind her back. She struggled but was unable to break free. At that moment, Jorge and Ai reappeared beside her, both with their arms behind their backs, a glowing white band connecting their wrists like handcuffs. Of course there would be more camouflaged guards. How could she have been so careless?

Chief Donald Buhl stood in the hall next to them. He stoppered a glass vial that contained some kind of murky brown liquid in it, then grabbed Ji and Kellan's upper arms. Was that the tincture used to camouflage the guards from Shifters? Now that it had been used on all of them, they could see each other.

"It's a good thing Chairperson Peters sent me here when she did," Donald said, his glare landing on Eric. "To get things done right."

Eric's jaw muscles flexed as he took hold of Nivi's arm. He and Nicola exchanged a glance as she grabbed Ai's and Jorge's arms. It was true; they would've all gotten away if Donald hadn't shown up, but why did Donald blame Eric specifically? Then she remembered Eric talking to Nicola after their interrogation at the Shifter Academy.

He only treats me like that because I'm not a big cat like the two of you. I thought our job was to protect our people.

Maybe she could sway Eric to their side.

"Are you going to let him treat you like that?" she whispered. "To treat us like *this*? I thought you were supposed to protect us. We're only kids."

"It's not my call," Eric said through gritted teeth.

The double doors opened, and Chairperson Ariana Peters walked through, causing the guards to halt their procession. Ariana wore her light brown hair in the same simple, low ponytail. She wore a light gray suit, slim and tapered.

The chairperson scanned them, her eyes flashing silver in the overhead lights. When her gaze paused on Nivi, it sent a chill through her. There was something familiar about that silver color.

How was Ariana able to see them through their camouflage? Had she put the same camouflage on herself? A glint of something around Ariana's neck caught Nivi's eye. Two stone pendants. One was the typical mottled green camouflage stone that all Shifters were required to wear, but the other was a mottled brown that Nivi didn't recognize. Nivi suspected the second one gave her the ability to see through the specific camouflage being used on them.

"Where are the others?" Ariana said.

"We're not sure, ma'am," Eric said, releasing his grip on Nivi's arm.

Ariana's placid expression cracked for a moment. Her nostrils flared with the intake of a deep breath before her gaze went vacant as if she were suddenly somewhere else.

Donald addressed Ariana. "This could work well for us. The school's been worried about them missing. We can spin it as an attack by the Statics, just like we did for that girl Vera."

"It was you!" Ai shouted, struggling against their restraints. Jorge tried to shush them, but Ai continued. "You hurt Vera for some agenda?"

Ariana didn't respond. Her eyes glowed, ever so slightly, enough for Nivi to recognize the source. The silver! Fortunately, it didn't seem to recognize Nivi. Maybe it wasn't as cognizant as it seemed and only had a basic desire to survive.

A calmness returned to Ariana's demeanor, and her eyes focused on Donald. "There's a disturbance in the Yuras forest. They might be headed there."

Or maybe Nivi was wrong. Somehow the silver was communicating with itself about its surroundings. The disturbance Ariana spoke of must be Ling's run-in with the Statics. Was she okay? Nivi pulled at her restraints. She needed to nullify the magic holding them captive and break the silver's hold on Ariana, but she was depleted from her last outburst.

Ariana waved at the guards. "Lock them up until we come back for a full debrief."

"Please let us go," Ji called out. "We didn't do anything wrong."

Ariana looked at Ji as if she were seeing her for the first time. A small smile touched her thin lips. "Don't worry. Everything will be as it should be soon enough."

Lukewarm heat trickled down Nivi's arms. It wasn't enough. The restraints remained in place.

Donald pushed Ji into one of the cells. She stumbled and fell to her knees. He closed and locked the door, and the binds dissolved from her wrists.

"Let her go!" Kellan cried.

He attempted to run after Ji, but Donald pulled him back and herded him into an adjacent cell.

Ji jumped up, ran to the wall, and pounded on the glass, trying to get the chairperson's attention, but Ariana was leaving.

Nicola started to push Jorge and Ai toward their own cells. Ai twisted, breaking from Nicola's grasp. Eric jumped forward to help. For a moment, Nivi was left standing alone.

Everything slowed. Ji's fist hung in the air. Kellan's mouth twisted mid-yell. The whites of Jorge's unblinking eyes shone with tears. Nicola's muscles tensed, arms outstretched. Ai hung in the air, mid-dive, escaping Eric's reach. Veins protruded from the forehead of Donald's beet red face. The edges of Nivi's vision darkened, and the world became a blur. They were taking away her family and friends, and there was nothing she could do. The realization shut her down. She couldn't be a part of this. She couldn't watch.

Guards pushed. Ai and Jorge resisted. Ji and Kellan banged on their cell walls. Yells resonated on both sides. Ariana took a step toward the doors and then another. Nivi backed away, her back and bound hands encountering the cold glass of a cell behind her. She slumped where she stood, sliding down the glass to the floor, her shoulders pulling painfully along the way, but she didn't care. Nothing mattered. She was alone. She would always be alone.

There was a flurry of motion in front of Nivi. Jorge shoved Nicola with his shoulder while Ai stomped on Eric's foot. Eric stumbled into Nicola, who immediately grabbed Ai, but it was enough for Jorge to break free. With his hands bound behind his back, he ran to Nivi, sliding onto his knees and skidding to a stop in front of her. He pressed his forehead to hers.

"You can do this, Nivi. We're in this together."

He sat back from her, and Nivi gazed into his warm brown eyes, his deceivingly soft demeanor that sheltered such ardent strength and steadfast loyalty. Warmth flooded her heart. These were her friends and family. Even if it was hopeless, she had to try.

Then Donald was there, jerking Jorge back.

Eric stepped up to take Jorge from Donald.

"Take it easy, Chief. He's only a kid."

Donald pushed him aside. "Stand down, Officer. I don't even know why I keep you around. I'm more capable than the two of you together."

Fear flashed through Jorge's eyes as Donald dragged him toward a cell, but his jaw remained set, and he nodded at Nivi. She could do this, and she wasn't alone.

Her heartbeat quickened, each beat pushing hot blood through her body. Her pulse thumped against the back of her eyes, sending a flush of heat through her face. She pressed her back into the glass wall and pushed herself up from the floor, a deluge of lava flowing down her veins. As she made it to her feet, the heat reached her wrists. Her powers wrapped around the binds and sank in, destroying their hold on her, their very existence.

Her hands broke free. She strode to the guards, fire licking up her wrists, sparks flying off her skin.

The guards' backs were to her as they tried to get Jorge and Ai into their cells. To their credit, Jorge and Ai were making it very hard for them, fighting and kicking. Nivi swept in between Nicola and Ai, and with a touch of her red-hot fingers, Ai was free. Without hesitation, Ai transformed into a celestial dog and sprang out of Nicola's reach. Their feathery black tail flashed blue and purple, glimmering under the lights like a galaxy of stars. Nicola leaped after Ai, stripes streaking her skin, hands elongating into claws. She landed on padded paws in her tiger form and growled.

"Don't hurt them!" Eric yelled. "We're meant to *protect* our citizens!"

Donald pushed Eric hard enough that he fell to the ground. "Out of the way, bird freak. Let the big cats handle this."

Donald stalked toward Ai, sleek black fur replacing his beige skin, his bulging biceps lengthening into powerful jaguar fore-arms. He joined the giant tiger to stare down the celestial dog. Ai backed up, their canine head looking side to side, their tail drooping.

Eric pushed himself up from the ground, mumbling to himself. "I knew it."

He spread his arms and gray feathers sprouted from his skin. A huge, bulbous, pinkish-gray bill formed on his face, the nail at its tip like the sharpened pick of an axe. Narrowed yellow eyes glared from above the beak as the bird clattered loudly. He jumped into the air, his great wings flapping, and flew at the big cats. Long dark legs extended, each one landing on a feline's head. The cats fell forward, growling and twisting from under the bird's feet.

In the distraction, Ai jumped into action, opening their canine mouth. Darkness flowed out, plunging the guards into a ribbon of pitch black. Each time one of the guards tried to step out into the light, the blackness followed like a sentient cloud. The sudden lack of visibility must've startled them out of their Shifter forms, because the hallway filled with angry and confused yells and the sound of bodies colliding in the dark.

"Watch it!"

"What was that about being more capable than the two of us together?"

"Shut up!"

Jorge sidestepped a leg that emerged from the darkness and then stuck out his own foot to trip the guard. A cloud of night followed the obscured officer's body as he fell to the ground with an angry cry. The celestial dog, sleek and muscular, with a flowing tail like the sky at dusk, expertly swept its head side to side, keeping the guards in the dark.

Nivi rushed to Jorge and dissolved his restraints with her glowing hands.

"Do you think you can hold them long enough for me to get to Chairperson Peters?" Nivi said. She hoped she could catch Ariana before she left the prison completely.

"I think there's something I can do," Jorge said. He pulled off his shirt. With his shirt on, he had been deceptively skinny. Without it, Nivi saw lean muscles like those of a Muay Thai fighter. Black, yellow, red, and blue swirled over his skin. "I've been practicing my mom's patterns, and I think I remember her party trick now."

A red handprint formed on the skin over his mouth. A red and blue human heart appeared on the left side of his chest, skewered with a sharp, yellow stick outlined in black. Across the rest of his face and upper body, linear geometric shapes formed in repeating patterns of red, blue, and yellow. Dispersed among the patterns were suns, split spirals, rabbits, and stair-step designs.

Nivi watched in awe. Could it be that there were multiple layers to his powers?

A mischievous smile curled Jorge's lips as he tilted his head back and raised his voice. "I invoke Mācuīltōchtli, god of pleasure, excess and... drunkenness."

The patterns on Jorge's skin shimmered, and energy filled the room. Nivi stumbled, her head suddenly light. She looked at Jorge, covered in painted designs, and started giggling. It was funny, right? This whole situation was funny.

Ai's celestial dog shook its head, also stumbling. The darkness from their mouth dissipated, and Donald, Nicola, and Eric reappeared from the shadows. Their eyes were bleary, and they swayed side to side.

"Hey, man," Eric slurred, a silly grin on his face. "I'm sorry."

"No," Donald said, returning the grin and emphasizing his words with a hand on his chest. "I'm sorry."

"No, no, no," Nicola said. "*I'm* sorry."

Eric laughed. "Why are you sorry?"

"Because..." Nicola burst into laughter. She swayed and began to sing.

"'I've been a wild rover for many a year. And I spend all my money on whiskey and beer... '"

Donald put an arm over her shoulder and sang the next line. "'But now I've returned with gold in great store... '"

"'And I never will play the wild rover no more,'" Eric finished, putting his arm around Nicola's other shoulder.

Behind them in the cells, Ji and Kellan clapped.

"This is messed up." Kellan laughed but continued to clap.

The guards continued to sing together.

And it's no, nay, never▢
No, nay, never, no more▢
Will I play the wild rover
No never, no more

Even the celestial dog looked like it was dancing, its front paws lifting in rhythm with the song.

"What's happening?" Nivi giggled into her hands.

Jorge nudged Nivi and whispered. "Nullify it."

It took Nivi a moment to realize what Jorge meant. She concentrated on summoning the heat through her body, giggling all the while, and eventually her head cleared. Suddenly sober, she watched the spectacle before her. They were all drunk! She gaped at Jorge, and he shrugged.

Nivi took off running down the hall and pushed through the double doors. The first cell block was empty. If Ariana exited the prison, she'd most likely take off for Yuras in her Shifter form or melt away into silver like Nivi herself had done earlier, and it'd be so much harder to catch her. She sped up, letting her spiraling thoughts fuel her pace.

Ariana. She was the one who had stolen Nivi's family away right when she had gotten them back. Her policies were destroying families everywhere.

Nivi fell onto all fours, her muscles stretching and growing, her joints popping. Iridescent green scales erupted over her skin all at once, snapping into place over her vanishing clothing. Gold hooves gleamed as they clacked against the stone floors and up the stairs. Fire rose up her legs. Sparks jumped off her skin. Flames and sparks coalesced into a bubble-thin shield around her body.

Just outside the prison entrance, Ariana stood, talking on her phone. Nivi leaped into the air just as Ariana turned around. A look of surprise touched the chairperson's face before Nivi was on top of her, her gold hooves knocking Ariana back and pinning her shoulders onto the ground. Ariana's body responded to the assault. Short, soft fur sprouted from her skin, and a membrane formed between her arms, legs, and torso. Her body shrank in size as her eyes became bulbous and round, still gleaming silver. Nivi quickly shifted into her human form to use her hands to grip the moth before it flew from under her.

Heat flowed from Nivi's body and pushed against the cold silver in Ariana as she fluttered in Nivi's grasp. Concentrating all her energy, Nivi exploded her remaining powers against that chill. Would it be enough this time? She hadn't been strong enough to go against the entirety of the silver pool, but this was just a small amount of silver in one person, right?

The moth stopped moving. Slowly, Nivi opened her hands. The silver glow left the moth's eyes. Silver oozed off the soft white body and seeped into the ground.

Drained again, Nivi sat down, resting her back against a rock. The moth lay still on the ground, wings spread as if frozen in flight. Fear flickered through Nivi. Had she hurt Ariana... or worse? But then the moth's head turned, the wings fluttered, and its limbs and torso lengthened and enlarged until Ariana reappeared, sprawled on the ground. Gone were those silver eyes that Nivi had first noticed in the school dining room.

"I—" Ariana began, patting her body. The color drained from her face. She shook her head, and her momentary dazed expression faded into her usual cool demeanor. She got up and brushed off her suit. "Guards!"

Nivi stiffened. It didn't matter that the silver no longer had control of Ariana; she was going to have them arrested anyway.

Singing traveled up the prison steps, and eventually the guards tumbled into the daylight, followed by a dancing Ai and a jovial Kellan and Ji. In their inebriated state, the guards must've released Ji and Kellan.

Jorge brought up the rear, waving his hands in the air as if he were a conductor. He was clearly enjoying himself. When he caught sight of Nivi with Ariana, he froze.

"Tell your friend to stop," Ariana said coolly.

Nivi waved over at Jorge who blinked several times, then nodded. He dropped his hands and the beautiful art on his body disappeared. He quickly pulled his shirt back over his head. The guards staggered, shaking their heads. Donald and Eric pushed themselves away from each other while Nicola smirked. When they saw Ariana, they straightened up and got into line.

Ariana addressed the guards. "We must return to the council headquarters, immediately."

Nivi could only stare in silence. How could the chairperson revert so quickly to business mode after all that happened?

As if reading her mind, Ariana spoke again. "If Davis carries out his end of the deal, we'll soon have many previous Shifters and council members regaining their powers. You can imagine the issues that would cause. We must be prepared to intercept them. We can't let things get out of control."

Control. That word sent a shudder through Nivi. What would happen once Ariana got back to the Shifter Council headquarters? Could she be trusted? Did it matter? She *was* the chairperson. If they forcibly tried to stop her, they'd be taking part in a coup, just like Davis had tried to do. And could Ariana even be blamed for how she'd directed the OT police? She'd been under the influence of the silver at the time. The silver had done the same to Nivi, hadn't it? Or had it only encouraged what was already there? How much of life was taking responsibility for one's own decisions versus blaming something else?

"What about Davis? And the silver?" Nivi said.

"I assume Meng and Iris will have things under control," Ariana said, "but I'll send one of the officers with you to Yuras."

Eric stepped forward. "I'll do it."

Nivi was glad Eric would be the one accompanying them, but she was also a little worried what Ariana and the others would do without his moderating supervision.

Ariana nodded at Eric. "I'll expect Meng to resume her position once all the powers have been restored. In fact, I look forward to stepping down."

Meng's position? Stepping down? And then Nivi understood. Meng had been vice chairperson when Davis attempted his coup. Even if sentiments changed and the council somehow allowed a Static to become politically involved, Davis would still be exempt due to his past criminal actions. Goose bumps pricked Nivi's skin. Meng would be the new chairperson. Despite everything, Nivi found herself respecting Ariana a little. She could've tried to maintain her position of power, but she was willingly standing down.

"Officer Okello," Ariana said. "Can you take us back before heading to Yuras?"

Ai stepped forward, seething. "So you're just going to run away from your actions, after all that you've done? You coward!"

"Ai..." Jorge said under his breath, pulling at their arm.

"You destroyed families!" Kellan added.

Nivi looked admiringly at those who'd spoken up, voicing the concerns and feelings she'd been too afraid to say aloud. Everyone grew quiet and watched Ariana.

"Everything I did," Ariana said with a deep sigh, "was for our people." She nodded at Eric. "Let's go."

Ai shook their head, not soothed by Ariana's words. Kellan made a sound of disgust. It wasn't fair, and it wasn't just, but they'd have to worry about it later. First, they needed to take care of the silver.

"Wait!" Ji said. "We need fast transportation back to Yuras."

"I'll take care of it," Eric said. "My secondary power is teleportation. It'll take me a few minutes each way to take the chairperson back. I'll be back with some water. Trust me, you'll want to hydrate before the trip. Getting to Yuras will take longer, maybe thirty minutes."

"Cool," Ai said, a little of their tenseness fading.

Eric nodded. Ariana touched one of his arms, and Donald and Nicola touched the other, and then all four of them blinked out of existence.

Ji and Kellan ran to Nivi, hugging and praising her. Ai and Jorge joined in. Nivi blushed from the attention, but she was so happy to have her friends and family back that she didn't mind it too much.

"You were so badass!" Ai exclaimed.

"She really was," Ji agreed with a laugh.

"So was Jorge," Nivi said, patting Jorge's back.

"I agree," Kellan said. "Even though I'm not sure what happened exactly." They all laughed again. "Maybe once all this has calmed down, we can sit down and you can explain it all to me."

"I'd like that." Nivi smiled, feeling happier than she had in a long time. She had her family and her friends. Everything else would fall into place.

Nivi sat in a circle with Jorge and Ai to wait for Eric's return. The sun peeked in and out from behind the clouds, and the ocean breeze rustled the cypress trees around them. Kellan and Ji stood nearby, looking out over the cliff's edge. At first they waited in silence, but at some point Kellan leaned over and said something to Ji, and Ji laughed. Watching them, Nivi no longer felt condemnation toward this previous stranger. It made her happy to see her mother happy, and maybe, in time, Nivi would be happy around Kellan too.

From the corner of her eye, Nivi kept catching Jorge staring at her. When she turned to look at him, he glanced away, his cheeks flushing. At some point, he touched her hand with his own. Nivi looked down at their touching hands and, realizing his intention, gently pulled hers away. Her heart fluttered again at his attention. Was this something she wanted?

"Jorge..." she began, hesitating. How could she tell him this without hurting him? "I don't—"

Jorge looked away. "I don't blame you. I mean, you're amazing, and I'm just—"

"No, it's not that. I don't know how I feel. I've never felt that way about anyone. Do you understand? I need time to figure things out. Please say we can still be friends." Jorge didn't respond right away, so Nivi continued, feeling the need to explain and justify herself, to hopefully save their friendship. "I've never *liked* anyone... at least... not like that. Sure, it'd be nice to have a partner, but—I don't know why I'm like this, I just am. I hope that doesn't change anything between us."

Jorge's face fell, just a little bit, but it still hurt Nivi to know that she was hurting him. He looked down at the ground. "I understand."

"So you're asexual," Ai said from the side. "Cool."

Jorge looked up at Ai, his brow furrowed.

"Oh," Nivi said. "I didn't know it was a thing. I just thought... I was different."

"You *are* different," Ai said with a wink. "And special, just like everyone else."

Jorge nodded slowly as if he was starting to understand. "Thanks for telling me—uh—us."

"So we're okay?" Nivi asked.

"Yeah." Jorge smiled.

Even with the lingering unease of what they needed to accomplish in Yuras, they continued chatting and were soon laughing together, just a happy group of family and friends, enjoying a beautiful day.

ARAV

YURAS, CALIFORNIA

ARAV GRIPPED THE DRAGON'S dorsal plate as it landed on the Yuras cliffs, his stomach jumping with the drop. Before their flight, Meng had introduced all the new people to each other, and he reviewed their names now while waiting to dismount. Those sitting at the front of the dragon were taking too long, using Meng's horns to lower themselves to the ground, so he ended up sliding off her flank.

"Davis is here," Iris said. "I'll go after him. You'll still have to return your powers to the silver, Meng. To restore the balance, they have to go through me, Davis, then back to you."

Meng transformed into her human form and nodded. "After I've helped Ling."

"Wait," Vera said to Iris. "Can you explain what you just said?"

Iris took a deep breath and spoke quickly. "If a transfer stone is used to transfer powers, it makes a disturbance in the magic, which creates this silver pool. Each transfer makes the silver bigger and more powerful. If a person with transferred powers touches the silver, those powers go back to the person who had them before, and the silver shrinks in size and power. If you don't have transferred powers and you touch the silver, it will try to possess you."

"Or eat you!" Amber added. "I saw it consume a whole man." She turned to Arav, her voice shaky. "I didn't tell you yet, but the silver got Mr. Pei."

Oh, no. That was awful. Amber took his hand, and he squeezed it. He swallowed down a lump forming in his throat. He had to focus on the current situation. He couldn't think too much about that right now.

"Got it," Vera said. "Stay away from the silver. A little touch and it might control you or consume you."

"It must consume anything that falls directly in it," Meng said. "Earlier, I saw it suck down a whole house and some trees."

Arav shuddered and changed the subject. "How do you know Davis is close?"

"By his shirt," Iris said with a smirk. "I committed it to memory while we were in the prison. I'm assuming he hasn't taken it off." She ran off into the forest with a wave.

Vera looked at Arav and Amber with a questioning look. They shrugged.

"Iris's secondary power," Meng explained, "is finding objects. She can't find people directly so she's locating him by his shirt. Let's hope Ling hasn't moved and is also easy to locate."

As they followed Meng into the forest, Arav regarded the cliffs. So much had changed since the last time he'd been here. When he'd left Yuras for Alaska, he'd been hunting *monsters*. Since then, he'd learned that *he* was actually a Shifter, as was his mother. So had his mother's death actually been an accident like the police had ruled? Or had it been murder like his father believed?

Images rushed through Arav's memory. The twisting of Kabir's body near this location as a dark figure slashed his torso. The slashes across his mother's body. And Davis's reaction when he first met Arav, the way his eyes had widened... Davis had recognized him. Arav flashed back to the strange visions he'd had in the prison. Every time he'd been angry, he'd been transported into a scene on the Yuras cliffs. Davis had been there. And his brother and mom. Were they just visions? Or something else?

They continued through the forest on a dirt road. A large crowd was gathered ahead, shouting at a group of four people. Arav recognized Ling at the forefront of the smaller group. A member of the crowd swung a bat at her, and Arav gasped, but the bat bounced off the air in front of her as if it'd hit an invisible dome.

"We aren't going to hurt you," Ling cried, her hands out in a placating gesture.

"Everyone back on," Meng said, her blue eyes flashing.

She transformed into a dragon, and Arav, Amber, and Vera scrambled onto her back. Meng lifted up into the air and flew over the four people at the center of the crowd. At the sight of the dragon, the crowd went into turmoil, pushing and shoving and yelling. Arav saw Ling look up and then motion to a young man beside her. The man raised his hands over his head, moving them in a slow circular motion, then waved for Meng to descend.

Meng landed beside Ling, and the young man waved his hands over his head again. Arav and the others got off Meng's back, and Meng transformed into her human form. At this closer vantage point, Arav recognized the other people with Ling were Maria, Shawn, and Alek, *The Crabby Lady* crew members.

"I secured the shield all around us," Shawn said, "including the hole I opened over the top to let you in. But I'm getting tired. I don't know how much longer I can hold it."

The air between Ling and the angry mob wavered as something else hit the shield. Meng ran to stand beside Ling. Amber and Vera followed.

"It's her!" a man in a red flannel yelled, pointing at Meng.

Arav recognized that voice and that flannel. It was his dad.

Shouts erupted from the crowd.

"Kill them!"

"They killed Fatima!"

"They took Arav!"

Ling tilted her head toward Meng. "What are you doing?"

"I'm here to help you."

"You're making it worse."

The wavering air in front of Ling and Meng shook violently again, blurring the crowd before them.

"I can't hold it any longer," Shawn said, his voice strained.

Then the air went still.

Arav ran in front of Ling and Meng. "Dad! I'm here! I'm okay!"

Frank looked at Arav with a silver glisten in his eyes. The silver faded and a look of pained surprise overtook his face.

"Arav?" Frank mouthed, then rushed forward to embrace him.

Arav hugged his dad tightly, burying his face into Frank's shoulder. He was actually here—home—somewhere he'd thought he'd never get back to when he'd been locked in the prison. And yet, the relief he should've felt was clouded by an ominous presence. He lifted his head from his dad's shoulder and looked out into the forest.

Something flashed by in the distance, past the crowd. *Someone.* A dark figure with a Shifter aura ran across the dirt road behind the crowd and into the trees. Arav didn't so much see the figure as feel it, and suddenly a memory clicked into place. That same dark figure who'd injured Kabir. Tall, slim, with black hair. Anger grew in Arav as he groped for more. He needed to know who the dark figure was. Was his mother's death an accident?

As in the prison cell, his consciousness pushed from his body and propelled through the trees toward the Shifter. And there he was again, looking into his mom's face. There was fear in her eyes. She was falling off the cliff. Down. Down. To the rocks below.

And then Arav was back in his body.

It was Davis! Arav had seen his mother fall to her death through *Davis's* eyes. All those things he'd seen in the prison... They were memories! *Davis's* memories!

Trembling, he let go of his dad and pointed in the direction of the Shifter glow.

"That's who killed Mom," Arav said. The tone of his voice was dark. Deadly.

Iris appeared behind the crowd, running across the road in the direction Davis had gone. Arav couldn't let her get him. Davis was his.

Amber grabbed his arm. "Arav, what are you doing? We need to stay here to help Ling and the others."

Arav pulled his arm from Amber. "This is how we help."

He broke into a jog, pushing his way through the crowd. Frank and a dozen other Statics followed him through the trees. Arav caught sight of Iris ahead of him. At the sound of the Statics' pursuit, she glanced back and made a sharp turn into the trees, disappearing from view. Good. Now no one was blocking his way to Davis.

Davis couldn't be allowed to run free to hurt other families. The loss of Arav's mother reemerged with a vengeance. Gone were the denial, depression, and bargaining. All that remained was pain and anger. So strong were the emotions that his bones ached, his joints cracked, and his muscles pulled unnaturally. He had accepted what he was going to do.

Somewhere behind, Arav heard the cries of his dad, and of Amber and Vera, but they were fading. Arav ran faster and faster, almost as if his feet weren't touching the ground. Something pinched and pulled between his shoulders. Wind blew by, above him and below. He looked down. The ground swept past under yellow eagle claws. The legs and tail of a lion hung behind. Brown feathered wings pumped to the sides, barely missing the trees with their enormous span.

Arav was so startled that he almost collided with a tree. He barely regained his balance just in time to avoid a full collision, but a wing clipped against the trunk of a redwood, causing him to lose control. Dropping to the ground, he caught himself on all fours, eagle and lion claws digging into the dirt.

Vera had told him what he was before, and he'd seen the claws fade from his hands, but he hadn't fully allowed himself to believe it. Had his dad or the other MHU members seen him?

From between the trees, a figure darted away, and Arav resumed the chase. He could see Davis's back weaving through the trees. That coward. That *murderer.*

In frustration, Arav swung a front claw at Davis's retreating figure. The force of anger jolted Arav from his body, and he was again in Davis's memories.

He hadn't meant to scare her. He grabbed at her as she went over the cliff edge, tried to save her, claws extended from his fingers to grip her shirt and skin, but she kept falling. Falling. Horror. Regret. Sadness. And a deep self-loathing.

Arav shot back into his body at a distant pursuit, but Davis tripped and went tumbling onto the ground as if Arav's intrusion into his memories had dealt him a blow. In a few more bounds, Arav closed the space between him and Davis. He leaped into the air and hovered as Davis flipped onto his back.

Davis threw his hands out in defense. Water sprang from his palms, but it had little effect on Arav who flew a little higher out of reach. Scales covered Davis's body, some kind of lizard or fish, but they wouldn't be enough to protect him from Arav's claws and beak. A kaleidoscope of colors rippled through Davis's skin. Sweat dripped from his pale face, his arms shaking.

This was it, Arav realized. Davis wouldn't be able to defend himself. Whatever powers he had now were no match for Arav's strength. He could finally get justice for his family and give them all peace.

His great wings rustled the nearby pine needles with their wind. The whites of Davis's eyes shone. Arav opened his mouth and screamed. A screech pierced the air. Sharp claws opened, closed, aimed.

Arav dove.

The tips of his front claws touched Davis's left cheek.

An electric shock hit Arav and knocked him to the side just before his claws plunged into flesh. He tumbled out of the air and onto the ground, banging into a tree trunk. The impact jolted him back into human form, and he lay on the ground, gasping for air. Footsteps ran up to his side, and he braced himself for Davis's attack, but it wasn't Davis. It was Amber. She dropped to her knees beside him and held him.

"I'm so sorry," she whispered. "But you can't hurt him."

"He killed my mom," Arav rasped, rage filling the void in his heart.

He broke free from Amber's embrace and struggled to his feet. Davis was just ahead, crawling away, wiping the blood that ran down his cheek.

"Please, Arav," Amber said, grabbing on to one of his hands. "Killing him won't bring her back."

Arav shook Amber off and kept moving. Another shock ripped through his body, and he fell back onto the pine-covered dirt. The tang of metal flooded his mouth, and his ears rang.

Amber stood over him, tears in her eyes. "I'm sorry. I can't let you kill him. Otherwise, we're all doomed."

Arav tried to sit up. Amber reached a blue-scaled hand toward him. Electrical sparks leaped from her fingers and arced into a bolt that slammed into his chest. A sharp pain seized his muscles. He fell back to the ground.

"Get out of here!" Amber screamed.

Arav furrowed his brows and realized she wasn't talking to him. She was helping Davis. A new pain hit his heart. Betrayal. The girl he had loved was helping his mother's murderer.

Amber turned back to him as if she sensed his pain. "If you kill him," she explained, "the silver will expand and destroy everything in its path."

Arav turned his head away, unable to respond. So much anger and pain threatened to burst from his body, but he lay unable to move from the shock to his muscles. He clenched and unclenched his fists, feeling the movement slowly return to his extremities.

Yells and footsteps came through the forest.

"He's getting away!"

"No, he's over here!"

Arav turned his head to see his dad standing halfway between Davis and himself. Frank turned back and forth as if torn about which direction to go in. The dappled lighting hit his eyes and made them appear silver. The other dozen or so MHU members who had followed stood in front of Frank, yelling and pointing at Arav.

Why were they all focused on Arav? They were letting Davis get away!

Because they'd seen him transform. They knew he was a *monster*.

Arav bent and unbent his knees. His muscles were working again. As the crowd advanced, Amber positioned herself in front of him in a protective position, as if she were suddenly on his side. The crowd hesitated for a second and then continued to advance. Amber glanced down at Arav, a look of fear on her face, but she stood her ground, blue sparks igniting on her fingertips. She turned to face the oncoming MHU members.

Behind the crowd, Meng's blue dragon whipped into view, roaring. It was the distraction Arav needed. He stood up and again took off after Davis. He wouldn't let him get away. He couldn't.

He ran as fast as he could, feeling his body transform and wings sprout behind his shoulders. He no longer cared if everyone saw him shift. All that mattered was getting Davis. Leaping into the air, he spotted his prey a short distance ahead. He aimed his eagle claws and dove down, shrieking.

Davis turned, hands raised in defense, as Arav's claws knocked into his chest. Davis fell back onto the forest floor. Blinded by rage, Arav dug his claws into Davis's flesh.

Claw marks.

His mom. His brother. They both had claw marks across their chests, just like Davis did now.

Arav pulled back, repulsed. He was a monster, just like Davis.

That bit of hesitation was enough for Davis to slip away. He rolled from under Arav, clutching his bleeding chest, and staggered to his feet. Tentacles sprouted from his waist to support his human legs. Darting between trees, he tripped and caught himself, his injuries obviously taking their toll. Arav shrieked and leaped into the air, preparing to attack again.

A gunshot rang out, and Davis fell. He lay there, unmoving.

No! This was supposed to be *his* vengeance. This was the moment he'd wished for, the moment that would get justice for his mother and bring punishment and pain upon the person who had caused all this. But instead of relief or satisfaction, a new dread settled in. Arav's pulse thrummed wildly, causing his ears to ring worse than the aftereffects of the gunshot. Someone had just been killed before his eyes. It was too easy. To be alive one moment and gone the next. He scanned the ground for the origin of the shot. Standing a short distance away was his dad, a shotgun smoking in his hands.

Arav plunged from the sky and hit the ground harder than he meant to, most likely due to his inexperience in his Shifter form. He shifted into human form and tried to get up but couldn't.

Davis stirred and got to his feet with the help of his tentacles. He began to limp away, still clutching his bleeding chest. So Davis hadn't been shot. He must have only tripped.

A heaviness descended upon Arav. His heart beat too fast. His leg wouldn't move. A dark stain spread from a hole in his left jean leg. The pain hit him all at once.

The silver cleared from Frank's eyes. He dropped his gun and ran to Arav.

"Arav! No, no, no!" He knelt beside his son, pressing down on his wound. "I thought you were a monster. I don't know what came over me."

"He *is* a monster!" came a shout from an MHU member.

"Finish him off!" yelled another.

The first MHU member picked up the shotgun that Frank had dropped, pumped it, and aimed it at Arav. A tall, lanky youth came up behind the person with the gun. Tom Ross! He wrestled the gun away and backed up toward Arav and Frank, pointing the gun at the two MHU members.

"Stay back!" Tom yelled. "You've gone too far! We're not here to hurt innocent people!"

"You shouldn't have done that," Arav said weakly to Tom. "You could've been shot."

Someone ran toward them, and Tom swung the gun in the direction of the footsteps. Amber yelped and raised her hands. Tom lowered the gun and nodded at her to join them. Amber ran over and dropped to her knees beside Arav.

"Oh no, Arav." Her voice wavered.

Despite his earlier feeling of betrayal, Arav was glad to see her. He took one of her hands in his, wincing at the pain in his leg.

"Hold on, son!" Frank yelled, still putting pressure on Arav's leg. He kept looking at Davis as if he wanted to go after him, but he stayed by Arav's side. His face contorted as if he were fighting internal demons, and his eyes vacillated between silver and brown.

More MHU members trickled in from different sides of the forest, surrounding them. They inched closer and closer, their mouths twisted and their fists clenched. One of them carried a bat, another one a shotgun of his own. Tom whirled around with the shotgun in his hands, unsure where to aim.

Through the forest came the sound of galloping hooves hitting dirt. A cloud of dust rose up between the trees and through it came a man riding a horse-like dragon. Iridescent green scales caught the speckled forest light in purples and blues. Gold branched horns shone on its head and fire rose up from the swiftly moving golden hooves. It jumped in front of the MHU member with the shotgun, knocking the gun from his hands with a rear kick. A white fox and two black dogs followed on the dragon's heels. One of the dogs was like a lean raccoon, and the other was the biggest, most muscular dog he'd ever seen. And it had wing-like purple and blue hair flowing off its shoulders. Wait, did the fox have a silver horn?

The fox picked up the fallen shotgun in its jaws. The smaller dog ran by the MHU member with the bat and grabbed it from his hands with the claw at the end of its tail. All the creatures skidded to a stop by Arav, Amber, and Frank, and the man dismounted from the dragon-horse. It was Kellan, but where had the other creatures come from? The dragon-horse shrank and reared back on two legs while skin and clothing replaced the scales. In an instant, Nivi stood in its place. The dogs transformed into Ai and Jorge, and the fox became Ji. Even though Arav had come to understand they were all Shifters, it was still a shock to see the transformations in person.

A large gray bird flew down from the trees and landed by Kellan, shifting into Eric, one of the prison guards. What was he doing here?

Soon after, Meng's blue dragon floated through the trees, carrying Ling, Vera, and *The Crabby Lady* crew on its back.

The MHU members in front of Tom backed up as the dragon approached. More MHU members emerged from the trees behind Meng, but their numbers were smaller than before, and they kept a wary distance.

The dragon landed near Arav. Ling, Vera, and the fishing crew dismounted from the dragon's back, and Meng transformed into human form.

"Here," Ji said, handing the shotgun to Ling. "You know how to use this."

Jorge handed the bat to Ai who held it over their shoulder and glared at the MHU members.

"Davis..." Arav said, pointing to where Davis limped some thirty feet away.

Davis picked up speed. Tentacles flung out, grabbing branches to help swing him over the ground. He was going to get away.

Suddenly, a giant white snake slithered in front of Davis, cutting off his path. The snake's tail lashed out, knocking Davis's tentacles from the branches on one side. Davis fell. He pushed himself onto his hands and knees and dragged himself away from the snake, trailing blood. Blood from injuries Arav had given him. Pain shot up Arav's leg, making his head swim, and with it, Davis's memories again flooded his consciousness.

For a second time, Arav saw Davis's reaction to his mother's death. It had been an accident. Davis hadn't meant to kill his mother. He loathed himself for it, even as he tried to cover it up through his obnoxious smugness and charm.

Arav choked on a sob as the memories faded. So what if it had been an accident? Did that change anything? But he could already feel a slight lightening in his body and soul.

Ji kneeled beside Arav and gently removed Frank's hands from his leg.

"I can help him," she said to Frank's protests. "Trust me."

The gray strip of hair above Ji's forehead shimmered, and a warm tingle spread across Arav's leg. He flexed his muscles. The pain was gone.

Across the way, the snake slithered around Davis. He wobbled on his hands and knees, then fell on his face.

The snake transformed into a human. It was Iris! Arav would need to process his awe at all the Shifter forms later.

Iris kneeled over Davis. She looked up and called out. "Ji! Help!"

"We need him to survive," Ji said. "I need to heal him." She turned to Nivi. "Go to Frank. Get the silver out of his system."

There was too much happening to fully comprehend, but Arav understood that whatever had had a hold of Nivi in the prison also had the same hold on his dad. He gave Nivi a pleading look. Nivi bit her lip. Why was she balking? Tears ran down her cheeks, and Arav realized she didn't want Ji to help Davis. Maybe Davis had also caused her pain. But no matter how Arav and Nivi felt, Davis couldn't die, not if they wanted to stop the silver.

One of the MHU members rushed Tom. Meng shot forward, instantly back in dragon form, knocking the member to the ground with the tip of her tail. A few more members ran forward, but the dragon hissed, and electricity seared the ground. The MHU members skidded to a stop and quickly retreated as the dragon turned its glowing blue eyes on them. Once Meng seemed satisfied at the crowd's distance, she turned around and rejoined Ling in her human form.

"Go, now." Ji's words to Nivi were gentle yet firm.

Nivi nodded, and Ji ran to Davis. Nivi walked up to where Frank knelt by Arav and put a hand on the top of his head. A warm glow shone where she touched him. Silver pooled in Frank's eyes and dripped down his face. It dropped to the ground and disappeared into the soil. He glanced around, eyes wide, tears rolling down his cheeks.

"I'm so sorry, my son."

"It's okay, Dad."

Arav pushed himself to a seated position and took Frank's hand in his own. All that anger and sadness and hate… They'd wasted so much of the little time they had in this world on those negative feelings. His mom wouldn't have wanted that, but now they had a chance to start again.

Amber stood up, her hands still sparking.

"So that's where my bit of power went," Meng said, walking up beside Amber.

Amber looked sheepish. "I didn't mean to take it."

Meng winked. "I know."

"What are we going to do about these other Statics?" Nivi said, pointing at the MHU mob.

"I think we're going to have to let the OT police handle them," Meng said, glancing at Eric.

Nivi shook her head. "No. No more."

"I'm sorry," Meng said. "It's not our call."

Eric looked at the Statics and then back at Nivi. The hint of a smile touched his eyes. "I didn't see anything."

"How are you feeling?" Meng said to Arav.

Frank jumped to his feet, positioning himself between Meng and Arav. "Stay away!"

Arav got to his feet. "It's okay, Dad." His dad looked at him with wild eyes. Arav put an arm over his shoulders. "We have a lot to talk about."

Ji reached Iris and Davis and kneeled next to them. She ran a hand over Davis's chest. A moment later, Davis vanished. Arav gasped. Ji shouldn't have healed him without tying him up first. They had been too distracted. Too foolish.

Ji ran back to them. "I'm sorry. I didn't think—he was losing so much blood."

"I'll find him," Iris said behind her. "He came here of his own accord, so I don't think he's a flight risk. I think he was just scared."

She glanced at Arav, and Arav felt a pang of guilt for his part in harming Davis.

"One of us should go with you," Meng said.

"No," Iris said. "Let me try first. I think he'll listen better to me if I'm alone. And if I fail, then I'll bring one of you with me to find him again."

"Can we trust her?" Nivi blurted.

"Yes."

Everyone turned to look at the muscular, petite woman standing behind Iris. Alek and Shawn flanked their captain.

Maria continued speaking. "We shared a form with Iris. Her intentions are genuine. She will be true to her word."

"Captain Maria's right," Ling said. "None of us have anything to gain by letting the silver go unchecked."

Iris looked around at everyone present. When there were no more objections, she ran through the trees and was gone.

At that moment, the ground began to shake. A fissure opened, cracking straight through the crowd of MHU members and ending about ten feet away from Meng and Ling. The surrounding trees fell into the crack with a crash. Silver bubbled from within the fissure, encasing and sucking down the trees. Arav spread his arms to his sides, trying to maintain balance. The MHU members ran back from the bubbling silver, stumbling through the trees as the ground continued to move.

"It's the silver!" Nivi cried.

"Amber. Shawn," Meng said. "We need to touch it."

Meng and Shawn approached the crevice. Silver bubbled out over the edge and slurped onto the dirt road.

Amber hung back, glancing at Arav, then ran to catch up with Meng and Shawn. The ground shook again, causing everyone to lose their footing. Meng fell to her knees and crawled toward the silver. Shawn and Amber followed suit. As they approached, the silver changed course as if avoiding them.

"This isn't working," Shawn said over the rumbling of the ground and the crashing of the trees. "We can't get close to it."

"Here!" Meng said. "Hold on!"

She took one of Amber's and Shawn's hands in each of her own. The back half of her body lengthened into a blue serpentine tail, propelling the three of them into the nearest glob of silver with sudden speed. White light erupted from where their hands touched the silver, coalescing into one localized haze that lingered above Shawn, and another that moved from Amber to Meng and then into the air, before they all dissipated. The remaining silver retreated into the crevice, and the ground stilled.

Meng, back in full human form, got to her feet and dusted off her dress and cardigan. She helped Amber and Shawn stand up. All their auras were gone.

"Let's hope Iris is successful," Meng said as she rejoined the group.

They all settled down to wait, bracing for potential doom.

IRIS

YURAS, CALIFORNIA

IRIS RAN THROUGH THE forest and toward the cliffs. Davis hadn't gone far; she could feel it.

She found him by the cliff's edge, near the same area where they had walked that moonlit night all those years ago. This was where it had all begun. The place she had fallen for a handsome, smooth-talking man obsessed with ambition, belonging, and revenge. The fate of the world depended on them now. Was it fate that brought them here together to close the circle?

He stood with his back to her, hands in his pockets, facing the setting sun. Brilliant shades of red spread up from the horizon, staining the clouds a golden pink and silhouetting Davis in a dazzling glow. It took Iris a moment to realize the glow also emanated from within him; the culmination of all those returned powers. Iris approached and stopped at the edge of his shadow. The elongated figure looked deflated. Davis stood tall and trim, but his shoulders sagged and trembled ever so slightly.

He must've sensed her presence because he turned, a sad smile touching his lips when he saw her. "Are you here to stop me?"

"Do you need to be stopped?"

Davis let out a morose laugh. "Even if I wanted to take over the world, I doubt there is anything I could do to gain the upper hand this time that the council won't be prepared for." He bent his arms and looked down at his palms. "Even with all this."

Iris stepped toward Davis, hope surging within her. "Then give it back. Come with me into the forest. Touch that silver pool. Stop it before it's too late. Don't you see? As long as you keep these powers, even a little bit of them, your mind is not your own. That silver will have power over you and through you."

"Don't *you* see? I'm nobody without these powers. Nothing. Inconsequential. Unworthy."

"That's not true. Look what you've accomplished in such a short time without them. All this time, you thought you were using your sister's allure to climb the political ladder, when in actuality, you naturally have a talent with people."

Davis turned away from Iris, put his hands back into his pockets, and looked out to sea. The last of the sun slipped below the horizon, and the bright hues thickened into blood. When he didn't respond, Iris walked up to Davis's side and tried again in a soft voice.

"If you don't, the powers will kill you."

"Why do you care?" His harsh tone took her aback, and she had no response. Davis sighed and continued, his tone still tense. "Why should I care what happens to a world that won't accept me?"

Iris couldn't help her voice rising. "That *world* you speak of is less than one percent of the total population!"

Davis's voice rose to match hers. "But it's the one that matters!"

"Says who? Your *father*?"

"Don't speak about what you don't know!"

"I know what it's like to be caught between two worlds and not fully belong to either. But it's time to stop playing the victim." Iris paused to take a breath. Her own words surprised her. She realized she was speaking to herself as much as she was to Davis. "Take responsibility for your actions. Empower yourself. You did this. You made a choice, and it was wrong. Learn from it and move on. You are in control of your life and your happiness and your belonging.

"You're working to please the wrong person. Your father was never going to accept you, Shifter or not. Other people will, just as you are, but not unless you accept yourself first. You've already risen to be the Static representative in the pro-integration cause. Now stop trying to destroy yourself and those around you. Find it in yourself to turn your platform and your connections toward good instead of destruction."

Davis was silent for a moment before he spoke again. "Does that mean you won't turn me over to the Shifter authorities?"

"I can't speak for others, but if you fix this, you'll make your peace with me."

Davis nodded thoughtfully and again stared out at the ocean. The ground beneath them shook. Davis didn't react, almost as if he'd expected it to happen. Iris's heart thumped and ached. If he didn't come with her, they were all doomed.

Heat rushed into her core and a tingly sensation across her skin made all her hairs stand on end. She glanced down at her hands. A smattering of blue scales shimmered briefly across her palms before fading. Sparks of electricity jumped from her fingertips. Meng. She must have returned her powers to the pool. More powers flowed into Iris's system, several this time. Shawn.

She and Davis had all the displaced powers now.

Davis spoke without looking at Iris. "You're still the same naive girl. You think I can change, but I haven't. I can't. I'm too far gone."

Iris shook her head. He had done some terrible things, but so had she. Were both of them beyond redemption? Beyond compassion? Beyond understanding and love? Maybe they would never fit in with the rest of society, but did that mean they shouldn't be given another chance?

"We may never be forgiven for our past sins," she said, a wobble in her voice, "but that doesn't mean we should let them dictate our future actions. We are human, prone to respond to our experiences and emotions, our circumstances and the random mix of chemicals that just happen to be passing through our brains and bodies at any given time, but we are also corrigible. We can learn and eventually—if we keep at it—change. We just have to keep trying."

The corner of Davis's lip curved up. "Still so good with the campaign speeches."

Iris hesitantly returned the smile. Was she finally getting through to him? She didn't know if it was the surge of new powers or the fear of extinction that made her suddenly brave and want to bare it all.

"Don't you realize you've always had people who care about you?"

Davis's voice sounded far away. "The only person who loved me died a long time ago."

"That's not true!"

Heat rose into Iris's cheeks. She was as surprised by her outburst as Davis looked at that moment. He met her gaze with a small furrow between his brows, but the anger was gone from his face. He didn't say anything for a while, just continued to look at her.

Iris's cheeks burned even hotter, and she felt compelled to explain herself. "I, uh, mean, your sister Anna for one."

What was she doing? Confessing her true feelings? Did she even know what those feelings were?

Something like disappointment flashed across his features. "Well, if that was once true, after what I did to her, it's not anymore."

There was something there in her, somewhere deep down, despite how wrong it may be. A flutter of affection, a mutual understanding, an attachment for time shared. He needed to know he was valued, that he wasn't alone. Her voice dropped to almost a whisper.

"You don't know that. People don't stop loving each other just because someone does something bad to them. She might be angry, but she didn't stop loving you."

Davis locked eyes with her, his black irises so intense they had their own gravitational field. No matter how red she must be turning, she couldn't look away. Did he suspect the sentiment behind her words? Eventually, he turned away, saving Iris from further embarrassment.

He was silent, and so was she, allowing the crash of the waves below to communicate the turmoil within. A silver veil swept across Iris's mind, like mist settling over the ocean. They should keep their powers, run away together, be powerful *together*.

No, Iris thought. She wouldn't allow herself to be manipulated or controlled any longer—by the silver, Davis, her mother, or anyone else. She fingered the transfer stones in her pocket, knowing she had to give them up. A wave of panic swirled the silver in her mind, and whispers flooded her thoughts, telling her to leave, to keep what was hers.

"Aren't you tired of being controlled?" Iris blurted in response to the compulsion.

Davis was quick to respond. "I'm not being controlled."

He thought she was talking about the silver, but she meant to dig deeper. "By the memory of your father?" Davis's jaw tightened, and Iris knew she'd hit a nerve. "Your father was a bastard who made up for his own insecurities by taking it out on his son. You were only a child, and he took advantage of his power over you to break you down, make you feel like you weren't enough. But you *are* enough. You were always enough."

Davis let out a bitter laugh. "Last time you were nice to me, you tackled me into the water."

"Who says I won't now?"

They locked eyes again, and a real smile touched Davis's lips, but he still didn't make a move to follow her.

If he wouldn't go willingly, she could force him, grab him like she had on the dock outside the Shifter Council headquarters, use another transfer stone to take his powers, and drag him to the pool. She could touch the pool and dunk him in at the same time.

If she forced him, she'd be crushing the last bit of self-worth that Davis was holding on to. Was there a point where one was beyond redemption? Had she passed it herself? If that was the case, maybe she could do some good for the world by committing a final bit of evil.

Before she needed to make that call, he finally turned to her and nodded.

"Okay," he said.

Iris felt her shoulders relax. Together, they slowly walked away from the cliffs, back into the forest, taking the long way around to avoid the group of Statics. All the while, silver swirled in and out of her mind and pulled at her subconscious. She knew Davis felt the same, but they didn't veer from their course. The closer they got to the pool, the less hold it had over her thoughts, until it faded into the periphery.

In the darkness of the forest, the silver pool glowed almost peacefully, as if resigned to its fate. As if it were content with the short time it was able to exist in this world.

The wind faded, and all was still and silent as they approached the pool's edge. Iris kneeled beside it and looked up at Davis. He kneeled next to her and nodded. She took off her suit jacket and dropped it—pockets full of transfer stones and all—into the pool. The splash was unremarkable, and the retreat of the silver was like a puddle drying in the sun. They stood and followed the retreating edge until it stabilized and then kneeled again.

Davis hesitated. "What about the powers that belonged to my mother and father?"

"What about them?" Iris said.

"They have no one to return to."

Iris gazed up into the canopy, envisioning the stars beyond. "Then they will return to the universe, like all our essence does after we pass. We are the last ones with transferred powers, so as long as we touch the silver, our job will be done."

She reached out a hand, and Davis took it. Together, they touched what remained of the pool until, in a haze of white threads and rushing heat, the silver ceased to exist.

Iris stared for a while at the empty, flat space of land that had been the silver; a strange, stark contrast to the surrounding density of pine trees and shrubs. Her mind was clear. Lighter. Free. She looked at Davis and knew from his bright eyes that even though he needed a moment to recover, he felt the same.

Eventually, the darkness forced them to move on. As they walked through the forest, they heard people talking ahead. The group of Shifters she had come with—and some Statics—stood around, saying goodbye to Meng, Maria, Alek, and Shawn. Davis hung back behind a tree while Iris watched. When everyone but Meng and the fishing crew had left, Iris turned to Davis.

"Stay here. I'll just be a moment."

He didn't need to wait for her—they'd be going their separate ways soon—but she hoped he would. She approached the remaining four people.

"Hi," she said.

"You did it," Meng said with a smile. "Thank you."

Iris shrugged. "We didn't have a choice."

Maria smirked. "I didn't know if we'd see you before we left. Meng's about to get us the heck home." She shook Iris's hand. "This was a life-changing experience. An adventure. And a nightmare. I have grown in ways I could have never imagined. I can't really thank you for any of it, but I can say it was nice knowing you."

Iris chuckled. "It was nice knowing you too. Thank you for saving my life,"—she looked at Shawn and Alek in turn—"even if you didn't really have a choice in the matter." She shook each man's hand.

"If you head back to Ling's and my place," Meng said, "they're organizing transportation to San Francisco. We'll need to hold a town hall soon."

Iris shook her head. "That's all right. I'll find my own way for now."

Meng glanced knowingly back at the trees behind Iris. "We'll see you around."

"See you around," Iris replied.

After they left, Iris walked back to the trees where Davis waited. She knew he hadn't left because she could still feel his presence—or at least his shirt's presence—with her finder ability, but her stomach still fluttered from happiness and relief when she saw him.

"What a heartfelt goodbye," he said.

Iris rolled her eyes, smiling.

They made their way to Main Street, where Iris stopped at a local market to call a cab. The TV in the market was playing the local news. A spotlight illuminated a reporter standing on a neighborhood cul-de-sac, a dozen people crowding behind him.

"I'm here at the end of Forest Lane where locals are saying they saw something incredible tonight," the reporter said.

A man in the crowd grabbed the reporter's microphone, his eyes unblinking and bloodshot. "A dragon! And snake! And *dogs*!"

The reporter pulled his microphone loose, but then a woman grabbed it from his other side. "I saw them too! There were two dragons, but they were different kinds!"

The crowd yelled in agreement, and the reporter's eyes darted side to side as he hunched toward the camera.

"Well, there you have it," he said with a hesitant laugh. "One person even claims to have proof." A man held up a camera by the reporter's shoulder and pointed at it enthusiastically. "I guess we'll have to wait to see what *develops*."

The market employee looked up from reading a newspaper and scoffed. "Do you believe this crap?" she said to Iris.

Iris chuckled nervously and backed out the door. "People will say anything to get on TV."

"I can't wait to see what *develops*," Davis said when Iris joined him outside.

She shook her head, amused yet uneasy. "We've opened quite the can of worms, haven't we?"

While they waited on the sidewalk for the cab to arrive, Iris glanced nervously about. Were the OT police watching her now? Or would they be busy enough with the local news and the restoration of powers to leave her alone? Would that crowd of Statics come marching around the corner at any moment? Would they recognize her or Davis?

It didn't take long for the taxi to arrive. Iris sighed with relief and pulled open the back door, pausing before getting in.

"You could come back with me," she said to Davis. "There will be more pro-integration sympathizers now, especially once all the original council members are restored, and they realize what Ariana did."

Davis looked thoughtful, and then a slight smile touched his lips. He met Iris's gaze and shook his head.

"They might sympathize, but I'll never be one of them. Not to mention they'll probably throw me back in prison. Better to continue my pro-integration work with my own kind." He took a few steps away, paused, and looked back. "I'm sure we'll be working together again soon, Representative Bai."

Iris watched him walking down the sidewalk. Before he got too far, she remembered something.

"Wait!" She ran after him and grabbed his arm, pulling him back toward the cab. "There's someone I want you to see."

NIVI

SAN FRANCISCO, CALIFORNIA

THE SHIFTER COUNCIL HEADQUARTERS was a bustle of activity. The Shifter police had been deployed with nullification tinctures, and, with Nivi's help, the majority of the affected Shifter population had regained their memories over the course of a week.

Nivi stood at the back of the room, anxiously awaiting the beginning of the town hall. Ji stood to her right, every so often placing a hand of support on her arm, and Arav stood to her left. Ling sat somewhere at the front of the room, and after several scans of the crowd, Nivi eventually saw what she thought was the back of her grandmother's head, her hair swept back in a sleek bun. It was confirmed when Ling's profile flashed into view as she said something to her neighbor. Ai, Jorge, and Vera entered the room but were stuck on the far side away from Nivi. They waved when they saw her.

A hush swept over the crowd as the now Chairperson Meng Zhang walked up the center aisle and stood on the podium at the front of the room. Meng welcomed everyone and gave a summary of the topics that would be discussed to determine potential future measures that would be put to vote.

Where was Ariana? In hiding? Locked up in the prison she'd locked them in? Awaiting trial?

Meng banged a gavel on her podium. "I will now open the floor to discussion about Shifter community safety and the use of oblivion tincture."

One by one, community members approached the microphone that faced Meng's podium, speaking their concerns, experiences, and questions. Rowdy conversations erupted through the hall.

"Ariana Peters should be jailed," the first speaker said. "She took away the rights and lives of so many people in the name of power."

A chorus of applause and jeers met the argument.

"She didn't have a choice," someone yelled out. "Shifters and Statics need to be kept separate, and the OT is the best way to keep us safe."

More cheers and boos.

Yet another person chimed in. "The purpose of the OT is protecting the few and privileged, those in power, at the expense of everyone else. None of us are safe if any of us can have our memories wiped at any time and our lives uprooted and replaced."

Nivi's eyes darted around the room, watching each speaker as they stood to be heard.

"But there will be no peace without mass oblivion. The knowledge of transfer stones will lead to a search for any remaining stones or the attempt to create more."

"All progress can be used for good or evil, depending on whose hands wield it, so are you saying all inventions should be erased from our memories due to concerns about how they could be used? Or are you saying we should stop innovating altogether?"

"I want to know why Ariana Peters is still vice chairperson!"

That demand garnered a round of applause, a few groans, and a standing ovation by a smattering of people.

Meng tapped her gavel. "Any thoughts on elected officials can be made known at the next election."

It was clear that there would be no agreement that day, if ever.

And then Mr. Cho stepped up to the microphone. He recounted how he witnessed the OT police abduct a student. He described how he was shot when he tried to stop them.

"Whether or not the use of oblivion tincture originally began as a measure to protect our people, it has morphed into something dark and ugly. A weapon to maintain absolute power," he concluded.

The hall once again erupted into pandemonium.

Meng banged her gavel. "Rest assured, there will be a full investigation into these matters."

Eventually, the argument turned to integration. There had been so much recent exposure to Statics. Ironically, that'd be easily taken care of with oblivion tincture, but how would they know if they got them all? And what about the pro-integration groups of Statics and Shifters working together? Recent raids had already nullified most of those. But there could be more.

A familiar person approached the microphone. Her straight, dark blond hair brushed the top of her shoulders, and her blue eyes shone above her round cheeks and warm smile. It was Rowena, the Shifter who'd hosted the pro-integration gathering at Kellan's bookstore.

"It seems to me," she began, "that many of these policies were formed out of fear. Fear of the other. Fear of the unknown. If we get to know each other, we can care about one another, and we can work together. So much more can be achieved if we work together than if we work apart. I'll be proposing a new measure on the ballot for the next election to allow focus groups between Shifters and Statics so we can begin building bridges. Thank you."

Applause followed Rowena back to her seat, and Nivi joined in, clapping loudly.

Of course, with integration talks, the subject of Davis came up again. What he'd done was unnatural. Statics were dangerous. He was just one Static, not all were like that. And so the two sides continued, neither swaying the other. It felt hopeless. How could any progress be made with two sides so staunchly set in their ideas and ways? But a careful review of the room soon revealed many more people sitting silently among the crowd, listening to the arguments like Nivi and Ji were doing at the back of the room. Those who were silent far outnumbered those who cried out. Maybe change could occur inconspicuously and quietly? It was easy to think that the loudest voices were also the majority.

And then someone at the podium made a comment that sent a chill of dread through Nivi.

"Davis is an example of why we need to keep Statics and Shifters separate. He was a *Static* born to *Shifter* parents!"

The topic hit close to home. If she was going to speak out, to sway Shifter politics, this was the time. She had discussed this moment with Ji, but the closer it got, the more unsure she was that she could do it, that she could bring that kind of attention to herself.

Meng spoke into her microphone. "There could be Static blood going back generations in many of our families that we are unaware of. Technically, we all have some amount of Static blood since Shifters originally developed from genetic mutations within Statics."

"Which is why we need to be more strict than ever about keeping our bloodlines pure. Statics will pollute us; our powers will cease to exist."

Someone yelled out. "No, they won't!"

For some reason, the force of that exclamation caused the arguments at the front of the room to go silent, and everyone turned back to look at the speaker. With horror, Nivi realized the words had come from her mother. Cold dread drained down the back of her neck.

"Do you have something more you'd like to add to that statement?" Meng asked.

Ji looked at Nivi and spoke quickly and quietly. "Are you ready? We don't have to do this now. We can wait."

Nivi only had to speak a few words: *My father is a Static.* Such loaded words. They would promote integration, especially since her Shifter powers were especially strong, but they'd also label her an illegitimate child and her mother an adulterer. They'd probably have to submit blood samples to prove their claims as well, and in the meantime, she'd be the center of speculation and gossip. She was still mourning the only father she'd ever known and the family she could've had. Could she withstand the fallout of those words? But it *would* be proven, and when it was, they would no longer be able to keep her family apart.

Arav spoke beside Nivi. "I'm ready. I can speak for both of us. You don't have to say anything."

Nivi shook her head. "No, I'm ready too. The more stories they know like ours, the better."

Side by side, they approached the microphone.

After the town hall adjourned, small crowds lingered outside, continuing some of the same discussions or making plans for lunch.

"How are you holding up?" Arav asked Nivi.

Nivi shrugged. "I'm not so angry anymore, but I don't know if I'll ever be able to forgive Davis, not fully."

"I don't think I ever will either. I don't think we have to. But we might eventually understand, and then he won't have a hold over us anymore."

Would she ever understand? She didn't know, but it felt nice that Arav would soon be at school, that she'd have someone there who knew what it was like to have Davis break apart their family. Nivi and Ji hugged Arav and thanked him for his support. He planned to return to Yuras for a few days before he was required to attend the Shifter school.

"If you see Amber," Nivi said, "tell her I said hi. And that I miss her."

"I will," Arav said.

He took off his camouflage pendant and walked down the sidewalk to a cream-colored sedan idling by the road. Frank got out from the driver side and Kabir from the passenger side, and they all hugged before getting back into the car. The sedan pulled away from the curb, and then they were gone. Nivi's heart ached for Arav. She knew the feeling of having to leave the only family you knew.

Nivi and Ji looked out over the water, waiting for Meng and Ling outside the Shifter Council headquarters. The thrill of speaking out was fading, and a hollowness took its place. Would her actions make any difference at all, or would they just put a target on her back?

Ji must've been thinking about the same thing. She turned and spoke to Nivi with such love in her eyes. "These things take time. I'm so proud of you. It takes a lot of courage to speak out, and I'm here to support you along the way."

Nivi nodded, fighting back tears. Fortunately, Ai, Jorge, and Vera emerged at that moment, giving Nivi an excuse to turn away and steady her emotions.

They ran at her, all smiles and screams, taking turns hugging her. What were they so happy about? It was disorienting.

"You were so badass!" Ai exclaimed.

Nivi shook her head, not believing it.

"You were!" Jorge and Vera said in unison.

Their excitement was contagious, and Nivi couldn't help laughing in response. Despite all she'd lost, she'd gained these wonderful people as friends. Jorge's gaze lingered on her, and she felt her heart flutter. It seemed it kept doing that each time she'd seen him recently. Maybe, over time, there could be something there.

They all made plans to meet up in Sequoia when they were back at school and said goodbye as Meng and Ling came out of the building.

Nivi approached Meng. She felt strange speaking to her in her new position, and she wasn't sure how to address her in public. "Hi, Chairperson. So does this mean Ariana gets to remain in power?"

Meng looked tired but spoke with a smile. "We won't know until the investigation is complete. And then if she isn't charged with a crime, it will be up to the voters to decide. Even with a vote, you can't just get rid of one side or the other. The best way forward would be to incorporate everyone's views."

Nivi nodded. How would she feel if Ariana remained in office? With Meng as chairperson, maybe it wouldn't be that bad.

"Well," Meng said, "I've worked up an appetite. Where are we going for lunch?"

"Actually," Ji said, and she sounded more nervous than during the town hall, "I was thinking we could all go to Kellan's for lunch. He's preparing a feast as we speak."

Ling glanced at Meng and then took in a long breath through her nose.

"Ling..." Meng said in a warning tone.

Ling put up a hand. "I know we've already discussed this to death in there, but I just want to say something. I can accept that Nivi is a Shifter, and a strong one at that, and Kellan is a decent man, but he *is* a Static. I just can't see a good way forward. How can he exist in our world without conflict? How can we exist in his?"

Meng took Ling's hand in her own and spoke words that brightened Ji's face and brought Nivi a surge of hope that threatened to again spill tears.

"We start... with lunch."

Epilogue

Yuras, California

Amber and Arav sat on the steps outside his house in the afternoon sun. So much had changed in so short a time. Part of him wished they'd never discovered that cave, but it wouldn't have mattered. It wouldn't have changed who he was. His powers would've emerged one way or another.

"When do you have to leave?" Amber said, breaking their silence.

Arav rubbed his hands together, his breath visible in the cool winter air. "In a couple of days."

Amber sighed. "I guess this is goodbye."

"It's not right," Arav said, "having to split my world like this."

"At least you'll be on the side of change now. You'll be able to influence the new generation."

So much was changing so quickly. He wasn't ready to lose her too.

"We could... try?"

Amber smiled sadly and shook her head. "No. I'm not the same Amber anymore, and you're not the same Arav, and not because you're a Shifter and I'm a Static. We're going to keep changing, and that's okay. You'll be okay, and so will I."

She squeezed his hand and let it go. He stared at her for a moment, then sniffed and nodded.

"Plus," Amber continued, "you've already made some new friends, right?"

Heat rose to his cheeks. Did she mean Vera?

"I guess. Not really," he stammered, trying not to upset her, but when he met her eyes, he didn't see any jealousy, only openness and warmth.

"I wish you the best. I really do."

He wished he could be as open to his future as she was, but he felt so confused and angry. He knew his mother's death had been an accident—he'd seen it through Davis's memories—but the hurt still lingered. "It's just hard knowing that Davis gets to just be out there, walking around, free."

"Oh, Arav." She rested a hand on his trembling shoulder. "I'm so sorry. I can't pretend I know what you're feeling, but please, try to find peace. Vengeance is an addictive drug. Talk to Nivi. She'll know what you're going through."

She was right. She didn't know what he was going through, but he didn't dwell on it, not when these could be the last moments they spent together. So he changed the subject.

"Nivi says hi. She misses you."

"Tell her hi back. And I miss her too."

They stood up and hugged, and then Amber walked down the sidewalk. She paused to turn around and wave. Arav lifted his hand in return from his doorway, saying goodbye to so much more than her, and then he closed the door.

As soon as Arav closed the door, Amber ran. Tears streamed down her face, obscuring her view as she turned onto Main Street. She collided with something warm and tall. *Someone.*

She stumbled back, mumbling apologies while hands gripped her shoulders to steady her.

"Amber," the person said, "are you okay?"

Amber wiped her eyes and nose with her sweatshirt sleeve and looked up. Tom Ross looked back at her, his brown eyes large and concerned, his dark hair tousled. He looked very proper in a high-neck, buttoned-up coat.

"Uh, yeah," Amber said. "I'm just heading home."

"I'll walk with you," Tom said. Amber tried to protest, but he was already chatting while keeping stride with her. "I get it. It's been crazy, hasn't it? First MHU, which—" he crossed his arms and swept them apart to create a dramatic X, "—I'm totally done with. I'm sure you are too. I mean, are they even still meeting? Maybe we should go to a meeting to keep tabs on them? Wait, I'm talking too much again. My mom says I need to ask more questions and listen more. How are *you* doing?"

Despite her tears, Amber chuckled. She wiped her face again. "I'll be okay, Tom. I think we all will."

He walked with her to her street, chatting all the while, and waved goodbye with promises to meet up sometime.

She entered her house where her parents were sitting on the couch. Before heading to San Francisco, Nivi had removed the oblivion tincture on them and briefed them on the situation. Since then, they'd been terrified every time she left the house. They stood up, with worried looks and tears in their eyes, and she ran to them and hugged them tightly.

She was so happy to be home, and she was so thankful for them, for so many reasons. For always being so kind and positive. For being such loving and supportive parents. For giving her space to discover who she was, and for always accepting who she was in each moment. For always being there for her, and just for being her family. But she was too overwhelmed at that moment to voice all those thoughts, so she just continued to hug them and simply said, "Thank you."

Monterey Park, California

Planter beds full of red, purple, and white petunias lined the lawn in front of the senior care facility. Spanish tiles roofed the three-story beige building, warm and inviting in the morning sun.

Iris and Davis walked up to the front door. When he realized where they were, he held back for a moment, worry on his face, but Iris smiled, took his hand, and led him inside. What a statement they made, seen in public together, a Shifter and a Static. Change would be slow, but this could be a start. She felt so much better now that all the excess magic in her was gone. She was excited for the future, and she finally felt like herself.

The interior of the facility continued the same color scheme as the exterior, although there was a more sterile feel to it. Iris signed in at the front desk, and an attendant led them to an open communal area where several seniors sat watching TV at low volume. Next to a window with a view of the front lawn and petunias, a frail woman hunched forward, nodding off in her chair, a warm glow radiating from her chest. Her black-and-white hair was combed back into a clean bun, and her chin rested against the front of her long, yellow dress. The dress was not attractive and could best be described as similar to a hospital gown, but Iris still smiled at the memory of having lunch with the woman wearing a similarly colored dress half a century earlier.

It was hard to know how long it would take for the woman to recover, if ever. The only other Shifters Iris knew who had been without their powers for a similar length of time were her parents, and they had never received them back.

The attendant tapped the woman on the shoulder and spoke into her ear, saying her name several times before the woman finally stirred.

"Ms. Sun. Anna Sun. You have visitors."

ACKNOWLEDGMENTS

There is so much hurt in the world right now. In these troubling times, I take comfort in my family and friends, as well as the wonderful people I've met through the book world. I have faith that through our shared community and mutual care for one another, we can create ripple effects that foster greater understanding in those around us. I can only hope that my storytelling has contributed, in some small way, toward that goal.

Thank you to everyone who has helped and supported me along the way. To my family and friends, you are the everyday joys that make life meaningful. To Karen—my friend, writing partner, alpha reader, and accountability manager—you are an integral part of helping me achieve all that I have. To James at Bookfly Design, thank you for being so receptive and responsive in creating an amazing book cover. To Zala, my editor, thank you for your hard work and attention to detail. I'm so fortunate you came to my stall at the *LA Times* Festival of Books. To Ryan at Outrider Creative, thank you for bringing Yuras to life with your stunning map drawing. And to all my readers: I am humbled that, out of all the books out there, you have chosen to spend your time on mine. Thank you from the bottom of my heart.

About the Author

Emily Renk Hawthorne writes fantasy inspired by mythology, hidden histories, and the world around her. She is the author of the *Of Mountains and Seas* duology, which explores identity, belonging, and the lengths people will go to for power.

When she's not writing, Emily can be found playing with her toddler or working on other people's kids' teeth. She lives on the California Central Coast with her husband, their daughter, and their dogs, Marshmallow and Toffee.